CROWTOWER

Book Two of The Sun Thief trilogy

DAVID RAE

Milton, Ontario
http://www.brain-lag.com/

This is a work of fiction. All of the characters, events, and organizations portrayed in this novel are either products of the author's imagination or are used fictitiously.

Brain Lag Publishing
Milton, Ontario
http://www.brain-lag.com/

Cover artwork by Catherine Fitzsimmons

ISBN 978-1-928011-50-7

Library and Archives Canada Cataloguing in Publication

Title: Crowtower : the twin of darkness / David Rae.
Names: Rae, David, 1962- author.
Description: Series statement: Book two of The sun thief trilogy
Identifiers: Canadiana (print) 20210107502 | Canadiana (ebook) 20210107510 | ISBN 9781928011507
 (softcover) | ISBN 9781928011514 (ebook)
Classification: LCC PR6118.A32 C77 2020 | DDC 823/.92—dc23

Content warnings: Abuse (child/sexual), death, gore (medical/graphic injuries)

The Twin of Darkness

Books by David Rae

The Sun Thief Trilogy
Crowman
Crowtower
Crowbait (forthcoming)

To my dear friend Des Dixon, author of the Cade Cannon series. Sadly gone.

Friend, comic genius, and one of the nicest people I ever met. I could not have done this without your support. You are much missed and often remembered.

The Dark Land

Riga

Basseriko

Fadu

Kota

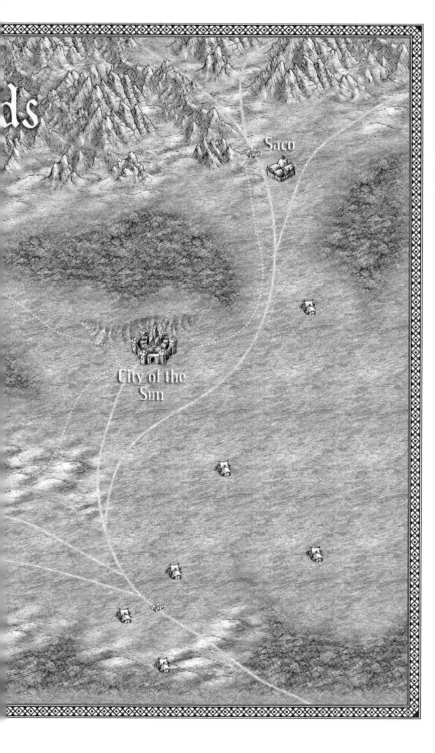

Chapter One
Reborn

I am Utas. I do not remember, but they came for me, the twelve. I die and am reborn. How many times? I am taken by the twelve from my home and taken to the tower. No more than a child, I remember nothing. The twelve came for me led by Vatu, by the Darkness, and brought me here to my home.

I remember nothing, just darkness. What does it matter, I grew, and the darkness grew within me.

The twelve fed me darkness. How they hate me. How they envy me. I will take from them all that they have for it is all mine. They will not keep me from it. They murdered me before, but I am reborn, and now when it is time I will murder them, each of them.

I will murder Zauria who took me for my first year. I remember nothing of that time, but still I will kill him when I can. I will take his body and burn him on the altar and sing the death hymn, but I will not shed tears for him. He is the least of the twelve.

Of the year spent with Zigoro I recall scarcely more. I survived. I suppose that Vatu would have made it clear that the death of the infant High Priest would displease him, otherwise Zigoro would surely have slain me. He is not to be trusted, but then again none of them are to be trusted. He is not strong, but he is cunning. He lies in wait until it is clear to strike; at other times he hides. He is hated, they are hated. I hate them all.

Beldura, Gorroto, Hondatu, Estira; I passed from one to the other each year. I was taken to the hall of Vatu. My sponsor would bring me to the echoing empty chamber. All of the twelve would be there, the twelve and Vatu.

"I have done with him," my sponsor would say. "I return him to the dark."

"Who will serve the dark? Who will guide the High Priest?"

"I will," and my new guardian will step forward and take my hand. Then the twelve retire from the hall, led by the new tutor holding my hand tightly. That is it; there is no great ceremony. I am handed over. I am led away.

Hilketa is my guardian now. He leads me to his chambers. They are not so different from the chambers of the others. They are large and dark. They have no windows. The moon does not shine here. There are four rooms, not counting the washroom and privy. Hilketa shows me to one of the apartments.

"This is yours," he says.

I look at it and shrug. It is a large, square room with black stone walls and floor. There are brass lanterns, but they are turned down low. There is a bed and a box and a table. The box is empty. Every year it is empty. My things are destroyed, and I receive new things. But I need few things anyway; perhaps a writing tablet and stylus, or a flute. They are easily replaced.

Hilketa looks at me. He looks me in the eye.

"Do you remember?" he asks, but I shake my head. I do not know what he thinks I will recall. I have been reborn, but I do not remember anything.

"We were friends," he says. I think it is a lie, but I say nothing. I am a child and I am in his care. I will not antagonize him needlessly.

"You are so like him."

It is a stupid thing to say. Of course I am like him. I am myself, who else should I look like?

"Go then, sleep, we will begin tomorrow."

"Begin what?" I ask.

"Your training, of course."

"The others did not train me," I state flatly.

"Yes they did," contradicts Hilketa, "you just don't know what you have learned."

"What will you teach me?" I ask.

"The same as the others; how to be yourself."

I think for a while and screw my face up. Do I need to be taught to be myself? I would like to ask him, but I do not in case he beats me. I am not afraid of beatings (who taught me that?). But I have no wish to be beaten for no good cause.

"What?" asks Hilketa. He seems amused.

"Why must I be taught to be myself?"

"That can wait, tomorrow is fine. We will speak then. You have much to learn. Sleep now."

With that, Hilketa turns and leaves. I am alone. I lie on the bed. It is firm and there is no cover. All the beds are firm and the tower is warm so there is no need for a cover. I sleep; sleep is the darkness's greatest gift.

In the morning I wake to find Hilketa in my room. He is seated and is looking at me. He is dressed in black robes, but he is not wearing his mask or his gauntlets. I look at him, but say nothing.

"It is time to get up," he says. "Are you hungry?"

He gestures to a bowl of blood and milk. I am hungry, and drink it with relish. It is slightly warm, and very satisfying.

"Do you know why we drink blood?" he asks.

"Estira says it is to symbolize our power and strength. Mighty predators drink blood and so do we."

Hilketa snorts. "Yes, mighty predators drink blood, and so do parasites.

"Come." He gestures and I follow him. He leads me to a broad hall.

"Stand on that mark," he says and points to a hieroglyph on the floor. I stand on the mark and Hilketa ties a blindfold around my eyes. "Walk forward," he instructs.

"Where to?" I ask.

"Just walk forward, I'll tell you when to stop."

I walk forward for about ten steps, then he tells me to stop. "Now turn and go back to where you were." I turn and walk back, counting out the ten steps in my head. When I think I have returned, I stop.

"Take the blindfold off," Hilketa says.

I am standing well to the left of the mark and about four feet too short. Hilketa looks disappointed, I can see by his face I have not done well.

"I will teach you to walk in darkness," he says. "It is not easy, not at first. You have walked with your eyes guiding you, now you must let the darkness guide you."

"I tried to count my steps," I reply sullenly.

"Yes," agrees Hilketa, "that was your mistake. Put the blindfold on again. There are many senses. No doubt you have been told we have five: smell, sight, touch, taste and hearing. It is a lie, we have many more senses. Lean to one side, that's right, a bit further. Now feel the difference, feel the change in your balance and feel the changes in your muscles. Be aware. Be aware of your movement. To walk in darkness, you must have faith. You must have faith in the darkness and in yourself, now once again."

I step onto the hieroglyph and replace the blindfold. Once again I step forward.

"Imagine that you are leaving a trail of silver behind you," says Hilketa. "Walk forward and then turn and follow that trail backward. In your head is both a compass and level. Feel each swing of the compass and each tilt of the level. When you go back you must repeat each tilt and swing. In your head you are building a map of silver trails that lead you through the dark."

Again I walk back.

"Now take off your blindfold."

This time I am only a short way from the hieroglyph.

"Good," says Hilketa. "What did you do wrong?"

I think for a while.

"Well, what is your answer?"

"I did everything as you said, I was very close to the hieroglyph."

"But not close enough. You must be exact. If you are even the slightest bit out, the gap between where you are and where you should be will get greater and greater and you will be lost in the darkness. When you are the High Priest you will have to dance in the hall of Vatu. Think, if then you could not find your way back to the doors of darkness, you would be trapped there."

"I could follow the wall till I came to the door."

"You could try, perhaps you would be fortunate and find it, but most likely not. The Hall of Vatu is not like this, it is vast and shapeless. You would not find your way out that way. Touch will not lead you out. Now again, what did you do wrong?"

Again I think for a moment.

"I compensated, I thought I had made a mistake and tried to correct it. I thought I had gone too far and stepped back. I put my faith in reason rather than in darkness and in myself."

"That is right." Hilketa nods. "Now, again."

Again and again I walk blindfolded. I get better but I make many mistakes.

"I cannot do this," I protest.

"If you could do it then I would not have to teach you," says

Hilketa mildly. "Again."

I try again and this time when I remove the blindfold I am standing directly over the hieroglyph.

"Good," says Hilketa.

"If I am the High Priest reborn," I ask, "why must I learn the things I knew before?"

Hilketa shrugs. "It is the way."

"Did you need to learn this?"

"Yes," says Hilketa. "You taught me."

I think about this for a while. It is strange to think that these men knew me in my past life.

"That was a long time ago," says Hilketa. "It was in the life before the last one. This is the second time I have taught you to walk in darkness, and other things."

"Was I a good teacher?" I ask.

"Yes, you taught me to walk in darkness. I am grateful," and to my surprise he bows to me. None of the others bowed to me. It must be a trick. He is trying to make me trust him. I am not such a fool.

We practice for the rest of the day, walking backwards and forwards. I get better, but I am still not perfect.

"Do not be discouraged, it is not easy to ignore reason and walk in darkness. Come now, that is enough for one day."

Chapter Two
Writing

Hilketa turns and I follow him back to his rooms. On the way we pass Kong. He is dressed in the robes of his priesthood and is wearing the black jet amulet of the chief priest, my amulet. He does not speak to me, but pushes past without a word. Hilketa has pulled me to him out of Kong's path. Kong has ignored us. It is as if we are beneath his notice.

I can feel Hilketa's grip tighten on my shoulder. After Kong has passed, he relaxes his grip and we walk onward. It is a trick, to make me think he is my ally against Kong. Hilketa is subtle. I must not underestimate him.

"Are you the oldest of the twelve?" I ask.

"For the moment. I will be reborn soon enough, and I will be the youngest. Then it will be your turn to teach me."

Good, let him think I trust him.

Day after day, Hilketa teaches me to walk in darkness. "Think of your body, think to every point of your skin, be aware of your own presence."

I get better, now I practice in total darkness. When I return to my room the light is not lit. I live in darkness, I eat in darkness, I sleep in darkness, I wash in darkness.

"Good," Hilketa says. "You have learned to walk in darkness."

Later we go to the top of the tower, mostly when the moon is out. Hilketa likes the moon. He stands staring at it. I look down into the inner court and out over the City of the Sun. I can see the people going about their business. The city is very busy.

"Why do we never go into the city?" I ask.

"We do go into the city. It is just you who does not, not yet anyway."

"When can I go?"

"Never mind about that, come and look at the moon."

I obey.

"How many times do you think the moon has travelled round the earth?"

I have not thought about that and shrug indifferently. It does not matter.

"How many more times do you think it will travel round the earth?"

"Thousands, millions."

"Thousands, millions," repeats Hilketa, "thousands, millions. Thousands and millions before and thousands and millions after. Thousands and millions."

I shrug. Why does he care about this? What difference does it make? I want to go back to watching the people down below. They look very small from the top of the tower. They look like ants. When I am High Priest I will get to play with them. They will do what I say. They will be mine.

"What do you do when you go to the city?" I ask.

Hilketa does not answer, so I ask again.

"So what do you do when you go to the city?"

"Lots of things, nothing important, you will see when you're older."

"Why do you always look at the moon when we come here?"

"You ask a lot of questions."

"If I am to learn, then I must ask questions."

"You may not like what you learn, you may learn nothing."

"Why, do you think I will be frightened of what I learn?"

"No, not frightened. I have known you all this lifetime and I have never known you to be frightened. Very well, I will tell you why I look at the moon. It is unchanging and ever changing. It is the same moon I have looked at in every lifetime. It is a different moon from the one I saw last moonrise. How many lives do you think I have lived looking at that moon, how many more lives do you think I will live looking at the moon?"

I shrug. What does it matter?

"Like I said, you have learned nothing. That is hardly surprising. Still, you will learn, you will remember. When you are yourself, you will know."

"What nonsense, I am myself. I am the High Priest."

Now it is Hilketa that shrugs.

"If you say so," he says. "Come, it is time to go."

We walk in darkness back to our apartment.

"What else do you have to teach me?" I ask. "Is this why I go to a new teacher every year? Is there only so much you teach me?"

"Yes, perhaps, or perhaps we can only bear to put up with you for a year."

At night I lie in my room looking up into the darkness. It is hot in the tower, always hot. I am glad I do not have to wear the robes of the High Priest. I am dressed in darkness. Bats chase moths and beetles in the dark. I lie listening to the flutter of wings, moth wings and bat wings. I can hear bats crunching the stiff carapace of beetles. Moth wings spiral down out of the night. When I sleep, I dream, but I can never remember my dreams when I wake. They are always just out of reach like the memories of my past lives. Who am I?

Hilketa is in the next room. I can hear the sound of him moving in his sleep. It seems he dreams too. Every night I can hear him muttering in his sleep, but I cannot make out what he says. What is it that disturbs his sleep? I should ask him, but I do not. In the morning it seems that night brought the gift of sleep after all.

"It is time to rise," says Hilketa. I rise and go to wash. There is the usual bowl of blood and milk for me to drink.

"What do moths eat?"

"What a strange question. Why do you ask?"

"Bats eat moths and beetles, but what do they eat? They must eat something. What do beetles eat?"

"They eat all sorts of things: human sweat, excrement, they eat clothes. They eat mosses that grow on damp walls. They eat the traces of blood and milk you leave. Why do you ask?"

"Can we eat moths and beetles? Can we eat bats? All I have ever eaten is blood and milk, can I eat other things? What do they taste like?"

"I see. Yes, we can eat bats and beetles and moths. They do not taste particularly nice. If you wish, we can catch some and you can eat them. There are other things we can eat. But blood and milk is what is brought to us at the tower from the outer court. It is brought to us because they are the most precious. Blood is given by the members of the court. It is taken from them. It is a sacrifice.

Milk is given too, it is stolen from their children. We are more precious than the children of the court. When we go to the court we eat other things. But blood and milk is more precious, and nothing is sweeter."

Hilketa has brought a lantern. It is the first time he has brought a lantern in weeks.

I ask him, "Why have you brought a lantern?"

"I must teach you to read. You must have light to read. You cannot learn without light."

He gives me a stylus and tablet. I have used them before and know how to shape glyphs. I know their names and their shapes. I tell Hilketa this, but he says this is not enough.

"I am teaching you to read and write. You say you can write, yes, that is true. But writing is a journey without end. Reading is a journey without end. I am teaching you not just how to write, and not just how to read.

"Now take your stylus and inscribe your name on the tablet."

I take the reed stylus and impress it into the wax tablet. I form the shape of my name.

"Good, that is your name, or at least the short version of it."

"What do you mean? This is my name, I don't have a longer version."

"Really?"

He is speaking in riddles. He is trying to confuse me. Sometimes I am good at riddles but this one has me perplexed.

"No, this is my name. It is the only name I know. It is the name of the High Priest and I am the High Priest, it is my name."

"Who am I?"

"Hilketa. Here, I can write the glyphs of your name. It means murder, to kill someone, to take their life."

"Is that who I am? Suppose someone who had never met me asked you who I was, what would you say? 'He is Hilketa,' but what would that tell them? Would they be able to know me from that name? Would they be able to pick me out in a crowd from that name? Who is Hilketa? What does that mean?"

"I suppose I could say you have grey hair, quite long, that you are one of the twelve priests of Vatu."

"Good, is that who I am then? Is that all you could say about me?"

"No, I could say more, maybe a lot more."

"Why don't you? Why don't you say more?"

"Well, because it would take too long to tell them everything I know about you, and even then it would not be enough to describe you, it would only be describing what I know, not what I don't know."

"Yes, that's right. No matter what you say, or write, it is never enough. If you are lucky, you have said enough that whoever hears and reads your words can fill in the gaps, not all of them for sure, but enough. A name is never enough, it is just a label. It is meaningless."

"So why bother writing, why bother with names at all?"

"Try and draw a picture of me."

I am not good at drawing. I form a round shape for Hilketa's bulbous head, I add some squiggles to represent his straggly grey hair, and some lines to represent his eyes, mouth and nose.

"It is not very good," I say and offer it to Hilketa.

"No, it is not very good," agrees Hilketa, "but it is good enough. If you showed this to a stranger, he would be able to pick me out or to find me from this picture. You have left out lots of things, but you have got enough. That is what writing is, it is finding enough to paint a picture, to say what you want to say."

"And what is reading?"

"Reading is filling in the blanks, hearing what has not been said and seeing what has not been shown. Reading what has not been written."

"That sounds impossible."

"And yet we do it, almost."

A tablet is set in front of me. I am asked to copy the words onto my tablet. When I do, I hand it to Hilketa and he reads it, then he runs a rule over the wax and flattens it again. I copy tablet after tablet. Then we stop.

"So, what have you been reading?"

"I don't know."

"So you copied tablet after tablet, but cannot tell me what you have copied."

I look at the blank tablet he has handed back to me, what was written there. It is the same tablet, but there is no trace of what I have written. I will not find the answers there. All of the glyphs, all of the words have gone from my eye to my mind and then through my hand to the tablet. Is there really no trace of what I have written left there either?

"Tell me what was on the first tablet I asked you to copy."

What was on that tablet? What did I write on the tablet? There is no trace of it now. I look down at the tablet again.

"You will not find the answer there."

"It was a report."

"They were all reports. But do not worry, I did not expect you to know the answer, I just wanted to show the difference between reading and reading well.

"You will learn, just as you learned to walk in the dark. It is just a question of knowing how. Again, read the report. This time, do not write it down, just read it aloud."

Hilketa hands me a tablet and I read.

> *Great ones, I hereby relate that certain citizens of our town have murmured against the order of things. These citizens being wealthy and influential did stir up discontent. It was necessary to conduct firm action to suppress the activities of these rebels. They and their households have been dealt with in the appropriate manner. All goods in the possession of the deceased have been confiscated and will be redistributed in due course. This will raise a small sum for the treasury to be sent shortly. As ever, we are loyal to the Sun and loyal to darkness. Praise Vatu.*

Hilketa listens to me as I recite these words. When I am finished, he nods his head.

"Well, what does this tell us?"

"A provincial governor has carried out his duties to keep the peace and sends his report. It is a routine report informing us and keeping us up to date on his action, and telling us that a sum of money is due shortly for the treasury."

Hilketa sniffs. I think he is displeased with my answer, but he says nothing.

"Have I done wrong?" I ask. I am not afraid to displease him, but I wish to learn; if I am wrong he should tell me, then I can do better.

"Not wrong, no... But..."

"Yes, tell me. I wish to learn."

"There are no wrong answers. What you say is correct, but it is not the whole of the matter."

I reread the tablet, but I cannot see what I have missed out and say so.

"I did not say you had missed anything."

"Then what?"

"What has the writer missed out?"

"What do you mean?"

"I mean you must read what is not written. But let us leave this for now."

He motions for me to pick up my flute, and from his robe he draws his own flute. He starts to play and I play along with him. It is a sad, mournful tune within a lingering minor key. We play together and his notes and mine twine together. It is as if we are one person playing one song. It is very sad but very beautiful. He plays slowly and steadily. I play softly and subtly, I let my notes lie over his like fallen leaves in a stream. It flows and eddies and circles around. Now he is playing softer still. It is like snow in moonlight. I play stealthily like wind drift shaping and brushing the music into waves and hollows. At last, he stops. I notice there is a tear in his eye.

"Good," he says. "You always did learn music quickly."

"Did I? I don't remember, I don't remember anything. Will I ever remember anything? Do you remember your past lives?"

Hilketa shakes his head.

"No. It is like the tablets, it is the same tablet, but once it is wiped clean, everything that was there is gone. It must be written again."

"So," I ask, "when I wipe the tablet and write on it, I do not have to write the same things."

"You are taking my analogy too far. We are the servants of Vatu. It is always the same that is written. There may be changes in the shapes of glyphs, but the content, the meaning is always the same."

"But," I say, "if the important thing is what is not written, then how can that always be the same? It could be different every time you read it."

"You always were too clever. I cannot answer these questions. I will ask you and you will tell me the answer in another lifetime."

I want to ask him more about myself. What was I like? What am I like? I know nothing. I must know everything. I wonder if he will tell me. Is this what he thinks, that he is writing who I am on a blank tablet? If he thinks that, he is wrong. I am not what he or what any of the twelve will try to make me. How dare he think he can shape me and mould me to his will. I am his master, he should not forget that.

Chapter Three
Games

It is late now and we return to the apartments. I retire to sleep. Bats flit in and around my bed. How do they get into my room? I have no windows and only one door which is kept closed. The tower is always warm and it is warmer than usual tonight. I lie awake in the heat.

I can feel a breeze, it is faint, fainter than breath. Somewhere air comes into the room. I suppose there must be some system to bring in air, otherwise the room would be stuffy. I suppose that the bats must come in the same way. Perhaps they come in chasing moths, but then why do moths come in? Every answer is followed by a question.

I am tired. Writing and reading is more tiring than learning to walk in darkness. I close my eyes, although in the darkness it makes no difference if they are open or shut. I am tired and will sleep soon. But I cannot. Why? I listen. I can hear Hilketa muttering in the next room.

Why can I not sleep? Trust yourself; that is what Hilketa told me. I am telling myself not to sleep. Why? I am alert, I am alarmed. I tell myself I am being stupid. I am safe here in Hilketa's rooms. I can hear Hilketa murmuring in his sleep. What else can I hear? Nothing. I start to relax. There is nothing here. There is no danger, I hear nothing. Trust yourself. I can hear nothing.

The bats have stopped flitting around the room. The moths too have stopped. The breeze is stronger, why have I never felt it so strongly before? Something is different. My door is open. I am alert, I am alarmed. There is danger.

I slide off my bed onto the floor and slip underneath. I am silent, as silent as the stranger in my room. Still I hear nothing. Wait, I hear something. It is not a footstep. It is the sound of a hand brushing the mattress of the bed. I do not move. I do not sleep. I can hear Hilketa in the next room. He is not murmuring and his breathing is irregular. I do not return to my bed. The bats do not return that night. In the morning I hear servants bring the jugs of blood and milk into the room. A lantern is lit. Hilketa has not come to wake me. I can hear his breathing in the next room. A servant enters my room and lights a lamp. Light spreads out.

"Where are you, Master?" the servant asks, but I do not answer, not at first. I wait to make sure he is alone, and to make sure that I am alone. When I am certain we are alone, I emerge from under the bed.

"Where is Hilketa?" I ask.

"Still sleeping."

"Does that not seem odd?"

"Yes it does, now you say it. He is usually awake when we arrive."

"Not usually," I correct, "always."

"Yes, always, as you say."

The slave looks at me with dull eyes. What is he thinking? It is like reading, what is not said, what is not shown. That is what I must know.

"You should stay," I say.

The slave nods. Is there fear in his eyes?

I go to the next room and shake Hilketa. It is with difficulty that I wake him. When he wakens, he understands.

"The slave is in the next room," I say.

With my help, Hilketa rises and I help him to the door. When we enter the room, the slave is lying on the floor. There is a white froth coming from his mouth. He is dead.

"Unfortunate," says Hilketa.

"It does not matter, it can only be him. It can only be Kong."

"Perhaps," agrees Hilketa.

"He was here. I hid under the bed till he left."

"He will not try again, at least not this way."

"I should have him killed."

"No doubt you will, but not yet, you are not strong enough."

Hilketa sits on my chair. He leans back.

"You could kill him."

"I should, but I will not."

"Why?"

"Because you will kill him, you will live and you will kill him."

"So till then I must walk carefully."

"You always had to walk carefully. He is not the only one that wishes you dead. I repeat, he will not come again, and if he does, he will not succeed."

To my surprise, he prostrates himself on the ground.

"Forgive me, I failed you and put your life in danger. I beg forgiveness and your leave to live."

I realize what he is asking. He is cunning. I would not have thought to ask him to take his life, and it would benefit me nothing if he did. He knows I must forgive him. To make him take his life would just bring me closer to Kong, but when I arrive I would be less prepared. He knows I must forgive him, and that by forgiving him I make him mine. He knows that if he is mine, then I am his. It is a trap, a subtle trap.

"Get up."

Hilketa rises.

That day we do not talk. Hilketa has been weakened more than he will admit by the poison. I wonder if Kong tried to kill him instead of just making him sleep. We wander through the tower in darkness, complete darkness. Hilketa leads and I follow, for now. That will change when I am High Priest. In the dark I stay a step behind Hilketa. He says nothing. I do not walk into him when he stops or lose him when he turns sharply into strange openings. I have never walked so far into the tunnels of darkness. We walk all day. As Hilketa taught me, I leave a trail of silver in my head. I leave a silver thread twined through the tunnels of darkness. Eventually he stops.

"Where are we?" Hilketa asks.

He thinks that he has led me on far and complicated ways and that I am lost.

"Where do you wish to be?"

"Anywhere but here."

There is despair in his voice.

"Are you lost?"

"We are lost, not that it matters. I must be somewhere. You have done well, you have followed me in darkness. Now we must return and you shall lead."

If he thinks I am lost, he is disappointed. I know exactly where we are and I lead him to our rooms by the quickest route. I do not have to back track. In my head there is a silver maze and I find the shortest way to our rooms.

"So you can find your way in the dark. That is good. But consider this, the quickest way is not always the best way."

I shrug as I light the lantern.

"What is wrong with the way I led you?"

"Nothing."

That night I sleep and the sound of an old man murmuring, the flutter of bats and the scuttle of beetles is my cradle song. I sleep soundly. I sleep with no fear. In the morning, Hilketa wakes me. Again he leads me through the tunnels in total darkness. We do not go the same way, but we end at the same junction.

"Now take us back."

I lead and he follows. It is easy. I can retrace the route I took yesterday. When we arrive at the rooms, Hilketa lights a lantern. I can see he is not happy.

"What is wrong with the way I led you?"

"Do I have to tell you? I thought you would be smarter than that. Last time you were smarter. Last time you would not have needed me to tell you."

He does not have to tell me, I know. I should not have come the same way, I should not have been predictable, I did not walk carefully. I should not let anyone think they know where I am. I have been a fool. I have put myself in danger. I have put Hilketa in danger.

"I am sorry, it will not happen again."

"Then it's a lesson learned."

Yes, it is a lesson learned, now I know why he took me back to the same place.

"Did I make the same mistake last time?"

I am annoyed at his suggestion that I am less than I was last time.

"What makes you think there was a last time? Now come and copy out these tablets."

I fetch a tablet and sit. Hilketa hands me a tablet and I start to copy it out.

Great ones, I hereby relate that certain citizens of our town have murmured against the order of things. These citizens being wealthy and influential did stir up discontent. It was necessary to conduct firm action to suppress the activities of these rebels. They and their households have been dealt with in the appropriate manner. All goods in the possession of the deceased have been confiscated and will be redistributed in due course. This will raise a small sum for the treasury to be sent shortly. As ever, we are loyal to the Sun and loyal to darkness. Praise Vatu.

It is the same report that Hilketa asked me about before.

"So what have you read?" he asks. Why is he asking this? I have told him before. I read it again. What have I missed? Who are these citizens? What kind of murmuring? What kind of discontent? What firm action have they carried out? What is the appropriate manner to treat them? What possessions have been confiscated? Who will they be redistributed to? What will be sent to the treasury?

"There is not enough information," I say.

"So what does that tell you?"

I think for a moment, then answer, "The governor has something to hide, otherwise he would have given me the information."

"So what does he hide?"

"He is hiding the nature of the discontent, he does not wish us to pay too much attention, he is suggesting that it is nothing, but if it was nothing, then why would he have executed the individuals? You do not execute rich citizens for nothing."

"Why do you execute rich citizens?"

Again I hesitate before answering. "Because they are a threat. Rich citizens can cause trouble, they can buy support from the outer court, maybe even from the inner court. They can have a governor removed, or assassinated."

"And which do you think is the reason this governor wishes to hide?"

"There would be no reason to hide either reason. Therefore it is neither, there was no discontent; the citizens are executed simply because the governor covets their wealth. He has murdered them and stolen their belongings, he offers a small bribe to the treasury to allow this to go unpunished."

"Good, now you are learning to read properly, now you are

reading what is not written. What should we do with this governor?"

"Kill him, he is a murderer and a thief, he has blackened the name of Vatu. He thinks a small bribe will buy him safety. Perhaps if the report had gone only to the outer court it would have been enough. He is also a fool. Does he think he can bribe Vatu? Does he think he can bribe justice? He must be stripped of his position and slain. Send for him. He must come to the tower to face justice."

"As you wish, but first consider. Is this wise to slay him? The land must be governed, should we not let the governors govern? If we slay every crooked official then we might have none left."

"Justice is not negotiable, it is not flexible, it does not consider what is wise or what is simple. But even so, if we do not execute those that misgovern, then they will all misgovern."

Hilketa is looking at me strangely.

"Why are you looking at me like that?"

"You are becoming yourself, great one. It is the right decision. It is the only decision that you can make. The order will be given and he will be brought here."

Then he hands me another tablet and I copy it out.

"Now tell me what this one says."

Most of the tablets I copy out are unremarkable, they are reports of the movement of goods, or production audits, or population tallies, or registers of tradesmen, or lists of official appointments within a province. I ask Hilketa why I have to copy out these tedious lists.

"How else will you know?" he asks. "If you will be the High Priest, you must know the land you rule."

"Do I rule? I thought Vatu ruled and that Vatu knows everything."

Hilketa looks away for a moment. That is how I know he is lying to me.

"Mighty Vatu does indeed know everything, but you are his servant. What he knows, he will not necessarily tell. He does indeed rule, but does not expect to be bothered with trivial things. If you think Vatu will run the administration or help you, then you are mistaken."

"Doesn't the outer court run these things?"

"Yes, indeed it does, but who runs the outer court? Will you let it just run itself? You will be the High Priest of Vatu, through you the power of the shadow is made plain in the land. You are the shadow of the shadow. What kind of shadow will you cast?"

A few days later, Hilketa hands me a tablet. "Read it out," he says.

> *Great one, it is as you thought, the governor Izain has been oppressing the people of Taiga. He has accumulated great wealth by taxing the people heavily and sending only minimal tribute to the treasury. He has threatened the citizens with execution if they do not comply with his demands. He has executed several notable citizens and confiscated their belongings. The people of the households have been sold into slavery and dispersed. We have imprisoned the governor and have appointed another in his place. We await further instruction.*

It is from the outer court.

"Well?" asks Hilketa.

"I wonder, who have they appointed as the replacement for Izain? Also, he could not have behaved thus without the assistance of someone within the outer court. That assistance must have been bought by bribes. He should be found and taken also."

"What you say is true. The outer court is very corrupt. If you wish to remove all that have taken bribes, then there will be many that will have to leave, perhaps all."

"Have you taken bribes?"

"I am one of the twelve, in my thousands of lifetimes, no doubt I have taken bribes."

"I ask about this lifetime, do not play games with me."

"What was written once is written over and over. If I took bribes once, then I will have taken them more than once. Yes, I have taken bribes. We have all taken bribes. Does that mean you will slay me? You cannot dismiss me, I am not your servant, I am Vatu's servant. For a thousand lifetimes he has not dismissed me, or any of the twelve."

He is right, I cannot punish him, not yet. I must wait, then I will punish them all. I take the tablet and wipe it clean. There is nothing else to do, not now.

"You are wise," says Hilketa.

I am not wise, I am weak. I must grow stronger.

"You say that Vatu has never dismissed any of the twelve, but how can you know? If you do not recall your past lives, then how can you know? He could have dismissed many of you and you would not know."

"That is true. I have no recollection of the first time Vatu called me to his service, or if he has ever dismissed one of the twelve. But the names of the twelve are written in the dark. These are deep mysteries that only you can know. Vatu will answer when you ask these things. He will show you as he has shown us. You will see that what I say is true. He has called us to him, and calls us to him still."

"So you know how we were first called?"

"No, I only know we were called. Vatu has told us that he called us, and that we are reborn to serve him. Only us, only the twelve and you are reborn. We live life after life, when all those around us are perished and go to the darkness. Only we are sent back by the dark. Only we live forever."

"It is a great gift from the dark one," I say.

"Is it?" says Hilketa. "It is," he answers his own question.

But then I think about him watching the moon. How many times has it travelled around the world? When did it first travel around the earth, when will it stop travelling? He is old and foolish, he is thinking about his rebirth. He is thinking about his death.

"What happens when one of the twelve die?" I ask.

"You mean what will happen when I die. You will go and find me; I will be reborn and Vatu will lead you to me. I will be brought back here and be raised by the remaining twelve until I take my rightful place as a servant of Vatu."

"Is that what happened when I died?" I ask, but Hilketa does not answer. It is late, I will go to my room and sleep. I turn to leave. Hilketa is sitting with his head bowed; he does not look up when I leave. In my room I lie down in darkness, but I do not sleep. All night I lie awake and I do not hear Hilketa snoring or murmuring in his sleep. It seems he does not sleep either. It is a gift the darkness does not give us.

Chapter Four
Justice

The same words are written on the tablet; that is what Hilketa said. That every time the tablet is cleared blank, the same words are written upon it. I have lived a thousand lifetimes, and I know nothing of any of them. My past is a mystery. In my room I look at my wax tablet. Is that really all I am?

Hilketa takes me to the tower again, to the top of the tower. The moon is like a blind man's eye. It is staring down at me. It sees nothing. It is a blind eye that opens and closes, blinking in phases from east to west, as it travels around the earth. It sees nothing. It can tell me nothing of my past lives. It will teach me nothing.

"Why must we look at the moon again?"

"Because it is beautiful."

"What is beauty?"

"It is something you know, something you recognize but cannot explain. I cannot tell you what beautiful is, I can only show you."

"Is that why you bring me here?"

"Do not you think the moon is beautiful?"

"I suppose. I have not thought about it. It is just there."

"Do you think anything is beautiful?"

"I have not thought about it. No, I can't think of anything that is beautiful. What is beauty, it is just a word."

"You are right, it is just a word, and like all words, it is not enough."

"What do you mean?"

"I mean that if I tell you the moon is beautiful you will not believe me, if I say a woman is beautiful you might agree or perhaps not. You might say 'yes she is pretty,' but you will not know what is beautiful about them to me. The moon is beautiful to me for all sorts of reasons. They are the same reasons you cannot see its beauty."

"I never said the moon was not beautiful."

"You said that nothing was beautiful, and that means there is no beauty in your life. I feel sorry for you, but you are young. Perhaps you will find it in time. Beauty is something you must search for, it must be found. Sometimes it finds you."

"Beauty is pointless nonsense."

"It is not pointless, although it can seem that way. It is only that too few of us see the point."

"What beauty was there in my past lives?"

"I don't know, perhaps none, you always kept things close. But there is beauty all around us, I cannot believe that you were too blind to see it."

"So it gives you pleasure to come and look at the beautiful sky and the beautiful moon. That is why you come up here. Beauty is pleasure. I understand now."

"Perhaps." Hilketa seems to shiver although it is not cold. It is never cold at the tower.

"Come," he says, "we should go back to our studies."

I follow him back to the apartments, and he lights a lamp. We will be copying more tablets.

"We will not be doing this much longer," he says. He is right, it will not be long now till my year with him is up. Is this all he has to teach me?

He hands me a tablet, again he seems to shiver. I ask him if he is unwell, but he shakes his head.

"Read it."

> Great Vatu, we have done as you have commanded. We went to the house as directed. The boy was there. We collected him. The mother objected, as did the father. It was necessary to dispatch both. Afterwards we burned their home and all their possessions. We took the rest of the household and sold the slaves. The money will be added to the treasury. The boy is now in the care of Zauria. All is as you commanded. Kong

Hilketa is shaking.

"What?" I ask. "This tablet is a report from Kong to Vatu. It tells of the taking of a boy into care. Presumably this is a report from when I was taken. Why has it been kept? Did you know it was in this pile? Is this why you are shaking? Did you think I would be angry when I discovered Kong has killed my parents?"

Hilketa shakes his head, but he is still trembling.

"There is more to this then, and I still cannot see it. You have kept this record and are showing it to me now. Why? Are you trying to make me hate Kong? I already know he is my enemy. But you are frightened to show me the tablet, it is fear that is making you shake. You do not fear to defy Kong. I know you do not fear him, although he almost poisoned you. What then? What do you fear? Who do you fear? It can only be Vatu that you fear. Why do you think he will be angry? What is written here that you should fear to let me read?"

I read over the tablet again. Hilketa is calmer but says nothing. This puzzle I must solve for myself. It would shame me if I should not be able to do so by myself. Why has he shown this to me? In fact, why is there a written report? How did Hilketa get the report? Is it a fake? Has Hilketa written this and is trying to pass it off as real?

"How did you get this?" I ask. "How did it get here? Tell me, what do you know about this?"

"You must ask Kong."

I must ask Kong. I will. I will ask him. I will be in his care in three years' time, then I will ask him.

"Are there records of all my rebirths?"

"No."

"No?"

"But there are some, not many."

"Then there are records going back to when? How many years do they go back?"

"Who can say? There are a great many records. They are kept in the library. I have read some but not all, not nearly all, there are a great many. They go back many years. Who knows how many years? Would you like me to show you the library sometime?"

"Yes."

"As you wish."

The next day I am told that there is a prisoner. Hilketa leads me to a cell. I did not know we had prisoners in the tower.

"How many prisoners do we have?"

"A great many come, mostly Kong deals with them. It is the High Priest's responsibility to dispense the justice of Vatu. Kong deals with it in your absence."

"How many are there?"

"Truthfully I do not know. It is not something I concern myself with. A great many come for certain, but they do not last for long. The justice of Vatu is swift and unerring... mostly."

"So will Kong deal with this man?"

"If you ask him, certainly. Do you wish me to let Kong deal with him? I'm certain he will. Perhaps it would be better."

"No. I will deal with him. It is right that I should."

"Yes, it is right that you should."

We enter a room. It is small but not rough. The walls are black glass with gold and there is a chair and a mirror, just one chair. There is a man sitting in it. He is tall and muscular. He is dressed well and has much gold draped around him. I can see he has not been maltreated. He has no bruising or injury on his dark skin. Nor is he any less plump than a governor should be. He has been fed well. I would guess that he has less gold than when he set out. He stands when we enter. He is nervous and forgets to prostrate himself before us. We do not bother to correct his mistake. There are more important things to deal with.

"What is your name?"

"My name is Izain."

"Indeed, Izain, and do you know why you are our guest?"

"No, lord. I know nothing about the workings of the court. I am governor of Urrunak. Why, may I ask, am I here?"

"You have been accused of stealing from the citizens of Urrunak."

"Great lord, I swear it, I have stolen nothing."

"Really? There is a report that you had executed some citizens and confiscated their goods."

Izain swallows. "Yes, lord, it is true. They were stirring up rebellion against Vatu."

"Rebellion against Vatu?" I laugh. "How is that possible? How is it possible to rebel against the darkness? He is everywhere."

Now Izain prostrates himself. "It is true, I swear it." His chains jangle as he drops to the floor.

"How can it be true? Tell us. If there is rebellion then we must know of it. Your report does not go into details. How did they rebel?"

"Through their words, they were caught. It was seen by many people and it cannot be denied. They were praying, to God, or to gods. I do not know all the details. But they met in secret in each other's houses and taught some nonsense that Vatu would depart, that the darkness would depart, that the Sun would shine day after day. It is true, I swear it."

"How can it be true?" I sneer. "No one can be such fools. No one can think that the darkness can end. Have you beheld Vatu? He cannot end. He is endless. The darkness is endless."

"This is true, great one. I cannot deny it. They are fools and like fools they deserved to die. They say the darkness is endless, but so is the light. They say the light is endless and that they will worship the light, not the darkness. Forgive me, great one, these are not my words but theirs. I only repeat them. They said many other things. They could not be allowed to spread their nonsense through the town. It was the only thing I could do. I had to kill them, all of them and their families and households."

Now Hilketa speaks. "It is easy to accuse, but what evidence do you have?"

"I have their own words, words drawn from torture. All of them confessed. All of them had to die."

"And you sold the slaves?" I ask. "Slaves who were taught this nonsense and able to spread it to their new homes. Nor did you seek to find where this madness sprang from."

"It is true, I swear it. The slaves are nothing."

"Indeed it may be true, although I doubt it. But if it is true, it is still clear that you acted only to make yourself richer. The houses should have been burned, who knows what heretical texts they have hidden in them, and their slaves should be killed. I am told the women were spared, is that true?"

"Yes, great one, it is true. They were allowed to live, but they were taken and given to others."

"Given to you, perhaps? I hear one of the women is in your own household. I hear that you have taken her to wife and put your old wife away. I am still young and in the tower we have no women. We do not understand these things. Why would you put away one wife for another? Is that a common thing to do; to take another man's wife and her become yours after slaying her husband and her sons? I wonder why you would do that. Perhaps you could help me understand. It sounds very strange to me, that you would wish to harbour this rebel in your home."

He does not speak. Instead he tears his gold from his arms and neck and pushes it towards me.

"You seek to bribe me. How strange. I had thought you would be cleverer than that. I have no need of your bribe. I can slay you and take all that you have. And even so, do you think it is a fraction of what the High Priest has?"

He is wise enough to say nothing, but stretches forth a hand in supplication.

"There is only one question now. Should only you die, or do I need to exterminate your entire household?"

"Great Lord, you have caught me in a lie. I beg that you spare me, and all that is mine. I coveted the woman, so I destroyed her husband and his allies. Now she lies with me. She is very beautiful. You are young, but the older one will understand. A man will do anything for love."

I turn to Hilketa, amused. "Well, old one. What do you say?"

Hilketa is dressed in the robes of his priesthood. His helmet covers his eyes and I cannot see to read them. The thought that Hilketa knows love, this kind of love, is laughable.

"What will you do for love, Hilketa? Will you betray Vatu?"

"They must all die," he says. "If this man will murder for this woman, he will lie for her too. She may be a heretic. As you say, the idea is ridiculous, but not so ridiculous that she can live. His household must perish, his name and line extinguished."

"The old one has spoken," I say.

I motion for Izain to sit on the chair. I walk behind him. He does not struggle as I wrap one of his gold chains around his neck. I pull it tighter and hold it, while his eyes and tongue bulge. It is hard work, Izain has a strong neck. He scratches at the chain but it does not break and towards the end he thrashes about. But I manage, I am strong. Hilketa watches and then comes forward.

"He is dead, let go, he is dead."

I loosen my grip on the chain and Izain slumps to the ground.

"I will have the officers of the inner court remove the body. I will write to have his household extinguished."

I nod in agreement.

"It was just," says Hilketa.

No doubt it was just, but still, it is the first time I have killed a man. I try to put the picture of his bulging tongue and eyes out of my head.

"It is hard," says Hilketa.

"No, it was not," I reply. "It was easy. All I had to do was hold on and wait."

"Yes," Hilketa says, "it is too easy, that is why it is hard."

He puts a gauntleted hand upon my shoulder but I shrug it off.

"Do you think I am weak? This is only the first I have slain in this life, there will be many others."

Hilketa nods. "Indeed, great lord."

The room now smells of death, cold and heavy like salt. It is unpleasant.

"Will you take the gold?" asks Hilketa.

"No," I reply. "Do you wish to have it? What will you do with it?"

Hilketa shrugs. But I know he will keep it. He will not let the inner court have it. We leave and he locks the door behind us. He will keep the gold. It is his weakness, one of them. We walk back, and I flex my hands. There are marks where the chain dug into my flesh as I pulled it tight.

Chapter Five
Graves

We speak no more of it, there is nothing to speak of. It is nothing, it is the work of the priest, it is my work to do justice and it was just. Now the tablet is truly wiped clean. The marks on my hand fade quickly. They fade quicker than the memory of the deed.

We return to our work of reading. It is necessary but not interesting. We read and write tablets for many days. But we find nothing that causes Hilketa to pause, nothing to make us read what is not written.

It is many days before Hilketa takes me to the library. It is a great hollow chamber. We enter towards the top of the chamber. There is a gallery that spirals downwards. The gallery is lined with shelves. Each shelf is filled with tablets. I look over the gallery and down. It is dark and I cannot see to the bottom.

"How far does it go?" I ask.

Hilketa shrugs. "I have never gone all the way to the bottom. It is very deep."

"So what is on the shelves?"

"Everything. Mostly as you go deeper they get older, or so I suppose, they are not in very good order. That is our fault, we should have catalogued them better, but we did not. Even now, we just bring the tablets in and stuff them where we find a space. I have seen some of the priests pull out old records and throw them over the rail to make space for new records. There is more space on the shelves further down."

We follow the gallery as it spirals down a few times. I pull a tablet from the shelf. There must be thousands of tablets.

"No one can read all of these."

"Then why do we keep them?" Hilketa asks.

I wonder the same question; why do we keep them?

"Cannot Vatu remember all things?" I ask Hilketa.

"Do you think that Vatu will answer questions for us? We are his servants; he is not ours."

"And you think that there are answers here, in this dusty place?"

Hilketa pauses, and I can see he is thinking.

"Yes," he says.

"What answers?" I ask and throw the tablet I am holding into the central space. It is a while before I hear it land with a clatter.

"It depends what questions are asked."

"How do I know what questions to ask?"

"What do you want to know?"

I have no answer. What do I want to know?

"The truth," I say, but Hilketa just laughs.

We return to the library every day for a moon turn. Each day we take a different route. Each time we come, we walk deeper into the library, going further down. As we walk, Hilketa will take a tablet and hand it to me. He will make me read it. Usually it is a pointless description of harvests or metal output or timber yields. Sometimes they relate changes in official appointments or are reports on executions. Hilketa will ask me about them. I tell him they are old, the events are from long ago. I do not understand why I am being shown these things. Are these the answers that Hilketa claims are to be found here? This is just dusty old facts about people long since dead. What good is that?

Once a screech owl comes flying at our heads, but Hilketa beats it away. There are always owls in the library. Their droppings are everywhere, small pellets filled with bat bones and fur. There are also spiders everywhere. You must check the shelves first before you put your hand there. Some of the spiders are poisonous. You do not want them to bite you. The floor is thick with dust. The first levels have not so much dust because they have been walked on, there are just layers in corners and by the edge of the gallery. Further down the dust is thicker and you can make out individual prints. Only the twelve come here. The servants from the outer court are not permitted, and anyway, they could only find it if they were accompanied by one of the twelve.

"Why are the servants not allowed in here?" I ask.

Hilketa looks at me. In the dark, I cannot see his face, but I can tell he is pleased by the way his breathing changes.

"How do you know that servants are not allowed in here?"

"I'm not sure, didn't you say so the first time we came?"

"No, I did not."

"Well, they must not be allowed, if they were we would have seen them."

"The twelve are allowed, but we have never seen them."

"That is because you do not wish to meet them, not here. I know you are cautious. Even so, it must be a risk to come so often. We might meet any of them here. Are you not afraid that one of them might come? Are you not afraid that Kong might come?"

"Has it not crossed your mind that the reason we do not meet others of the twelve may not be because I fear them, but because they fear me?"

I look at Hilketa for a moment. He is old and almost gentle. I realize that I have started to think of him as such. I have forgotten that he is one of the twelve.

"Do they fear you?"

"How do you know only the twelve are allowed here?"

I think for a moment and then it comes to me.

"There are only twelve different footprints. There must be countless different footprints from each of the twelve from their past lives, but the footprints of the twelve, the living twelve are all that I can see in the dust. The older prints must have been filled with dust or obscured by the footprints of those that are the twelve now. Look, here are your footprints and mine, these ones, these are Zauria. See how he walks hesitantly and keeps to the side as if he would hide. The heavier ones, slightly sparrow toed, that is Beldura. Some of the others I do not recognize. I do not know all of the twelve, not yet. But look, here, these ones, proud and arrogant, see how he strides boldly and quickly, these are Kong's. I know them because I have seen them once before. I will not forget them."

Hilketa nods. "I told you there were answers here, a great many answers. This is just the first."

After that we do not go back to the library. Whatever answers to whatever questions Hilketa wanted me to find, it seems can wait. I am taught to read and write and to count and divide. I am taught other things. Corpses are brought to our rooms, and

Hilketa peels back the layers of skin and muscle. Joints are exposed and we explore how they bend and turn. Nerves are traced from end to origin. Weaknesses are revealed. I learn how to stun and to cripple and how to kill. The human body is remarkably vulnerable.

"Mostly," Hilketa tells me, "you will wish to inflict pain without death or without the subject passing out."

"Why?"

"Because an unconscious man can tell us very little and a dead man even less. Mostly you will want to subdue a subject. That is why locking and immobilization is useful to you. But remember, to dominate a body is one thing, to dominate a mind is something different."

"Will you not teach me how to dominate a mind?"

Hilketa looks at me.

"What?" I say. "Do you think I am not ready? Do you think I am too young for such things? If you know them, teach me. You will not get the chance again."

"These are things you must teach yourself. There will be other teachers too. But never forget you are Utas, the darkness is inside you. It will show you all that you need to know."

Hilketa hands me the knife and I flay the skin from a corpse's foot. It is delicate work, I take the skin off in a single piece, rolling it back as I do.

"If you cut into my corpse, where would you find that part of the body that is me?" I ask.

"That is difficult to say. If you are dead, then the part of you that is you will be gone, so we would not be able to find it. Some say that the soul resides in the stomach, some say in the head and some that it resides in the brain. It is true that some emotions are felt in the stomach and heart, while the brain is the organ of thought."

"So in the brain then?"

"Well perhaps, but consider, your bowels churn because you are afraid, you are not afraid because your bowels are churning. Your heart races because you are in love, you are not in love because your heart is racing. So it is with thinking, do you think because your brain works or does your brain work because you are thinking?"

"What do you mean?"

"Stop and think of something, anything. Now tell me what it

is?"

"I am thinking of the moon."

"So where has that thought come from?"

"I don't know, you are too subtle for me, I wish only to know what life is."

"A mystery."

"That is not much of an answer."

"It is the only answer I can give."

Next day, Hilketa leads me into the tunnels again. We travel far and by routes I do not know. How many tunnels are there? Where do they all lead?

"This is Vatu's kingdom, it is endless and limitless. There is no end to darkness," says Hilketa when I ask.

Nevertheless, we come to an end, or at least to a stop, a destination. The tunnel opens out into another vast cavern. How many of these dark caverns are there?

"Countless, or perhaps none, perhaps Vatu creates each tunnel anew each time we walk through them and each cavern anew when we enter them," says Hilketa when I ask.

I point out that this cannot be right. When we return to the library, everything is just the same as when we left, even the footprints in the dust, just as we remember them.

"If Vatu can create a cavern of darkness, he can create footprints in dust, or memories."

I do not agree, but I say nothing more on the subject. This cavern is not like the library. It was deep and narrow, going down in a seemingly endless spiral. This cavern is low and vast. When Hilketa holds up the lantern I can see roots coming down from the roof. We must be near the surface.

"Perhaps," agrees Hilketa, "or perhaps the roots are very deep."

The floor of the cavern is like a shallow bowl sloping down to the centre. There is a wide path leading into the centre and paths radiating out. I think the paths are circular and come back to the main path but I cannot be sure because I cannot see all the way to the other side of the cavern. It is too vast, the light does not shine far enough. There are low walls following the sides of the paths forming a series of terraces descending downwards. In the walls are a series of niches; in the niches there are old urns. As we walk I can see that the urns are made in a wide variety of materials and styles. Some are made of bronze, the older ones are mostly made of clay. Some of them look quite crude. As we go nearer the centre, the urns look older and some of them have fallen over or have cracked. Where the urns have broken, ash and bone have spilled out, and there are fragments of bone strewn over the path. We have to tread on bone to walk. It crunches as we step on the path, bits of bone cracking and breaking, then ground into the earth as we walk.

"What is this place?"

"Do you need me to tell you?"

"I can see it is a boneyard. I can see that each of these urns is filled with funeral ashes. This must be where the remains of the twelve are laid at rest."

"The twelve are not laid at rest here. Even in death, we are beneath you. Can you see now why we hate you so?"

"So is there a graveyard for the twelve?"

"Yes, our ashes are taken to another place. I can show you if you wish. It is not like this, it is not here."

Hilketa leads me along one of the paths and stops. There is a tall clay urn decorated with a white slip glaze. It is tall and cylindrical with a white lid. The glaze is very fine and lightly crazed. It has no markings on it, no name or date.

"Who is this?"

"No one, it is no one. None of these are anyone, they are ashes, they are nothing. This urn contains ashes, nothing. It is the nothing that was you. It is the nothing that was you when I was a child. It is the nothing that was my friend. Now my friend is you."

I am not his friend. I do not believe him.

"Yes, I know; you are not my friend. You will not say it, not out loud. But I know."

I stand and a weight seems to rest upon me.

"Why have you brought me here?"

"Because you must know."

I nod my head. I understand.

"Do you wish to see the place of the twelve?"

"No, there is no need. I will see it soon enough."

"You mean when I die. Yes, I suppose that will be soon enough."

There are so many, so so many. I have walked over my own ashes. This is nothing. What I was is gone. This is nothing. It is like the ashes of a fire, the fire is not the ashes, although if one stirs the ashes while they are still hot, the fire could start again, but not so with these ashes. They are very cold. I am here, I am now and I will be forever.

Hilketa leads me on to another urn, it is more cone shaped and is decorated with combed motifs. It is unglazed clay, but the body of the clay is mottled ochre with marks of iron oxide. It is simple and plain, and very elegant.

"Why are they all different?"

"Do you think we have a store of pots just to put ashes in? When you died the first time you had the pot. The second time you died unexpectedly. Kong chose the pot. He is the leader of the twelve. I think he chose well, I think you would have liked it. I think you should like it."

"I do like it. I am surprised."

"Yes, it is very elegant, simple but elegant. Why are you surprised? Kong would only want the finest for the ashes of the High Priest."

"So he has chosen all of these, or at least most of them?"

"I don't know. I can only say he chose that one."

"You say I died unexpectedly. How did I die?"

"I don't know, I was not there."

"But you know."

"Not for sure."

"But you can guess."

"I can but so can you."

I reach out and touch the urn. It feels rough to my fingers. The top of the urn is open and I can see bone and ash. I am crying. Why? I am not dead. I am not ashes stuffed in a jar. What am I?

"Do you want me to leave? I can leave for a while."

"No, why would I want that? This is nothing."

"I remember the first time I visited the grave of the twelve. It raised thoughts and feelings, difficult feelings. Later not so much, but still it is a strange thing to think about."

"No. I am fine, there is no problem. Is there anything else you want to show me here?"

"Is there anything else you want to see?"

I look around me again. Everywhere I look is the same, urns filled with ashes and bone. What else is there to see? I could walk forever and not see every urn. Many are broken. I wonder if the earliest bones were even put in a pot.

"Do you know where the first bones were laid?"

"The pots do not have dates, you can guess which ones are older by how worn they look and some of them are broken. Some have roots growing through them. The older ones are probably in the middle, or so it seems to me. Some of the pots are very beautiful, as is fitting for the High Priest. It might be that the first bones were not even laid here. Parts of the cavern have collapsed, the tree roots have caused the roof to fall."

"Why are there tree roots here? Why build the tombs here?"

"I would guess that there were no tree roots when they first laid your bones here. I guess that over the ages the roots have grown. It may be that the earth above has worn away and that this is nearer to the surface than it used to be. That might be why there are roots now. Perhaps this is not even the first tomb chamber, perhaps there was a chamber above that the earth has worn down to and exposed. In time, this chamber might collapse and we will build a new one below it. Eventually, even this cavern will be full."

I close my eyes and think of darkness, endless darkness.

"I have seen enough."

Chapter Six
Footsteps

When we return to the rooms, I fill the bathing pool with water. I slip into the pool and sink down into the lukewarm water. It is good to feel the cool water after the heat of the tower. The tower is always hot. Air is funnelled through the tower to cool it, but is never enough to make it comfortable. The heat of the Sun makes the air hot and dry; it is only in the tunnels beneath the tower that it is bearable.

I want to wash the dust and ash from my body. I want to wash all traces of my dead selves away. I put my head down under the water. I stay under for as long as I can hold my breath. I am in a different world, a world of water. When I can hold my breath no longer, I break through the surface. I return to this world.

Hilketa is there in the dark, waiting.

"Drowned," he says. "They say he drowned, the older one. You would have thought he knew better. You cannot hear underwater; you cannot hear someone approach. Perhaps he just died in the bath. It is not a bad way to die. We all die sometime, somewhere. We die more often than others."

I am ashamed. I should not have let him enter unaware. I think he will correct me, but he does not.

"There is no need to fear. I would not have drowned you. If I would kill you, I could have come to your room any night for the last year and smothered you. You are right to trust me. I come because you have been in here so long. I wish only to make sure you are all right."

"Why would I not be?"

"Indeed, why would you not be, you are the High Priest."

"If I am the High Priest, then why am I not taken to Vatu? The only time I have been with him is when I have been handed over from one of the twelve to the next. Even on Sunday, even in summer, I am not present. Why am I not with Vatu?"

Hilketa sits at the edge of the pool. He draws his robe around him to keep it dry.

"You are the High Priest, and you are not the High Priest. It is like a tablet. We are writing down what must be written, but there is more to write. You are the start of the High Priest but you are not the end. When all is written, then you will be the High Priest and you will be with Vatu."

"Why can Vatu not write what must be written?"

"I'm sure he can. He chooses not to. He does not answer to the twelve, or even to you. He will do as he wills, and we must follow."

Why, why must we follow, I think to myself, but I say nothing. I stand up in the pool and let the water fall back. I walk out and stand with my arms outstretched and let the warm air dry my skin. The water runs down my back. I step away from the pool.

"The Sun will rise soon. Then after that, I will hand you over to Arraio. Our year will be over."

"Yes. I will move on and learn more. Soon I will be the High Priest. Soon the tablet will be written."

"Yes, soon it will."

"I want to go back to the library."

"Why?"

"I want you to show me something."

"As you wish."

Hilketa turns and goes to his room. I leave and go to mine. I lie awake thinking. It is no use. Why must we do as Vatu says? Why must we do this same thing over and over again? How many times have my ashes been placed in a vase and laid in the dark? I feel like I am drowning in ashes, I feel like l am lying on a pile of bones. I have burned. I have burned. I have burned, and I am ash. I rise up from my bed and lie underneath it. I curl up into a ball. Why, I do not understand, why am I doing this? My fingernails dig into my forearms. I drive them in deeper and deeper until there is blood. I feel better and lie down on my couch. As the blood flows, so do my cares flow away. It is a blessed relief, and sleep comes at last. I sleep obliviously.

In the morning, Hilketa comes to wake me as he has every day, except the one when Kong attempted to kill me. I rise and eat. He indicates the wounds on my arms.

"Did it help?" he asks.

"Yes, it helps."

"It is not the answer."

"What is the answer?"

"You must find the answer, I cannot tell you."

"How do you cope?" I ask.

"What makes you think I cope? What makes you think any of us cope? Have you not seen that we are mad? Soon, you will be mad too."

We do not go to the library that day, despite my request. Instead, I am led through familiar passages to an unfamiliar door.

"What is this?"

"It is the place of the twelve, where our bones and ashes are laid."

"There is no need for me to see this."

"Yes, there is," says Hilketa, and opens the door. We enter onto a gantry. It is only a few feet wide.

"I cannot see any urns."

"No, you will not see any urns."

"Well, where?"

"Go to the edge."

I am hesitant. I think it may be a trick. From the edge, he can cast me down. But if he had wanted me dead, he has had better chances than this. So I walk to the edge and look. It is not a big cave, but it is deep. At first, I can see nothing.

"I don't understand."

Looking down I see a large pile, like a mound or bigger, a heap. At first, I think it is dirt collapsed down from above to form a great pile. Then I see there are bits of broken earthenware and bone. It is a pile of ash and bone and broken pottery. It is all tossed over the gantry to fall into the pit. They must land on the great pile of ash and shatter and bounce. Bones and ash must scatter and mingle. It is the ashes of the twelve mingled into a great pile. They are not interred nor respected. They are discarded, like trash. The ash and bone of a million heaped in disrespect. This is where Hilketa will be discharged, into a great pile of trash.

"Why?" I ask, but there is no answer. There can never be an answer.

Hilketa stays away from the edge. He does not approach me. I see it was necessary to bring me here. I do not know how long we stay. It seems like barely a moment.

"My ashes are mixed with Kong and with Arraio and Irruzura and Zauria, all of the filthy disgusting scum that make the twelve, and is just. I am filthy just like them. It is just that we are discarded."

"It is a hard justice," I say.

"All justice is hard," replied Hilketa, "and cruel."

We leave and close the door. We want no ghosts to follow us. Can there be ghosts of those reborn? Can we haunt ourselves?

Later that night it is hot and I think I hear footsteps. I realize that I am sleeping and that I am dreaming of footsteps. Whose footsteps do I hear? They are moving around the tower. At first they were quiet and I could only just hear them but now they are loud as drums, and they come quickly as if they are running. Faster and faster they come. Whose footsteps? Where are they going? They are coming for me. I know they are coming for me.

In the morning, I hear footsteps, but they are Hilketa's footsteps as he comes to wake me and bring me food.

"Today we must go to the library," I say.

"Yes," agrees Hilketa, "we will go to the library."

We walk to the library. I walk in front, and Hilketa follows me. We walk down into the lower levels of the library. As we go, the footprints in the dust get fewer and fewer. We keep going. Now there are fewer footprints still, but still we go deeper down into the library. As we go deeper, the air is cooler. It is good to escape the heat. Hilketa follows as I walk. We walk in silence. Our path is lit only by a single lantern. Our footsteps leave a trail in the dust, but still there are footsteps ahead of us.

Now there are only two sets of footprints. I can recognize one of the sets, but not the other. I keep going until I see one set of footprints stop, turn to a shelf and then turn back. Now there is only one set of footsteps going forward. I stop and turn to Hilketa.

"Tell me, whose footsteps are these?" I ask, pointing to one set of footprints.

"Yes, it is as you guess. These are mine. Only we two have ever come so deep." He points to the footprints that have stopped. "I will wait here."

I step forward. I put my feet into my own footsteps. I step forward, following them down and down. From the space between steps, and from the size of the steps, I know I was older, much older. I was fully grown, and I need to stretch out each stride so that I can reach each print. For some reason, I do not want to leave a trail. It is because I do not want Kong to see where I have gone. He must not know. It is enough that Hilketa knows. I walk deeper and deeper. But still, the footsteps do not end. I notice that there are no footsteps going backwards. There is only one set of steps. I follow them and then suddenly they stop. I stand in my footsteps and look around. By the light of my lantern, I can see the rough stone roof of the gantry above and I can see the shelves to my left. I look across. The room has belled out and is quite wide. I can see the room goes on down for at least four more stories, perhaps more. To the other side, I can see the shelves lining the wall. There are some tablets sitting on the shelves. I write the last few lines on the tablet I am carrying and place it on the shelf for me to find some other time, some other me. Then I lift a tablet from the shelf and trace my steps backwards.

When I return, Hilketa is waiting for me.

"Did you find what you were looking for?"

"No, not yet."

In the morning, I go and wake Hilketa. It is Sunday and Hilketa will go with the twelve to open the Sun. I must stay here. I do not open the Sun until I am High Priest. I will sit and wait for the Sun to go down. I am alone in the rooms. Tomorrow I will be gone. In the room, I cannot see the Sun, but still the darkness seems lighter. I can see light coming in under the door. It might be from lamps. There is a noise like a distant roaring. The air is hotter than ever. I take the tablet from under my pillow. It is of wax, like the one Hilketa used to teach me to write, like the one I have left on the shelf in the library. I run my fingers over the surface and feel the indentations of the stylus. I can read it just by touch, but I turn on the light and start to read.

You have come, I knew you would. Why would you not? To find the answer, you must know the question. Do you know the question? I wonder how many stand between us. Is it years between us or decades, or centuries or longer? Maybe now, there are piles of tablets on this shelf. I must leave something for me to find, something for the new me. I must speak to you. What question would you ask? Who can I trust? That is easy, you know to trust no one. Trust none of them, especially do not trust Kong. We struggled in the dark, blade to blade. Twice now I have slain him. But Vatu will not let him go. I have seen each of the twelve die. Soon I will die and be reborn. My spirit enters a child, but how? I have no answer. I cannot see the beginning of things. Are you as tired of blood as I am? Kong will try to kill me soon. I will slay him. There will be blood once more on my knife. The moon will keep turning. The beautiful moon.

Chapter Seven
Dirt

The next day I am taken to the hall of darkness. Hilketa leads me into the darkness. There is no light here, and I can see none of the others. I cannot see Vatu, unless all of the darkness is Vatu. I open my eyes but I can see nothing. Hilketa is holding my hand.

"I have done with him," he says. "I return him to the dark."

"Who will serve the dark? Who will guide the High Priest?"

"I will," Arraio says and steps forward and takes my hand.

It is always the same order that I am passed from one to another. It is Arraio's turn now. Then he leads me back to his rooms.

Arraio is a filthy pervert. I will not write what he has taught me. It is not worthy of me. I take the bowl that holds my blood and milk and drop it to the ground. It breaks into jagged and sharp pieces. I take a shard and wrap one end in cloth torn from the coverlet of my couch.

When Arraio comes into my room again, I wait until he is close and then I strike. I plunge the shard into his loins and twist. I can hear Arraio scream in pain. I rise up and light the lantern. It takes perhaps an hour before someone from the outer court comes. No doubt they had thought to come and clean, or to remove the remains of my breakfast. He comes rushing in to see Arraio rolling naked on my floor screaming. He is bleeding profusely. The servant looks and says nothing, then rushes away. It is some time later that he returns. Hilketa is with him. Hilketa looks at

Arraio without concern.

"So soon?" he says.

He motions to two servants and they carry him to my couch.

"No," I say. "He does not lie on my couch. Take him next door."

The servants are confused and look to Hilketa for guidance.

"As you wish," he says, and motions the servants to carry Arraio back to his own rooms. I follow.

"Give me something to stop the bleeding," says Arraio.

"It is better if you bleed out," says Hilketa. "The blade will be poisoned. I will have to fish out shards of glass. Glass shatters in the wound. If I do not get it all out, it will fester and spread poison." Hilketa turns to me. "He will not be visiting in the night again, not for some time. What have you poisoned him with?"

"Excrement, from his own pot. I smeared the blade with it."

"Fitting. I will stop the bleeding now and clean the wound. It will likely still putrefy."

Hilketa motions, and the servants hold down Arraio while he washes the wound. He prises the wound open and removes some splinters of glass, then washes it out. There is a lot of blood. Perhaps Arraio will die. I hope he does. If he does not, I may kill him anyway. Hilketa heats wine over a small stove and pours it over the wound.

"Come and see," says Hilketa. "It is a good blow, but not fatal. You have pierced the inside of his groin, just past the major ligament. I suppose you timed the blow to when he raised his leg. It has gone in deep, but has missed the artery. If you had hit the artery there, it would have been fatal. You have nicked the ligament, but not severed it. He will be hampered but not crippled. You might have also pierced the bladder or bowel. I think he will survive the blow, although any infection may still kill him."

Arraio looks at Hilketa. "Don't let me die," he says. Hilketa does not answer him.

"If he dies he will be reborn, you cannot rid us of him this way. We cannot be rid of him."

I nod in agreement. I will not kill him, yet. Hilketa washes his hands and then leaves. Arraio is still lying naked on his bed. He does not speak, but makes small whimpering noises like a child or a wounded animal. I am still tempted to kill him, but instead I return to my room. I practice writing. Arraio has nothing to teach me.

The next day, Arraio is unable to get up out of his bed and is moaning and crying in pain. Hilketa returns to check his wound. As I had hoped, the wound is putrid, and the infection seems to have entered his blood. His body and left thigh are red and swollen. Hilketa has to lance the wound and drain pus. He squeezes and lets the pus fill a copper bowl. He gives Arraio wine to drink laced with poppy syrup. I watch him dosing the patient.

"Yes," he says. "Come and see, this much and no more. It will keep him sleeping."

"How much to kill him?"

"It is not an exact amount. To poison someone is always about judgment. For a large man like Arraio, the dose would have to be more, in general the higher the better, but if the dose is too high, there is more chance of the victim noticing. Poppy syrup is not a good poison to use, the fatal dose is high, and it has a distinctive taste. There are much better things to use."

"Such as?"

"It depends. Do you wish it to be quick, do you wish it to be undetected, do you wish it to be tasteless? Perhaps you want to tip a needle or an arrow. In that case it must be stable. Or maybe you want a powder to blow in someone's face. Do you want it to be absorbed through the skin? If you wish to kill Arraio, then why not smother him or sever an artery?"

"I will not kill him. It would be inconvenient. He is my guardian."

"Yes, if you slay him then we will have to find the reborn Arraio, then you will have an infant as your guardian. It is not ideal."

Hilketa is correct, it would not be, although the servants would care for Arraio.

"None of it is ideal."

Arraio stirs and moans. I wonder if he is really asleep. I wonder if he is listening to us. Many of the twelve have built up immunity to poisons. He may have immunity to poppy syrup. It is a good reminder. Trust no one, trust nothing.

"How long will he be like this?"

"It is difficult to say, probably weeks. You should give him syrup of poppy for the pain. The servants from the inner court will see he is cleaned and fed. You should be careful how often you dose him with syrup."

"Can the servants not dose him as well?"

"They could if you wish it."

I think for a moment. I want as little to do with Arraio as possible. He disgusts me. But if I give him the syrup, then... Enough, I will give him the syrup. He will have to beg me for relief.

"No, I will do it."

Hilketa hands me the vial of poppy syrup, and turns to go.

"I will have to return, to check him. He still might die. But even if he does not, he will suffer. He will never be whole. He will hate you, but he hates you already. You have done such terrible things. We have all done such terrible things."

"Except you, of course, friend," I say.

Hilketa does not reply. He leaves without another word. Does he think I am a fool? Trust no one. I will not let him fool me. I hold the vial and look at it. I am tempted to empty it out. Let Arraio suffer. I wonder if Hilketa has poisoned the vial. It is one of the reasons that the twelve wear gloves; to prevent them from being poisoned by the things they touch. Although as I have said, the twelve are immune to many poisons, most poisons.

Arraio seems to be sleeping. He is snoring loudly and breathing heavily. The room smells bad. It smells of sickness. How fitting. The servants have changed his covers, and they have placed a light cover over him. The bowl of pus has been removed, emptied and washed, and now it is returned. It stands by his bed. Arraio is flushed and sweaty. He is muttering in his sleep. I sit by him and listen. I cannot make out everything that is said.

Arraio is sick many days. He is in great pain. When he sees me, he grimaces and begs for the poppy syrup. Sometimes I give him some. I give him a generous dose so that he sleeps. In his sleep he is restless and delirious. I sit and listen to his words. When he comes to himself, I leave. I wander through the tower, but I do not go back to the library. Not yet, I cannot go just yet. I should go. When I return, Arraio is moaning in pain. I give him a small dose, enough for him to leave me in peace. It numbs his pain but does not make him sleep. I go to my room, and he begs me to leave the bottle with him. I will not. If I did, I do not doubt he would take it all; perhaps it would kill him. I must keep him alive, at least until the next handover. Hilketa comes and cleans his wound. Each day he draws more pus from the wound. I stay and listen to Arraio screaming. No matter how much poppy syrup he takes, he still screams. Hilketa does not speak. He comes, tends Arraio and leaves. Arraio does not say much either. I can see he is getting stronger; it looks like he will survive. Hilketa suggests that I should reduce the amount of syrup I give Arraio.

"The syrup is addictive, you should start to reduce his dose. He will need to be weaned off it slowly."

"Why does he need to be weaned off it at all?"

"Because it is a poison."

"Do we not all dose ourselves with poison? You suggested it to me. Not in so many words, but it is what you meant when you told me the others of the twelve are doing so to make themselves immune," I say.

"It is not quite the same. The body becomes dependent on the syrup. It numbs the nerves, and when it wears off, the nerves are very sensitive. There is always a price to pay. The price of this is that pain is taken away, but when the syrup wears off a greater pain comes. Those addicted to the syrup will do anything for it."

"So he will do what I say to get more," I tell Hilketa. "Now he will do what I say."

Hilketa does not agree. "Yes, for a bit, but he will also do what others of the twelve say. Is that what you want? He will go to Kong, and Kong will give him syrup if he does what he says."

I see he is right.

"The twelve are all necessary," says Hilketa. "We are all vile, but each of us cancels out the others. If Arraio is not here, then others are able to act unhindered. I know you think he deserves to die, but so do we all. It is Vatu who decrees that we do not. Will you argue with him?"

I know I cannot, and I know he is right. The twelve are necessary.

When Arraio recovers he is still weak, perhaps he was always weak. Now that he is stronger, I have to take care. I sleep with a blade under my pillow. I walk with a blade in my hand. I stay alert. I take my food directly from the servants, not from Arraio. I will not let him poison me. For his part, Arraio seems to give me little heed. He starts to leave his room early in the moon round, and returns late. At first I think nothing of it, but then I start to wonder what he is up to. I start to follow him and see that each day, his wanderings always lead out into the inner court.

I do not follow him into the inner court, not at first. I am not sure why. Am I afraid? I stay in the tower and don't go out into the moonlight, I do not leave the tower. Instead, I wait in hiding for Arraio to return. When he returns, he moves erratically and smells of alcohol. I follow him back to the room. When he arrives, he goes to sleep.

Some days when he is gone, I stay in the rooms and look through his things. Arraio is an artist. In his room I find small carved shapes, there are a great many of them. They are surprisingly fine. They are small and intricate. They are carved from bone and ivory and fine woods. Some of them are made from black stone. Some are moulded from clay, or cast from bronze. But each is clearly the work of the same hand. I have not seen Arraio work. It is hard to believe that they are made by him. I hesitate to admit it, but they are beautiful. Most of them are of the human form. He has carved a skull the size of a thumb joint, or hands, or feet, or just shapes hard to describe and hard to understand. Some are shapes that twist and turn back into themselves in ways that do not seem possible. There are many carvings of him, but most are of boys, boys my age. They are obscene, but still beautiful. I am careful to return each to its position after I touch it. Arraio's tools are left out on a table.

I spend days trying to carve an image like his. I take wood and try to shape it, but I do not have his artistry. The figures I create are crude and ugly. After I have shaped them, I destroy them. I take them and burn the wooden figures until they are nothing but ash. I am ashamed of them. If Arraio saw them, he would laugh and mock me. If Arraio notices that I have used his tools, he says nothing. Every day, when he leaves, I go and carve a figure. I no longer care to follow him. But every day I burn my handiwork.

One day, Arraio does not leave. Instead, he stays and hovers around. I realize he is hoping that I leave. I slip out and wander through the tower. When I return, I realize that he has been carving another small figure. It is a face. The features are familiar, are they mine? It is beautiful. I hold it in my hands.

"You can have it if you want," he says. "Do you like it?"

I hold it in my hand. It is smooth and cold. It is made of bone.

"Where did you get the bone?"

"There is no shortage of bone in the tower."

"I did not ask that. Where did you get it? Tell me. If you lie, I will know."

"It is your bone. I have taken it from your grave. I have carved you from your bone. It is you. You should keep it."

I am angry and turn to throw it at him. He has defiled me. He has found a way to defile. He will always defile me.

"Stop. Do not be angry. It is beautiful."

He is right, it is beautiful. It is as if I have come back to life.

"Why do you do this? Not just this one, all of it. Why do you do it?"

Arraio shrugs. "Why do I do anything; it is because this is what I am. It is what we all are. It does not matter why. We do it because it is what we are, we do not change."

I run my fingers over the carving, smooth and cold, like eggshell.

"Why do we not change?"

"I don't care why. What does it matter? It is not important."

Is he right? I put the carving back on the table and turn to leave.

"Don't you want it?"

"No," I say. "What is it; it is nothing."

"As you like," says Arraio.

There is nothing else to say.

The next day I go out again. I wander aimlessly through the tower. I arrive at the library. I hesitate but then I decide to enter and walk carefully, following my footprints. I follow them right to the end. When I get to the shelves, I turn on my light and look. On the top shelf there is a row of carvings, small carvings made of bone. They are carvings of a face, my face. They are staring out at me.

Chapter Eight
Strong

Not long after, I am taken to the Hall of Darkness. It is time. I have spent my time with Arraio. I have learned much. I have learned bitter lessons. The year is over and now a new one begins with another teacher. That is the way of my life until all twelve have taught me.

"I have done with him," Arraio says. "I return him to the dark."

"Who will serve the dark? Who will guide the High Priest?"

In the dark I hear strong, steady footsteps. A strong hand takes mine.

"I will," says Greba, then I am led back out and taken. I know where Greba's chambers are, they are at the bottom of the tower. When we enter I am surprised to see that there is a small window. Moonlight enters. It gathers in a pool in the middle of the floor. Greba steps into it. I see he is tall and muscular. He pulls me into the moonlight, but I pull away. He cuffs me until I am standing in the light.

"Stay still, damn you, what do you think I'm going to do? Stand there and let me have a look at you."

I stand while he looks at me, and I glare defiantly back at him. Abruptly and without reason, he cuffs me again and sends me sprawling.

"Don't look at me like that."

"I will remember these blows when I am High Priest," I tell him.

"Good," says Greba.

"I am not afraid," I say.

"No, neither am I. You think you can threaten me, but you can't. I'm not afraid of you. I'm not like the others, I'm not a coward."

So, at least he will not pretend to be my friend. At least he is honest enough not to hide his hatred.

There is food on the table. He gestures to me to eat. I sit and drink blood.

"Do you know why we drink blood?" he asks.

"Estira says it is because we are predators, Hilketa says it is because we are parasites."

Greba grunts, "It is the same thing, in the end."

"How so? A parasite is weak and a predator is strong."

"If you say so. It does not matter. They will both die if there is no prey."

"What do you mean?"

"I don't mean anything. I mean if there is no food, we die. If there are no slaves, then we die."

"I don't understand."

"So why do you need to understand? Do you think you can understand everything? Some things just are, too bad if you don't understand. You don't have to understand."

"Then what will you teach me, to not understand things? There is plenty I don't understand."

"You're a fool. Who said I'm going to teach you anything? Vatu says you have to be here so you're here. You can understand all you like, you'll still be here."

"So my time with you is just a waste."

"That depends, doesn't it? It depends on what you do with it. If you waste it, then it's a waste. Anyway, all time is a waste."

"What do you mean?"

Again he strikes me, hard.

"I don't mean anything."

I get up and spring at him. He should not strike me. I will not let him strike me. With a fluid grace, he slips to one side. He does not strike me but instead he leads me on and past him so that I go flying into the wall. I hit it hard and fall back dazed. I can hear his mocking laughter.

"You thought you could fight me."

The next morning, I awaken and eat. Greba is gone. I sit and wait but he does not return until late.

"Where have you been?" I ask when he returns.

He ignores me. I sit with him while he eats. After he has eaten, he tosses my flute over to me.

"Play."

"Why?"

"All right then, don't play."

He turns his back on me. I sit and then decide to play after all. I play a simple melody. Greba sits and listens. After I finish, he nods.

"Why did you stop?"

"It's the end of the tune. I can play it again if you like."

Greba does not reply.

"Can you play?" I ask.

"No," says Greba. "I cannot play, I can sing a bit."

"I can teach you to play, if you like."

"What's the point? I can't play. I've never learned to play. I'm told in all my lives I've never learned to play. What makes you think I can start now? It's like Hilketa says, we rewrite the same things."

"If you like. You could write something new. Have you ever tried?"

"No, I don't know. Not in this life anyway."

"Here," I say and pass the flute to him. He holds in his large hands, looking at it.

"What do I do now?" he asks.

"Put it to your lips and blow."

He holds it to his lips and blows, it is a hollow whistling note, off key.

"See," he says. "I cannot do it."

"You've barely tried. It took me ages to learn how to do it. You can't expect to just pick it up and play it straight off. You need to learn. Look, hold it like this softly, and when you blow, blow just as soft, and even."

He tries again, it is better but not much better.

"Gentle," I say, "gentle, let it build up gently."

He tries again and this time there is a single note, soft and sweet.

"Good," I say, "that is it, try again."

We try this over and over for about an hour, just that one note, over and over.

"Enough," I say, "that is enough, it is a good start. You should get one of your own, then you can practice anytime during the day."

"I will not be practising, not during the moon rise, but I will get one, then I can practice and you can show me. Here."

He hands me back my flute. I play for a bit, then I go to my room. In the morning I wake early. Greba is eating. He does not speak. He leaves and I follow. He turns and looks at me.

"If you wish you can come, but keep up and stay close."

I hurry after him and we come to a door. It is a cell. He opens it and walks in. He does not close the door behind him. There are maybe twelve prisoners. They are not chained. Mostly the prisoners are men, they look well fed and muscular, as if they are used to hard work. They shrink back when Greba enters the cell. I follow him in. Greba does not lock the door behind us, or even pull it closed. There are no other guards, just him in a room of prisoners. I think he is mad, will they not rise up? Is he so confident that he can subdue them all?

"Why are they here?" I ask, but Greba does not answer. Instead he walks towards one of the prisoners. He is a tall man with sandy hair and pale skin. Like all the prisoners, he is dirty and smells bad.

"What is your name?" snaps Greba.

"Please, your greatness," replies the prisoner, "my name is Takur."

The prisoner bows but does not say anything else.

"You arrived yesterday evening."

It is not a question. Takur says nothing.

"Who are you?"

"No one, a prisoner. I was a minor member of the outer court."

"What did you do there?"

"I was a guard, a chief guard. I worked as a guard, I served the darkness diligently."

"Too diligently."

Again it is not a question, so Takur says nothing. Greba is looking at him.

"You are hoping to be set free."

"Yes, great one. It is always the wish of prisoners to be set free."

"Not always," says Greba, but I think the prisoner is right. Why would a prisoner wish to stay imprisoned? Of course they wish to be made free.

"But you also hope to be made free," says Greba. "You believe the darkness can be merciful."

"I am innocent, I believe in that."

"Why are you here if you are innocent?"

"I am here because my lover is dead. They say I killed her, but I did not."

"If not you, then who?"

"His name is Larrak, he is in the guards too, but he is senior to me. He thought to take my lover but she would not have him. So he slew her and seeks to blame me."

"Is he here?" asks Greba.

"No, he is not here."

"Then he shall be brought."

Takur bows his head. "Thank you, great one," he says.

"Do not thank me," says Greba.

He turns and walks away. His back is turned to the prisoner. He walks on and one of the prisoners grasps his robe. Greba turns and looks at the prisoner. It is an older man. He is lying prostrate.

"Who dares touch me?"

"I am innocent too, great one," says the old man, but Greba does not listen, instead he lashes out and sends the man flying across the cell as if he were nothing. The man hits the far wall with a sharp crack. The other prisoners scurry away from him. I know now why Greba has no fear as he walks amongst the prisoners. The old man is not dead, but he is winded and gasping. I think Greba will kill him, but he just ignores him. He does not need to kill him.

Later, Greba asks me to teach him to sing and I agree. We spend many days going over scales and pitches. Greba has a surprisingly good singing voice. It is deep and steady. He learns the flute quickly too. I wonder why he has never learned before. When I ask, he just shrugs.

"What does it matter?"

It does not matter. But...

"Why did I not teach you before? Do you not have to play for Vatu like the rest of the twelve?"

"You did not teach me. I do not know why you did not. Do you know?"

I shake my head.

"You see, you think we know why things are as they are. We do not. We know nothing."

"We must know something, we must know."

"There is nothing to know. It makes no difference, we live in this life, this life only. The rest does not matter, there is no point."

He is right. There is no point.

"Will you teach me how you do it?" I ask.

"You mean the fighting? Why do you want to know how to do that?"

"It might come in useful sometime."

Greba laughs, it sounds joyful and honest. Is it?

"It might come in useful, eh? Why? Do you think the High Priest has to get his hands dirty, you think you will have to fight?"

"Won't I?"

"You'll be the High Priest."

"But Kong will still murder me, or try to."

"And you think this will help, when he comes for you in the dark. You think he will come at you like an assassin in the dark. That is not how he will do it. This will not help you."

"How will he come? How did he kill me last time?"

"Do you think he killed you? Really, do you think he did?"

"Then how did I die, why do they all say he killed me?"

"We all die, over and over again. Kong hates you, we all hate you. We all want to kill you. We hate each other."

"If you want to kill me, why don't you? I'm sure you could."

"Course I could. Kong drowned you in your bath."

"How?"

"Because you let him. Do you think he could come creeping into your room and you not know? I will teach you to fight. Why? Because I always teach you to fight. I taught you to fight last time too, almost as good as me. You let Kong kill you."

"I don't believe you."

"I don't kill you because I don't want to. I don't want you to escape, not from this. You can't anyway, none of us can."

"It is a blessing," I say. "To live forever in the service of the dark."

"Yes, a great blessing, praise Vatu, praise the shadow."

After that he agrees to teach me to fight, to move like he does. It is not easy, but I learn. Greba is a surprisingly good teacher, he is patient and never raises his voice or strikes me without cause. He is very thorough in his teaching. Every day he teaches me. I learn fast but I am never able to master him. It is not because he is bigger or stronger, at least not physically. I try to match him.

"Do you think you can learn in a year what I learned in a lifetime?"

"I do not have a lifetime."

"You will learn. And one day you will teach me. Only you can do this, you and I. It is our bond. It is why I do not kill you. One reason, one more reason."

I learn how to move, to dodge and avoid. I learn how to pin and immobilize, to throw and strike. To perfect violence, you must find stillness within. It is that stillness that I must learn. To learn stillness, I need to know how to move without thinking. To move without thinking, it is necessary to know what I will do. We practice simple movements over and over again. Each time we refine the move. Sometimes I exercise with the prisoners. The trick is to think they are not there, to think it is just an exercise, to just carry out the movement and when we touch to think there is nothing there and just carry on with the move.

It is not as easy as it sounds, to be aware and unaware, thinking and not thinking, moving and yet still. But it is possible. Every night when I go to lie down I run through all the moves in my head. I do not need to think when I carry them out because I have already thought them through.

I continue to teach Greba to play the flute and sing. I do not know why he has never learned before. Why did I never teach him before? He will never play as well as Hilketa, but he is competent. By the time I am ready to leave, he can sing and play well.

We return to the hall of darkness.

"I have done with him," Greba says. "I return him to the dark."

Chapter Nine
Kong

Now I am with Kong. His hand slips into mine, and he leads me from the darkness. In his chambers, I sit and glare at him. Will he try to kill me?

"I will not try to kill you, not now. You are safe for now. You need not be afraid."

"I am not afraid."

"No?"

We sit and stare at each other. I am not afraid. I do not care what he says, I am not afraid.

"There is no reason to be afraid," he says. "I have said I will not kill you."

"You could try, you will not succeed."

"I could try, I could succeed, but do not be afraid. I will not try to kill you, not yet."

I turn away, I look away from him.

"Yes, there is no need to fear," he says.

But I remember that he has betrayed me a thousand times and will a thousand more. Although my back is turned, I am wary. I am not afraid but I am not a fool.

"We should be friends," says Kong. He always takes things too far. I am full of darkness, it wells up inside me and overflows. It seeps between my teeth like vomit. Darkness spills down my throat, it tastes of bitterness. I will kill Kong, I will be avenged.

"How did you kill me? How did you defeat me? How?"

"Why should I tell you?"

"Why should you not, are you afraid?"

"What, afraid that you knowing might stop it happening again? Don't be stupid. Do you think I killed you in every lifetime? Do you think that your life is like a tablet that is written before you were born? Did Hilketa tell you that? I bet he did. I bet he told you that everything is set in clay. It isn't. Some lives I kill you, some lives you kill me, some lives no one is killed."

"But always we strive against each other."

"Do we? Why? I can never prevail. I can kill you but what then? You are reborn, and always you are the High Priest and I am nothing. Vatu favours you, he does not favour me. There is nothing I can do. You are the High Priest."

"Then why did you kill me?"

"Because you wanted to die. Do you think I could slay you without your aid? I drowned you in your bath this time. It is the only time I have slain you and I do not remember the other times. Perhaps you can find something in the library. I understand you like to spend time there. But I don't think you will find anything to help you. Remember, when you wrote these tablets, you knew no more than you know now. Feel free to spend as much time as you like there."

"You mean I came to you and asked you to kill me? I don't believe you."

"No, of course not, but you stopped caring whether I killed you or not. I will always be there waiting for when you need me, when you want me. I will be death, I will be your friend, as you have been mine. And will be again."

"Why should I kill you?"

"Because I want to die, not now, but I will and you will kill me. I will give you reason to."

I do not spend time with Kong. Sometimes he comes into my room at night, but each time he does, I am ready. I wake and move, we play a game of seek in the dark. I hide from him, I hear him, I feel him. I move as silently as I can and he seeks to find me. He has not come to abuse me. His vice is not the same as Arraio. I fashion a blade from bone, a long thin blade with a sharp end. It will pierce the robes that Kong wears and go deep enough to slay him. I do not doubt he holds a blade as sharp as mine. We move in silence through the dark. It is like a dance. He cannot find me. He does not find me. It is not real; it is practice for when we will do this for real. Then one of us will die.

"Remember, hate is power. It will give you power," he calls, mocking as he leaves. I do not answer. Sometimes he tries to poison my food. But I can smell or taste it. He will not poison me. Besides, I have dosed myself with most of the poisons he tries since I was a child. It is just a game, just a test. When I taste the poison, I leave the blood untouched for the servants to remove. I do not know if Kong even checks to see if I have taken his poison.

During moonrise we seldom speak. Sometimes I go somewhere and sleep if I have been awake all moondown. Kong goes about his business, sometimes I follow him, but mostly not.

In the library, I follow Kong's footsteps and rummage among the records he keeps. He has stowed them here and there throughout the library. If he has a system, I cannot discern it. I think he just looks for a shelf and puts his tablets there. They are of little interest. I find the tablet that Hilketa made me read once.

> *Great Vatu, we have done as you have commanded. We went to the house as directed. The boy was there. We collected him. The mother objected, as did the father. It was necessary to dispatch both. Afterwards, we burned their home and all their possessions. We took the rest of the household and sold them as slaves. The money will be added to the treasury. The boy is now in the care of Zauria. All is as you commanded. Kong*

I look, but I do not find any other reports from when the twelve are reborn, or when I am reborn, just this one. There is just this one and no other.

I turn and Kong is there. He has followed me to the library.

"What are you reading?" he asks.

"I am not sure," I say.

"Let me see it."

Reluctantly I hand him the tablet. He reads it and grunts.

"It is a report of your rebirth. Why are you interested?"

"I'm not, should I be? I found it. Is it about me? There must be hundreds of these reports."

"And yet this is the one you read."

"I just read it. I read lots of tablets."

"Why?"

Why indeed? Because I am looking for something. I am looking to make sense of things. I am trying to understand. I want to know who I am. I want to know why I am here.

"I don't know. I just do. Do you wish me not to? You said I should read some tablets."

"I did," he says. He is looking at the tablet in his hand. "What do you want to know?"

As we speak, he has placed the tablet back on the shelf and is tracing patterns with his finger in the dust, a circle of twisting and intertwining lines. He turns and looks at me.

"What do you wish to know? What do you seek?"

"Why did you write this? Why bother with a report?"

"Is this what you wish to know?"

"No, I know why you wrote this, you wrote it because it is a lie. Somewhere on that tablet is a lie. You seek to hide the lie by writing it down. Do you think that writing it will make it real? There are lots of lies written. It does not make them any more real."

"Good, but this is no lie. Why should I lie, why should I lie to you or to Vatu? I would be mad to try and deceive the Great Spirit."

"But you are mad, we are all mad, and liars."

"If you say so, this is a lie then," says Kong and he takes the tablet and tosses it over the side of the gantry where it falls. It takes a long time, but eventually I hear it clatter to a stop many feet below. Kong looks at me as if daring me to challenge him.

"If it is a lie then it is of no value, I suppose all these must be lies, all of these are of no value," and he tosses another tablet over the gantry, "a whole cavern of no value, you should spend more of your time here, all of it."

But he cannot be bothered to throw more tablets off the shelves.

"Anything else you wish to know?"

"No. You have told me all I need to know."

"You know nothing, and if you did, it would do you no good. There is nothing to know, not now."

"If you say so."

He is right, I know nothing. But I will, it will come to me. I must read what is not there. Why did Hilketa fear to show me that tablet, why did Kong wish to hide it from me? I remember it all. I will unlock it. It will come to me and I will know.

Kong turns and leaves. He walks heavily, leaving his heavy

footprints in the dust. Eventually, he is out of sight. I douse the light and follow him for a while, but then stop. Let him go where he will. There is no reason to follow him, not now. Besides, I have other things to do, other things to think about.

What do I want? What do I seek? I will be High Priest of Vatu. I have been High Priest of Vatu a million times. It is what is written, it is what I am. What else is there to seek? I am the High Priest, I will be the High Priest; I will always be the High Priest, a million more times.

I wander in the darkness. I pay no attention to where I go. Perhaps it is as Hilketa said, the tunnels form as I move and as I turn. Reality is defined by the edges of my perception. Everything else is simply void and darkness. Everything is simply shaped by my mind. I write on the tablet and it is. I erase the tablet and it is not. Vatu, great dark one, you have given me the power to shape reality. What do I do with that power, what kind of reality do I make? I have absolute freedom, but it is an illusion, I can only be what I am, whatever that is. It is not reality I shape, it is myself, if I am not moulded already. But it is ridiculous. I turn and walk straight and the tunnel wall does not open and form a new tunnel for me, instead I walk face first into it. There, I do not shape reality. The tunnels are fixed and real. They were made a long time ago and these are the trails along which I must travel. I can choose my trail, but I cannot make new ones.

How can I choose which way to go if I am blind, if I cannot see what is ahead? I walked every path before, which is best? Unless I know, unless I can see what I have done before, how can I choose? Fear fills me up like water. Before I can stop I am crouched down and crying. The darkness is no comfort. There is only emptiness. There is nothing for me except darkness.

That is all darkness, it is all I have. Every day I walk in darkness.

Finally, Kong leads me to the hall of darkness. All the twelve are there, each of them. They have done with me, now I will return to the darkness. Kong walks forward.

"I have done with him," Kong says. "I return him to the dark."

No one comes forward to claim me. Now I am left in the dark, the twelve leave me. There is just me and the dark. There is just me and Vatu. There is just me and nothing. I have prepared for this moment and for this time. I am alone in the dark. I walk into the darkness. There is only me, they are all gone. I am alone. I stop and stand still, alone in the emptiness. I am High Priest of this. I am High Priest of emptiness, of darkness, of nothing. I turn to leave this empty place. I walk forwards and I am lost. I am in total darkness and I cannot see or feel anything. It's as if I am suspended in the night. I walk forward, but I am going nowhere. The twelve have left, I am alone in the dark. It is as Hilketa warned me. I cannot find the way out.

"That is because there is no way out.

"You have returned. Have you nothing to say? It must be because you have forgotten. Yes, you always forget."

I reach out and touch the darkness. It is solid and hard and cold. I touch it and it parts with my touch like a waterfall. Darkness seeps inside me. It fills my stomach and my lungs, it runs through my veins and into my brain, it travels along my nerves and saturates my skin and muscle. Darkness enters every part of me. It is like dark water entering the hollow space that is me.

It draws me in and I feel myself dissolve. I feel myself stretching out, expanding, the darkness is my flesh, my flesh is the darkness. I have been swallowed by the dark. My mind expands out into the darkness and the walls and floors of the great hall are like a new skin, and on that skin my mind sees paintings in shades of black that no eye has ever or will ever see. I see, I know everything the dark conceals. I feel the darkness beyond the great darkness under the sky and over all the earth. I reach out to it.

"No, come back."

It is the voice of Vatu. He is calling me back.

"It is not time to go. Not now, not ever. You must stay with me."

I am drawn back to myself and the darkness withdraws to the surface of my skin. I am trapped in black jet. Set in darkness. I cannot move or breathe.

"You are mine, you are always mine, you will always be mine."

I am High Priest to darkness, and what is that, other than to be the slave of Vatu? I am never free, I will never be free, I was never free. I know now what I sought, and why I could not find it. I will never find it, I will never be free.

"Yes," says Vatu, "that is right. We will always be together. I will keep you and bring you back."

And I see that the darkness is a stain that I will never be cleansed of. So be it. I am the High Priest.

I walk to the chamber door. I am led by Vatu. I swim in a dark current.

Outside the chamber, the twelve are waiting. They dress me

and cover my nakedness with the robes of my priesthood. Kong cedes to me the amulet of darkness that is the symbol of my power. Now I am myself. Now I am the slave of Vatu. When I am dressed, when I am High Priest, dressed in my robes and wearing the amulet and mask of my power, they bow to me. They are my slaves. The whole world is mine now, mine and the dark's.

Chapter Ten
Vice

Nothing has changed and everything has changed. Nothing can change. How could it possibly? Now that I am High Priest, things are different, but I am always High Priest. Now I can do whatever I will. I am limited only by my imagination. The dark, all reality will do as I will. This world is my plaything. It exists only at the whim of the darkness, only at my whim. It blinks in and out of existence. And then I let it go, a perfect world of darkness like a black bubble floating through space. I have made a world. I have remade the world. Vatu has made the world.

I step into the bubble, into the world. I step in to see my handiwork. I go forward a man, to live in my world, a world of my making.

I am standing on the top of the Tower of the Sun, the Crowtower. It is some years since I have become myself. I am looking down into the inner courtyard. The people below me are like ants. I remember thinking that when I became High Priest I would play with them like toys. It is true, I rule over them, and every whim is obeyed, but it is not like I imagined. I had thought, as a child, that to rule was some grand thing that I could trifle and meddle for amusement. But it is not so. It is an estate in need of constant attention. I must check and watch, and correct and repair. I see now why the twelve write tablets, they write so that I can read and for that reason only. These tablets are pictures into the world, and into their doings. I must command and instruct, otherwise, like a neglected garden, it will go to ruin. It was ruinous when I took command. The twelve fear me, but do not fear each other; without me they all went their own way. I have corrected them. Now there is order and things are maintained. People are fed enough to live and flourish, but not enough to be idle. There is order enough for safety, but not enough to bring despair. I am benevolent enough to be loved, but not enough to be scorned. I am firm enough to be feared, but not enough to be hated. It is balance, all balance. The twelve are my servants, to me only do they answer, and through me to Vatu.

But it is hard to balance things, even for me. My eye can only look in one direction at a time. It is not how I imagined things.

I have lied, I am hated and there are those who do not fear me. There are those who starve, and those who idle. I am scorned by some and by some, feared. There are some that groan under my oppression and some that feel free of all restraint. The world is not one thing, it is many things. It is a terrible and wonderful thing that I have made.

Now that I am the High Priest, I visit the inner court daily. It is a chore. There is always some request or favour to consider, or some dispute to resolve. They are children who look to me as their master. There is also justice to be done. Much of this I leave to the twelve, but I cannot leave it all. So every day I go to the inner court and listen to the whining of servants. They know what needs to be done in the main, and know how to do it, but still they seek my assent. They can do nothing without my word. My words create this world. It is my words and my commands that fashion this world.

What is my duty as High Priest, to obey? All must obey. I must do as Vatu commands, as must all. What does he command? That is my duty; to know what Vatu desires. To know his will. I am the High Priest, I know his will. That is my duty. How do I know his will? Does he whisper to me in darkness? Does he haunt my dreams? Does he summon me? Does he appear before me and issue his will? Yes, all of these he does and more. It is more. It is inside me. I am the High Priest, what I do is his will. He has willed me to be. He has called me back from the void uncountable times. I am his will. What I do, he will sanction. I am everything he wishes me to be.

There is ritual and worship. It makes his will, to my will. It is one and the same. Every word is his word and mine. Every deed is his deed and mine. I am his shadow and he is mine. There are no words for it. I cannot say how it is. I am one with the darkness. The darkness is one with me. He is darkness made man. I am man made darkness. It is as if I see myself in a black mirror. I am a void made in the void. I hold the darkness in me, and darkness has wrapped its wings around me. But it is all darkness. Darkness is everywhere.

And yet I am a man too. Like other men and unlike. I have the vices of all men. All men have vices. The twelve are men also and each of them has vices also, weaknesses for me to exploit. I will not speak of Arraio's vice. But each has one. Hilketa covets gold, others covet women or wine or food. Or violence, or are filled with the need to inflict pain on others, or themselves.

What is vice but a way to fill the darkness? Men think they can fill the darkness with pain or pleasure. Is that what they think? That darkness can be filled with the pleasure of flesh. Nothing can fill the darkness; no river of blood or torment or exquisite pain or joy can fill it. It is endless. It will engulf all your vices and all your pleasures, your whole life is swallowed and barely noticed by the dark. You are nothing, and it is that nothingness, the knowledge of nothingness that vice seeks to hide. In the end, nothing can fill it, nothing can conquer it. Darkness cannot be filled, it is endless.

And what of my vices? They are the vices of any man. It is the same. It counts for weakness. I am weak. But the darkness makes me strong.

Always one of the twelve will come with me when I visit the court, sometimes more than one and even sometimes them all. The twelve like to come and leave the dark tower. They do not love the darkness as I do. They love their vices more. Sometimes they invite me to share their vices and sometimes I go with them. I go with some of them; there are those whose vices I will not share and those whose vices I share only once. But it is all the same, women, alcohol, money, gambling, the thrill of the fight and chase, none of these can fill the darkness. Most often I go with Beldura. He takes me to watch duels. When we go, we must dress not as priests. Duelling is against Vatu's will. Only he can take another's life. Still, we go and watch. The duels are fought with swords. Sometimes the fights are short and quick. Often this is so. The fighters are mismatched. Then it is not so much a duel as simple murder; the strong taking the life of the weak. There are some who often duel and they duel with great skill. For them, the sword is a way of life. It is part of them. For others, it is as if they have never held a sword before, and they simply wave it in front of them. Usually, they die quickly but sometimes they get lucky. Beldura seems to like these fights the most, quick ones, short and cruel and bloody. I realize that it is not fighting he has come to see, but death. Death is his vice.

Other times the fighters are more evenly matched and fight with great skill. These fights can go on for hours. Or the duel can, the fight is often only seconds. Perhaps they are even quicker. They are subtle. The difference between victory and death is a half second's pause, or a stretch a fraction too long. Some fights are longer, but mostly these are fights between two who have not mastered the blade. They slash wildly, and the fight is like the clashing of beasts. They fight until one is too exhausted to continue and then death comes.

Greba comes to these fights too, but not often. I had thought he would share Beldura's vice before I understood the true nature of Beldura. And then I realized they are not alike. Greba does not come often and watches as if he is looking for something. I ask him why he comes. He glares at me, even now he does not hide his hatred for me. Now I am the High Priest and he cannot strike me as he did when I was a child. If he did, I would have him killed, slowly.

"Why do you come, great one?" he asks.

I am not sure, but anyway, it is not his place to question me, and I tell him so.

"Indeed, great one," he says. "I come looking for something, but have never found it."

"For what do you seek?"

"For my equal."

I watch the two fighters. They are very skilled. Neither makes a mistake. They are still like two sleeping men, but they are coiled to strike. They are good fighters, but not the best I have seen. Even the best of them together, fully armed with sword and dagger, could not harm Greba if he were unarmed. He has no equal, not here.

It is not love of violence that is Greba's weakness, nor love of death, nor pride. What then is his secret vice? If I am to control him, I must know, as I know and have learned the weaknesses of the others. I will know his weakness. I will find it and use it against him. I will make him mine.

Greba is careful. He does not invite me to go with him into the inner court, and takes pains to ensure that I do not follow him. If I do, he is careful. He has a secret, and I will find it.

I cannot spend too much time trying to find Greba's secret. The life of the High Priest is measured and unmeasured. It is unmeasured because it is endless and is endlessly renewed. Only Vatu can know how long it is. It is measured by ritual and custom. It is measured by the passing of the moon and by the opening of the Sun. It is measured by steps in the dark and by ashes buried far below the ground. Every day is the same and every day different. I praise Vatu and worship him. I attend the darkness far below. I do his will, I hear his will. I proclaim his will. I have no time to wander in the dark. I must do the bidding of the dark. I must worship the dark. I must read and attend to the outer court. Hilketa seeks to help. He administered the court while I grew; now the burden falls on me, and I cannot let it go. That is Vatu's will. It is my will. It is one and the same. I must try the guilty and deal justice. Greba dealt with that before. If he could, he would deal with it still. But that is not Vatu's will. It is not my will.

When I go to the cells of prisoners, Greba is always there. He is watching me. I command him to deal with the prisoners. To torture this one and to execute this one. He listens but says nothing. When I return, he has always done as I have commanded. He makes no comment on my will, never challenges or makes any suggestion. But I can see from his eyes that he is judging me. How dare he; I am the High Priest and my will is the will of Vatu. Will he seek to judge the darkness? Sometimes I ask myself what Greba would do with this prisoner and command him to do it, knowing that it is what he would have done when he was master. Other times, I think the same but then command him to do differently, knowing it is not what he would do. Regardless, his eyes are flat and show nothing. He is judging me. He has no right. One day he will slip up and his judgment will show in an action or in a glance, and then I will have him. Then I will punish him. He dares to judge the darkness; he has no right.

But Greba is not the one I seek to destroy. He is not the one I hate. Kong is the one I hate. I will destroy him. He, who once stood in my place, now he is moved aside. Now I am the High Priest and he is nothing. Kong is jealous and seeks only for himself. It is his vice, he seeks to fill the darkness within him with praise and glory, and with the envy of others. It is an easy vice to use against him.

Chapter Eleven
Rivals

Today I visit the inner court and Kong is with me. There is a dispute between two courtiers over a woman they both desire, and they have brought the dispute to me. They do not wish to share the woman. Instead, they both wish the woman to stay in their quarters. It is sentimental and foolish. There are plenty of women in the inner court; if they do not wish to share then there is no need, there are plenty to go around. Perhaps this is another vice. It is amusing and more common than is supposed. Both men are guards. It is surprising how often strong men have a weakness for soft things. They wish the woman to be there when they return to their quarters and to make them comfortable. They wish to have children that they know are theirs. It's a foolish notion to recreate the home they were born in, or some idealized version of it. It is amusing to hear them profess love. If they truly loved the woman, they would let her choose her fate. They have fooled themselves, but I am not fooled ever.

The woman has been with one man longer than the other. She is brought before us and stands with her head bowed. She is not beautiful, or at least not so beautiful that her place could not be taken by another. She is not tall, and is slim. Her hair is straight and dark. She answers my questions simply and directly but she does not indicate favour to either of her suitors. That is wise; she should have no wish to anger either man. Even if I give her to the one she favoured, the other could find her and punish her, and if I give her to the one she did not favour, then he also would punish her.

It is simple. I listen and then rule. The woman should go to one and not the other, the one who is senior, it is always so. The woman belongs to the senior officer. It cannot be otherwise. It is a fair judgment.

Even so, the other guard does not agree. He does not challenge my decision, and I do not see the disobedience in his eyes, but he springs forward. He has a knife. He pushes it into the throat of his rival. Blood flows, lots of blood. The stabbed man gasps and tries to speak, but blood and not words come out of his mouth. He clutches his throat as if he thinks he can stop the bleeding with his hands. He sinks to his knees and then his eyes roll back. The other guards hold him and try to stop the bleeding, but it is useless. Hilketa could perhaps save him, but Hilketa is not here. He is dying and his eyes are filled with fear. The killer steps back, he still has his knife and tries to drive it into his own throat, but before he can, he is grappled to the ground. Pinned beneath the weight of four guards, he is unable to kill himself. He will suffer for defying my will, for defying Vatu's will.

The woman screams, but it is a scream of fear for herself, not sorrow for the death of her lover, both her lovers. She had feared the scorned guard would slay her. Now that she is safe, she is sobbing from relief. Perhaps the dying man imagines they are tears of sorrow for lost love. It may be a small comfort to them as they die. One dies quickly, the other will die slowly.

"If I cannot have her, then neither shall you," says the killer. These are the words of a dying man. They are the words of a man who cannot bear to be beaten by a rival. His love is a lie; a lie he has told himself until he believes it. His eyes do not turn to the woman, but stay focused on his rival as he dies.

His rival does not look anywhere, his eyes are unfocused. He had not come here expecting to die. He has no final words, even if he had breath to say them.

Murder is common in the inner court; it is less common to find the killer. I am angry that my judgment should have been denied, that the will of Vatu is denied. I will make the killer suffer for his foolishness.

To think it better to kill his rival and himself than to lose a woman. There are plenty of women in the inner court, he could have found another, many others. And why not wait and poison his rival in secret, or poison the woman? They are all such fools.

While the man is dying, I think the woman would weep and cry, or run to one of them. But she does not. She only stands. I watch. She did not care.

This is how I rule, I utter the words but they do not run true. They turn and deny me and make a different world than the one I wish.

Kong is with me.

"Foolish man," he says. He pretends his words are for the murderer but they are for me.

He is saying this to taunt me. He has seen my words denied. He would deny my words too if he could.

"It is the woman, she has bewitched them no doubt."

He is wrong. The woman does not care. She knows that there will be another man who will want her. It does not matter to her. She is wiser than the men, she does not let passion rule her. Wisdom is this, to deny passion, to do only what is best. That is wisdom.

I say so to Kong.

"Of course, great one," he says, but I know he is mocking me again.

"Are you prey to passion?" I ask.

He says he is not, but I know he is. Murder is a passion, a madness, and he has fallen prey to it many times. It is good that he is here. Good that he sees how futile passion is.

"This is how you will die, driven by madness to destroy yourself. You think you will destroy me, but you cannot, not even for a while. I cannot be destroyed, Vatu will not allow it. Yet still you hurl yourself at me and perish."

"As you say, great one." He bows as he speaks. His face is white. He knows I can slay him if I will. I am tempted, but then it is I who would be driven by passion. I will not give in to passion, I will be wise.

I reach a gloved hand to his face. He does not turn away.

"What secrets do you think you can keep from me?"

"None, great one, there are no secrets from the dark."

And yet my justice has been denied. There are secrets even in the lowest of men's hearts. I can reason and understand but cannot comprehend this, the passions of men. It is a mystery to me. It is why men are senseless and unpredictable.

"Why did I not foresee this?"

"Because this is madness, you cannot foresee madness, unless you are mad."

"Is that why Vatu keeps you with us, because you are mad?"

"We are all mad, every one of us, except you, great one."

He is mocking me. Does he seek death by my hand? One day I will grant his wish.

The body has been carried away. It will be bled and later we will drink the blood. The killer is taken away. I will deal with him another day. The woman also is led away. It may be that she is an accomplice. In any rate, she will be questioned. There is no more reason to stay here, so I turn and return to the dark tower. Kong does not follow me.

I spend less time in the library. There is little need for me to go there. Records are brought to me. Not old ones from long before, but new reports from all over the dark land, many, many reports for me to read, and to read what is not written. When I write, I write not to inform, but to instruct. My words shape the world. When I wish to compare my instructions with what has been reported to me, I go and read the words I have written.

I am in the library now. I am looking again for the record of my rebirth. In all the times I have been reborn, that was the only record made. Why did Kong write it? He wrote it for me to read. I see now; he hopes to raise my ire by telling of his brutality to the parents of my flesh. I hear him approach, I feel him move through the darkness. Turning, I find he is there behind me.

"Can I assist you?" he asks. I shake my head. I have no wish for his assistance or for his company.

"What brings you here?" he continues.

"I do not have to answer to you. I go where I will."

"Of course, great one, I merely ask."

We are alone. Has he laid a trap for me and seeks to kill me? No, he is not such a fool. Instead he draws patterns in the dust. The same pattern he drew before.

"What are you doing?" I ask.

"Nothing."

"Nothing, you say, but I can see you are writing something. Let me see."

"If you wish," he replies and moves aside. I can see the pattern. It is the same circle of intertwining lines he drew before.

"What does this mean?"

"Nothing, it is nothing, it has no meaning. Why should it?"

I look again. I am sure it has meaning, but it is not one of the shapes I learned or that we use while writing on the tablets. The symbol is curved and joined, not sharp and angular. I am certain it has meaning, but I cannot comprehend. It is no word that I know.

"What does it mean?" I ask.

"Nothing, it means nothing."

He is lying. I know he is lying; he always lies. But I cannot read the word.

"Why did you write the report on my birth?" I ask, thinking of the tablet he took from me and cast away that time in the library.

"So that you might read it."

"There are no other reports from past times I have been reborn. Why was there only that one?"

"How can I say? I have seen only this rebirth. If I have erred in writing then forgive me."

He kneels and bows as he says these words.

"Why write them, the tablet contained only lies."

"How so, great one? I did indeed do as Vatu commanded, I did indeed bring you from your home to the dark tower. I did indeed."

Now that I hear the words, I know he is lying. He has defied Vatu. How; it is unthinkable. It is beyond belief. That report was written only because it is a lie. In all our lifetimes, only in this lifetime has Kong defied Vatu. I step back, and in doing so betray myself. He knows that I have discovered him. He looks around in panic and seeks to rise, but I do not allow it. Kong is not my equal, especially not here in the dark. I spring forward and knock him to the ground. My foot is on his neck. He gasps in pain, and clutches my foot, but he cannot rise, the weight of the darkness is too great for him. He tries to squirm away but I have him and he cannot escape.

"Go on then. Kill me," he croaks.

I am tempted. I just need to push harder with my foot and his neck will break. Then I could simply kick his body over the edge of the gantry into the centre well of the library.

"Tell me," I say, but he shakes his head.

"Kill me now. I know you want to. Just push down. Then it's finished."

"Tell me."

"No, never, I'll never tell you, and once I'm dead you can never know."

"The others know," I say. "One of them will tell me."

He laughs. "Why have they not told you? They are afraid. They will never tell you. They know nothing. Kill me, let me live, it makes no difference, you will never know."

"The darkness knows, he will tell me."

"The darkness knows nothing, I have cheated him and I have cheated you. Kill me now."

"I should, then you will be reborn knowing nothing. Knowing nothing, your secret will die with you."

"If you say so."

"I do say so. I say you are very pleased with your little secret, whatever it is. When you are reborn, you will know nothing about it."

"As you say, great one. You knew my secret once, and then I killed you. Now you know nothing. Now you will never know."

"If I discovered it once I can discover it again."

"Maybe."

"Not maybe, I will find out."

"Perhaps, but not this way. Kill me now. Kill me now and see if you can find my secret. You want to."

He is right. I want to kill him. I want to give in to my passion, to my hate. I want to crush his skull beneath my heel. I want to kill him. To give in to passion is weakness. I am not weak. I will not kill him. It is what he wants, I will not give him what he wants. I will not set him free. I will find his secret. I kick him away. He disgusts me. He is weak and cowardly. He rises and leaves, quickly enough to show his fear but slowly enough to pretend he has some dignity.

"I will know," I call after him. He does not answer.

Chapter Twelve
Defiance

The man is brought to me. He has been stripped naked. He has been beaten. I did not command it and question the guardsman about his bruises.

"He has tried to kill himself several times and has attacked his guards. He has had to be restrained."

I am not fooled. It is possible to restrain a man without beating him half to death, and say so. The guard bows his head and falls to his knees.

"Forgive me, great one, you are correct. I will look into it and give you a full report."

"Do not bother, I will ask him myself." I turn to the killer and ask him who has beaten him.

"It is as the sergeant says," he replies. "I have been fighting with the other guards."

"I do not doubt that, but that is not what I asked. I asked why you have been beaten, why you have been allowed to fight."

"Agana, the man I killed, had friends. They think that to beat me is to show loyalty to their friend."

"How were they allowed to?"

Again the sergeant bows. "Great one, you did not order that he should not be beaten, also to beat him helps to make him more manageable."

He is right. If I punish the soldier for beating the killer, then it will go down badly with the guards, and why should they be punished? It is of no great importance. They have not disobeyed me. I should not care so much for the health of a killer who will die soon.

"Tell me your name," I command the killer.

"My name is Amantae."

"So tell me, Amantae; why do you think that you can defy Vatu?"

Amantae is not cowed; I see now why he was beaten. He is proud and fearless. He will need to be beaten more.

"I do not seek to defy Vatu, I seek only to ensure that my rival does not have my woman."

I let it pass. She is not his woman, not then or ever. She is one of the maidens of the court, and she belongs to Vatu. They all do.

"But if Vatu decreed that she should be his, then to take her from him is to defy Vatu."

"Great one, do you think Vatu concerns himself with such small things?"

I do not let this pass and motion for the sergeant to strike him. The sergeant strikes him hard in the mouth and draws blood. Amantae's head rocks back, but he does not cry out or complain.

"I have concerned myself with these small things. My will is Vatu's will. Who are you to say what Vatu will or will not concern himself with? Now tell me why you seek to defy my will, Vatu's will. What you say is heresy."

Amantae bows. "Forgive me, great one. I did not seek to thwart your will. I acted out of foolish impulse. It was foolishness, nothing more. I see now my error and ask only a quick death."

"Indeed, but you are a guard in the inner court, you are not the kind of man to act on impulse. Such men do not rise to the inner court. Neither do fools. If you were such a man you would have perished long since."

"I do not know what you wish me to say, Great One. I acted on impulse, out of hatred and anger. Agana has long been my rival and I his. To lose the woman to him was more than I could bear. I could not stand it, so I struck him down. He is dead. I will not pretend that I do not rejoice in that. The woman is nothing but another thing he sought to take from me. She is not beautiful or skilled. She is nothing. Kill me, let me die, it is fair that I should. I have defied Vatu. I see that I must die. It is just."

I nod; it is just that he should die. But he must die slowly, publicly and in great pain. It is not enough that he dies; his death must discourage others who think to defy me. He can have had no hope for any other outcome. Is he trying to protect the girl? Why? He has said she is nothing.

"She must die too," I say. It is true, but I wish to see his reaction. I wish to see if she is really nothing to him. He tries to hide his feelings, but I see he wishes to save her.

"Is it truly necessary?" he asks.

I raise my hand to stay the sergeant from striking him. I wish Amantae to speak freely. I wish to understand. He may question me if he wishes. Each question he asks reveals more.

"Why should you care?"

"I do not, at least not really. It's just that I feel that I'm responsible."

"You are, she is dying as a result of your actions. It is you that has killed her. But why do you care, you have killed many I'm sure, men and women. In the dark and in the light. Why are you concerned about a woman? Why are you so concerned about this woman? She is nothing; is she not?"

He does not answer, again I motion to the sergeant to stay his hand.

"We must see this woman and see how remarkable she is. Bring her here. It would be fair to let the prisoner see the woman whose life he has taken one last time. After all, she has taken his life."

Amantae throws himself down before me.

"Please, great one, spare her life, I beg you."

"And why should I grant your wish? You have defied me and even now seek to sway my judgment. You, who I have condemned to die; why should I listen to a dead man? There is more to this. Much more and I will know it all."

I think of Kong and how I have spared his life because he kept a secret that I will discover. It is the same. Now, I must keep this man alive until I have found the truth. But afterwards he will suffer, as will Kong. He will suffer, they both will. Do they think they can defy me and not suffer? It is not so. They will be punished. They will die.

I am inching forward. I am discovering the truth. I am discovering what is hidden from me. I will make it plain and clear. And when I know all, I shall have revenge. I will make it plain and then I will kill them all, all those who defy me, those who question me, those who taunt me. I am not weak, I am the master of this world; it is shaped by my words. Those caught in my net can twist and try to escape, but there is nowhere to escape to. The whole world is mine and mine alone. I will go on and on until the end.

"I will tell you," he says.

"Tell me what?"

"Everything, I will tell you everything. All I ask is that you are merciful to her."

"You seek to bargain with me. You seek to bargain with the dark. The darkness makes no bargains. You will tell me. I will know. She will tell me, if you do not. I will draw it from her."

"She does not know. She does not know anything. Only I can tell you. There is only me left, and him, and he will not tell you."

"Who?"

"Him, the chief of the twelve, Kong. He knows but he will not tell."

"How can you know? If you know, there must be others."

"There are no others, they are dead. He has slain them all, and now I will die. He will have me dead, and then there will be no others that know."

"Why should I care, what do you think that I wish to know? It does not matter, it does not matter at all."

"If you say so, great one. If you have no wish to know, then I have nothing to trade, no gift to lay before you. I have nothing to say."

He stays lying prostrate before me. He does not move or speak. I look at him. There is silence for a long time.

"Leave us," I say to the guards.

They would protest, but I am adamant. They leave reluctantly. No doubt they wait outside the door listening. They are fools. If Kong knows they have overheard his secret, he will kill them. But I do not care. Their lives are nothing to me. I have many guards and soldiers, and the darkness needs none of them. When we are alone, I wonder if Amantae will try to attack me. The thought amuses me. I almost wish he will, but he does not. He stays prone, lying motionless and silent, so silent I wonder if he is dead. But he is not. I hear him breathing and see his body swell and contract as he does.

"Are you asleep? Have you nothing to say to me?"

"What can I say? I can tell you, but it is like a stone in my throat. It is something I swore I would never say. It is buried deep within me. I never knew it was buried so deep."

"Never mind, what have you to say? Get up. Get up now."

I reach down and grab his shoulder and pull him up. I see his eyes, they are wide with fear. It is the first time I have seen him afraid. Is he afraid to tell me? Is he afraid even to say the words?

There is a commotion outside. Someone has come. Someone will defy my commands; there can only be one who will do that.

"Stay here," I say and walk to the door. Kong is here. He is seeking entry, but the sergeant has denied him. He is afraid. He has no wish to anger Kong. That is wise. But he has no wish to anger me, and that is wiser still.

"I have commanded that no one enters."

"As you wish, great one," says Kong, but he cannot hide the rising panic in his voice. "Would you not wish your adviser present?"

"You are not my adviser."

"I could be, great one, I could give you much advice, good advice. Kong always gives good advice to those wise enough to listen. It is good advice. I should be with you to advise you. Yes, let me in. The criminal is dangerous, you should not be alone with him. You need your adviser."

"You think me unwise. You think me weak."

"Yes, no, no, great one. I am loyal, loyal to the dark. I am always loyal. I seek to serve, to advise. You should let me in."

"Why; in what way do you think you can help? You cannot help. I do not wish you to enter. Do you question my commands?"

"No, never. But consider, he is a liar. He is a heretic. He will seek to lie to you, to deceive you. You must not be deceived. You must not listen to him."

"I know everything," I tell him.

Kong steps back and looks at me. He sees that now he is discovered, that all his schemes are undone, that there is only darkness.

"It was not as he says."

I motion to the guards and they hold Kong fast.

"Strip him and search him."

They remove his priestly gown and mask. They remove his gauntlets. One of the guards rifles through his robes as the others remove his small clothes. When he is naked, they search his beard and hair. They search inside his mouth and in his ears and nostrils. They search under his fingernails and between his toes. They search his buttocks and genitals and armpits and when they have collected all his pellets and needles and darts and powders and cords, they let him stand.

I suppose Kong always has these instruments with him. Murder is his trade. Did he really think he could slay me with these foolish toys? I am tempted to laugh at him, but he looks pitiful, short and naked. He is far less impressive now. I feel pity for him and contempt. He is weak. He is nothing.

"Do you still wish to visit your accuser?"

"I am accused of nothing, great one. I am innocent. I seek only to serve. I am loyal."

I hear the words that are not spoken. I know he has betrayed me. I know he has betrayed the dark.

"Bring him," I say and motion to the guards to follow me.

We enter the room, and as we do Kong tries to free himself. He shakes off one of his restrainers. He is not trying to escape. He is trying to reach Amantae. I strike him, hard, and he falls to the ground. Even now he seeks to defy me. He has learned nothing. Amantae is still crouched on the floor. When he sees Kong, they glare hatefully at each other.

"I should have killed you long ago, heretic," says Kong. It is the first honest thing I have ever heard him say.

"You could not; you tried often enough. I am alive," says the soldier.

"Not for much longer."

"Perhaps, if I am lucky. If I am fortunate, my death will be brief. I am not sure yours will be. But no matter, it will come soon enough after mine, if not before."

"Enough. I have no wish to listen to such nonsense. I will decide who lives and dies. Me, the priest of Vatu, the sayer of his will. The doer of his will."

Amantae bows and is silent, but Kong looks angrily towards me.

"You are nothing," he says and before I can speak, the sergeant has struck him.

"Gag him for now. I will not have him interrupt with his wise counsel. Later we will hear him speak. I will guess he has much to say."

I turn to look directly at him.

"How does it feel to lose? You have lost everything. I have won and you have lost. You always lose. Even when you slay me, you lose. You can never win. You lose, over and over again. Is that why you did it, because you cannot bear to lose? You are a fool."

The gag is not yet in his mouth and Kong spits at me. "It was not like that, not like that all."

And then the gag is in his mouth. The guards hold him tight; he struggles, but he is neither strong enough nor skillful enough to escape. He is held fast. My words hold him tight. He cannot escape my commands. How can he possibly think to defy me? This is my world, I am master of it.

I turn to Amantae. "Stand," I command and he does so. I notice as he stands that he has drawn a circle in the dust, a circle of intertwining lines. It is the same circle that Kong drew in the dust in the library. I crouch down and trace the circle with my hand. I let my fingers memorize the shapes, then I draw the exact same shape in the dust next to it. It is a beautiful and intricate design.

"So," I say to Amantae. "You are a heretic. Is the girl a heretic too? Tell me, do your gods help you now? Are you praying to them inside? Do they bring you comfort?"

Amantae does not answer.

"I am not mocking you. I am curious. What have your heretic gods done to deserve your loyalty?"

"If it is deserved, then it is not loyalty, it is repayment."

"Of course, but think of Vatu, he is due repayment. The dark will have its due, willing or no. It will take what is owed."

"The darkness is owed nothing."

"Really, all life comes from the dark. It was in darkness you were conceived and grew. Darkness to which you will return."

"I hope for better things."

"That is all that is left to you now; hope. Is it enough?"

"Yes, in the end it is enough; there can be nothing more."

"If you say so."

"Will you spare the girl?"

"Why should I?"

"Very well, as I said, in the end hope must be enough. I will hope for mercy for her. But if not, then I will hope the gods intervene."

"They will not. They cannot. There are no gods, only darkness. Let there be no heretic nonsense here. I am the priest of darkness. Only darkness is eternal. There are no gods. Your hope is foolish nonsense.

"Why do you seek to draw this out? Eventually you will do what I say. You are just wasting time. Is life so precious that you want to eke it out longer? Bring the girl, we must take this to the end."

The girl is brought. When I see her again, I realize she is younger than I had supposed, and prettier. She does not look up when she enters. When she comes in, all the fight goes out of Amantae. I have won. He will speak. He will tell me everything. Kong struggles to free himself, but cannot. Why? Does he wish to silence Amantae? Does he wish to attack the girl? Does he wish to attack me? I am surprised at his foolishness. To think that he can struggle now. He is trapped in black amber.

"Now, you must tell me everything, now you must speak. She will hear. Kong will hear. I will hear. The darkness will hear."

I let the darkness seep out of me. Dark bands wrap around the three prisoners. I motion for the guards to leave. There is no need for them to hear.

"Now I will hear it. Now you will speak."

Chapter Thirteen
History

The prisoner says, "I will tell you everything. I will tell you the truth. I am as you say, nothing, or I was a nothing. I was brought up in a town far from the Sun. Saco, it is a small place, but it is on the river and so many people travel through it. I was a guardsman, a good one, or at least not a bad one. What makes a good guardsman? Well, that depends I suppose. I was good at what I did, and what I did was fight, or train to fight. You probably think that guardsmen don't have much fighting to do. That's true up to a point. Mostly people don't fight back. When the guard comes, they mostly do as they are told. Most people, that is. Mostly they are docile, like cattle. They live comfortable lives and want to keep things comfortable. But there are others, those that don't live comfortable lives, those that are desperate, and there are capos.

"So yes, there is some call for fighting and more than you might think. The darkness is everywhere, but there are many things in the darkness. I was young and I was ambitious, and talented. I was quick and nimble on my feet. There is only one place for someone like me, and that's here, at the City of the Sun. That's what I wanted. I wanted to leave that small town on the river and head towards the Sun."

"Is this really necessary?" I ask.

"Yes, yes it is; necessary for me anyway. If you are going to hear it, you should hear it all, every last bit of it. I will tell it all, all of the things that make me what I am and all of the things that make me real. This is what happened, this is all of it. It is who I am, it is what makes me.

"I am a good fighter, I am quick like I said, and I had a good teacher. Not only that, I trained hard every day, and I trained because I knew that the better I was, the more likely I was to get here, where I wanted to be. I wanted to be here at the centre of things, where things happen. I thought that to be here was better than to be in some distant outpost that no one had heard of. In some ways I was right.

"It seems so silly now, but I wanted to get to the top, to be the best. So eventually I got my chance. There was a troop of guards coming through, and one of the captains saw me training. He asked if I wanted to join his troop. Of course I said yes. My own captain wasn't so pleased. He said I was being stupid and that it was a daft thing to do. I never understood why he said that. He was bright and capable. I'm not sure why he never tried to get to the City of the Sun himself. Anyway, I went with the captain and came with him to the City of the Sun. My teacher was leaving Saco anyway, moving further away from the Sun. Said he was getting old and wanted to settle down. Shame, he was a good swordsman. Might have been one of the best I've seen. But then I hadn't seen many back then. Anyway, there was no one there who could teach me anything. If I was going to learn, I had to move.

"Once I got here, I realized why the captain wanted me to come with him. It was about my fighting skills all right, but not to use them for guard work. He wanted to use me as a fighter in the duelling bouts. When I got here, I was in no way the best swordsman in the guard, not even close. Those others had trained with teachers much better than mine. And they knew a trick or two I'd never seen in Saco. I fought a few fights, I won a few, mostly because I was quicker or more determined. But I lost a good few too and have the scars to prove it. When we fight, there is a surgeon near. Even here we don't want too many bodies turning up. And if we did kill every time we had a bout, we'd run through guardsmen at quite a rate for sure. You'd have to be recruiting all the time. Even so, I was lucky to live through those first few years. Just dumb luck. I bet there are thousands just like me that come here and last a few years. Then they're dead or crippled, or they just get fed up and limp home. I know I thought of going back to Saco more than a few times. But I never did go back. I told myself I would never go back to that dump, and it looks like I never will. Although right now I wish I had, that I could. It would be better than what is coming, that's for sure. Still, dumb luck or whatever got me through those first years, and I started training with the best teachers. I still trained every day. I was still quick. Eventually it was me that knew a trick or two when I was in a fight. I started to win. I won more and more often, and when I lost I made sure that I survived. And if I lost I'd think about the fight, and how he beat me, and learn from it instead of just being mad and angry. I've not lost now for years in a fight, and it's me that does the teaching now. There might be a better swordsman than me here, but I've never seen him, and I've seen all the guards."

"There is a better," I say. Greba would not break sweat against him.

"Perhaps. Like I said, I ended up being a big fish in the big pond. I was, I am, the best swordsman here. That didn't do much for me in other ways. I'm still only a sergeant, never made captain, much less general. And never got a chance to move into the civil ranks, you know, chancellors and dukes and all that. Some of the guards do. I'm not mad about that. If I'm honest, it's probably just as well, I'd most likely be terrible as an officer or functionary. I'm not even a particularly good sergeant. Still, everyone wants to get on, so I started getting on in other ways. He'll tell you more about that."

With this Amantae indicated Kong with a glance.

"I'm not sure quite how we met, most likely in one of the taverns. When I was younger, I liked to drink. I liked to think I could drink better and fight harder than anyone else. But it's not a good mix; fighting and drinking. You think it's giving you an edge, but it's taking everything else. Can't remember the first time we met. But there he was. You were old then. Very old, you were going to die sooner or later. No one was going to hitch their wagon to you, not then. So, when the chance came to work for him, I took it. Why not, nothing wrong in it. If it meant extra gold, or better land coming my way then so what? I could make extra gambling and duelling and teaching, but this was better. I could make real money now, money like a captain and more. I could have my own lodgings, good ones, not shitty army ones, and women, as many as I wanted. I told myself that was it. That this was what I came to the city for. And it was.

"So what if a few courtiers or guards disappeared in the dark?

Things like that happened all the time. I can't remember the first time I killed for him. But I did, again and again. Lots of them; all put away quickly and with no fuss. Some he wanted to disappear, that was no problem. Others he wanted to be found, in certain places and positions. That was no problem either. I guess they were left as messages for someone. Either way it was no problem to me. I had no worries. A few times it was people I knew that had to go, but that was all right. You don't get too attached to anyone here. That's not wise.

"Anyway, soon I'm his right hand man. His most trusted lieutenant. No, not trusted, but you know what I mean. I'm doing well. Or I was then. Things were great."

Amantae stops. He is remembering those times.

"No doubt you wish you could go back to those times," I say.

"What, no, is that what you think? Well, I suppose I can understand why you would, but no, never. Don't you see that life, this life is nothing? I'd made it all the way, as far as I can go. And I was nothing. I was a true servant of the dark. Nothing, less than nothing. I had given in to the dark and was nothing. I didn't know it then but I know it now. I would not go back to that for anything. If I could I would go back to Saco, to those times before I gave myself away for gold, ambition and pride. Of course it's too late now.

"No, those were times when things seemed great on the outside, but inside I was empty. I know that now but not then.

"Eventually you died. They say that he killed you, and I know he wanted to. He hated you so much. Him and me; we were alike then. We both wanted to be top dog, but of course neither of us could be. He thought he could be top dog if he got rid of you. Perhaps he was for a bit. I wonder how that was. I wonder if he was like me: empty. Who knows, perhaps the twelve are different the same way you are different. Perhaps they were good times for him.

"He told me that he did it, that he killed you. That he came into your chambers and drowned you in your bath. He told me how he held you under and how your eyes looked up at him as he smiled and how he pushed harder. He told me about the last bubbles of air that came from your mouth and how your eyes were suddenly empty. He told me you were old and pathetic, that you did not have the strength to fight him. He told me he urinated in your bath water and left you there for the servants to find. He laughed as he told me. He said he'd killed others before, but never enjoyed it as much as he enjoyed killing you. You were dead, and he was glad. I have never seen him so full of glee. It was as if he had been born to kill you.

"I think this was the first time I started to think about things. I mean, I'd killed loads of people too, but I wasn't exactly happy about it. I never had a problem with it, true. But to take so much joy from murder. It was not right. Even then I knew it was not right."

"But," I said, "you took joy in killing the other man. What was his name, Agana?"

"Yes I did," he admits, "and it is wrong of me, but it is not the same thing. I am glad because of what I have done, not because I killed him. It is not the same."

"If you say so; it does not matter." I wave for him to continue.

"No, it does matter. You think I am the same as him. Well, perhaps. If I am, then may the gods strike me now. I am not like him, and if I am, there is still a difference. I do not wish to be like him, but he does. If I am evil, then I wish to be redeemed. He is evil and wishes only to do evil forever."

"Evil, who mentioned evil?" I sneer. "There is no such thing as evil. It is a word we use only to describe those things we wish would not happen."

"How can you walk in darkness and not know evil? How can you stand by him and not know evil? It is simply a lie you tell yourself. I cannot swap words with you. I'm only an assassin. But I am right."

"If you are right, then continue," I say, losing patience. "I already knew Kong was my killer."

"Yes, I'm told that the twelve kill each other all the time. All right. All the others swore to secrecy. I did it too. For all the good it did them though, they're all dead. I killed a few of them myself. Not sure who did for the others. Maybe Kong, that's when I finally gave up on him and began to see this world for what it is."

"And what is it?" I asked.

Amantae looks at me startled, as if he is amazed. "Hell, of course. Or at least one of them. There's more than one, and this ain't the worst of them by any means, but it's bad enough."

"Hell, you think this is Hell." I am astonished. "Heretic nonsense."

"What else can it be?" he asks.

"It is my world. It is Vatu's world. It is a perfect world," I tell him. "This is not Hell, it is just the world. There is no Hell or Heaven, just this world. Hell... What a stupid thing to say."

"It is Hell, it is Hell for you too because there is no escape for you." It is the slave girl who speaks. It is the first time I hear her speak. I am surprised. I had not thought she would speak without a great deal of persuasion.

"Why should I want to escape? I rule everything, I am all powerful," I tell her.

No one answers. They cannot answer.

"It is Hell to me," says Amantae. "I wanted out. I wanted to change. I wanted a way out and I found it."

"There is only one way out," I tell him. "And I will give you it. I will give you oblivion. I will give you death."

"You think this is all there is," Amantae says. "This is all you know, but there are things beyond knowledge. It was not enough to die, to just stop being. That was not what I wanted. I wanted more than that, I just did not know what."

"So you became a heretic," I say.

"Not then. I was still the right hand man to the right hand man to the right hand man of Vatu. Not the top, but close. A man like me could not get higher."

"I will hear more of this," I say. "I will hear it all."

"Very well," Amantae says. "You want my secret. I killed you, not even you, the real you, not the fake. I have told you my secret and you know nothing. Why should I fear you? I killed you. I crushed your head between my hands. Your blood has seeped between my fingers. And now you think I should fear you. You should fear me. I was your death. Can't you see? Kong has won. He came to see me straight after he killed you. After he told me you were dead, he told me what would happen next. That he would go and find the reborn High Priest. That he would be led by Vatu to where your spirit would now reside.

"When you die, your spirit leaves your body. Or so I am told. For the rest of us, we go into the void. But you, High Priest of Darkness, you do not go to the void. The darkness brings you back to this Hell. Vatu brings you back here. You were reborn an infant. Vatu led us to you. Kong was guided to the place you are reborn, to find the child.

"Kong led. I and the guards followed. He is the only one of the twelve that comes. He should wait for the others of the twelve, but he does not. 'We must go now,' he says, and sends me to gather together a squadron of the guards. I am not a captain, but the guards know that I am in favour with Kong. They do not question me. Kong has told me to select twelve. There were twelve of us that set out with Kong to bring you home.

"We travelled far. Kong seemed to know where we were going. We followed him. This is how it had been done many, many times. This was something slightly different, but not much. It is the same when one of the twelve are reborn.

"We went very far up the river. I thought we might be going to Saco, but we turned and went west, towards the mountains. It was strange to be away from the City of the Sun, everywhere we went was just a pale shadow. It was a long and boring journey. Kong seemed to know where we were going. Eventually we came to a village. Kong told the troop to stay there and off we went, just him and me. Kong led me straight up to the house. There was a woman sitting outside with a baby. You could not be more than a few weeks old. When the woman saw us, she started screaming and screaming. Just straight out screaming. I don't know why. Her man came out of the house and looked at us and then the woman. 'What's all this,' he asked. He went to the woman, but she wouldn't stop, and then suddenly she did. She just went limp. 'We've come for the child,' said Kong.

"'Yes, I thought you had,' the man replied. The woman handed you over. Your parents just gave you up straight away. Just like that. I could see the man was glad to see you gone. Maybe he just did not want to feed another mouth, or maybe there was something spooky about you even then. The woman was a bit less keen. Women are like that. You can tell that she wanted rid of you just as much as him, but she felt bad about it.

"There was no small talk, no debate. They must have known somehow. I don't know how, but it seems that they knew we were coming. They must have known who you were. I don't know much about kids. They all look the same to me.

"They just handed you over and off we went. The mother gave Kong some clothes and stuff. She wanted to come with us, but Kong said he had brought a wet nurse. So she was not needed. All this was going on while we sat out in the yard. The moon was up. You could see all round the clearing.

"After a bit, we headed off. The woman snivelled a bit, but the man told her that you were never theirs so it made no difference, they could have more. That's the thing with sprogs, he said, if one dies you can always have more. I don't think the woman felt the same. I guess it's easier for a man to lose a kid than for a woman. I guess after all she's gone through she thinks she should get something.

"Things are going fine. Off we go, no problems, everything as smooth as milk. We march off a few miles down the road back to Sun Valley, and then Kong comes up to me. 'Now,' he says. That's all he said, one word, but I know what he wanted. It was all he had to say. I guess that's why he wanted me along. I grumble a bit about having to go back. Why couldn't I have just bumped them off when we were there? But Kong does not want that. I'm not sure why, but he didn't.

"Do you want me to tell you how it went? I came back. The man was waiting at the door. He was surprised to see me and even more surprised when I stuck my blade in his ribs. He died quick— your father, no pain. I can't say the same for your mother. She died in the end. There was a lot of screaming and blood. No one was around. It went on for a couple of days. Eventually she died. I didn't kill her, she just couldn't take any more. After, I thought I'd burn it down. But I never, it had started to rain and I didn't think the house would burn. Besides, I needed to get back to Kong. I'd had enough of travelling around."

"I thought we'd be heading back, but when I caught up, Kong was waiting behind. 'You took your time,' he said. I could tell he was not pleased, but I did not care. 'These things take time to do properly,' I said. 'If you wanted it done quick then you should have told me.' I asked where the others were. 'Still at the village,' he said. He had you with him, and he handed you over to me. What's this, I say, I thought you had a wet nurse. What do you want me to do?

"'Nothing for now,' he says. I have to keep you out of sight. Kong and the rest of them move on. They come to a town, it's quite a nice one. I still have to keep out of sight. I still don't know what the plan is, but I do as I'm told. In the town Kong comes up to a house, there is a woman and child. 'This one,' Kong says. 'We take this one,' and the boys take it. The woman is bewildered and so is the man. The man keeps crying and saying there is some mistake. 'No mistake,' says Kong, but the man will not let it go. He is pleading and pleading, eventually Kong gives a signal and the soldiers step forward. They kill the man and then burn the house.

The woman is raped in the street in front of everyone. Then they slit her throat. The child is given to a wet nurse. And we head back. The townspeople are shocked, but they know better than to resist. The local guards stare at us. They would like to fight us, but they know better. The boys I brought would carve them up. And how can you fight against one of the twelve? It can't be done. They can't take arms up against their own. But you could see the disgust on their faces, hate.

"So still I had to stay hid. Even now, when there was two of you. That one that he'd picked up in town and the real you. I'd been with you for some days now. You were only a few weeks old, but you could tell it was the real one. In all that time I never fed you, but you did not cry. Instead you just looked at me with dark eyes.

"Kong came. 'What's this all about?' I wanted to know. I still hadn't figured it out. What he was up to. I still thought we were going to take you home, back to the tower, the real you, that is, not the fake. I guess it was just too much to think of, too much to imagine. I mean, it's unthinkable."

I have not said a word. I want to strike him and tell him he is a liar. "I am the High Priest. I am no fake. I am reborn, over and over again. The darkness is within me. I am a blank tablet and what is written on me is written. Even if it is true, it makes no difference. I am the High Priest and no trick of Kong's will change that. Can you not see; Vatu directed all your actions. I am the High Priest. The child to be chosen was me."

"Yes, I thought of that too," says Amantae. "It could be right. It could be that you are the High Priest. But you are not. I held the real you. I looked into its dark eyes. It was born with darkness inside it. I held you also, later. The darkness was not in you. I know I've scorned Vatu, defied him. But I've seen the child, and I know he was the one and not you. You can tell yourself what you like, but I know the truth and deep down, so do you. You are not of the darkness, you are simply a man, a child.

"Kong laughed and told me what was up. 'Why don't I just kill him,' I said. But he said no, that would be no good. You'd just escape again, just be reborn. We had to keep you alive. If we killed you, maybe your spirit would jump into the other boy; who knows. I don't know how all that mumbo jumbo works. Neither does he. He thinks he does, but he does not. He knows nothing, I'm surprised he came up with this. Although I suppose he had a thousand lifetimes to think it up. 'Well, what then?' I asked, I can't look after him. If you want him to live, then I'm not going to be much use. You should have told me this before. I might have got twitchy and killed him before now.

"He said that he knew I wouldn't. Why would I if I thought you were going to be the High Priest? I had enough smarts not to mess with that voodoo. 'Give him up to someone,' he said. 'Tell them he's your bastard and his mother is dead. Give them this to look after him. That way you can go and check on him, make sure he's alive, that he's not escaped.' He hands me gold, lots of it. He thinks he can trust me with it. 'I'll need more,' I say. 'What for?' he asks. 'For me,' I reply. He scowls and then he hands more gold over. I nod. 'This will do,' I tell him. 'This will do for now,' I think to myself.

"'Take him and go,' he says, so I do. 'What am I to do with you?' I wonder. That's the real you, not the fake one, not the false one that's here."

Chapter Fourteen
Questions

I want to scream. I want to lash out. He is wrong, he is a liar. I will not let him speak. I send a dark gag across his mouth. Amantae does not flinch. Kong is cowering, muttering over and over to himself. The girl is standing but her head is bowed. All of them must die. This heresy must not be spoken of ever. I will die in this room.

"Then why has Vatu not destroyed me? Why has he accepted me and filled me with darkness?" I demand and let the gag slip from his mouth.

"Isn't it obvious?" Amantae answers. "It's because he is not all knowing, not all powerful. He is a dark spirit. He has power, but he is a fraud. He has stolen the Sun from us and cloaked us in darkness and ignorance. One day the Sun will be free, and when the Sun is free, we will be free also. I am loyal to the Sun, but I am no longer loyal to the dark."

"So you are indeed a heretic," I sneer.

"No, not a heretic, a believer," he says.

"So what happened to this child that you were given?" I demand.

"I have already told you," Amantae says. "What does it matter what I did with the child? If it is reborn, then it is reborn. As long as you are at the Tower of the Sun, he will not be found. Why should I bother to keep you alive? Why should I spend gold on keeping you? If you were really my bastard, I would have drowned you. If I send you to someone to look after, then they would know you were not mine. I have had other bastards, real ones. Why would I treat a pretend bastard differently to how I treated them? I could keep all the gold and not just some of it. I could even go back every year to Kong and tell him that I needed more gold. I did too."

"So what did you do?" I shout.

"I'm not afraid of you," he says. "I'll tell you what I did. I took your infant head between my hands and squeezed until it popped like a melon. Your infant brains and blood ran over my hands. I told you what I was like. I told you. I stared into your black eyes, and squeezed, and all the darkness in you made no difference. I squeezed until you were dead. You are dead. You died at my hands, like I said. If you were reborn, then so what, somewhere you live miles away, it does not matter. No one came to get you because you were here at the Tower of the Sun. No one even gave it a thought."

"You fool," I tell him. "When you killed me, you released me. I was reborn here. I am the High Priest."

"No, you are not. I have seen the High Priest. I have seen the darkness in you. Even now, while you hold me in bonds of darkness, I can see you are not him. You are not the son of darkness. You are nothing, you are a fraud. You are truly dead, and you are just a ghost, a nothing."

I am struck now by the sheer effrontery of Kong's scheme, to defy Vatu.

"How could you have done such a thing?" I ask Kong. "How could you even imagine such a thing?"

"I did not," says Kong. "In all my lifetimes such a thought never came to me. It came to you. It is your deed. You sought to escape this life and now you have. You came to me, not I to you. Like all of us, you were wearied of darkness and service. You came to me. You always come to me. You had endured enough and wished to depart. As ever you wished to depart. Eventually we all wish to depart. But we cannot escape, not ever. Vatu will not release us. Not ever.

"'Yes,' I tell you, 'I will release you.' I will take your life. But you shake your head. 'It is not enough,' you say. I do not understand. I say that straight out, I don't understand. What more do you want, and you tell me. You want this. You want me to kill you, not just that one, but all of them, all of you, each and every one. I can scarcely believe it. It is staggering to kill each and every one of you. I am amazed. Can it even be done?

"But you say it can, that all I need to do is kill you again and again. If you are never High Priest, then you cannot be reborn. You tell me what to do, exactly what to do, to swap you for another child. I can scarcely believe it. 'He will know. He is all knowing.' But you say he is not. You say he can be cheated, you say this is how to cheat him. I can scarcely believe you.

"Do you know how many times you begged me to do this? I was your friend. I am more afraid of Vatu than I am of you. 'It will be me that has to pay for this,' I say. 'Yes, it will be, if he ever finds out. He will find out,' I say. But you promised me he will not. That was your promise, and you have been true to it. 'He does not need to know. You do not need to tell him.'"

I need to think. It is too much. I cannot believe that I would do such a thing. Stop now, I am the master of this world, this cannot be. I will not allow it. I will rewind. I will bring the world back to where it should be. I will change everything. It cannot be right. And yet, have I known this all along? Is this the secret that I have hidden from myself? If so, then why reveal it now? Why reveal it ever? If it is a secret, then why have I let it be revealed? Can I go back and start again? And if I can, what will I change? I have been hiding this from myself. The prisoners are silenced by a gesture. I cannot believe it, I will not.

"It is lies," I say. "Clever lies, but lies nonetheless. Do you think for a moment that I would give up what I have, what I am? Do you imagine that I would betray Vatu? I am the High Priest. I alone share his power."

"Yes, that is why only you can betray him," says Kong.

"You are a boy and know nothing," says Amantae. "If I could, I would kill you again."

He is seeking to goad me. But I do not act on a whim. I have more that I will know from him still. I will know it all, even if it is lies. The lies of my enemy cannot harm me. I will know them all and laugh at them. I will tell Vatu of these lies and we shall laugh together after we have stripped the truth from their bones. Yes, I will speak with Vatu, I will enter his darkness and commune with him. He will tell me what to do. He will make things right. He is all powerful.

"I should take you to Vatu. I should take you now. He would devour you," I say.

"He devoured me long ago," says Kong. "He devoured me and remade me in his image. He devoured us all. He devoured Amantae when he came to me and asked me to raise him up. He has devoured you."

"What nonsense," I tell him. "You know nothing of Vatu, even after a thousand lifetimes."

I pause again. There is still much for me to learn here. I will know it all. If I go to Vatu now, then I am weak. I will be strong and force it open, I will know my secret.

"There is more," I say to Amantae. "You have told me some of it, but not all. You have told me nothing of the girl. Who is she? Why should you care for her? Why risk your life for her?"

Amantae is kneeling and his head is bowed. He looks up at the girl. He stares at her as if he is seeing her for the first time.

"Forgive me," he says. "I hoped to save you, but I have not. You would have been better off if I had killed you rather than Agana. I tried to, but could not make myself do it. I will tell him all. Not to betray you, but because it might save you. He might let you live."

"It does not matter," she says. "It is too late for that. It is too late for anything."

"Then I will tell him. It might change things."

"If you want, but I doubt it."

"I was in hell, I am in hell, but I came to know it. This land of yours, I want no part of it. So I wish to escape. And that is where it started. I wish to be free of the darkness. Have you never wished such a thing?"

"No," I say.

"Neither had I. I could not even imagine such a thing. But I watched and saw that only those who die escape the darkness."

"They do not, they enter the darkness."

"If you say so," Amantae continues. "Anyway, Kong had started to remove the others that had been on the journey to collect you. At first I never noticed what he was doing and one or two of them I bumped off myself under his instruction. But then I started to notice. They were almost all dead and those that were still alive were jumpy. It got me to thinking I should be jumpy. I knew why he wanted them dead of course; dead men tell no tales. I kept telling myself that it was different for me. Kong trusted me, or so I thought. But I knew Kong never trusted me, not really. It was only a matter of time before he came for me, and come for me he did.

"I went swimming. I used to go swimming a lot, I love the water, especially when it is hot. Lots of us would go down to the caverns. There's a river that runs right under the Valley, through a big cave. I'm not sure you've ever been to it. There are steps that go down so you can collect water. There are steps cut from most of the houses. From my house there's a gate that leads down and I go swimming there. I'd unlock the gate and there, where I was alone, I'd strip naked and go swimming in the dark.

"It was when I was swimming, coming naked out of the water, that he struck. Not Kong, but one of the fencing masters working at his command. He had snuck up behind me and grappled me. How he got in, I don't know. I suppose it is easy enough to unlock a gate if you know how to do it. I came up thinking I was all alone and there he was. I'm good with a sword but I'm not the biggest and so he held me under. I struggled of course, but he was too strong. There was not much I could do. I was drowning. I did drown. Let me tell you, it was not nice. You try and hold your breath until you just can't anymore, and then you're gulping in water, into your lungs, not into your throat. The water goes into your chest and it gets heavier. It feels like a fire. You get weaker and weaker until you can't struggle any more. There is so much pain, I think there can be nothing like it and then suddenly it's not about the pain or even about your body, it's only about your head. Everything is about your head, the whole world is in your head. It's not like going to sleep, it's like waking up. It's this world that is a dream and dying is waking up. You're getting out of it. I was dying. I did die, but I never went to darkness, suddenly there was light everywhere. No darkness, just light, and I realized that everything I thought was important was nothing."

"But you never died," I said.

"I think I did. I think I was dead. It was the best thing in my whole life. But I never stayed dead. I woke up. I was lying on the steps face up. The assassin was floating face down. How could that be? It was like we had switched, but then I saw that I had managed to bash his head in. I think I must have picked up a rock and brained him. Even then he would be on top of me and too heavy to move. We should have both died."

"Why didn't you?" I asked.

"I don't know really. I should have. Like I said, I think I did, but he must have drifted over the top of me with the current, at least drifted enough for me to float up and get air. That's one explanation, but there is another. Maybe it was meant. Maybe some other reason brought me back. Like I said, I died and when I was dead I could hear a voice. It said it was sending me back. Why? I asked. Why can't I stay here? It's nice."

"What, you think that some divine hand interceded and sent you back? Superstitious claptrap."

"Sure it is, that's what I kept telling myself. I kept telling myself that it was all nonsense, and sometimes I even managed to convince myself of that. But then I realized that even if it was all nonsense, I wanted it to be real. I didn't want it to be nonsense, I wanted the voice and the light and everything to be real. Otherwise what? I just got lucky or unlucky and would die at some point anyway. So even if it was nonsense, I started to do things that the voice had told me to do. The things that it said it was sending me back for. If it is nonsense then so what, it's all nonsense anyway. This world is nonsense. You're nonsense, Vatu is nonsense. And him." Amantae pointed to Kong.

"So what did the voice tell you to do?"

"Change."

"And how did you change?"

"I stopped working for him for a start."

Kong turns and hisses, "I should have killed you myself."

"You could have tried. You never did though, did you? You were always too scared to get close."

Kong does not reply. There is no need. Everyone knows that Amantae is correct, Kong is a coward.

"So you became a heretic?" I ask.

"No, not at first. In some ways I'm still not a heretic. Not the way they want me to be anyway. I've changed but maybe I've not changed enough. Some things are too hard. At first all I did was try to... well, I'm not sure what. Not to be me I suppose. Not the old me anyway. It sounds like nothing but it was the hardest thing I ever did, harder than learning to fight and harder than killing people. I've tried so hard, but in some ways I'm still the same. Deep down, I'm still the same and all the time I have to fight the same battle over and over again. It gets easier, but then you forget, you think the battle is over and you let your guard down and then you have to fight the same fight all over again. Do you understand?"

"No," I reply, "I don't understand. But I am not interested in this. I want to know about the heretics. They must be crushed."

"There's not much I can tell you, to be honest. There are always plenty of heretics in the cells. Vatu likes them all brought here to question. Not that most of them get questioned. Most of them just get tortured and killed. Most of them are not really heretics. Most of them are just people accused so that their property can be confiscated or for some other reason. You know, like girls that turn down someone important or for revenge. There are some real heretics out there, but mostly people are not."

The girl looks up. She is going to say something and then stops.

"Go on," I say to her.

She looks down again and shakes her head. I think she will be silent but then she speaks. "It is not right, what he says. Everyone is a heretic, deep inside. Or not a heretic, that's not the right word. No one really believes that Vatu is anything other than a demon sent to torture us. Everyone hopes to escape. They may not know the truth, but they know that Vatu is false. They recognize that this world is a lie."

It is a pointless diversion. I motion her to be silent. I will hear the end of this. I will uncover the treachery of those around me.

Amantae continues. "I suppose that she is right, and wrong. Having something inside is all very well, but it's what you do with it that counts. But anyway, that's not what you mean by heretic. Just hating Vatu does not make you a heretic, not the way you mean. You mean those like her, that teach hope. Those that are organized and think they know the way out of this hell. There are much fewer of them than you think. But now I was looking for them, the real ones. Like I said, there were not many, but there were some. I'd take them and question them. If anyone asked I'd say I was interrogating them. I suppose I was. What's the difference? It's just two words that mean the same thing. So I'd question them. Yes, I'd ask about who taught them, who their leaders were, but then I realized I was asking the wrong questions. So I'd ask them other questions, about what they believed and why. Some of it made sense, but not all of it. I learned a great deal about what they thought and what they think. Some of it I knew already, I knew for sure that this world was hell, created by some twisted crazy mind for whatever bizarre reason. But they began to show me something else. They began to show me the way out."

"There is no way out. It is all lies. It is a trick and you have been fooled," I say.

"If you say so, but tell me, will you spare the girl?"

"Why do you want me to spare her?"

"I don't really know. I've met plenty of heretics; like I said, I don't buy into everything they say. Maybe I should, but I don't. She is one of them. You learn to recognize them. She was brought here as a slave girl for the pleasure houses. I still went there from time to time. Like I said, even with the voice, I had to fight those battles over and over. I went there and maybe it was just as well I did. They brought her up to me and I could see she was barely more than a child. She hid it well, but she was terrified. I knew then that I couldn't do it. I mean I could, but that I knew I would hate myself afterwards, and I knew I couldn't leave her. So I bought her. I had plenty gold. She was not even that expensive. I took her home, and she was still afraid. I suppose she was right to be. I kept her safe. It was as if by keeping her safe, it made up for the others. I don't suppose it does really. Not really. But in my head it makes a difference. The voice, it said to help her, so I did."

"So that is all then, is it," I say. "You want me to save her just for sentiment. She's not important at all."

"Everyone is important. That's what you don't get. I can't help everyone, but I could help her. I've kept her safe. She works around my home. People think she's my servant so I let her act like one, but she's not, not really. When Agana picked her up I knew I had to get her back, even if it means this. I had to do something."

After that he is silent. He is weaker than I had thought. I see he is bleeding. I call for surgeons to come and bind his wounds. I do not want him dead, not yet. They take him away, and I let them take the girl too. She is unimportant. Now there is just the two of us.

I let the darkness slip from Kong. He lies huddled at my feet. He does not speak again. I do not let him. I let black ropes of power twist around his throat until they choke the life from him. I am the darkness, I am death.

Chapter Fifteen
Searching

Kong is dead. I have burned his body and thrown his ashes in the pit. They are all dead. The others, I have fed them to Vatu. They are with him in the great darkness. He will do with them what he will. It is just. It is right. No one can defy me and live. There is no escape from the vengeance of Vatu. When he is dead I am angry. He did not suffer enough. I have slain him too quickly. His corpse is ground to ash, and cast into the pit. There is no funeral pyre and none of the twelve see his corpse. I will not have it. There is nothing to see anyway. Now when I walk through the tower I see fear in their eyes, and hatred. That is as it should be. They should fear me. They are right to fear me. I will destroy every one of them. It is good to remind them of their place, of their fate, that dark pit of bones, that is their fate. They cannot escape it any more than I can. There is no escape. This is the justice of Vatu and there is no escape from justice.

Vatu is angry. He wishes to know why I have slain one of the twelve so soon. I have only been High Priest for a few years and now I have slain Kong. Because I hate him, is that not reason enough? Together we reach out into the void and catch his soul before he can escape. We send it into a host and plant it. We must act in haste and plant it in the first host we find. Then we return. It will be many months, nine months before Kong is born. I cannot sense him now, but I will find him and bring him back. There is no escape, not for him or for me. This is where we will be forever.

Hilketa takes over Kong's duties. But he still makes reports to me. Hilketa grumbles but not too loudly. He does not want to face my wrath. It seems he is not yet tired of living.

Eventually, he asks me why.

"There does not have to be a reason."

He cannot doubt it. And he cannot know the reason, no one can. There is no reason. Somewhere Kong is growing inside a womb, a black comma of spite getting larger and larger, eating away at the inside like a worm in an apple. He is getting bigger; soon he will be big enough to live outside of the womb. Soon it will be my turn to fetch him and bring him here. It will be my turn to torment him. My turn to fill him with hate.

"Will he also be a blank tablet?" I ask Hilketa.

"Yes."

"What if we choose to write something else on it?"

Hilketa is speechless, and then he says, "Vatu will not allow it."

"Will he not?"

Soon, Kong is reborn. I can feel him. I can sense him. It is time to bring him back.

It is the first time I have left the Valley of the Sun. I don't take all the remaining twelve with me, I take Greba and Hilketa. There must be witnesses, especially now. Kong will not escape. I will find him and bring him back. Greba and Hilketa both complain. Hilketa claims he is too old and that he will be needed to administer the city in my absence. But I do not listen to him. There are others that can do that. Greba does not say anything but just looks at me with sullen resentment. I am not sure why I brought him along.

It is the strangest feeling. I am being led by some strange impulse. There is no direction or vision, just an urge forwards. What is driving me on? It is Vatu. He is irresistible. I am doing his will. Greba and Hilketa are both in a wagon following me and the guards are on horseback, but I am the High Priest. I have no need for a carriage, darkness drives me on. I walk ahead and the rest follow me. It is as if the whole world is full of light and I am drawn to one spot of darkness, a fish swimming upstream in a river of darkness. The world is a well of darkness and I am a stone plummeting downwards. I can no more resist than a stone could fly upward, or fish walk on dry land. There is only onwards.

We travel quickly but we travel far. I do not know how far. When we stop I am like a caged beast, eager to go on. But the rest cannot keep going. They are tired and hungry. Darkness cannot sustain them.

I know now that it was all a lie. I feel the drive within me and I know that I cannot resist. How could Kong resist the urge of Vatu? It was a poor lie. Perhaps Kong even believed it. Amantae did. I am the High Priest. I am the chosen of Vatu. It is plain. It cannot be denied.

Hilketa is grumbling and complaining. We have stopped in a town; I do not care what it is called. It is not important. We are staying in the townhouse and have taken over the best apartments. It is necessary to remind everyone who we are. It is necessary to remind them that everything belongs to Vatu, to me. The whole world is mine. I am driven and can hardly notice the apartment. It is not very grand. I would be as happy to camp outside the town, but that could not be allowed, we must remind all that I am High Priest.

This is why we are reborn away from the City of the Sun, so that we show everyone our power, so that we remind them that the world is mine. Greba is still saying nothing.

"Why so sullen?" I ask.

He looks up, but does not answer. He knows that I do not care, he knows that I am desperate to be on the road again. He turns back to the fire without speaking.

"I am too old for this," says Hilketa. He too is sitting by the fire. He is wrapped in black fur. He looks old. And frail. Perhaps he will die on this trip. I do not care. If he dies I will find him too. It is nothing.

"Maybe we should be going," I say. But I know that they cannot leave now. I know that they will need food and sleep.

The governor enters the room. He feels he must give us his attention. He is worried that we may take any oversight as a slight. He does not want to offend us, he is afraid.

"Is there anything I can bring for you?" he asks. I do not answer but Hilketa assures him our needs are adequately attended to.

"Food, wine, dancing girls or boys?" he asks.

"No we are fine, I am too old for that and Greba's tastes do not run in that direction," Hilketa says.

I stop and listen. What direction do Greba's tastes run?

"Maybe the High Priest? He is young."

He thinks my restlessness is the restlessness of youth that can be sated by flesh.

"I think not," says Hilketa. "The High Priest has other things on his mind. Perhaps when we return."

The fat little governor nods and bows as he leaves us.

I should reprimand Hilketa for speaking on my behalf, but words are like stones stuck in my throat. They will not come, and he is right anyway. I have no interest in these things, not now. I am like a hound straining at a leash.

In the morning I am still driven to go on. The troops are assembled as quickly as possible. I let them eat quickly before we depart. They are on horseback. But even so it is difficult for them to keep with the pace I set. I could run and run and they could not keep up. The darkness gives me a power they cannot match, cannot imagine.

The moon is almost full. It seems to float slowly and serenely overhead, and yet no matter how fast I go, it will pass me. We are walking far from the Valley of the Sun now. There are some roads, but mostly there is woodland to either side. There are some fields and small cottages. Some of the cottages are grouped into small villages. It is poor people who live here, people who cannot afford to live in the towns or on the large estates and seek to eke out an existence on their mean patches of land. Sometimes they will come out of their homes and look at us. There are few travellers in these parts. Still fewer are visits from the High Priest and ruler of all the land. We stop at mid moon. The guards make camp and start to cook gruel.

Hilketa comes. "You must eat," he says.

I have not eaten since we left the Tower of the Sun. I do not know if Hilketa has eaten.

"There is no blood," I say.

"There is always blood," he replies.

"Then give me some."

"Not here," he says and points to a group of cottages in the distance.

"Will you feed with me?"

"Yes," he replies, "and so will Greba."

"How have you fed till now?"

"The soldiers have given us blood, but they are weak now and you will need more than they can give."

He is right, I am famished. I have never been so hungry. I did not realize it till now. But now I am starving. Greba is with us. I set out towards the cottage, and they follow after me. I set a good pace, but they are able to keep up, just. When we reach the cottage I stop. I am shaking.

"What is wrong?" It is Greba who speaks.

I can barely keep myself in check.

The cottage is small but surprisingly well built with walls made from rounded river stones that must have been carried up from the stream. There are no windows, and only a small door. It is thatched with reeds that have not yet turned fully silver grey. There are low walls around the cottage garden that are too low to keep stock out.

"Perhaps there is no one here," I say, but even as I speak the door opens. There is a woman who looks afraid.

"Who is it?" she asks.

I say nothing, but step forward. She is looking straight at me. I grab her by the throat and force her to the ground. There is a shout from the cottage and a man comes running out. Greba slays him with a single blow, like you would snuff a candle. I am holding the woman down and Hilketa brings a bowl and a knife. We fill the bowl with her blood. She weeps as she bleeds to death. And then we feed.

After I have fed, I stop shaking. Next, we bleed the man. His heart has stopped beating so we must hang him upside down to drain the blood. I feed on his blood as well; it is less sweet than the woman's blood. Hilketa and Greba do not share it with me. They are already full.

After I have eaten, I stand. Greba will not look at me. Is he ashamed? This is what I am. I will not be ashamed. There is nothing to be ashamed of. I return to the camp and they follow after me. The men are ready. They have been waiting for our return and we move out. I lead and they follow. That is the way.

Chapter Sixteen
Finding

We arrive at a farm and I know he is here. I can feel it. There is a man sitting on the step to the farm cottage. He does not appear surprised, it is as if he has been waiting for us. He stands but says nothing. I ignore him and push past him into the cottage. It is clear they are not prosperous. The cottage is meaner even than the one we fed at and much less clean. There is a fire in the middle of the floor but no chimney. The room is full of smoke and is very dark. I can see a bed of sorts. It is little more than a pile of rags. There is a woman lying as she is feeding a child. It is him. He has returned.

"It is not milk he needs but blood," I say.

It is true, but the woman is fearful. She thinks I will feed Kong with her blood. She shrinks back. Hilketa and Greba enter the room. Greba, who is taller, coughs in the smoke and bows his head. Then we are all silent, we are silent for a long time, or so it seems to me. The only noise is the soft breathing of the woman and the fire.

"What will you do?" she asks.

"We will take him."

Hilketa says that she can come and nurse him on the way back, but she shakes her head.

"No, I do not want to. He is not mine, never mine. I do not want him. I do not want to leave my husband or my cottage."

"You misunderstand," says Greba. "Hilketa is merely being polite. You will come with us and feed him."

The woman begins to cry. She is older than I thought and far from beautiful. Why should she wish to stay here in this mean holding? Life must be hard. But then life is hard most places, I think.

"Your husband will come too," I say, but she only cries harder.

"No," she says, but her voice is soft and resigned. Insignificant.

There is nothing more to say. There is everything to say. Greba reaches for the child and the woman does not resist.

"What is your name?" he asks.

I do not hear her reply. It is unimportant; she is only a vessel for darkness. She is not important. Greba hands the child to me. I almost fear to touch it, but I fear nothing. I hold it.

"Not like that," says Hilketa, "you must support the head, he cannot do so on his own. Not yet."

I slip my hand up behind his neck and realize how weak he is. I could dash his brains out on the floor in an instant, and I want to, but I know that if I do, I will have to find him all over again. It is better this way. Kong looks up at me. His eyes are twin black holes filled with malice and hate. I realize now why the woman weeps. She had hoped to escape from this hated infant.

"Yes, it is him," I say, although there is no need for words. There is no need for me to say anything. I hand him back to the woman. She shrinks away, but takes him.

That was not so hard. It is nothing. There is nothing. It is just him and it is time to go. It seems like something is missing, but I cannot think what.

"Is this it?" I did not mean to speak out loud.

"Yes," says Hilketa. "This is it."

But Greba laughs. "No, this is not it. What are you talking about, this is only the beginning. It begins again. For him at any rate, and for us. And you don't forget this is a beginning for you too."

He is mocking me. Does he seek to die? I turn at him and I see that he is not afraid. Why does he not fear me? All the others do, even Kong, especially Kong. Why not him? I will destroy him, I will make him afraid. He will not mock the darkness.

I leave and let the others deal with the child. As I step out I see that the father is being held by two soldiers.

"He tried to run off," says the captain, by way of explanation. But none is needed. We would all run if we were not bound in some way. Why does Greba not run? What binds him?

The father is crying. "Please, great one, spare Katilu."

"Who?" And then I realize that he is talking about his wife. That must be her name.

"What should I spare her from?" I ask. The man only stammers and is too afraid to answer. It was brave of him to speak, but foolish. I consider having his tongue ripped out. It is too much bother; I am bored with all this. I walk away. The dark urge has left me, and now I am tired.

"We stay here for now." I drop to the ground, but Greba catches me. When did we leave the cottage? He leads me to a tent and there he leaves me. I am so tired and must sleep.

When I wake, I feel empty. I am alone and I rise and leave the tent. The guards part but say nothing. As ever, they say nothing.

"Where are they?"

They point to the cottage and I make my way back to the cottage. The fire is out and it is dark, very dark. I have brought a torch and I see that they are sleeping. When I wave the light, Greba opens his eyes.

"Are you ready?" he asks.

"Yes, let us get going."

He nods and stands up. He kicks Hilketa awake.

"Get up, old man."

Then he turns and shakes the sleeping couple.

"You will travel with us," he says, "in the coach."

The coach is ready. The horses are fresh and hitched up. Greba and Hilketa lead the couple into the coach. It is open-topped and offers little protection from the weather. There is plenty of room in the coach even with the two parents and the infant.

"Will you sit with us?"

I shake my head. I have too much to think about.

Later as the hare moon drops below the horizon, they are asleep. We are camped. Still, I feel a yearning I cannot explain. What is it that steals rest from me? It is late and early. The moon will rise in a few hours. Everyone sleeps. I walk out into the camp. I enter a certain tent. Yes, the tent in which the infant lies. But it is not him that is drawing me, nor is it the sleeping woman who is lying face down. It is something else. It is not here. I walk out of the camp and I am led straight uphill. At the top of the hill, I stop. He is here.

So it is true, and it is a lie. I am alive and I am here. I am standing in the darkness but I do not need eyes to see. I can hear my breath, his breath. He is here, I am here. It is true. I am not dead, I am alive, both of me.

"Do I remember?"

"No, I remember nothing."

There is nothing to remember. There is only darkness. Everything else is a lie, everything else is dead.

It is not true, I am not dead. Amantae has lied to me, or if he has not, then I have been reborn and still live.

"We cannot escape. Not this way."

I reach out, we reach out, but our fingers do not touch, instead they hover a bare inch apart.

"Tell me everything."

But I cannot, there is not time, nor are there words. It is him who has drawn me here and I came. I have drawn him here and he has come. We are like two halves, but we cannot be made whole. I stare into darkness, into my own eyes and the darkness stares back, I stare back.

"Can you not speak?" I ask and I find that I can.

"You are not me." But I am. I put our hands forward and they touch, gently brushing fingertip to fingertip. No sparks fly between us. I do not find his voice in my head. I see no visions of his life. But his finger is soft and warm and real. It is real. How can I live like this?

"Do you know?"

"Some things, enough, I know enough."

"He must not know. He must never know."

"It cannot be done."

"Will you come with me?"

I shake my head. I cannot leave. Where would I go? There is nowhere I can hide. And we cannot escape.

"Not now, not yet. Maybe never."

"I will not go back."

And so I leave and he walks down the hill into the camp. I wish him well. Where shall I go? Freedom is a hard gift at first. I walk for days and days in the dark, empty land. It is like walking through the empty tunnels of the Tower of the Sun. Tunnels I will never walk again. I will never walk through them again. I am free. I am glad.

When he gets to the camp, when I get to the camp, I say nothing, but stand waiting. They begin to awaken. There is a child crying.

"Why is the child not fed?" I ask, and a nurse, perhaps his mother, begins to suckle him.

"Should he not be given blood?" It is the stout well-built man who asks. I see he does not fear me. That is good. It is his weakness. They cannot tell the difference.

"You have blood. Let him feed."

The stout man stares at me. He moves as if he will fight me. But he is not foolish. That is his strength. He cuts his wrist and lets the child feed. The child's black eyes look at me. Even though he is newborn, they are filled with hate. So this is Kong. This is my killer. Our plan failed. You failed me. I should kill you. I will kill you.

An old man brings me a bowl to eat. I smell the tang of blood mixed with sweet milk. I take it and look at it. Is this what I should eat?

"Drink, lord," the old man says. And so I drink and the blood curdles in my insides. It is foul, and I want to throw up but I do not. I have eaten things more foul. After I have eaten, I wash and then the camp is broken. I follow the old man and the stout man into a large wooden carriage.

"Move on," I say. And we travel onwards.

Chapter Seventeen
Dining

This is my life, this is what I have escaped to, this is what I have taken and won. I realize that my every command will be obeyed, either by men or by shadows. They obey me.

The old man attempts to engage me in conversation, but I will not let myself be trapped by words. I say nothing, I only listen. The other man only watches silently. I can tell by the way he carries himself he is a warrior, perhaps a great warrior. That too is a weakness.

We come to a town by the river; it is a large town. It is larger than any town I have lived in. I have never seen so many people. They are holding torches and lining the road. As we go past, they look at us with sullen empty eyes and cheer. The carriage stops outside the townhouse. It is large and very finely decorated. Hilketa leads me into the house and we are led to our quarters. There is a man following us and promising us wine and dancers, a great feast. Hilketa is assuring the man that it is not required, but I stop him.

"You do not speak on my behalf."

He is startled but says nothing, only bows. I turn to the busy man. I assume he is the head man of this town.

"I will bathe first, and then we will dine."

"Very good, great one." The headman also bows and I am led to a suite of rooms. There are maidens there that remove my clothes, and I am led into a silver bath of warm water. The maidens pour water over my naked body as I stand upright in the bath with my arms outstretched. Oils are poured onto my head and massaged into my skin and hair. More water and gentle rubbing with pumice. The dirt of my travel, of my old life runs and collects in the silver basin. The water is turned to darkness. The dirt has left my skin, a lifetime of dirt has left me. By the light of a glass oil lamp I stare at my skin; it is dark but it is clean. I have never been clean before, never.

When I come out of the bath, I am dried. I raise my hand to my neck and find a necklace of black jet. I cannot recall where it came from. He must have placed it around my neck. Dark robes are placed upon me, the dark robes of my priesthood, our priesthood. There is a knock on the door and the two priests enter. They are also bathed and dressed.

"Shall we go?"

We are led into a hall. It is big. Bigger than any I have seen. It is lit by white candles that do not smell of lard, nor do they smoke. The hall is brighter than a full moon. We are seated at a table laden with food. It is amazing; I have never seen so much food. It must have taken a great deal of time to make such a feast and it is only for us. We will not eat, not all of it or even most of it. What a waste. Perhaps the servants will get to eat what we do not. Hilketa and Greba are sitting on either side of me and the headman is sitting beside Hilketa. Perhaps he thinks that the old man is less dangerous than the warrior. If so, he is wrong.

Neither Hilketa nor Greba eat before I do. It is clear that they wish to, and so I wait and eat nothing. Perhaps I will eat nothing; it pleases me that they should know hunger even if it is just for a short time. I have known hunger for days. We sit and no one eats.

Finally, Hilketa asks, "Will you not eat, lord?"

I had thought the stout man would have asked first, or perhaps the headman if he was brave.

"What do you recommend?" I ask the headman.

"We have fish," says the headman. "Sturgeon, we pull it from the river. I'm sure you have as good or better at the Dark Tower, but in our modest town it is the best we have to offer."

So, I will have flesh. It is a fine, rich life I am to live. I motion, and one of the servants cuts a piece and places it on a disc of silver before me. I reach down and eat it. The headman is correct, it is sweet and tender. It is like eating water, it is finer even than meat. The fish melts into nothing in my mouth. I have only once tasted fish before, and it was nothing half so fine; a few thin strips of some bottom feeding pond fish that tasted of mud. But this tastes of waterfalls and salt and mayflies buzzing in the summer air.

"It is good," I say, and the headman smiles, then motions for the servant to serve us all. Hilketa relaxes, but Greba is still tense. Hilketa speaks to me with a familiarity, as if he thinks I am his friend. Greba says little, and when he speaks he makes no effort to hide the contempt in his voice. Well, if I deserve contempt, so too does he.

The food is very good. There are vegetables I have never eaten and then fruit, not wild berries but big cultivated fruit about the size of my fist. It is very sweet and juicy. I eat more than I thought I would, but still not anything like the amount placed before me. Hilketa eats about the same, but Greba eats less, as is often the way with stout people.

After we have eaten, cups of glass are brought and wine is poured into them. I can see the golden colour of the wine as it sits in the cup. It is surprisingly soft to taste and not at all sour.

"Shall we bring in the dancers?" says the headman and claps his hands together before I can speak. Boys and girls enter, they are not naked but are dressed in ways that make their sexual organs more pronounced. It is ludicrous. They are like crude sketches of men and women. They gyrate and thrust in a caricature of mating. Do men find this erotic? I look to my left, and I see that Hilketa does not, he is bored and uninterested. He is old. So perhaps he no longer has stirrings. Greba is looking down away from the dancers. He is ashamed. Only the headman appears to be fully appreciating the dancers. He leans forward to speak to me.

"Are there any of interest?"

At first I do not understand what he is saying, but then when I understand, I laugh. There is a part of me that thinks why not? I have flesh and it must be fed and warmed and cared for. Is this not just another need of the flesh? I have appetites. But I see Greba looking at me out of the corner of his eye. I see the contempt he has for me. How dare he? Sitting there looking away, too afraid to trust himself, but still he thinks he is better than me. He imagines he can judge me. He knows nothing.

"What do you think, Greba? Are there any of interest to you?"

He does not bother to hide his anger. He knows I am mocking him.

"What should I be looking for?" I continue. "I'm not as experienced in these things as you. Should I select a few and see which is best? I would not want to take any that have caught your eye."

"I have no interest in any of them."

"Really? Are they not up to scratch, do you think the headman is holding back on us? Perhaps he is keeping the best of the slaves for himself?"

The headman interrupts, "No, Lord, no, not at all. If they displease you I will send them away, but they are the best in the town."

"Now see what you've done, you've offended our host. He's done his best here and you just turn up your nose at them. You must have very high standards to expect better, especially in a little place like this. I think the headman should be commended, he's clearly done his best."

"I intended no insult to our host."

"Then you should apologize."

Greba turns to the headman. "My apologies, I meant no offence."

The headman's face is white, and he bows desperately to Greba. "None taken, lord, if there is a need to apologize, it is I that should for my incompetence. I will find finer than this if your lordships will stay tomorrow also."

It is too funny. We should stay tomorrow. There is no need to travel to the Dark Tower as quickly as we came.

"It is not displays of this sort that appeal to Greba; he is master of the gladiatorial arts, it is in that his chief interest lies." Hilketa is trying to keep the peace, to cheat me from my fun.

"He is indeed a master," I say. "Perhaps it is he that should give us a display."

"I fear there will be none my equal here," says Greba. None but you, great one, he should say.

"Lord, you are of course correct," says the headman, "but we have many criminals here that we could give trial to, it would be a great honour and service. They will not be your equal, no matter how many you fight."

It seems the headman is either very stupid and does not fear to offend Greba, or he is even stupider and does not see that I am taunting the priest.

"If you stay tomorrow then it will be my delight to do so," the headman says.

"Well then," I say, "let us stay one more day. The troops must be weary after so many hasty marches. It will do them good to have some rest. And they will surely enjoy watching Greba butcher his opponents."

"It is agreed then," says Greba. "If it please you, then may I retire? I shall need my strength tomorrow."

"No, no. You will be fine. It's not trained fighters you'll be facing. Besides, should you not take one of these with you to stir up the blood?"

"If you command it."

"Yes, yes, I do command it. Which will you have?"

"It does not matter."

"Well in that case, Hilketa, you choose. You're so much more experienced in these things than I am."

Hilketa cannot hide his pleasure. He has tried to keep the peace between us, but he is also glad to be able to rile Greba. There is no love lost between any of the twelve. They have only hatred for each other. Hilketa surveys the dancers. He selects one, female. She is pretty enough, slim with smallish breasts. I would have thought that Greba would prefer a fuller figure. The headman motions for her to come forward. She is dressed in thin blue gauze that barely conceals her modesty. Her face is covered with a blue feathered mask so it is difficult to judge her features. Her skin and hair are dark but not as dark as mine, and there is a hint of red in her hair. She is passable I suppose.

"You must go with this man," says the headman to the dancer. She shows neither surprise, nor shock, but looks towards Greba and bows, then moves forward and kneels by his feet.

"Not here," he says. "May I leave now?"

"Yes of course," I say, and he rises. The dancer follows him from the hall. I should have made him stay.

"Is my lord tired too?" asks Hilketa.

So he wishes to retire.

The headman immediately starts to get servants to lead me back to my quarters.

"It is late," I concede, "and I know that you are old and feeble. It is rude of me to keep you up so late."

"Not at all, great one, I merely wish to ensure that your health is not affected by the travel."

"But we will not be travelling tomorrow. Come, you should

have more wine."

The headman frantically gestures for Hilketa's cup to be filled, but he puts his hand over it to indicate he will have no more.

"Too much wine will make an old man foolish," he says.

But he has already been foolish.

When he has gone I rise and retire to my room. I have no interest in dancing bodies and wine. The maids undress me and I retire to the bed. It is very soft, much softer than the camp beds I have slept on. It is good to stretch and sleep. I dream of me and of him.

Chapter Eighteen
Fighting

I am walking in the darkness. The moon has gone down but I keep walking. I am walking over black ash. I have walked this way many times and I can see my footsteps. I follow them and catch up.

"You have come at last," I say. "You have come again."

I nod, one of us nods.

"Where is this?"

"It is our handiwork." I reach down and pick up a handful of ash. I am the destroyer.

"Once that was flesh."

I agree, it is the end of all flesh. One of us is kicking the ash aside. There is a red ball buried in the ashes.

"Where will you go?" I ask. "Will you stay here?"

But I know the answer, I cannot stay here. There is nothing to eat or drink, no warmth or shelter, there is nothing, not another human soul. If I stay I will die. I will perish, I will turn to dust.

"I will go with them to the tower."

I nod. Where will I go?

"There is a place, there are many places. Do not stay here."

The black ash has covered my mouth and nose. It has caked my nostrils and throat. My eyes are rimmed with black ash and it has sucked all the moisture away. I try to clear my throat and spit but there is no moisture. I am dried out.

I wake up where I went to sleep, a few miles away from the hilltop where we met. I am very hungry. I have not eaten since we parted. He has eaten. He is sleeping in a fine bed while I lie on the ground, but I do not envy him. What do people eat in the darkness? No one will bring me blood and milk, or meat or anything to eat. I must find it myself. It is not hard, I tell myself. I have fed myself for many years now. There are things buried in the earth that can be eaten. Here, look, this plant has roots that are edible. I dig in the earth and find a small tuber about the size of the first joint of my thumb. It takes me a while to gather a handful, and my fingernails are broken and dirty. I follow the sound of water and wash them before I eat. They would have been better boiled, but I have no way to make fire. Yes, it is easy enough to make fire, I will teach you if you like. I reach to my waist and there is a small bag with flint and iron. I have no kindling but there are many things that I could use. I curse myself for not thinking of this earlier while the other me laughs.

After I have eaten, I feel better. What will I do now? I can do whatever I like. But what do I want? He told me there is a place I could go. I will go there. I step forward in the darkness and as before, I can find my way, only now it is another thought, another thread that is leading me. I do not know where it will lead. I should have asked more. I should have known more.

I am in bed and now I awaken. It is good to rise and wash and then to eat. Smoked fish is brought to my room, just a small amount, and rice. It is enough. There is knocking at my door, and the headman is there to enquire after my health and needs. I tell him I do not require his assistance and send him on his way. Later Hilketa and Greba enter. They do not knock, and I find that I am annoyed that they should be so familiar. Is this the way the twelve treat the High Priest of Vatu? It does not show much respect.

"The fight is ready, will you come?"

"We fight at high moon. It is better to fight when there is light."

Of course he is right. I follow them out of the place to a quadrangle where there are torches all around to give extra light. There are about ten men of various ages armed with swords. Greba has stripped to the waist and is slashing a blade back and forth. The men are eyeing him nervously, as they should. Although he is called the Whip, Greba is not thin, not especially thin. He is well muscled and tall. However, he moves with grace and poise. The victims do not look especially dangerous. I suspect it is the first time that some of them have ever held a sword. They will not have been given any choice. The headman has promised some sport, and if this is the best he can provide, then they will die whether they wish to or not, fight or die, fight and die.

"So how will we do this?" I ask. "Will they all come at Greba at once or one at a time?"

The headman has not thought about this.

"I will take them one at time," says Greba. "If they want to attack in a group then so be it, but it would just make it easier for me. Most likely they will just get in each other's way. To be fair, this is not going to take long. I can see that none of the prisoners are familiar with sword play."

He is right, the fight is short and bloody. Not a one lays so much as a scratch on Greba, and if any watching had any doubt about his prowess, then there could be none now. Soon there are ten bodies dispatched, crumpled and bleeding. Greba has been merciful at least and has killed them as quickly and as painlessly as a butcher would kill a calf. It is not good sport. Not for him or for the watcher. Dull sport indeed, we should have left.

"We should have them bled."

I nod in agreement. We will drink blood tonight.

Greba has cleaned his sword and is now wiping his body with a sponge.

"You are indeed a great swordsman," says the headman, "the finest in the whole land."

"Yes," agrees Greba.

There is none here that will challenge his claim. He sheathes his sword and approaches me. Do not get foolish, Greba, I do not need to use a sword to slay you.

"Only one is my equal," he says.

Is he daring me to fight him? I look around. Hilketa is staring at us; the headman has bowed his head.

"Do you wish to test that?"

"There is no other test for me. Only you could test me. It is what I have been trained for."

He is right, why else should he be trained other than to kill me? I am certain he has killed me in the past, probably many times. I am certain I have killed him many times too.

"Is this where you wish to test me?"

He shrugs. It does not matter; in the end we will have to put it to the test.

He has me at a disadvantage. He does not know it, or does he?

"Bring me a sword," but even as I speak a black blade, an edge of darkness forms in my hand and I step forward.

We spar gently to begin with. I have never trained with a sword, not in this body, but the teaching that the other me had floods into me. I reach for them and they are there. The sword is a thing of my mind, but it sits easily in my hand like a soul mate. Greba is indeed very skilled and has trained very hard. He is quick and strong with a good eye for an opening. We are testing each other. He is not certain he can kill me, but he thinks he can. We are evenly matched. I am quicker and stronger and younger. I could wait for him to tire, like a matador with a bull. He knows this, but also knows I am too proud to kill him that way, that I wish to show him that I am better than him. He knows I will attack and use all the skill that he has taught me to defeat him. He knows that is my weakness, that every trick and feint I know I learned from him. He is smiling now, he is confident that he will kill me. He is toying with me. He knows that he is far more skilled than I am. He feints one way and when I counter, I find it is not a feint but instead a thrust. I spin out of reach, as he taught me, only to find he has countered my movement. This is how he will win because he knows every move I will make, because he has taught me every move he will make. He has drilled them into me. Every step he has taught me is leading to this, leading to the one error he has drilled into me that will leave me open to my death. It is clever. I see it now. There is no way I can beat him, none. Our swords glance off each other, my black iron and his shining steel. Every eye is on us. They have never seen anything like this. Blades of darkness and light flick in and out, twisting and dancing like... like nothing, they are swords and there is nothing like a sword, it is death held in a man's hand.

I can see Greba staring at me. I can see hope and triumph and hate. When I kill him, I will have to teach him to fight all over again. It is I who has taught him to fight; no wonder he is so skilled. I have taught him to kill me. It is good that when I wish to die I can die by the sword. But I do not wish to die now, not yet. I have things to do yet. He comes at me with a flurry of strikes that fall gentle and cool like snowflakes. I drift out of the way, letting the strikes fall around me. It is like dancing between raindrops.

He is surprised. I should have died, the other me would have, but I am not him. The darkness alone has been my teacher. He tries again with another pattern of blows I taught him long ago, but it fails him too. I promised him it would not. I am a liar, I always was. Now he thinks he will die, he hates me more than ever. I could kill him.

He moves and now he is moving faster than ever. It is desperation that is driving him onward. It seems he too is not ready to die. But is no use; perhaps if I was the boy he taught to fight he might be able to kill me, but I am not. He cannot know my mind because he has never taught me to fight. Only darkness has taught me, and he cannot know darkness, only I can, only I and the others. I know now that I can kill him, if I wish. Greba, your life hangs in the balance. Do you know that? I must decide. And then I decide no. I do not wish to have to find another of the twelve, not yet. Besides, you still have secrets kept from me that I will know. Far away there is another voice. Kill him, it says, but he is far away. If he wished to kill Greba, he should not have left. It is my choice, not his.

Now Greba is tired. He has used all his energy in those desperate lunges. It is fear I see in his eyes now, and resignation. He is proud.

"You lied to me," he says.

"Yes," I agree.

He is looking at me, waiting for the final blow. But it does not come. Instead I step back and lower my sword. No, it has gone, I no longer need it.

"Do not pity me."

"I don't," I say and turn away. I wonder if he will be foolish enough to attack me when my back is turned or if he is wise enough to take his own life. But he is neither wise nor foolish, like most men.

Hilketa speaks first. But I do not listen, nor do I listen to the cheers of the crowd that has watched. The headman's eyes are shining as he cheers and claps. The crowd is just a dull roar. They have never seen anything like this before and never will again.

In my chambers there are more maids to wash me. I am tired and dirty. They anoint me with oil. Later I will feast with the headman. A slave comes to invite me to the feast; I rise from the couch and the maidens come forward and dress me. When I am ready, I enter the hall. Hilketa and Greba will not meet my glance.

It does not matter. I sit and we eat in silence. The food is not as fine as yesterday. The headman too is silent. There are no dancers or musicians. I turn to Greba and he bows his head.

"You fought well, great one."

It is praise, of a sort.

"You have defeated me in the past and will again in the future, but only when I wish it. Did you not understand that?"

"I do now."

I doubt it. He must die soon, otherwise when he trains me again he will not teach me all I need to know. I must replace him and teach his replacement, and in his teaching I must plant the seed of his defeat, this defeat, and every other. There is another way. I could teach myself. If I live and die then I can teach my replacement. I wish to unthink these thoughts. I wish to unmake this world. I am faithful to the darkness. But I am not faithful. I have no reason to love the dark or anything in it. I have lived another life, not this soft one of maidens and feasting. It is a soft life. Mine was harder, is harder.

Hilketa thinks we have made peace. He looks relieved and starts to make small conversation. He will die soon, I will not need to assist his departure. He is old, very old.

"How old are you?" I ask.

"Seventy-two summers," he replies.

It seems like forever, and then I remember he has seen more than one of me.

"How many have you seen?"

"You mean incarnations of yourself? Just two, two previous to yourself. Three in total."

"And how many of him, how many of the others?"

"I have not thought of it before, I must think. I am the oldest and so have seen them all die, but some died when I was very young, they lived at the same time as me but I do not remember them, not all of them. Some have died a great many times, died young and did not live to take their place among the twelve. It is a lot, maybe fifty. Kong and Arraio are the ones that have died the most. I think Arraio has died five times in my lifetime, and Kong four. But I could be wrong. I am old now and do not remember these things. I only remember the last Greba, but he was young when he died, maybe thirty summers, about the same age he is now. May I ask why you wish to know? It does not really matter, in a way we are all the same. I know only the twelve, and you. You are no different than you were before, none of us are. He is just the same as he was, I will be just the same as I am. It is as Vatu wishes."

"You also remember me," I say to Greba.

"Yes, it is as he says, you are just the same." Greba looks up. I cannot read his expression.

The headman is looking alarmed. The mysteries of the dark are not for him to know or hear.

"No dancers tonight?" I inquire.

"Great one, yes, if you desire it," he says and immediately rises but I motion him to stop. Our dance is of more interest.

"How can this be?" I ask. "I am not even the same person that you taught. I am no longer the child that was in your care. If I am no longer him, then how can I be the same as a dead man?"

"Because it is Vatu's will."

It is the headman who has answered me, not Hilketa nor Greba. I should be angry with the headman that he thinks to answer me, but I am amused. And besides, he is right, or at least it is the right thing to say.

It is enough; if they cannot see it then so be it. It is enough, it is time to retire. I motion and rise. Tomorrow we will leave and return on our way. Greba and Hilketa also rise.

"You do not need to retire," I say. But they also wish to be alone.

Chapter Nineteen
Ghosts

I have walked for miles, more miles than I care to count or think about. My feet are sore and I am dirty. The moon is full and is floating ahead of me. It is high in the sky and will stay there for a good few hours yet. I have left the ash fields behind me and now I am walking through dense forest. I do not know where I am going, or why. I am alone.

Where am I going? Does it matter? There is only one place I am going, away from there. I will never return. Never, not to that place, I do not belong there. Clouds surround the moon and choke its light. Darkness surrounds me and falls like flakes of black snow, like soot, a warm covering of dark feathers. I close my eyes and open them again and again until I cannot tell if they are open or closed. There is no difference, there is only darkness. Now all I hear is the sound of my own breath and the beat of my heart. I hear the earth shift under my weight.

Am I alone? I stop to think. Surely this is darkness, Vatu is here with me. But he is not. He is not here. I am alone. And yet I stop and hear the flutter of wings and the call of birds. I hear the rustle of mice and voles moving in the dark. Still there is no human here, I am alone. But then I smell smoke from a fire, cooked meat. It is far distant. They are strangers to me and will not welcome my presence. I am alone. I lie on my back on the moulding leaves of distant summers and look up at the empty sky. It is not empty. Stars are draped across the sky. Clouds veil and unveil the darkness. I am not alone. I am never alone. I do not know how long I have been walking, travelling alone. No, not alone, never alone. There is always something with me. The moon shines once more.

I am hungry; I cannot recall when last I ate. Yes, it was when I left. I could find more to eat, but I am eager to keep going. It is far and not far to where I will go. The earth is soft beneath my feet. It makes walking comfortable but slow.

When I arrive, he is waiting.

"So you have come back."

No, I have not; it is not me that stands here. But I do not explain it to him; he would not understand. You can explain nothing to ghosts.

The house is not dark, or at least not as dark as the wastelands I have walked through. There are a great many lanterns, one at every window and door, even though the moon is still up and almost full.

"Am I welcome here?"

He stares at me. "How can you ask?"

"I am hungry."

He motions to the house. "She is in there waiting. She will feed you."

I enter the house. She is sitting by the fire stirring a pot.

"Are you hungry?" she asks and turns to me.

"Yes," I reply and she dishes out a bowl of oatmeal. She hands it to me and as she does she ruffles my hair.

"I knew you'd come back."

"I won't always."

"We'll see."

"You won't always be here."

"Why do you say that?"

"Well, you won't, will you? You should have left, really. You should not be here. You should have gone."

"Eat up."

The oatmeal is good and very filling. I am hungrier than I thought. It is warm and sweetened with honey.

"Where did you get honey?" I ask.

"He found a swarm last summer and followed it to the nest. Once the summer was over, he cut out some of the comb. He was lucky the bees did not wake. He kept it. He could have sold it, but he said no. He said he wanted me to have it. I thought he should have sold it. But he said they'd only swindle him out of any money, or worse, cut his throat on the way back here."

"He's right, they would have."

"He'd have found a way to get the money. He's smart. I know you don't think so, but that's because you're young. You think everyone is foolish except you. No, he could have sold it. He'd have kept the money. We could do with it too. We still have some. You know from where. But he said no. He wanted me to have it."

He enters the house and looks at us. She puts a hand out and holds his.

"There's oatmeal here. I put some of the honey in it."

He accepts the bowl she is offering him with a polite nod and sits to eat it. He is staring at me.

"How long will you stay?"

"I don't know."

"You should sleep."

When I hear these words a great weariness falls upon me. I go through to the next room. There is a cot painted with roses. It is too small for me to sleep on. Beside it is a larger bed. I take some blankets and lie on the floor. Sleep comes almost straight away.

When I wake up, they are gone. There are no lights nor fires nor food. But I am rested and I am full. I leave the house and walk onwards. I do not look back. I will not come back.

I am walking onwards. There is a village and there is another house I will visit. It is a long walk.

Will you let me take you there? There is no need to walk. Whose voice is this?

But I am angry and I do not reply. I will walk. I want nothing from you, nothing.

I am not to blame.

I must see it all. There is much still to see.

You have seen it already.

Yes, but not with these eyes. You want to hide what you have done, but I will see it all. I will show it all. Everyone will know what you have done.

I am not to blame.

Then who is?

We do not speak.

How do I know this is the place? How do I know this town and this house? How do I know that the man and wife and child are the ones I seek? I should walk past them unaware. They should be nothing to me. Blood does not seek after blood. We know nothing of who we are and less of who others are.

We are all one blood. If we knew this, if we felt it in our blood, then the world would be better. But we do not.

I know this is the town, the house, and that these are mine. How is it so?

Will you have me answer?

You have seen these places with your eyes and lived in these places. You cannot forget.

Why can I not forget? We all forget, it is the only way we can live with the past, it is the only way we can live with ourselves.

No one forgets, not truly, they just choose not to remember.

There are things I would choose not to remember.

Like what?

But he does not answer.

I stand and watch for a long time. The man is running a small store. He sells corn and wheat. The woman and the child help, or help a little. She is busy going in and out of the house. She brings the man a bowl of rice and he eats it sitting on the step of the house under the lantern.

"Are you going to stay all day in the shadow?" he asks.

Chapter Twenty
Home

"No," I reply and step forward. He does not know who I am, or pretends not to.

"Do you wish to buy some grain?"

"No, I have come to see you, and them."

"Ah. I never thought you'd come back. You look just like him, now that I can see you clearly. You've grown up a lot, but you've not changed, at least not much, to look at anyway. She'll be pleased to see you, you have a sister now."

"A foster-sister."

"If you like," he says and looks down. "I..."

What? What will you say to me; that you treated me like your own, that I was your own? That you tried to stop them, or that you tried to stop me. It is just words and it makes no difference. And he does not say them anyway.

Instead, he turns and shouts for the woman to come out of the house. She comes, and the girl follows behind her. When she sees me, she stares and looks at me. She also has no words.

"Who are you?" It is the child who speaks. She steps forward smiling, but her mother holds her.

"It's all right," I say.

"Yes, of course," she says and lets the child go. But the child does not come to me. Now she is afraid. I think she will cry, but she does not.

"You are different."

How could I not be? The man stands and comes towards me. I

laugh.

"I don't even know your name."

"Does it matter?"

"Yes, of course it matters. Of course it does. I don't know your name or hers, or my sister's. Do I have other family? Of course it matters. I know nothing, I don't even know who I am. Nothing."

"What can I tell you?"

"You could start with a name."

"Yes, yes, of course, my name is Huneko. I live here. I run a small shop. I don't make much money but we make enough. You would have lived here in this house. It was my father's. He started the business with a small cart. He went out and collected food from the farmers and brought it to town to sell. I still go and collect food and sell it here. We don't have much, but we never go hungry or cold. This is..."

"Tanden, my name is Tanden, and this is Nino, she is nine."

Now the words have stopped. There is nothing to say, there is too much to say. No words can carry what needs to be said.

"You are like him."

"Who?"

"The man who brought you here."

"Where is he?"

"He returned to the Tower of the Sun."

"Who is he?"

"We don't know. He used to send money but that stopped. It was never very much. We think that the soldiers that brought it stole most of it. Perhaps he still sends it, only now the soldiers steal it all."

"Why did you not complain?"

"We were told never to seek him out. If people knew, you would be killed. You are so like him."

"I should go."

"Will you eat with us?"

"No."

I turn to go but now she is holding me back. She is holding me tightly and crying. He is holding me too.

"Let me go."

It is quite a sight, the tower. When you approach the city,

climbing up the valley in moonlight, it looms ahead of you and dominates the city below. We have almost arrived. I stop and look. The old man comes and stands beside me.

"It is something," he says, and he is right. It is something, it is ancient and massive. It stands many-tiered. This is my home. Here is the place of darkness. It is to this I am born.

"No matter how often I see it, it is still a sight."

I have never seen it. Not with these eyes. And yet I am not afraid. It is home. It is where I belong. The other cheated me. This is mine, all of it.

The old man is familiar, too familiar. He thinks I am his friend. It is time to show him I am not.

"I could make sure you never see it again."

That silences him. Good. They must learn to fear me, to fear me more. I see that he was soft. I will make them fear me.

Greba, the well-built one, speaks. "What of the child?"

Yes, the child, Kong. What of him? He has travelled with his nurse, now he must be given to the twelve to train.

"We must take him to Vatu first. It is he who will decide his fate."

His fate is already decided. It was decided the moment he was born; he is one of the twelve. That is his fate, he cannot escape it. But he must come to Vatu, as must I. I am the High Priest. It is I who decides things here.

The old man, Hilketa, leads the way. But the paths are familiar to me anyway. It is the same as before. An urge leads me on. I want to push the old man out of the way and race into the darkness. I want to trample him underfoot. Why does Vatu waste his time with these twelve fools? They are unnecessary. As we walk, the others follow. All twelve are here. I must learn their names, and then their weakness, and then crush them. They are fools.

Through dark tunnels we travel and when I reach the doors of darkness, I reach and touch them. Cool bronze lies under my fingers. One of the twelve walks forward and gives me a key. As if I need such a thing. The door opens and the dark invites me in. I carry Kong, and the others follow me. Immediately I am home; darkness is my home, my birthright. It has been stolen from me, now it is mine.

There is no voice, no sound, but the darkness welcomes me. I reach out and place the child before the dark, in the dark. Then I step back. The darkness is like a current of dark water swirling around the child. It is accepted. I am accepted. I am welcome. I have been gone too long. I have been gone a lifetime.

I motion for the twelve to leave and take the child, take Kong, with them. I am alone. I know everything. Everything I once knew is now mine again. I am whole.

When I leave the darkness, Hilketa is waiting for me. But I am not afraid. I know everything. He does not need to know, and soon he will die.

"You have changed," he says.

"Yes," I agree, "I have changed."

"Once, I thought you were my friend, but you were never my friend."

"No, never, not in this life or any of the past ones."

"It is my weakness."

"Yes, and I have exploited it."

He nods.

"Only one has escaped me."

"You will find his weakness."

"You could tell me."

"You think I know."

"Do you not know?"

I am walking through the city. I am dressed in yellow robes of a servant. No one looks at me, not even other servants, not even guards, not even courtesans. I am invisible, as invisible as if I were clothed in shadow. I am walking to the edge of the city, through narrow alleyways where moonlight does not fall. They are lit only by light that comes through door jambs and through shuttered windows. The wooden clogs I am wearing pinch my feet, and the sound of them striking the cobbled path echoes through the alley. I stop. This is the door. This is the house that Hilketa told me of. This is where Greba's weakness lies. I stop and listen. But the house is quiet. I knock softly and after a few moments I can hear a stirring and some footsteps. I can hear the door latch being lifted and the door opens. I have shrunk into the shadows.

I can see a woman outlined in the doorway.

"Is anyone there?" she asks. But I do not answer. She is looking around but cannot see me. She is not young. She is at least as old as Greba. Nor is she beautiful.

"Who is it?" It is the voice of a child.

"No one, it must have been the wind or perhaps a cat."

"When will Daddy come?"

"When he can."

The door makes a clunking sound as she turns and closes it. I am alone in the dark.

We enjoy women or men as we see fit. No doubt children are born of these unions, but it is a weakness to love them. It is such a weakness, to love a child. I turn and head back to the tower. I must think more on this. It is a weakness that I can only use once. Hilketa was wise not to tell me before. I would have killed the child. It is better this way. Who else knows? No one, I am certain. Not even Kong would keep this from me if he knew. Now I know everything.

What will you do?

It is none of your concern, you left and now it is up to me.

True, but do you not wish to ask what I would have done?

I know what you would have done, you would have killed them all.

Yes, perhaps. But what will you do?

I don't know. It is a great power to have over him, but I must be careful. I must think. I must know how to play this game.

I knew.

No, you did not.

Yes, I knew. I did not know where, or who, but I knew. It is obvious. Yes, I am right, it is obvious. Not knowing was wiser, you should not have come here.

I did not know what I would find.

Yes you did.

Then why did I come?

You will return.

No, I will not.

Yes you will, you will see why.

I am right, he is right.

Why do I care, it means nothing.

I am helping Huneko with the wagon. Every day I help hitch up the horse and light the lanterns, then we trek out to the farms to collect food. Huneko lets me drive the cart and sleeps. But when we get to the farms, he does all the bargaining with the farmers. Of course there is not much food to buy and prices are high. But the farmers always have some food they have hidden away from the collectors. Mostly it is grains, buried in stone lined pits. Huneko is not the only one looking to buy, but there is always enough. The farmers grumble about the prices and call Huneko a thief. But they always take his coins. They are happy enough to take them. As the winter goes on, the prices get higher.

"Why do you not buy more and come out less often?" I ask.

"I would," says Huneko. "After summer I buy as much as I can afford and don't come back out until I've sold out. But now prices are high, they get higher every day. I can only afford to buy a day's load. I need to keep coin for the summer too. It will come soon, then all of the old crop will be worthless."

It makes sense, I suppose. I am not a merchant, or a farmer. But it seems there should be a better way. I am aware that I am a burden. They say nothing and make me welcome, but it is clear that they are not rich, and although I help as much as I can, there is not much to do. Huneko does not need my help. It is only out of politeness that he lets me do what I can. He can hitch the wagon himself easily enough, and drive the cart. I am another mouth to feed. I should go. I am a burden.

"It is good to have you here," says Huneko.

I turn and look at him. I wonder if he is trying to tell me to go. I should go.

"Your mother is very pleased that you are here. I am too. You should not have gone."

But he is wrong.

I have been with Huneko and Tanden for some moon turns now. They are friendly and kind but there is still a distance between us. Maybe there is a distance between all of us. Nino is curious and likes having a big brother, even if it is only a pretend one. They are not my family, they were never my family.

When I come back from the farms with Huneko, it is mid moon up. I unload the cart onto his barrow.

"If we had two days of food, we could go and collect the next day's and Tanden could sell what we have in the morning. "

He says nothing but just smiles. It is strange. He does not seem to buy or sell very much and yet they always seem to have plenty. Perhaps they make more money at different times. Are they still getting money from Amantae, I wonder? But then I remember that Amantae is given to the darkness, he must be dead by now.

Tanden has made a broth for us and we sit and drink it in the moonlight.

"Will you stay?" he asks. "She would like you to stay. We all would."

"No."

"Then what will you do? Will you go to the City of the Sun?"

I say nothing but I will not go. How could I? It is there that I am running from. I am running, I had not known it till now. I seek to escape the darkness. You cannot escape the dark, it is madness.

"You could stay," he says again.

"Why, why would I stay; to load wagons?"

Now it is his turn to say nothing. He simply shrugs, as if that is reason enough.

But I cannot stay. At some point I will be hunted. I cannot allow myself to live. The two of us cannot live. One of us must die. If I stay here, I will come and burn this place like all the others have been burned. There will be more ghosts.

"The world is full of ghosts."

He turns and looks at me. "Yes, ghosts and devils."

"The broth is good."

"Yes, it is made with rice, wine and barley."

Later, Nino comes and makes me play with her, a game with string. It is looped around her fingers and changes into many patterns. The game is to take the string from each other and to make new patterns. She has played it many times before, and tells me that she wins all our games, although I do not know the rules and think she might be cheating. I have never played this game before. Tanden is watching us while we play and smiling. I turn and look at her, but Nino climbs on my lap and makes me pay attention to her game.

"Don't you have other games?" I ask. "Or other friends?"

"Yes, lots, what do you want to play? You're not very good at strings. Look, I bet you can't make this shape."

I turn and look. The string between her fingers make a pattern of interlocking loops that form a circle in the middle. There is a loop around every one of her fingers and thumbs. It is the sign.

"Where did you learn that one?" I ask.

"It looks like a star," she says.

"Play something else," says Tanden. "Go and play in the

moonlight, with the other children."

When Nino is gone, Tanden asks, "Will you tell anyone?"

"No."

Now it makes sense. He goes out every day not because he is a trader, but because he is a preacher, a heretic preacher.

"They will find you eventually."

"Maybe, but they will not find us all. They never find us all. They can never find us all. In the end, we are all heretics. Because we are right. Vatu is a devil, and we are all ghosts."

"If you were a ghost, you would not need to fear death, or torture."

"Can't a ghost die? Can't a ghost torture another ghost?"

It is heretic nonsense. I will not answer, instead I say, "You have seen what they can do. If you were right, then they could not do it."

"It is because of what they do we know they are devils. Only a devil would murder and torture."

Does that make me a devil?

"Men or devils; what is the difference? It will make no difference when they find you. If it is a man or a devil that burns you, still you will die. If you are right, then it will not help you. If Vatu is not a god, then there are no gods. There is no one to save you or to usher you into the dark."

"We are saved, and we do not go into the dark. We leave here and move to a new life, a true life."

"Is that what Huneko tells those farmers? I'm not a farmer. I do not believe it."

"That does not change things; it is the truth."

Why do they cling to these beliefs? Can they not see the power of Vatu, my power? Have they no inkling what I am? Born over and over again to the darkness, I am darkness, nothing else is possible. Almost I wish it were the truth, that I could die and escape this, but I have died a thousand-thousand times and still I am here. What great crime have I done to merit this punishment?

"Do you know who I am, who I truly am?"

"Yes, do you? Or do you just know the lies they told you?"

"What lies are these?"

"That you are trapped, that you are a slave, that you are a devil."

"I have killed men, many men. I am a devil. It is possible I will kill you and Huneko and Nino. I will have to kill you all if I go back. Do you know who I am, or who they say I am? If they are lies, do you know the lies they tell me? But they are not lies, I have seen him, Vatu. I have stood before the dark and in the dark, and the darkness has been inside me. I am reborn."

But she is shaking her head.

"It is lies, all lies. It is just the dream of a madman, the words of a devil that seeks to trap you. Do not listen to him, the author of all darkness. He is nothing, he has no power, only here in this play that he performs, and even that runs away from him."

"How do I fight him?"

"It is enough to wish to fight him. Everything springs from that."

"And if I do not wish to fight him?"

"Then you would not be here; you would not have returned to us."

Have I returned, I ask myself, and for what?

"I still cannot stay."

"I know. Huneko wishes otherwise, but he is blinded by his love for you. In the end no one stays, no matter how they are loved."

"He does not love me."

"Because you do not accept it, does not mean it is not there. When they took you and gave you to us, it was he who loved you first, not me. My heart was filled with devil words, but he helped me pluck them out one by one."

"It did not seem that way." I remember his harshness, his hard, unyielding presence. I remember his disapproval, his disappointment.

"He was afraid. He is afraid."

"Of what?"

"Of losing you."

"I was never his."

"All the more reason to fear losing you."

Chapter Twenty-One
Heresy

I have watched the house for a full moon turn. On each quarter moon day, full moon and no-moon, a tutor comes to the house. He tutors Greba's daughter for a morning. Today he will not come. Today I have come. I knock on the door and a servant opens the door to me.

"Who are you?" she asks.

"Master Hoga is indisposed; he has sent me in his place to tutor the child. My name is Karo."

She is unsure. "Wait here," she says and returns shortly with the mistress of the house.

"What is the problem with Master Hoga?" asks the mistress.

I bow and hand her a letter written by Master Hoga. I say nothing, as would befit the station of a scholar. She reads the first few lines, then looks at me. She motions for the servant to hold up the lamp.

"When will Hoga be better?"

"Not for some days." Not ever.

She bites her lip. "Perhaps I should hire another tutor?"

"Master Hoga is most anxious to retain your custom. He has offered my services for less than half his fee. It is in the letter."

"Are you not a bit young?"

"Yes, mistress, but very diligent."

She reads more. "Karo, the letter says you are called; he speaks highly of you."

"Yes, mistress."

"And what is wrong with him?"

"Old age, mistress." And other things.

"Very well." She motions for me to enter, but remains irritated. "I will sit with you this time. If you do not please me, I will find another tutor. There are many scholars in the city."

I bow my head and follow the mistress, three paces behind. The child is sitting by a table. There is a lamp on the table and the room is brightly lit. The room is elegant but not rich. I bow to the child, then unpack my tablets and quills. The girl is surprised but shows nothing other than a slight widening of the eyes.

"This boy will teach you today," says the mistress.

The girl is quick and intelligent. Her mother sits but pays little attention as I go about my work. She is fanning herself from the heat. It is always warm in the City of the Sun, even in winter. I follow the lesson that Hoga would have given: calligraphy, some arithmetic, then she reads from the histories, and I correct her errors. She makes few errors, but every time she does, her mother looks up and scowls.

"Darkness has lasted forever and always will," she reads. "Vatu searched in the darkness and found all things. All things are in the darkness, and all things are in Vatu. The Sun, the moon, the stars, the earth; all things are in the darkness and all things are in Vatu. There is nothing that is not in darkness and nothing that is not in Vatu."

I follow her words as she reads, but hardly need to. I wrote these words a hundred thousand years ago and have spoken them every day for a thousand lifetimes.

"All things come from the darkness and return to it. Life, fire, light, all come from darkness and return to it. There is no hope except to hope for the dark. Light, fire, life are darkness, there is no life, fire or light except for the dark."

Her voice is clear and sweet. And she reads without error.

"Well done," I say.

"Yes, well done," says the mistress of the house and motions for me to rise. The servant enters; it is time for me to leave.

I bow and follow the servant. "You may return at full moon if your master has not recovered," the mistress calls after me.

Each day I return. The mistress does not sit with us. We read and write. The girl has a steady, clear hand. We read the histories and the classics. I teach her to play music as befits a woman. She strums softly on a stringed lyre. She is not adept at playing, but she is passable. We do not speak of other things. That is not befitting. But when I pack my tablets and stylus back in my satchel, I always leave something behind: a cake of bean paste, or a small sprig of night jasmine, perhaps a bird feather, tiny and brightly coloured.

Huneko is ill. He has come back from the farms in the rain. I should have gone with him and helped with loading the cart, we would have been quicker. Tanden says it is better only one of us is sick, and that it is work enough to nurse one without having to nurse two. Nino is worried and sits by Huneko all day. Tanden chases her away and says she is in the way.

I sit by the stall to let Tanden look after Huneko. Nino comes to sit with me. She does not say anything.

"What is wrong, little one?" I ask.

"He will die," says Nino.

"What makes you say that?" I ask. "Tanden says he's getting better."

"He's not," she says, "or at least not much. He doesn't know me when I sit with him. He did at first. Now he doesn't. My mother has started to make sure I don't get too close. She does not want me to see he is dying. She knows. And there is the shadow."

"Don't speak like that," I say.

"Why not? It's the truth."

"We don't want to scare the customers away. Cheer up. I'm sure Huneko will get better." But even as I say the words I know it is a lie. I know they give Nino no comfort.

"I don't care," she says. "I just don't want him to die."

"Huneko says that this world is all a lie, and that when we die our eyes are open and we see the truth."

Nino looks at me for a while, biting her lip.

"Do you believe that?" she asks. "Do you think he is right?"

"Yes," I say, and I realize it is not a lie, not completely, not even a bit, not the smallest bit.

She takes my hand, my foster sister, my sister, my little sister.

I have been coming many moon rounds. When I arrive this moon up, the servant asks me to wait, and to my surprise, I am led to the mistress. She is sitting on cushions in a pavilion overlooking the courtyard. It is open on all sides and cooling winds make the room comfortable. She is looking out at the full moon and I can see why Greba finds her desirable. She is beautiful.

She does not turn around. Nor does she motion for me to sit. "When will your master be well?" she asks.

"Mistress, he is no longer in this darkness but in another."

"That is unfortunate, for me at any rate. No doubt he has gone to glory in the dark, but I shall have to replace him."

I think now I should have kept the old man alive, but it would have been too great a risk. Greba might have found him.

She turns and looks at me, and I avert my eyes. "You have done well," she says, "but now you have no master. I paid you half thinking that the master would return, now it is clear he will not. I will not pay half a master's fee to you."

"What will you pay, mistress?"

"Four silver." There, she is a money grabber, this is barely half of what she paid the master. It is her weakness. That is good to know.

"That will be enough," I say. If I were truly a poor scholar, I would be glad of the fee, but also outraged. "I can find other students," I say. I would have to.

She shrugs; it is of no concern to her. It is simply an inconvenience taken care of.

"I am told you are a gifted musician."

"With the flute? Yes. Also, somewhat with the lyre. My voice is passable."

"I entertain some evenings. As no doubt you understand, music is pleasurable to my guests' ears. I myself have little skill at such things. There are times when musicians attend, discreetly of course. Would such a task be of interest? If so, then your payment could remain as is."

"There are finer musicians than myself," I admit.

"Yes, but discretion is very important. You have shown yourself discreet."

"Then yes, mistress, I accept."

The mistress turns back to watching the moon. She has lost interest in me. "Two moon ups, when the moon is almost full. Come when the moon is setting in the west."

Huneko is dying. Nino comes and tells me he is asking to speak with me.

"I'm busy with the shop," I say and turn away.

"It's all right," says Nino, "no one will come today. Everyone knows he's dying."

And I realize I am afraid.

"Come," she says and slips her hand into mine. There is nothing else for it. We walk without speaking. There are no words left for this. I should comfort her, tell her things will be fine. But I cannot lie to her, or to myself, not now. Lies will come later. For now, truth is enough.

Nino is leading me into the house. The moonlight fades as we enter. There is one lamp shining downstairs and she takes it and leads me up to Huneko's bedroom. What am I afraid of? I am darkness, death should fear me.

The room is lit by candles and by candlelight I see Tanden's face, but even in full Sun I could not read what was written there. There is no surface, no emotion. What is she thinking?

"Can you see it?" asks Nino.

"What?"

"Here, look through my eyes," she says and when I do, I see it. It is not a shadow, it is a veil or curtain that keeps brightness from this world.

"What is it?" I ask.

But there is no answer, none is needed. When the vision fades from my eyes, Huneko calls for me. I go and sit by his bed. He looks up at me.

"Don't cry," he says, but I'm not crying; why would I cry?

"Will you look after them?" he asks.

Tanden scowls.

"We've been over this," she says. "You know he can't stay, not for long."

"But for a while," he asks again.

"Yes, for a while," I agree. Tanden is strong and still young. She will marry again. There will be many men that would wish for her. I will stay till then, and after, I will be asked to leave. No man would want me to stay, no man except Huneko.

He is moving in his bed and Tanden goes to quiet him. He is looking right at me.

"Did she tell you?" he asks.

"Yes, she told me everything."

He seems to gasp, to drink air, and then again when he has found his breath, he speaks.

"I was too harsh, I drove you away. I am sorry."

"I'm sorry too." The words come without me speaking. "I came back."

He nods and then starts to cough violently. Tanden motions for us to leave. Nino slips her hand back into mine and leads me away.

When I return I have my flute and lyre, or a flute and lyre. My own instruments are too fine for a poor scholar. The ones I have brought are fine instruments, but worn and old and made of pinewood, not gold. I am led into the room and shown a place to sit behind a screen. I seat myself and play gentle, soft music. Neither the mistress nor Greba are present. Not yet. But I hear doors open, and footsteps.

I continue to play. After a while another person arrives. It is Greba. Even though I cannot see him, I recognize his footsteps. Wine is brought to them. I hear them drinking and muttering to each other quietly, but not so quietly that I cannot hear. I hear everything. They are talking of unimportant things. She is telling him how she has missed him, and he is telling her how beautiful she looks. More wine is drunk. Now she is complaining of the heat, even though the wind is cool. He makes a suggestion and she giggles. Although I cannot see, I hear the silk of her gown brushing against silk as she lifts her hand to cover her mouth. There is more rustling of silk but it is different. Pillows are moved and gowns adjusted. I do not need to see. I continue playing slightly louder to mask the grunts and moans, and the rhythmic creaking of floorboards. It seems Greba is a gentle lover. Soft and slow, they pause from time to time and then begin again. Eventually the soft sounds include snores, and I cease playing. I pack my instruments away and leave. As I leave I can see they are lying wrapped in each other's arms and her hair is covering his face.

I continue to teach the girl as agreed and to play for the lovers maybe twice a moon turn. As promised, I am discreet, very discreet. Each time it is Greba that comes to her. I think his mistress is faithful, which surprises me. She calls him husband and he calls her wife. It may be that they have less formal meetings, but I am not privy to them. They do not argue, nor is money exchanged. From time to time he will ask about his daughter. Once, the mistress calls the girl into the room.

"Come, let your father see you." The girl bows and then stands.

"You are beautiful," says Greba. It is clear that he loves her. It is a great weakness. "How is your education coming?"

The girl does not reply, it is her mother who answers. "Well, she is better at writing and history than music. Her tutor is good, but she has no aptitude for it."

"What does she have an aptitude for?"

"Perhaps it is time she should attend a seminary or scola?"

"No," says Greba, "she cannot go, it is too dangerous."

"If you say so, husband," says the mistress meekly. "Are there no other young ladies that can teach her? I have taught her some things, and her tutor has taught her others, but is hard on her to stay here alone each day with only servants for company. Are there no gentlemen of a certain age that could visit? It will soon be time for these things."

Greba sounds uncomfortable when he replies. "I will think on it. But she is young still."

"Husband, she is," agrees the mistress, "but not for much longer. If you wish well for her then you must find her a suitable match."

"Yes, but not soon, there is time yet."

"As you say, husband."

"Come now, Irid, have you no kiss for the cheek of your father?"

The girl steps forward and leans to kiss Greba, then turns and leaves, bowing.

The whole time I have not stopped playing on the flute. I realize I am shaking ever so slightly.

Greba has not seen me even though I have played to him behind that screen many times.

When he has gone, I return to the tower. I have much to think on.

The next day I return to the house. It is not one of the days when I am supposed to tutor the girl. When I knock and the door is opened, the servant is surprised.

"I have come to see the mistress," I say. The servant makes me wait and then returns.

"She will see you." The maid ushers me through and up again to the moon-viewing tower. The mistress is very beautiful in the moonlight. Her skin is fine porcelain, it is delicate and breakable. It would be a crime to break that spotless, perfect skin and neck.

"You listened."

"Yes, mistress."

"And what do you wish to say? If you seek to blackmail us, you will be killed, you will not leave this house."

I do not doubt she can defend herself. She will have poison hidden up her sleeve. And the servant will have been trained by Greba, but the whole household could not stand against me. She suspects nothing, thinking I am just a boy.

"I wish t-to..." I stammer, a false stammer, I am still playing a part.

"To what?" She still has not turned towards me.

"I am not poor," I say.

"Oh, that? You think we need money? You think we need your money?"

Nonetheless, I take a bag of coins and place it on the table, bowing. She turns when she hears the gold chink as I drop it. She looks at it, but does not move to take it or to count it.

"He will not allow it, not for a thousand times that."

"Your words could sway him."

"No, they would not, not my words. But there is another who could."

I understand her words. "I will speak with her."

"You are confident she will agree?"

"Mistress, if you were not confident, you would not have spoken. Your confidence is my hope."

A smile; does it touch her eyes? It barely touches her lips.

"I wish only the best for my daughter. Afterwards, if he agrees, you will stay here."

I say nothing but bow as I leave. I do not pick up the coins.

At our next meeting, Irid is agitated. She stumbles over words while reading, and when she writes, her hand is weak and uncertain.

"Here," I say and move behind her, "let me help you."

I reach over and put my hand on hers to guide it, and I know I have won.

Huneko is dead. It was not an easy passing. It was harsher than some of the passings I have made for other men, for men who deserved to die in pain. I could have eased his going, but I could not, I could not say the words, and besides, I knew what Tanden would have said, what Huneko would have said. And they would have been right, death comes soon enough. And when it comes there is no going back. Even if he is in a better place, he is not here with Tanden and Nino, with us.

He is buried in the graveyard under a full moon. It is strange how often death comes by moonlight. Many of the villagers have come to send him into the darkness, and many lanterns are lit at the head of his grave. They recount his kindness with thanks and commend him to the dark, and later when the moon has dropped below the horizon, the heretics gather. Tanden has brought a vessel of water and she pours it on his grave.

"Spirit and water."

It is the words of heresy. They all repeat the words. I look around. Maybe half the village is here, and many from the farms around. Do they have no fear? Do they not know that death is the punishment for what they have done, what they have said and what they believe? Do they not fear that someone will betray them, that I will betray them? I look around at their faces; each of them has their eyes closed. They have no fear. I close my eyes and repeat the words.

"Spirit and water."

There, I have said the words. I am a heretic.

Chapter Twenty-Two
Family

At first, nothing has changed since my meeting with the mistress. It is much as it was. When I arrive I am shown to the place of study and lessons continue. As I have said, she is studious but not brilliant.

Nothing I have said is true. It has all changed. She is no different, but now she is mine. When I look at her, she has changed. She is still barely more than a child. She is barely the age I was when I left Kong's keeping. Neither Greba nor his mistress have spoken to me, but I know she is mine. There are little changes. She will not look at me. She is like a shy bird. But I am different too, in some ways. I visit now as much to see her as to trap her father. He is already in my trap. For now I will view my prize. I do not force attention upon her; there is no need for that. As she works, I watch her from the corner of my eye. I realize she is beautiful. I had not thought on it before.

"How old are you?" she asks me.

I am taken by surprise; she has never spoken other than about her lessons till now.

"Fourteen Suns." Why should I lie to her?

"I am thirteen Suns, or will be soon." She is younger than I thought.

"Why do you ask my age?" I inquire, but she still does not look at me.

"It is my duty," she replies.

"What?" I laugh. "You have a duty to ask my age?"

"No, not that, a duty to find a place, not to be a burden."

"A burden to who?"

"To the house, to my mother and father. I should find a place."

"I don't understand."

"I know."

"Know what?"

"I know you have spoken to my mother. But it is no good. I have a duty. Father will find a place for me. I know I cannot sing or play well, but I am pretty."

"And you think that is preferable? You think your father would rather that?"

"When they sell me, they will get some coin and be rid of me."

"Who has told you to say this?"

"No one. You must understand, it is all the daughter of a courtesan can hope for, to be a courtesan."

"And not the wife of a humble scholar?"

"It is not that, a wife is honourable, but I have a duty."

Again I ask, "Who told you to say this?" but I know the answer.

"No one," she says again.

"Things are not what they seem. This is a game they are playing. Do not let them use you this way, it will not end the way they think. That would be bad for you." I do not mean it as a threat, although when the words go to my ear I can hear the threat in them. She looks at me, turning her face towards me and lifting her head. Her mouth is open slightly with shock.

"My father is a very important man," she says. Yes indeed he is, but I am more important. You are more important.

"If he is wise, then he will do wise things," I tell her. She turns back to her calligraphy. Her head is bowed and I can see the nape of her neck, fragile and delicate.

There is a letter come from the mistress. It is blunt, my services are no longer required. When I knock at the door, the maid hisses when she sees me.

"You should not have come, she will not see you."

"She will," I say and hand her a purse. "Take this to her."

When the maid eventually returns, she is flustered.

"Come quickly."

I am taken again to the moon viewing pavilion. All the drapes are down.

"I should kill you," she says.

I bow and wait.

"Very well, I will let you speak with him, but most likely he will kill you. I am sure of it. She is pretty, but is she worth dying for? Come and play for us, then I will introduce you."

It is agreed.

I come as usual and set up my place behind the screen. I begin playing my flute, and wait for Greba to arrive.

I do not have to wait long. He enters alone.

"Come and show yourself," he says. I lay down my flute and fold the screen back then sit and kneel in front of him.

"Well played," he says.

"Thank you, master," I reply.

He snorts derisively.

"Sit up and stop mocking me. What is this all about?"

It is about power of course, about my power over you. I say nothing.

"So now you know; now you know everything. I suppose you think you have won, but you have not. You hid your face behind that screen, but you did not hide your talent, there are not ten players in all of this city that could play like that."

"So you knew."

"No, not until she spoke to me about you. A scholar with gold, wishing to speak to me; the idea of it."

"I could have just taken her, I suppose. I could have just killed everyone and taken her."

He shrugged. "Why didn't you?" He never did understand subtlety.

"I do not need you to hate me, I already have that."

"What do you think this will gain you?"

"Power, power over you. I have found your weakness. Now I will use it. The girl will not be harmed."

"I could kill you, I could kill you now. Here."

"No you could not," I say and the darkness enters me. "I am not a child anymore, I am the High Priest of darkness."

"But you have been killed before." He attempts to spring forward and draw his sword, but ropes of shadow reach out and restrain him. "You are a coward, why will you not fight me like a man?"

"Fool, do you think you can goad me into fighting you? You think I will let you fence with me? Even then, you would lose. It would be your death, is that what you seek? No, I will not let you escape me that way. I have you now and I will keep you."

He struggles for a while and then goes limp. He is like a fish on a line, or a moth in a web. He is mine to do with as I will.

"So what now?" he asks.

And then I realize, fool that I am. I jerk him out of my way with a motion of my hand and send him spinning across the pavilion. I sprint out into the courtyard, hoping I am not too late. I should have foreseen his plan; I should have foreseen that he would be desperate. He is laughing and his laughter follows me. I enter the room where I have sat as a teacher many times. The girl and her mother are lying together. I tug the dark cords I have bound Greba with, and I drag him into the room.

"I would rather that they die than that you hurt them."

Both of them are still alive. I smell their breath, it is sweet with opium. Greba wished to give them a pleasant death, not a quick one. It is his undoing. They are both breathing and I open Irid's mouth to make her gag. I shout to the servants and they come running. The maid screams when she sees her mistress.

"Stop that. If you want to help, then prop her up; try and waken her."

As she does, I light a fire and heat a blade. I place it on the mistress's skin, and the shock causes her to wake.

"Keep her awake. If she closes her eyes, then burn her again."

"No, stop," Greba is saying, but no one listens. The servants take turns walking the women around the room. They are talking gibberish, fevered dream talk. From time to time they have to be slapped or burned until they awaken. Eventually it is over. They will live, although both of them are weak. I have cheated Greba of his triumph, as he attempted to cheat me of mine.

"What now?"

Yes, what now. I must think on this. There is no time. I must decide now. It will do no good to delay. What are my choices?

"If I leave them with you, what will you do? If I let them live? If I let this pretense continue?"

Greba is broken, he bows before me unbidden.

"I will not harm them, not if you will let them live."

Can I believe him?

"I could take them," I say. "I could take them to the tower, there are places that I can keep them where you cannot reach them. I can keep them in the dark and do what I will to them. You should not have tried to cheat me. How can I know you will not try to cheat me again?"

He is broken completely; there is fear in his voice.

"Great one, no, I beg of you. Let them stay with me."

Can I trust him? But then I think what if they die, it is nothing to me. I know his weakness now. I should have let them die. I should have made him watch them die.

"I could kill them both now. That is what you wanted, for them to die quick and easy, is it not?"

He does not answer, not in words. Instead he shakes his head over and over. He has no words, instead his pleas are unspoken. It is just as well, words are too easy, so many are lies.

This has not gone as I hoped. If I let them stay with him, then I will have to trust him. That would be a weakness, it would give him some small power over me. But to slay them would leave me with nothing, no hold over him.

I must not be seen to hesitate, it would make me seem weak. It is too difficult to take them to the tower, then the others would know. It cannot be done; this must be my triumph alone. If Greba will slay them, then he will pay; he will be broken. I do not need to fear anything.

"Very well, they will stay here in your keeping. We will talk more of what the price shall be." With those words I release the black bands securing him. I half expect Greba to try to attack me. But he is broken now. I have won.

He crawls to his mistress and cradles her head. She is still drowsy and looks at him. She does not speak, but her hand moves towards him. She tilts her head towards her daughter.

"She is well," says Greba, and then he looks at me. "It will be well."

Now the servants are moving the two women to their sleeping chambers.

"Call a wise woman," says Greba.

"No," I stop him. "No one comes, no one else knows of this." He meets my eyes and nods. The servants are his trained men and women. They are pledged to die for him, and now that is what they must do. No one must know of this.

"I will see to it."

"Good."

The darkness has shrunk back and now I seem again a simple scholar.

"I will return soon," I say as I leave the courtyard and head back to the dark tower.

I do not believe, I do not have faith. I have nothing, but I wish to believe. Even if it is all a lie, I wish to believe. It is a better lie than the one that I have been told till now.

"Spirit and water." A different kind of rebirth; reborn to what, though? I ask Tanden. At first she does not answer me. But, after many days of asking, she stops and motions for me to sit.

"What do you wish me to tell you?"

I pause and think. There is so much I wish to know.

"What have I done?"

She does not laugh at me, my almost mother. Instead she takes my hand in hers and looks at it.

"You have done a great many things," she says at last. "But that is not what you are asking, not really. You are asking what will you do, and why."

"I am changed, but I do not understand it. I am not what I was."

"You were never what you were, nor what they tried to make you. No one is. It was all a lie to deceive you. It was a trick. It is the cruellest trick the darkness can play, to make you believe the darkness inside you."

"Darkness is inside me," I say.

"Yes," she nods, "it is. But that is not all. And you do not need to believe in it. You can turn away from it. It does not define you. You are more than darkness, much more. You have defied it."

That is what I want to believe, even if it is a lie; I am more than darkness.

"I have done terrible things."

"Have you?"

"I have tortured and slain both in this life and in ones past."

She is nodding her head and then she stops.

"But now, you have turned away from these things."

"Is that possible?"

"It is what we believe. Huneko turned away from the meanness and greed of a merchant, from the anger of a husband, from hatred for oppressors."

"These are small things."

"If you say so, but it was not easy for him; to have a child not his forced upon him. A child not his to feed while struggling to provide for us, it was difficult, more difficult than you think. It is easy to say they are small things. They were his things. He turned away from them. There was nothing more he could do."

"I do not mean it like that. I mean only that these are not things that can be..."

"Can be what? Forgiven? Did you know he beat me once? Just once, never again, but still, you think that was easy to forgive? I was angry with him over that; the anger was a darkness within me. I had to turn away from that. It was a small thing too, perhaps. He turned away from his anger. It took him a long time to put what he did behind. All darkness can be overcome, even the darkness they planted in you. Let me tell you a secret, a big secret. When they handed you to me and I looked into your eyes, I hated you. But then I saw something, I saw that you were no different than any other child."

I do not know what to say. Can I believe her? Do I want to believe her? Yes, I wish to be free of the darkness, and I can see no other way to do it.

"Then what will I do?" I ask.

Now she does laugh at me. "You think I know the future?"

"Do the gods not reveal it to you?"

"No, the gods mostly keep quiet, at least to me. I have no insight. I have only faith."

"I have done so much."

But then I think, if this world is just a ghost world, a play, a story written on a clay tablet, then even those darkest of deeds, are they not just ghost acts, play murders and words that mean nothing? If so, then maybe those deeds can be washed away, erased. Even if they are real acts, it might be possible.

"What should I do?" There is no answer.

I return to the house. When I do, the servant, the new servant, opens the door to me immediately. Although I am still dressed as a scholar, he bows and takes me immediately to the moon viewing pavilion. The mistress is now better, but still weak. Even through her face paint I can see her skin is pale and her eyes have lost some of their lustre. She is waiting for me and is standing when I enter. She bows and averts her eyes. She says nothing. I am cruel to keep her standing. Eventually I motion for her to sit. Her eyes are still averted. It seems that Greba has not the courage to face me. He is broken.

"Does the great one wish refreshment?" the new servant ventures, but I wave him away. There is much to say, and I have no wish to be overheard.

"Are you well?"

"Yes, great one, as well as can be expected. I grow stronger every day."

"And the girl?"

"A smaller frame, the same dose, she was nearer to death than I. It will take her longer to recover."

"What does she know?"

The mistress hesitates. "She knows as much as I, which is nothing." Although she guesses more, I am certain.

It is a strange feeling, this triumph. My heart does not sing with joy. It is almost as if I regret crushing Greba. I realize that I found pleasure in my time here, an escape from darkness, even though there can be no escape.

"You know who I am?"

"Yes, great one, my husband has told me."

"And you know who he is?"

"It seems I do not. I thought him a great one from the court, but he is more than that."

"He is one of the twelve."

"He is, my lord." Now she falls silent again.

"You have power over him," I say at last.

She is distressed at my words. "Great one, only the power of a woman over a man, a wife over a husband. That is nothing, it is a thread of silk that can be broken at a whim." Or like the thread of a spider, I think to myself.

She is thinking about Greba and his demand that they drink poison. They had no choice not to obey. It must seem to her that Greba wished to break that thread.

"Has he returned?"

"Yes, no. He has come to remove the old servants and instruct the new, he has stood outside in the moonlight looking up at the pavilion, but he has not entered the house. I have waited for him. I have stood looking down on him, but he will not enter."

In time he will. He is angry with himself, ashamed, but men always forgive themselves and forget their shame. He will too. I know him. I know he will do this. I have him.

What now? Those two words again. I have decided, I will use that power.

"So, mother-in-law, what is your name? I cannot call you mistress, not now."

There is a soft exhalation of breath. Is it of surprise, or of something else?

"My name is Unead, great one."

"There is much you will need to do to arrange our wedding."

She bows.

"I suppose it will be unseemly for me to visit before then. I will return on the day. He will have to be here. I cannot have my father-in-law absent at my wedding feast. Send to him in the usual way. It will get to him."

Again she bows.

"It would be unseemly for a suitor not to visit the sick bed of his betrothed. It would be most seemly for her to be brought here."

"As you wish, great one." She hails the servants, who come running. She motions to them and shortly Irid is brought into the pavilion. There is a manservant at each corner of her litter and they bring her in and lay her down before me.

It is as Unead has said, she is very ill. She is as frail as a mouse skull and as white as bleached bone. But her eyes are not averted, she is looking straight at me. Her eyes are strong, and angry. That is good. She will live. I am glad she will live.

Her voice is soft and barely louder than the flutter of moth wings. I cannot make her words out and lean in to hear.

"You have lied to me."

"Yes," I say, "I have lied to all of you, and I have caught you. Now you are mine. You had better get used to it. If your father had not tried to defy me, there would have been no need for you to know, but now you do. You are my hostage and will be my wife. Your father will be mine because of you. But do not be afraid. I will not harm you."

She starts to cough, and Unead motions for the manservants to carry her back to the sleeping pavilions. Irid's eyes stay fixed on me as they carry her out. It seems I will have to tame her also.

When Irid is gone, I turn to Unead.

"Two moon rounds, then I will return."

Chapter Twenty-Three
Dark

What have I done? I have mastered them all. When I return to the dark tower, Greba comes to my chambers. He is not proud; he is broken. He bows and enters. It is not low enough, but is lower than he has ever bowed before. I will teach him to bow lower, later. For now it is sufficient.

He does not speak but waits. I sit silently for a while. It is a childish game, but it gives me satisfaction. Victory is always satisfying.

"What do you wish?" I ask at last.

"Safety for my family." When he says the words, his full weakness is revealed. My family is dead. They were murdered by Kong. Perhaps he has done me a favour. I have no attachments to weaken me. I am strong. I cannot be touched, nor harmed.

"I hold them in my hand, like sparrow chicks in the claws of a cat. It is nothing to close my hand. It is what you wished for them. Safety. Is death safety? Would death make them safe from the dark? I must ask Vatu, but I would think not. Is this the kind of safety you would have me give them? I have better poisons than the one you used on them. I have poisons that will not fail. Do you wish me to give them to you?"

I watch him. I must know if he will slay them. But I already know the answer; I already know that he will not slay them. If he had truly wished them dead, he would not have waited until I came before poisoning them. He would have made sure—a blade is quicker and more certain than any poison. He would not have needed my help for that. There is no antidote to a knife thrust through the heart.

So, it seems I truly have him under my heel.

"It is not that I wish," he says.

"What do you wish?" I demand.

But he shakes his head. He does not know how he can keep them safe, nor does he know how to keep them his.

"No one else must know," he says. In this he is correct, none of the others can be trusted with this. Some, like Arraio, would simply kill and then abuse the women.

Others, like Kong, would seek to use the knowledge for their own advantage. They would make Greba their servant. I will not allow this. Greba shall be my servant and none others. It is possible that Hilketa already knows, but the old man will be dead soon.

"I will keep your secret," I tell him. He seems to stand straighter, taller, as if a weight has been lifted from him.

"That is one thing, but not all," he says.

"What else do you ask of me?"

"I wish them to stay at the house," he says. "I wish them to be safe." He pauses, but eventually he says it. "Safe from you."

"I give you my word that I will not harm them," I tell him. The words are meaningless. My word means nothing; we have no honour—we are liars and murderers.

"You must stay away," he says.

"Must I?" I say and poison hangs from my tongue. I must do nothing, except the will of Vatu. It is not for Greba to command me.

"You have harmed them enough," he almost shouts at me.

"Have you come to bargain with me?" I say. "It seems as if you have. I must keep your secret, and I must stay away from your family. These are not the words of a penitent. I had thought you had come here to plead with me, but all I hear are demands. You are in no position to demand anything."

He is silent.

"You live a lie," I continue. "Your life is a charade. Loving husband and father, that is not what you truly are. You are one of us, one of the twelve. You are a monster, the same as us all. Does your wife and child know the truth?"

"I have told them, and now they know. They know who you are too."

He is glaring angrily at me. It is a new thing for him; to be powerless.

"I hold them in my hand, and I will not let them go. I have said I will not harm them. You do not need to believe me, but it will give you some comfort if you do. All of us have our little delusions; what harm is there in one more? I must be close to them, as close as ever I was. I must see them often, at least as often as before."

"What will you do?" he asks, and he does not keep despair out of his voice. I savour it.

"Surely there is only one course that will satisfy us both," I answer. He looks up uncertainly. He really has not guessed what I will do. It is surely obvious.

"You will not bring them here?" he asks. I refrain from laughter.

"That would suit neither of us," I reply. "I have a better plan, father-in-law."

With Huneko dead, I had thought Tanden would give up the market stall, but she does not. I take over Huneko's role collecting food from the outlying farms. I go less often, and I make poorer bargains. It is clear that I am no merchant. Still, we make enough to live on. I have started taking Nino with me on my rounds. It is good to have company, even the company of a small child. But more importantly, she must learn to be a trader, she will be the merchant when she is grown and I have left.

Even though she is nine, she is better at making a deal than I am. Sometimes she will tell me that I should have held out to pay less. Other times she will tell me I have done well. When I am making a deal, I usually get better prices when she is with me. This may be because the farmers are reminded that there is an orphan child to be looked after, but mostly, it is because I pick up her subtle prompting; here and there a slight shake of the head, or a nod. But she is too small to drive the cart and load it. I am needed for now.

No one speaks to me about the heretic faith. I am not trusted, and it is right that I am not. It seems the faith is not very organized, and that the main tenet of the faith is to reject this world and the darkness within it. The faith is less sure what should be accepted in the place of the dark. That is why it is a faith, because we do not know. In many ways, my life has barely changed since the death of Huneko and my adoption of heresy.

I eat, sleep and work just as before. But in other ways, things are very different. I no longer have hate inside me eating me up every minute. I no longer have darkness within me prompting me. I no longer wish to harm those around me, or hurt people just because they are fools or because they are weak.

I think back to my time at the dark tower. The words written within me have been erased. I am truly a blank tablet, and the words that will be written upon me will be the words I wish to write, not those that Vatu wishes inscribed upon me. I have given up my strength, because it is the strength of darkness. I must find the strength that I possess. I must find the strength within me.

Soon it will be Sunday. The thought brings up bitterness. In this world, the light is barely less toxic than the dark. This far from the Sun, we will only get one harvest. Still, the farms are hiring labourers for the whole day. They will plant and harvest in a single day, then they will store corn and barley to dry before threshing the grains and storing them for the long night.

I will not work in the field, but I will drive workers out to the fields in the cart and use it to bring grain back to the barns and granaries. Both Tanden and Nino have come with me. Nino will work in the field, but Tanden will work with the women threshing the grains. We are waiting for daybreak at one of the farms. The farmer's name is Tuathan. I think he has eyes for Tanden. He is not young but is unmarried. His brother inherited the farm, but he died childless. Normally, you would expect Tuathan to marry his brother's widow. That way there will be no disputes about the ownership of the land, but either the widow is not to Tuathan's liking or Tuathan is not to hers. Either way, the widow returned to her father's farm and remarried with another man. There is some bad blood between Tuathan and the new husband. But it seems that the arrangement suits both men. Tuathan gets the farm and can marry who he wishes, the new husband seems happy to marry Tuathan's sister-in-law. Some talk amongst the country folk suggests that the new husband is not such a new thing so to speak, that there was a closeness between the couple even while Tuathan's brother was alive.

Whatever the truth of it, Tanden does not encourage Tuathan's attention. I had not thought on it before, but I can see that Tanden is an attractive woman for her age. She will have many suitors.

Perhaps it is just too soon for her to think about other men. Huneko has left her well provided, so she will not have to marry if she does not wish to.

We are awaiting the opening of the Sun. All of us are outside, waiting in the field. We are facing towards the dark tower. We are ready to plant. The field will be planted with barley. There is some bread and beer passed around. I have been carting seed, workers and tools all night. When the Sun is up, I will rest while the workers plant and harvest. Because we are farther from the Sun, we will not need to water the crop. But later I will cart more food and water out to the fields for the workers.

The Sun blinks open, shedding its brilliant gaze across the land. Warmth and brightness engulf me, and the gathered workers set to planting. I have made a bed of blankets in the back of my cart, but I stand in the morning light and watch the work. It is the first time I have seen the Sun from so far away. It is strange to think that I am standing before it now and that Vatu opened his box of darkness at my bidding. But I do not think of it, not much. Instead I think of sleep, or Sunshine, and lie on a bed of harsh blankets dozing in the Sun.

The opening of the Sun is a great event. I stand on the tower and the twelve cower before me. Vatu coalesces within me and together we open the box. Darkness retreats for a while. Life cannot flourish in darkness only; we must give them some light, one day. On this day, crops are grown and harvested. For the rest, we protect them from the burning light.

The twelve retire, leaving us. They cannot endure the brightness of the Sun; they cannot endure its burning rays. But I can endure. I am shielded by Vatu. He engulfs me. The brilliance of the Sun cannot harm me. I am the chosen one. I am the reborn one. I am the High Priest.

There is another; I put the thought out of my head as quickly as it enters. Besides, I am he also. We are one, and he is here with me as I have been with him. We are united in darkness. My eyes see for miles. They see to the edge of the light. I am all knowing.

The heat of the Sun blisters the black stone of the tower. It is well that this lasts only one day. Cocooned in darkness, no harm can come to me. I pity those who must endure the burning rays unshielded. Even the twelve cannot endure this.

So you are there.

Can you see me? Do you serve him still? I will not. I have stood where you stand now, but I have turned away from it. I will not be one with the dark.

But you are one with me, and I am one with the dark.

Yes, but I am one with something other, something greater, something I do not understand. You must be one with that too, but you are not. You wish to stay in darkness, or so you claim.

I do not believe it.

You will be free. One day, we will both be free.

The thoughts fade, they are far away.

I turn and watch the women working in the fields. It is always women who work the hardest.

I lie by my cart and move grain and water. When the workers are tired, I bring them bread to eat. It is a long day. I work hard enough. The Sun is warm but also tiring. The heat is strong. Later, I cart the workers back to the field. Nino is sitting beside me. Her head is resting upon my shoulder. She is very tired. Tanden is in the wagon with the rest of the workers.

"I am ten summers now," says Nino. I nod and think nothing of that. She is barely younger than I am. There are five summers difference, but it could be a thousand years; it is a thousand years and more. I am ageless, I am eternal, or at least I was. Now, I have decided to die. My age is not the passing of summers in this body. I am ageless and ancient.

There are no secrets from the dark. I should have known. I should have left. I should not have listened to Tanden or Huneko.

The soldiers come.

I come; darkness has come.

It is only two days since the harvest. The villages are merry and glad. There is plenty to eat, for now at least. And then the soldiers come.

They surround the village and they say not a word. When I see them, I shout. There are screams and panic, but there is no way out. Why? I should have left. I have brought this upon them. They do not enter the village. The headman goes and asks why they have come, but they say nothing. Is it possible for any of us to leave? Again, they say nothing.

"They have come for me," I tell Tanden.

"No," she says, "they have come for us because we are heretics." She will not see what is plain.

"I will go to them."

"No," she says, "you are not to blame."

"What else can I do?" I ask. I do not hear her reply; I have turned away. There is nothing else I can do.

I walk up to the soldiers. They barely look at me.

"I am the one you are looking for," I tell them. But, they say nothing. They just point spears to my chest. I could kill them all. I could kill every one of them. Instead, I walk back to the village.

We must wait.

Is there nothing I can do? I sit and look at the stars. There is only darkness after all. But I know that that is not true. The villagers will die, and they will live. I think about Tanden's words. They sounded wise and brave, but now they just sound foolish. They have thrown their lives away.

You could save them.

I could, but they would not wish it. I can save them only by turning back to the dark, and even then, it would only be slavery that I could give them.

Can you think of no other way?

What other way is there?

There are many, many ways.

That may be true, but I cannot see one.

I can, will you listen to me?

I do not even know who you are.

Does it matter? You will listen; at the very least you will listen. I can save them. You can save them. Will you listen?

Who are you?

I am the author of all things. There are many darknesses. Vatu is not the only darkness, and there is also light.

You talk in riddles, can you not speak plainly? Tell me how to save them.

You cannot save them; they are ghosts.

So they will die; you said you would save them.

I said that you could not save them. I can, if you will listen.
Speak then.

But he does not speak. It is not with my ears I listen. Words, unspoken words form and shape me; they shape the future. I can barely speak them.

Darkness has come. The soldiers do not move from around the village. There is no sound, but the darkness creeps like mist through the village. It is toxic. It is poison. It fills the lungs of the villagers and smothers them. Some try to escape, but the soldiers will not let them pass. The darkness is burning. The skin of the villagers blisters and peels from their bones. I hold Tanden and Nino, and watch with horror. The darkness does not, cannot, harm me. It is my punishment. They look up at me with smiling eyes as they choke and blister. Nino holds my hand.

"Don't be frightened." It is her voice, not mine. I cannot stop tears. She lifts a bleeding, skinless hand and wipes them away. "It will be all right."

But it will not be all right; they are dying—they are taken from me. Eventually they are all dead, and their suffering is over. Where were you, author of all things, you said that you would save them.

And I have. Look closely.

I look and I see nothing, just corpses. The soldiers have left. The darkness has gone. That darkness has gone, the choking, burning darkness. This is my handiwork. But then I remember looking with Nino's eyes.

I look and I see the curtain drawn back. They are all there: Tanden and Nino, and Huneko and all the villagers.

I have taken them to another place, a better place.

Can I go too?

No, not yet.

Will it be soon?

Yes, although it may not seem so to you. There is still much to do.

I walk out of the house, and you are there. You are dressed in the robes of the High Priest and are wearing the amulet of jet. We have done this. It is our handiwork. We have done this many times before, a hundred thousand times.

"You will come with me."

We nod.

I have put him in a dark place where he cannot be found. I should have killed him, but Vatu will not have it. Now he knows. I will not give up my place, not to him or any other. I have trapped him in darkness, but he does not seem to care. He is weak. How can he not be weak? He is a fake. I only am real. I am the true High Priest. How could anyone think he was me? He will die in the darkness. He will starve. Let his gods save him if they will. They cannot, any more than they could save the villagers he sheltered with, or the soldiers that were disposed of afterwards. It is the way of the dark, there is no escape.

I have allowed myself to be brought here. I am in darkness, but the darkness cannot hold me. I am placed here in the dark. I wait. They come to me and comfort me. What can I do? How long must I wait?

Chapter Twenty-Four
Wedding

The wedding will be in private. It will be at the house of Unead. There will be no guests. I am dressed like a bridegroom. I have bought clothes at the market. Not too fine, I am only a scholar, but far finer than a scholar can really afford. It should appear that I am in love, and so spend more than I can afford. I have bought gifts for the bride and for her mother and father: a fine sword for her father, a bronze cooking pot for her mother, and a dress for Irid, my bride.

Although there are no guests, the servants have decorated the courtyard. A bower of red silk, rose petals, and sweet smelling incense. They have been cooking rice and fish. That is traditional, for those who can afford it. So soon after the Sun opened, food is not very expensive. The rice will be spiced with cardamom and saffron. When I approach the house, there are beggars waiting. They will have heard in the market that there will be a wedding here. I will feed them with the rice not eaten by the wedding party. In the meantime, I hand them small copper coins worth almost nothing.

When I approach the gate of the house, there are lanterns all around. The servants are waiting for me and shout as I approach. The gates are flung open to greet me, and musicians start to play. I smile to think that none of them is as gifted as I am.

I enter the courtyard. The smell of incense and jasmine is over-powering. There is a priest there, a poor priest from the local temple. There has been nothing to show who is getting married;

the high priest of Vatu and the daughter of one of the twelve. Such a thing is unheard of. In all my thousands of lives, have I ever married before? And in all Greba's thousands of lives, has his daughter ever married before?

He is there. His face is smiling, but his eyes are not. There is nothing he can do about it. There is no other way, but my way. He cannot escape. She will be mine, and I will have power over him. But Unead is smiling. I have never seen her smile before. Always she has kept decorum. It is right that she should smile at her daughter's wedding. Not to do so would be an insult. She has learned it is not wise to insult me.

We are seated together, Irid and I. She is gowned and hooded, and I cannot see her face, but I know it is her. As she walks to our seat, I recognize the lightness of her step and the softness of her breath. There are no secrets from the dark. She cannot escape me.

The ceremony is short. Unead has only paid the priest for the minimum. He joins us together and, pushing back Irid's hood, he anoints us and blesses us. Then, walking backwards, he leaves.

The feast is adequate. The rice is well cooked and nicely spiced. The fish is salted and slightly fermented. It is fine, but not too fine. There are no words uttered. Unead does not speak. Greba, my father-in-law, should welcome me to his family.

I smile, and he glares at me. But the pretense continues. He stands and hands me a glass of rice wine.

"Welcome, my son." The words must choke him. But he says them nonetheless. It is done.

The servants retire; Greba and Unead retire. No doubt they will rest in the moon-viewing pavilion. Now there are only the two of us. She is frail and delicate. The moon is shining into the courtyard. By the light of the moon and lanterns I watch her face. How long do I wait, hovering? It is delightsome. She is like a moth, or a mouse fluttering and trembling. She will not raise her face to me. She will not look at me.

"Are you afraid?" I ask.

She does not answer, but her head tilts forward. She is wise enough not to lie to me. She knows I can be terrible.

Her mouth opens in a perfect little circle. "Why?"

The sound is soft as the scent of jasmine, it is like a breeze pushing through silk. It is the fall of a rose petal. Still she will not look at me.

I could force her. I could take her to the bower as is my right. Why; because I will it, because I will use her to master her father, because it amuses me. I could tell her all that and more. I am the High Priest, and she is nothing.

"Because I love you," I say. And she looks at me. I have started with a lie.

I am sitting in the tower. I know the place. I am right to put me here. None of the twelve will find me. The darkness will not part for them. Only I even know this is here. Only those most dangerous are here. I am here and so is she. I should have killed her. Instead I have brought her here. She is in the cell next to mine, except it is not a cell, it is a vast darkness that we wander in and yet cannot meet. The darkness cannot hold me.

"Are you there?" I ask.

I hear only a low moan. I ask again, and she breathes heavily. She is afraid. She has been in the dark for such a long time. The oubliette, the forgotten, but I remember. She is right to be afraid. I was very cruel to her, and to Amantae. He is here too, at least his bones are. I did not let him live. I cannot remember her name.

"There is no need to be afraid," I tell her. But why should she believe me? I stand up and the shackles fall from my wrists. The darkness cannot hold me, at least not this darkness. I walk and the door opens at my touch. I enter her chamber. She can hear me coming in. In the dark she can see nothing, as can I. But I do not need to see. She is chained, and I have not been generous with food and drink. She is alive, but only barely. I wonder if she is sane. Alone in the dark, the mind goes so quickly. I have tormented her. I have tested her faith. She needs food and drink. I am healthy and strong. I make a small cut at my wrist and press my wrist to her mouth. She tries to resist me, but she is too weak and too hungry. I let her feed, but not too much. I do not want her to be sick. After she has eaten, her breathing is slightly stronger. She would wish a lantern, but I think that would hurt her eyes. She has not seen the light for over a year. Is that all? Is that all it was since I killed Kong? It seems longer and yet it is almost as if it were just the day before.

"Why have you come?" she asks.

"To make things right," I reply.

I find that I wish to spend more and more time with Irid. I no longer give her lessons. Instead, we sit and drink tea, or else I will play music for her. We do not sit in the moon-viewing pavilion. I have paid for the construction of a terrace to one side of the house, and these are our quarters. They are humble enough to be the quarters of a scholar, even a jumped up scholar who has married above his station. Irid calls me Karo and that is what I am to her. We will keep up the pretense.

Greba still does not come to the house. Unead waits for him in the moon-viewing pavilion. Sometimes, he watches her from the street and she watches him, but he does not enter the house, nor does she call to him. I do not speak to her about it. I seldom speak to her. When I do, I see reproach in her eyes. It is not my fault her husband is a fool. The house may as well be mine, except I do not think that Irid is ready to run the house. She honours her mother, and her father, even though he tried to kill her.

I know it is my presence that keeps Greba away. It is possible that he comes when I am not here. I cannot spend every day here; I have the duties of a high priest to attend. When I am not here, it is possible that he comes. I will ask Irid.

Irid says that Greba comes sometimes, like I suspected, but never when I am here. I am thinking that he does not wish to see my victory over him. I can only come a few times in a moon turn. So I suppose there are many other days for him to visit, but every time I am here, he is out there watching. He is a fool. Does he think that he can protect Irid from me? He cannot.

There are a great many duties to perform. Now I am finding less joy in them than before. They are empty rituals that keep me from time with Irid.

And there is one other thing.

It has been many moon turns since our bond was broken. It is not broken, that is not the word. I had thought that Vatu would slay him, or me, but he has not. I know he sits in the dark. Even now I can hear his breath and feel his heartbeat. When I close my eyes I can see the darkness around him. Vatu will not have him slain. Vatu will not make me the sole High Priest. I am diminished. I am halved. I am divided. I am a tablet, but I am written on two sides.

I am standing on the top of the tower and there is a full moon.

The moon is shining down upon me. In all the turns of the moon, here is something new. I am but half a man. No, I am two men. No, I am a myriad of men. This is not so new after all, it would seem.

Hilketa is here. He is looking at the moon, as is his habit. What is he thinking? I know better than to ask. If he were not here, I would let my gaze fall down to the city and to a certain house, and to a certain wooden terrace hanging from one of its stocky walls. But I dare not. He must know nothing. If he discovers me, I will kill him. He is old and will die soon in any case. But he is subtle and dangerous; of all the twelve, he is the most dangerous.

"I am thinking I will die soon," he says.

Why does he say this? It is true, but why does he say it to me?

"Yes," I agree.

"There are things I would say," he tells me.

I dare not look at him; what does he suspect? Even if he knows everything, then what of it? He is powerless. Vatu knows all now. I have been exposed. Kong has been exposed. If Vatu will do nothing, then what can the others do? They can do nothing. They have no power over me.

"Schemes come to nothing in the end," he says.

"What schemes?"

"Forgive me, words come hard now after almost a lifetime of silence."

I laugh. Hilketa is not known for his silence; quite the other.

"You have said much, old one," I tell him, my voice a mixture of feigned affection and respect.

"Yes," he agrees, "but not as much as I should have. Each of us, even Zauria, even Arraio could have killed you, but we did not. Why do you think that is so?"

"Because Vatu would not allow it."

"Vatu would allow it. He has allowed it, many times."

"But it is pointless."

"Yes, it is pointless, but that has never stopped men from doing many things."

I am growing tired of this. What does he wish to tell me? That is the problem with Hilketa and his subtlety; in the end he says nothing. Perhaps he has nothing worth saying.

"What do you wish to tell me?"

Hilketa stops. It seems there is a long pause, but I may have imagined it. It is difficult to judge time.

"I know," he says.

That is unfortunate, I think.

"Know what?" I ask.

"Many things," he continues. "Right now, you are thinking about throwing me from the tower. Perhaps you will throw me from the tower. You are quite right, I would not survive. And my secrets would die with me. You think that would make you safe, but it would not. I am no danger to you. At least, not the danger you think I am. You have some reason to fear me, but not much."

"I do not fear you," I reply.

"Good," nods Hilketa, "then perhaps you will not kill me just yet. That is good; I have no wish to die just yet."

This is tiresome, but slightly amusing. He first tempts me to slay him and then tries to trick me into sparing his life.

"What is it you wish?" I ask.

"Your last question is better; what do I know?"

"Then tell me, old man, what do you know?" I do not raise my voice; I do not have to.

"I know about him."

I look in his eyes—is he trying to trick me?

"Then tell me about him, whoever he is."

"He is in a dark place that only you can go. I know you have watched gladiators fight. Did you know that all the weapons are held in a single rack? Each is identical, at least to me. I am told that each gladiator has a favoured weapon, one that looks no different to the eye, but feels different. The balance or the heft or whatever is different."

"And?" I ask.

"Did you think it would be different with me? Did you really think I would not know the change? He was in my charge for a year; I am not deceived."

I think about his words. I should kill him now and end this game of his. It would certainly be simpler. He thinks that I will not and is bold.

"And?" I ask. This will give you no power over me.

"Is sitting in the dark the best use you can make of him?"

I think for a bit, and then I cast the old man from the tower. He does not scream or make a noise, until he crashes on the courtyard below. He misjudged me.

The darkness surrounds us. She is brave, but few have ever faced this. I have done this to her. There is water here, it drips from above. I catch it in cupped hands and wait until there is a scant mouthful. I had never thought about there being water here before. I had only ever thought on the darkness, on Vatu. He does not speak to me. He does not come to me. The sense of emptiness fills me. It is as if Vatu was just a dream, as if he were less even than a demon.

I am surprised she is alive. The girl has endured much. I take the skull of Amantae and leave it to catch more water while I dribble the handful I have collected between the girl's lips. I let my fingers brush along the floor until I feel soft moss and I collect as much as I can. I chew the moss until it is a soft paste and then I put it in her mouth. She is almost too weak to swallow it. Here in the dark, even in the dark there is life.

"What is your name?" I ask.

She still cannot speak. Not yet, but as time passes she grows stronger. I speak to her, I ask her small things; would you like some water, or moss. She has started to communicate with little mute movements of her head. I cannot see them in the dark, in the total dark, but I can sense them. After all, I was master of the dark, once.

"What is your name?"

I have asked her many times, and I no longer expect an answer. It is as if she has forgotten how to speak. I am not surprised. I still do not know why she is alive. Vatu is playing games; I will bring her back to health and then he will take her. So be it. I cannot stop making amends as best I can just because he will make things worse.

She can stand now, and with my help she can walk a few steps. Our diet is still water, moss, beetles and for her, what blood I can spare. When she sleeps, she reaches out and holds my hand. But when she is awake, she still shrinks from me and I have to persuade her to let me feed her, or help her walk, with soft words.

"What is your name?"

She still does not answer me, but makes soft moaning noises when I speak. Has she forgotten how to speak? She is getting stronger, and I am afraid. Vatu must know all that I have done here, and in other places. He is toying with me, and with her. She has stopped fearing me, but still she will not drink water from Amantae's skull. When I hand it to her she pushes it back and says no. It seems she can speak after all.

"What is your name?"

"What does it matter; the dead have no names."

But she is not dead; she is alive and getting stronger. How can she rise and walk without my aid? She collects her own water, standing for hours catching the soft droplets. I have taught her how to find moss by running her fingers over the stone floor.

"What if I get lost?"

We are lost. It will make no difference.

"Can you not hear the drip of water? Follow that back here."

"What if I cannot hear the water?"

"Then I will find you."

The darkness cannot keep her from me, at least, not that way.

Are you faithful to the dark?

No.

Can I trust you?

No.

I have slain your friend, the old one.

Why are you telling me this? He was not my friend, or at any rate, I was not his. He was not our friend. But then I remember he was kind when I was small. You killed Tanden and Nino and all of the villagers. They were my friends, and yours. You will have to leave for a while, to find Hilketa.

Yes, I will have to go.

In my dreams, I am in a wooden terrace built hanging from the wall of a house in the City of the Sun. It is built of fine wood, cedar rather than pine. It is not old, it is fragrant with the smell of fresh cut cedar. It is open on one side, facing towards the setting full moon.

I am leaning against the cyclopean stone work looking out as the moon falls over the mountains. I am seated on cushions of silk, and there are gauze curtains draped around. Now that the moon has gone, a girl comes and lights a charcoal brazier. She is very pretty but I do not know her.

"Are you cold, husband?" she asks. Her voice is polite, but there is a coldness in it. I shake my head. I am not cold. The moon may be gone, but the fire is warm.

"Who are you?" I ask, but she does not answer.

Chapter Twenty-Five
Caged

In my dreams, I am with Irid. We are sitting on our terrace watching the moon setting over the mountains. Once the moon has gone, she lights a small fire. She is as beautiful as ever. She is more beautiful by far than her mother. I breathe in the scent of fresh cedar. There is a hint of jasmine drifting into our abode from the courtyard. I sit and look at Irid in the lamplight. She does not look at me, but I can see she is blushing under my gaze. I reach up and let the gauze curtains fall closed.

"Are you cold, husband?" she asks. Her voice is stiff with formality. She speaks as a proper wife should. But when she looks up at me eventually, I do not recognize her. She is not Irid.

"Who are you?" I ask, but I know the answer, and she does not speak.

It is the time of the hunting moon and far away I find the reborn Hilketa. I have travelled fast and far to find him. The infant mews and struggles when I take him. How strange to see the ancient now reborn. I take him and return to the tower. I am gone so long it seems. So long since I visited Irid.

When I return to the tower, I must take the infant Hilketa to Vatu. I am not afraid to do so. I lead the rest of the twelve into the dark. I know he is here, and her. But it does not matter, Vatu will not let them speak. He will shroud them in darkness and keep them secret.

I unlock the door to the darkness and push it open. I bow and enter, and one by one the rest of the twelve follow me.

"I have brought him," I say, "and I give him to the dark."

Vatu's voice is heard in every ear. "Who will foster him for the dark?"

Zauria steps forward and takes the infant from me and then the twelve retreat from the dark. I am alone with Vatu, and with him.

Vatu leads me to him, and my fingers twitch to reach out and choke him. I want to strangle him to death. She is with him—the girl from my dream. I had thought her dead. I look around for the other one, the soldier. I can see his bones scattered through the dark. His skull is turned upwards and is being used to catch drips of water. He at least is dead.

There are no words, not now at any rate.

"You betrayed me." Is it me or him or Vatu who speaks—there is no way to know. Is it me or him or Vatu who has betrayed us?

I turn and leave them in the dark.

No more dreams. I have returned to my home, to Irid. She welcomes me, but I think she is not pleased to see me. I could force her, but instead I wish to win her to me. It is a game I will play. I played it once and won. I do not forget her trembling like a bird as I guided her hand to draw the characters of the history she copied.

It is just time I need. In time, I will make her once more that trembling maid. I will find her weakness, and I will conquer her.

"Shall we sit and watch the moon setting?" I ask.

"If you wish it," she replies. I motion for her to lead me through the courtyard and onto the wall; from there we descend to the terrace. It is just like my dream, only this time she does not turn into the girl in the dark. I sit on the cushions and motion for her to bring my flute. I will play as I watch the moon setting. She kneels before me and I watch the moon shadows play across her bowed face and the delicate nape of her neck.

When the moon is set, she lights the charcoal and draws the curtains. She sits beside me obediently.

"I have brought you a gift."

"How kind of you, husband," she says.

From within my robe, I fetch a brass cage. The sides are closed by glass, but the top has small holes to allow air to pass in and out. In the cage is a black and violet winged moth. The violet glows like moonshine through clouds.

"It is very beautiful, husband," she says, but she does not smile or show any signs of pleasure. I hand it to her, and she hangs it from the window frame. There are some few withered leaves of willow in the cage.

"On what do I feed it?" Irid asks.

"It will feed on willow; you can find fresh leaves in the market. Send one of the servants. The leaves will need changed every few days. But even so, it will not live long. Moths do not live for long. If you wish, we can set up a tent of gauze and the moth will lay eggs. That way, there will be more moths to watch."

"It seems very cruel, husband; to keep a thing in captivity."

"It will die just as quick in the wild," I tell her, "and this one is not from the wild. It is from a moth farmer. Many people keep moths; it's pleasing to watch them fluttering in moonlight. It gives me joy to watch them beating against the glass of the cage."

Irid bows. "Yes, husband, it will be as you wish."

We are alone in the dark. He has left us once again. The girl will live, or at least she will not die soon. All of us will die in the end. Those of us who are lucky do not return.

"What is your name?"

How many times have I asked that question, but now it is her who is asking me. Do I have a name? Does it matter? There are only the two of us here. There is no need for names in the dark.

In the dark, we cannot see each other, but still she can recognize me, and I recognize her. She is well. She is much stronger.

"Can we escape?" she asks me.

How can I answer? There is no escape from the dark; I have said those words many times. I have seen it with my own eyes. I had thought that I had escaped, but I had not. Tanden and Nino died because I could not. And yet, have they not escaped the dark? Even now, here in the great hall of Vatu, prisoner to darkness; I am not his. We have escaped the dark. And if we die here, and our bones are mixed with Amantae's bones, we will be free. Our flesh will feed beetles and worms. It will provide nutrients for mosses and lichens. But we will not belong to the dark. We are free.

"Close your eyes," I tell her.

"They are closed."

"What do you see?" I ask.

"Darkness," she says.

"Now open them. What do you see now?"

"Still darkness."

"But," I say, "it is not the same darkness."

When I close my eyes I am there with him. It is dark and I see nothing, but he is waiting for me.

"You cannot escape," I tell him, but he does not listen. Why has Vatu not consumed him? I reach and turn on a lamp. Light pools around us. We are in my chambers, our chambers.

"Why did you not run?" But why run; there is no escape from the dark. He is not listening to me. He is walking around. He goes to the basin and washes his face. I stop and look down at our reflection in the still water.

"Which of us am I?" Why does he ask that?

He is drinking water. It is very hot in our room. That is why I am not sleeping.

"What will you do?" I ask.

"She is not dead. I will not leave her."

"You left her once before. It is you that put her there."

"Yes, I have done many evil things."

"To talk of evil; there is no evil—there is only Vatu's will," I tell him.

"But you have defied Vatu's will. We have defied him."

"I have not, I am faithful to the dark."

"You are trapped in darkness, you cannot escape."

How can he say this to me when his body is far underground, and when he will die at Vatu's whim? I am free to do the will of Vatu. I am the High Priest, and he is nothing. He is a fool.

"Why are you here?" I ask.

"I am not here," he replies, but he does not leave. I lie down on my bed. When I close my eyes, he is still there.

"Hilketa is dead," I say out loud. "I threw him from the tower. He knows about you, about me, us. Or rather, he knew. Reborn, he knows nothing."

"So he is dead, that is why you came to me. You were afraid to come before."

I am not afraid. I fear nothing. When I tell him that, he laughs.

"What are you afraid of, then?" Will he tell me that he has no fear?

He stops then and seems to think. At last he speaks.

"Fear is like darkness, it vanishes when you shine light upon it. All things are in the author's hands, and we should fear nothing that he does. I had thought I feared death, or that I feared the deaths of Tanden and Nino and the other villagers you slew. I thought that I feared the death of the girl trapped in the dark. I thought I feared the tortures and the agonies that Vatu would heap upon me. I thought I feared Vatu."

Is he saying he has no fears? If so, then he is a fool.

"You must be very brave," I say, mocking him. "You have no fears."

"I did not say that. I only said that when I look at my fears, they vanish. They are shadows that seem great and terrible, but when you turn towards them, they are only shades."

"You sound like Hilketa. I should cast you from the tower."

"If you like," he says, "but you will not. And it is fear that will stop you."

"It is not fear that stops me; it is wisdom."

He laughs. "Now you sound like Hilketa."

Then he is gone.

It is difficult to judge time. We measure it by the movement of the moon, the fall of water, and by the opening of the Sun. We call a moon round the time between the two moon risings and we call a moon turn the time between two full moons. A year is the time between one Sun opening and the next.

In the dark, where there is no moon, or Sun, does time still move? Is it counted only by the drip of water from above? And if you do not count them, those measureless drops, does time stop?

Those drops, each one starts where? Do they start in the clouds or in soil above me? Does it take an instant to fall, or does it take an age to rise from the sea and to drift above me and fall, then to seep through rock and dirt and then gather and fall through the dark, endless cavern and land upon my tongue? There is no time here. And yet there is. It can be measured in heartbeats, or in breaths, or in the shift from waking to sleeping. But even there time plays tricks. Does my heart race, or does my breathing cease? How can I know? Is dreaming waking, and is waking dreaming? It is so hard to tell.

In my dreams I am with him, but he is not there. We are together. I am sitting in a wooden lodge built hanging from the walls of a great house. The same one I have sat in before. I have sat in it many times. The girl is there. I am sitting in the light of soft lanterns watching the moon, and by my side is my flute. Hanging at the window is a glass case; in it flutters a moth with wings of black and violet. Moonlight plays on its wings and they are startling in their beauty. The scent of cedar has faded. Now the scent of woodbine and violets fills the room. The brazier is not lit. In my hand is a cup of rice wine. The beautiful girl is there. I try to remember her name, but I cannot.

"What is your name?" I ask.

"My name is Irid, husband."

Yes, that is her name. I remember now. But she is still formal and cold.

She is kneeling beside me with her head bowed. She is very beautiful, but she is sad. I have made her sad. I can feel her sadness; it is like the cry of a bird on the seashore. Only I can hear it, far away and soft. I must listen hard to hear it.

"Why are you sad, Irid?" I ask.

But she will not answer me. She will not tell me. Instead, she looks at me with a forced smile.

"I am always happy when my husband is here."

So, it is I that has made her sad. Then I realize that there is a wall between us. I do not know who built it, but now I am sad too. And I am sad for him also. He has done this. He has robbed himself of joy. Is there nothing to be done? I wonder if I should leave.

"How old are you?" I ask.

She shudders slightly when I ask. Now I wish I had not.

"Fourteen Suns I have seen, husband, as you know well. Soon I will fulfill all my duties."

It is this she fears, and yet I am surprised that he has been patient. No, it is not this she fears at all, it is something else. It is me.

"Who am I?"

"You are my husband, Karo. You are a great scholar."

"Where is this?"

"This is the home of my father, Greba. Husband, are you well? Surely you know all these things. Have I displeased you in any way?" So much fear.

"You do not need to fear me." The words are softer than breathing, and yet they strike her like a fist. Is it true? Perhaps she should fear me. Perhaps she should fear him. She has raised a hand to her mouth, but now she is letting it glide back to her lap. She says nothing.

I can feel her presence in the dark. Why has Vatu not slain her? Does he seek to mock me?

"Who are you?" she calls.

I have brought bread, and I cast it to her. It will be better eating than moss and worms. She eats it. At first she is eating greedily and then she stops.

"Will you have some?" she asks.

"You think it is poisoned, do you?" I say and take a mouthful to show her that it is not.

"No," she says, "I thought only that you might want some. If you wanted to kill me, I don't think that you need to use poison."

"I might find it amusing," I replied.

"You might," she admits, "but it wouldn't really be very funny, just mean. You didn't answer my question. Who are you?"

"How can you say that after we've been trapped here for so long?"

She stops and thinks.

"You're not him," she says. "I don't know where he is. He goes and leaves me from time to time, but you're not him."

"How can you be sure?" How can you know this when no one else can?

"I can't be, not completely, but you talk differently, and you breathe differently. I can't see you, so you might look the same for all I know, but you feel completely different. Besides, where would he get bread? He couldn't just magic it out of thin air."

"How do you know he couldn't?"

"True, I don't know. But if you were him, then you wouldn't say that. He would say, how do you know that I can't. But I think if he could, then he would have done so before now."

"I can't argue with your logic," I tell her, even though I could.

"Why are you here?" Why are you here; that is what I wish to know. Why are you not dead? Why has he kept you alive?

"For answers," I tell her.

"From me? I'm not sure I can tell you anything. If I try, will you let me go; me and him, both of us? Will you let us go?" she asks.

"No, of course not, but I can bring more bread. If I want to; if you answer my questions," I tell her.

"All right, I suppose that is better than starving. I forgot how good bread is. And what it's like to feel full. Ask me what you want and I'll try and answer. What do you want to know?"

"Let's start with your name," I say.

"That's easy enough, my name is Algria."

"There is no way out. At least there is no way out for me. I know you have left me, although I don't know where you have gone."

She is right. I have been and left her, but it was not by design. I have found myself pulled from this place to another and then pulled back. Have I really escaped? She says I have. But I still feel trapped.

"You do not have to stay with me," she says.

"If I leave you, I think you will die."

She does not seem to mind. She just shrugs. It is not important.

"Perhaps I am dead already," she says. And perhaps she is; perhaps we both are.

"If you could leave here, what would you do?" I ask her.

"I don't know. I wasn't doing that much with my life before you put me here. I was treated well by Amantae, but I was really little more than a slave. The other man, the man he killed, would have raped me. He would have kept me, and forced himself on me. Lots of the guards do it. They keep girls in locked rooms or in brothels. Some of the girls say it is not too bad. It is better than working in a brothel."

"Is that what you would do?" I ask.

"No." In the darkness I can hear her hair falling as she shakes her head. "That would be hardly better than this. I'd be fed and at least get a lantern and a softer bed, but I'd be no less of a prisoner."

"Maybe you would grow to like the man?" I suggested.

"Yes, that is possible. Some of the girls do, especially if the man is kind. But I don't think Agana was a kind man. There's as many men murder their slaves after they've had enough of them, or if the girls give them children they don't want. I think Agana was like that. I think once I was older, he'd have either killed me, or sold me to a brothel." She is saying these things in a flat voice.

"Did you love Amantae?" Why am I asking that?

"No. Like I said, he was kind. I think it was hard for him. The whole time I was with him, I was safe. He kept me safe. He was kind to me, but I did not love him, not like that. And he never asked me to anyway. He would not have been my first. Agana was not my first, but he was rough and violent. If I had been in a brothel, they would not have let him treat me so, or at least not without paying a great deal." After she finishes speaking, we sit in silence for a while.

Chapter Twenty-Six
Mocking

"You had no marks when you stood before me?" I say.

"Yes, I had no visible marks," she agrees.

"You must blame me for this."

"No, not at all, you are just as much a prisoner, a victim, as I am. It is this world, this Hell that is to blame. It is Vatu that is to blame."

I nod. "And the author of all things. He too is to blame."

She starts slightly. I can hear her sharp intake of breath.

"You have become a heretic too?" she asks.

"Once, you told me that all men are heretics. Not because they believe, but because they wish to believe."

"I told you that?" She laughs, and her laughter is like sparks of fire in the dark.

"You did. I thought you very brave to speak, and very foolish. You still have not answered my question," I tell her.

"What would I do if I could escape? Run, there is nothing else I can do. I cannot fight the darkness." I wonder where she would run to; there is nowhere that the darkness is not. When I tell her this, she hesitates.

"Tell me about how you became a heretic?" she asks.

I have to think for a while. I am not sure exactly how I became a heretic. Was it because of Huneko or Tanden? When I think about it, I realize it is none of these things.

"It is because the author spoke to me," I say at last, and realize finally that he has spoken to me. I had thought it just my own thinking before.

"He speaks to all of us," she says, "but not all of us listen. Perhaps that is why I am still here, because I have not listened to him. I wonder what he will say."

I try to remember the words he spoke to me, the words he put in my mind and in my mouth, and in my ears. But I cannot think on them, they were for another time. If he will speak to me, or through me, he will have new words to say. And if he will speak to her, then he will have words for her only.

"Where do you go when you leave here?" she asks.

"I do not know," I reply. "Mostly, I come to a house and to a girl. She is no older than you, younger most likely. She calls me husband, but there is no love for me in her eyes, only fear. I am not who I am. I am someone else. Or maybe that is not true, perhaps it is here that I am someone else, and there I am truly who I am."

"I don't know what that means," she says. "I don't understand that at all. You leave here and go to your house and your wife. Is she pretty?"

"Yes, she is very pretty. She is young and delicate. She is like a cherry blossom in moonlight."

"Is she prettier than I am?" she asks.

"I don't know," I reply, "I cannot remember your face." I try to remember her. But she was too unimportant for me to have thought much about her appearance. Still, she must have been pretty—two men died because of her. She was young then, she may be prettier now. I will never see her face. We will never leave the darkness.

It is strange to think of Hilketa as young. For so long I thought of him as old, ancient even. It was wrong of me to think of him so, the reborn are ageless. We are all ancient and we are all infants. Even if I had lived just one life from the moment Vatu called us to this world, I would be young compared to the darkness. It is the oldest thing of all.

Now he is here. He is but a child. He is younger than us all. He has no wisdom or trickery. He is a blank tablet. It is I who will eventually teach him wisdom. As he is dead, many of his duties come to me. There are a great many reports to read. How unimportant they are. They are the mindless babble of bureaucrats. It is important only that they are written. It is the thing itself that is important.

It is vital that stores are kept, that soldiers are fed and paid. It is vital that sewers are cleared and maintained. It is vital that tribute is taken and that criminals are punished. But recording these things is important only in that if they were not reported, they would not happen. If a governor does not need to report his tribute, then he will send none. If a general does not need to report the training of his men, he will do none. If a building maintenance official does not need to report his efforts then the buildings will fall into disrepair.

It is important that they are read and that they are checked. Otherwise, they will do nothing, but they will report it anyway. So I read the tablets, thousands and thousands of tablets. It is a burden. It will be many years before Hilketa takes that burden from me.

Sometimes, some few times, there is information of importance within them. I notice that soldiers are not being trained enough, or that governors are sending too little tribute, or that too little maintenance is happening to roads or city walls. My direction, my wisdom; it is important, but less important than you might think. A city is not built by architects or planners, it is built by labourers and masons. If there was no head to lead the dark lands, then maybe things would go less well. But, if there were no farmers or labourers or street cleaners or cooks, things would go much worse. I see now that the dark lands are not built by me or Hilketa, or even by Vatu, but by a million nameless labourers and farmers.

Still, it is necessary to do what I do. Many long hours spent reading and directing—it is necessary.

Now that both Kong and Hilketa are reborn, Greba is first of the twelve. He has no skill, nor inclination for administration. It is his duty. He does as I command, but he grumbles constantly.

"Why kill them both?" he says, meaning Kong and Hilketa. "If you had thought, we would not be weighed down with this nonsense."

When he says these things, I consider killing Greba. But I do not. To kill him now would be to set him free. He is mine to control. My foot is on his neck, and on the neck of his child.

"It is not so different from dealing with the prisoners," I remind him. "If it is too much work, I can have Arraio or Estira take care of the prisoners."

He snorts. "Arraio would be too busy buggering the prisoners to get anything done, and Estira would be having his own fun, in his own way."

"Why does that matter?" I ask. "They are prisoners."

He looks up at me. He is still impudent even though I hold him as mine. Perhaps I will beat Irid just to remind him that I hold him so.

"Great one," he says. "There was a time when you taught me. You taught me all that I am. All of the twelve are your handiwork, including me. You taught me the value of justice and that even a prisoner should be treated with justice. These are not my thoughts and thinking. It was you that told me that justice was the highest virtue."

He is right; justice is the darkness's highest virtue, its only virtue. I will not let those that are not just deal with the prisoners. It is what I made Greba for, and he is good at what he does. He is a monster, but a monster with uses.

How long have we been sitting reading the reports? The lantern is dimming. I should call the slave to come and trim it and refill it. But I do not, instead I let my fingers run across the inscriptions on the tablet. It is a trick Hilketa taught me—to read with my fingers by brushing them across the indentations in the clay.

> *Great one,*
>
> *As you commanded, we have kept watch on the place where you slew the heretics. No one has approached or come near. The village is completely destroyed. Nothing grows and even birds will not fly over the land.*
>
> *As you commanded, we have sent out children into the land. When they returned, they were sick and later, their skins started to peel off. All of the children have lost their hair. They cannot hold down food or water. Most are now dead, and most likely the rest will die soon.*
>
> *As you commanded, we will send more children after the next Sunrise. I shall report the outcomes and if anyone attempts to visit the area, they will be arrested and sent to the tower.*
>
> *I await your further commands as always.*

Some reports are more important than others.

In the darkness I close my eyes. She is there. I hold her hand; does she take my hand? When I open my eyes, I am still in darkness, but there is a soft breeze cooling my brow. There is the sound of fluttering wings and of curtains blowing in the wind. I hear soft breathing. There is a small hand in mine. It seems fine and delicate, like a lady's hand, but it feels rough and strong.

"Where have you been?" she asks.

"Here mostly," I reply. "I'm not sure where else. It's just like suddenly I'm not here anymore. I don't know how I go, where I go or how I get there."

"Can I come with you next time?"

"Maybe," I say. "I know some of the places I've been to. Some of them you don't want to go to visit. I've been to the dungeons. This isn't a dungeon."

"What is it then? At first when you put me here, it seemed just like a dungeon. There were four walls and I had chains on. Now it's like a great big cave."

"That's exactly what it is, or at least in part. This is the hall of Vatu. This is the place of darkness. It is a cave, I suppose, but it is bigger than any cave. It is vast."

"Is there a way out?"

"One way at least, but Vatu keeps it locked," I tell her. "I used to have the key, or at least I used to be able to open it."

"Have you tried?" she asked.

"No, I haven't. I don't know where it is. We're right in the middle of the darkness, the door could be in any direction and miles away. I can't find it. Vatu will not let me find it."

She thinks for a while and then says, "If we could find the wall, then we could follow it till we came to the door."

"It's not like that; you can't find the door that way. You'd have to run your fingers over every inch of the wall and even then you could miss it. There are ledges and folds and you can't find it that way. Even if you could, Vatu would fill your mind with confusion. You'd just end up going round and round in the dark."

"Still," she suggested, "it's got to be better than this. Surely it is better than doing nothing."

"But we're not doing nothing," I tell her, "we are staying alive.

We have water and can find food. We might not find any if we go too far. We could die of thirst and starvation."

"When he comes, you could follow him."

I stare into the darkness. I do not stare at her, because I can see nothing.

"He has been here?"

"Yes," she says. "I hope you're not angry. He came and gave me bread. I tried to save you some, but you were gone for a long time, or it seemed like a long time anyway. I should have kept you some, I'm sorry that I never. If he comes back with more, then I will try and keep you some."

"No, I'm not angry, not at all." Why should I be angry with her after what I have done to her? She is only here because I brought her here.

"What did he say when he was here?" I ask.

"Not very much," she says. "He asked me about all sorts of things. I told him that I'd tell him whatever he wants to know. But he never asked much. He never asked about the heretics or about all that stuff Amantae did with Kong, not that I know much about it anyway. To be honest, I don't know very much about any of this, but if he had asked, I would have told him everything I know for more bread. I feel a bit ashamed now."

"There is no need to feel ashamed," I say; no need for her to feel ashamed anyway.

In the dark, she is just a voice. She is only a sound. I cannot see her, and she cannot see me. I know she is real. I have touched her and fed her. I have dribbled water into her mouth. She is real and yet she sounds like a voice in my head, and the echoes in the dark are like echoes in my skull.

"I wish there was light. I wish there was some way to see you."

Why does she say that?

"There is no light here. There has never been light here. Here the darkness is eternal. This is Vatu's domain." I say the words, but do I believe them? Here in the centre of his kingdom, I doubt him. I am a heretic indeed.

The moon has risen just above the horizon. It is a thin sliver of light, we are still in darkness. I am standing in the dark looking up. What is it I wish to see? I am the High Priest and all things happen at my command. I have moved around to look at the hanging pavilion. From the outside of the house, it looks like a cage hanging from the wall. In some ways, it is a cage. It is Irid's cage. In the dark, workers have awoken and have started to clean the streets of night soil. They will take it and use it to feed the land. As they sweep, the fetid scent of excrement is everywhere. They move quickly and quietly, but they are not silent. In the terrace above, there are signs of waking. A light is struck. I can see the glow of the lamp through the veiled curtains. In silhouette, I see Irid rising from her bed. Even her shadow is beautiful. She will wash and then feed on rice.

The curtain is drawn back, and she stands at the window. I look up to her and feel longing. Why am I here? It is my right to be by her side and in her bed. I have won that right. She is looking out into the dark; can she see me? I am certain she cannot. But still she looks out. What is it that her eyes are seeking if they are not seeking me? What is it she hopes for; what does she hope to find?

Why do I not go to her? It is my right. If I wish it, then it must be. All things are mine to command and she is mine also. I have lain in that bed with her, and she has obeyed my commands. Why is that not enough? What is it that I seek? I have made her mine. She is my captive. She is my wife. What more do I want?

Answers do not come. Only more questions come. Now they are coming faster and faster.

Enough, this must stop. I am the High Priest, all things are mine to command. How is it that she has escaped me? How is it that she can keep something from me? What is it that I am denied?

There is no stopping them, the questions. They rise unbidden, like flies from dung. I command them to stop, but they do not obey. What do you wish? Why are you here? What is it you want? Do you even know what you want? Do you even know why you are here? Why do you not go to her? What is it that you are afraid of? Who dares to question me?

There is a ghost at my shoulder. I do not turn around to look at him.

"You remind me of someone," he says.

"Who do I remind you of?" I ask. But I know the answer. He is mocking me.

"I am not like him," I say.

This is no answer and for a minute I think he has gone, then I hear slight laughter. When I turn around, he looks at me and smiles.

"Why do you think he stood like you do now?" he asks.

"Because I broke him," I reply. "I broke him, I destroyed him and all that he held close to him. I discovered his secrets and made him mine. He stood outside and looked at his wife because he was ashamed. I made him ashamed. I did. I broke him. He is mine."

The ghost nods his head. "That is correct. Now you must ask yourself; who made you ashamed?"

I go to strike the ghost, but my hand passes right through him and then he is gone.

I will not be denied. I will make him pay. I will make them all pay. I arrive at the door of the house. I do not wait for admittance. It is all mine now. When I enter, Unead is there. She bows and welcomes me but does not speak. That is wise. She may be a money grubbing courtesan, but she is wise. She knows to fear my wrath.

Irid comes running into the courtyard. She is dressed in fine silk, as if she were expecting me. Perhaps she is always dressed so. Perhaps she is always expecting me.

She bows and kneels when she sees me.

"Husband," she says, "it is a pleasure." But her voice is hollow and bland. There is no pleasure in her voice. It is the voice of duty, of obedience and of fear. I look at her. Her makeup is faultlessly applied. Her hair is perfect. She is graceful and delicate. I want to reach out and touch her, but I restrain myself. Again, why do I deny myself what is mine?

Unead has brought me wine. She is beseeching me to sit. I allow her to lead me to a cushioned chamber, and she places the wine before me. Irid has followed me and is sitting beside me as a wife should. She is offering me food, but I am not hungry.

The ghost has come back. He is standing in front of me. Neither Irid nor her mother can see him, or hear him as he laughs at me.

"Everyone is a prisoner," he says. They cannot hear, and I do not reply. I close my eyes and he is gone. I turn and look at Irid and she looks back at me with empty, disinterested eyes.

"How may I bring you joy, husband?" she says. Now it is she who mocks me, all unintended.

Chapter Twenty-Seven
Time

There are no such things as ghosts. The dead do not rise. If they did, then I would have the ghosts of a million people haunting me. And if they did haunt me, what then? Ghosts cannot harm me. They have no power over me. I have power over them. I am the High Priest of darkness. In the dark, there are a thousand ghosts ringed around me.

"What do you want?" I ask, but they do not answer.

Algria stirs in the dark and crawls towards me. Her fingers wrap around mine. She is afraid. I reach in the dark and brush her hair. I have forgotten what colour her hair is. Why do I think of that now? Why does it matter?

"What is it?" she asks me. She cannot feel them or see them or sense that they are there. Are they there? Is it all just my imagination? If I could not sense them, would they even exist? They do not speak, nor move, nor do anything except wait. What are they waiting on? Why do they follow me?

"Stay here," I tell Algria. She shrugs and I can feel the movement of her muscles ripple down her arm and fingers. What choice does she have?

"Where are you going?" she asks, but I do not answer. I step forward and the ghosts crowd even closer to me. I cannot see them or touch them or hear them, but I know that they are there. The whole cavern is filled with them.

"Who are you?" I ask and a thousand unseen ghost fingers raise and point in answer. I am you. We are your ghosts; they do not speak. But they are not. They are nothing. They are stage props placed around me. They are empty images and imaginings. They are decorations placed for effect but have no reality.

"You cannot harm me," I tell them.

Why would we harm you? they ask without words.

Then what is their purpose, I wonder. They have no purpose. They are simply a distraction. I walk through them. They do not part to let me pass, but they do not need to. They cannot stop me. They are as insubstantial as water, or air. They are as insubstantial as darkness. They are as real as I choose to make them. They fade back to nothing. They were never here.

"What is it?" Algria asks me.

"It is time that we left this place," I tell her.

I walk in darkness through the tower and visit the place where the two infants are held. It is not like my childhood. They are not farmed off to the other twelve to be raised and taught. Instead they are cared for by slave girls. Kong's birth mother is here to feed him. But he will be weaned soon. Then she will leave. When I enter the chamber, she puts Kong down and then comes and bows. He is growing. He is able to walk now, clumsy steps. The other, Hilketa, is still too young. Why have I come?

The girl is wondering the same thing. She wonders if I have come to harm Kong, or her. I see that some of the guards have used her harshly. She is thinking that I will use her in the same way. A peasant girl is of no interest to me, especially not one as plain as Katilu is. I will not harm the child. He walks up to me and looks up. Kong is in his eyes. It is there; all the hatred of ages and of countless lives. The eyes say too much. I cannot write but a tenth of what they say or less.

Greba is with me. He is with me often now. He does not like to be with me but it does not matter. He also is looking down at the infant Kong. Why has Vatu done this to us? What have we done to deserve his honour? Why does he love us so much that he cannot let one of us slip away? Why does he keep us with him, over and over again? It is a great honour and a great gift to live eternally with the dark.

In the future, I will be called to teach Kong what he must know, but that time is still far distant. For now there is no reason to be here, other than to look and see the future. I turn and look at Greba. He is watching Kong and in his eyes there is more hate for him even than he has for me. Why do we all hate each other? The question drifts into my mind. The answer is simple; it is who we are. Hate is what makes us.

Later that night I am alone in my chambers. I lie down to sleep. When I close my eyes, I see his face again. It is not so different from the one he had before. He is the same. Kong will be the same and look the same and act the same. He will die the same too. There is no escape from Vatu's will.

An overwhelming sadness engulfs me. Where has this sadness come from? It has come from within. I am struck by the pointlessness of it all. Eternal. Who would have thought that word would be a curse? Where do I get the energy to hate? It is like a black fire within me that consumes everything. In the dark I find no comfort. I almost wish that Kong would slay me and free me from this sadness and from this endless life. But death is not a release, it is a rebirth; a rebirth into the endless squabble that is the twelve.

There is more, a voice whispers to me. *Will you hear me?*

It seems as if I must. Who are you?

I am the author of all things.

What does that mean? That is meaningless. You have no power, no reality, no substance. Can you touch me or even hear me? You are a figment of my imagination. There is no author of all things. There is only Vatu and darkness. Is this what you have written, author of all things? Is it you who has trapped me here? Are we your playthings? Why speak now? You have been silent for long enough; why are you not silent now?

Do you wish to hear me?

No, I have no wish to hear you. There is nothing you can say to me. Anger has swallowed my sadness. Sadness and anger; you are the author of them both or you are nothing. You are nothing. You are a trick that I have played upon myself.

The voice is gone and when my anger fades, I find sleep.

We are together. It is just us two in the dark. She is sleeping and does not even know that I am here. Starlight tints the darkness into shades of black. It paints a picture in darkness of beauty. She is beautiful. For that she takes after her mother and has surpassed her; there is also something of her father's strength. She looks frail as eggshell or bone, but she is strong. Why have I come here again? Why do I always come here? And when I come here why do I do nothing but watch, look?

When I speak to her my words go wrong. And yet words are all I have.

There is another way, the voice says.

Why have you returned? It is the same question I have asked myself.

I have never left, the voice says.

Is this some madness that is upon me?

If Hilketa were not a child I would ask him. He would tell me some nonsense. Action is the cure for too much thought. It is time to stop playing and act. I reach to waken her.

There is another way, the voice says, and I stop with my hand poised to wake her roughly.

There is no other way. This is madness, but then if I am mad, what of it? Why should I hide it? I am the high priest of Vatu. If he wishes me to be mad then so be it, I am mad, it is his will. All things are his will.

There is another way.

Then let me hear it. Show it to me that I might see it and know it. There may be many other ways, but not all ways are desirable.

What do you desire? I ask myself. The voice asks what I desire.

I do whatever I desire. There is no one who can stop me.

Is that what you desire, someone to stop you? I could stop you. It is the whisperer.

His words wash over me like icy water. No one can stop me, not even myself. It is like a rushing fall of darkness, a landslide of black stone. I am merely a puppet to my emotions and desire. I am helpless to resist.

If you can stop me, then stop me. I reach out to touch her and as I do I am frozen. Time stops. The light of the lamp fades to nothing. I can no longer hear her gentle breath. I have stopped. I have been stopped.

I am not alone. I am in the darkness. They are nearby.

"Why are we here?" I ask.

His footsteps echo as he walks towards me. The girl says nothing, but I can hear her moving on the floor.

"What do you mean?" I ask.

"I have been brought here against my will," I reply.

"By who?"

We have not been together for maybe a year, maybe longer, not since I brought him here. I reach out and touch his face, my face.

"You need to rest."

I am tired. I have fought for so long. Here I am safe.

"They have done this to you."

Yes, did they do it to you too? Is that why you handed me the amulet willingly?

"Do you wish to stay and rest?"

I think he is trying to trick me. He is trying to steal back the amulet of Vatu.

"You cannot trick me."

The girl has crept closer and she is listening to us speak. I do not know why he has kept her alive, why I have kept her alive. And then the voice says that it is not us that have kept her alive but him, the author of all things. Then why does he keep her alive? The author of all things does not answer.

"I am not trying to trick you."

Then what are you trying to do? Why has the author of all things brought me here?

In the darkness I feel comfortable. It is cooler in the Chamber of Darkness than in the rest of the tower and the city. I am handed a cup of water. It is heavy with minerals and warm. It tastes like tears. I should be drinking wine or blood. Neither of us needs to stay here. I should leave. Why has he not left also?

"Why are you here?"

"Because I am not ready to leave."

"Vatu will not let you leave."

He does not answer and neither does Vatu. He is silent. In the dark I can hear breathing, mine and his. Then I reach out and touch him. My fingers brush down his face, my face.

"It seems we are one."

But does it seem so? Are we one? We have lived apart for so long and even now, whether he is my shadow or I his, we stand facing each other, separate and distinct. Have not the same words been written on both of us? If I bleed, then he will not. If I feel, then he will not feel also. If I die, then he will not die. In what way then are we one? We are not one at all. It is all a lie.

Kong lied and so did Amantae. I am the High Priest and this is my birth right. He is nothing, not even a shadow. He is only a lie. Or I am only a lie. I can no longer remember which of us is real and which of us is fake. It does not even matter. We should not both live. One of us should die, it does not matter which. I thought we could both live and that I could take my place in the hall of darkness while he lived a life of sorts. But it cannot be. I will live and he will perish because I wish to live more than he does.

"If you kill me, it will only start again." It is my mouth and my voice.

"I have no wish to kill you, even after what you have done."

"What have I done?"

"You have slain those that we cared for most: Nino and Tanden."

"Does their memory haunt you?"

"No, it comforts me. Did you love them very much?"

Love, the word is like ashes. I love no one; the dark loves no one. It is a trick, it is all a trick. I will not be deceived, there is no love.

"They loved you."

More lies, more tricks. None of them loved me; they just sought to get gain from me. He knows nothing. He was not there and I was. I remember it all. There was no love. It was business, only business. They are all dead now anyway. Their bones are poisoned and blackened. They are dust and ash. They have gone into the final darkness. There is no love there; even if there ever was any love to begin with, then there is none now. I have killed love, I have ended it. It cannot reach me; I am beyond its touch.

A hand reaches to brush a tear. Why? A black pearl brushed away.

It does not have to be so.

It does if I wish it to be.

Is this what you wish?

This no longer haunts my dreams. Six thousand things need to be said. I wish I could curl up in the darkness and lie here doing nothing except let time pass. Each second counted as a drip of water falling from above to the floor of the cave; a black pearl falling in darkness. Above, the white pearl moon rolls around the sky over and over again. That is what he has done; he has stayed here in the dark. He has pretended that he is trapped but it is only himself that holds back. He could leave anytime. He could leave and take the girl. Why did I bring him here? It is madness. I should not be here. He should not be here.

"What is it that you wish? What are you waiting for? You have killed those around you and they have returned. I am here. We are here and the girl. Her name is Algria. She should be dead but is not. It is the author of all things that has kept her alive. She is nothing. She is less than nothing."

But as I say the words I shake my head. I know that I will not kill her nor leave her. I should leave this place but as I turn to go I stop. He is behind me now. The two of them are behind me. I wish I could stay here forever. I wish Vatu would keep me safe.

Safe from what? There is nothing that can harm me. I cannot die, nor can I feel. If I die, I am reborn. There are a thousand tablets that recount my life story and thousands more.

What is it you wish?

What does anyone wish? Can you tell me that, author of all things, can you tell me what is wanted?

I can tell you all these things and more but not in words. I cannot write them or whisper them to you. You may know all things but you must know them for yourself.

The words are trite and cheap.

All words are cheap. There is nothing that can be said that is not weakened in the saying. Everything that needs spoken is weak and feeble.

What is it that I wish? I have spoken it. Did you not listen? Is it beyond your power?

No. It is done. It is done as you wished. Now you may leave.

I step forward and darkness peels back before me. I step to the door of the cavern and exit. I have returned.

It is as he said. He has more power than I thought. When I ascend, I am met by all the twelve. They bow low before me. I scan their faces. Kong and Hilketa are here. They have grown. In Hilketa's eyes there is no wisdom. It is strange to see Hilketa look so young and to look in Kong's eyes and see neither hate nor madness. I have not yet put hate or madness or wisdom in their eyes. Still, there is enough hate and madness in the eyes of the others.

"You have returned." It is strange to hear words spoken once again. It is Greba who speaks. I wonder how many Sunrises I have missed. They have grown and are now young men. I will have to teach them. The lanterns are lit and I can see my reflection in their eyes. Not my real reflection, but from their eyes I can tell that I have not aged. Fourteen years! It is a wonder. My first thought is of her. She will have aged. I smile. Now she will be older than I am. My first thought is of her.

Greba speaks again, or moves to. I see he will not in front of the others. That is wise. They are not to be trusted. I am worried that she is old or ill or sick or dead. How could I stay away for years and let her wither and waste? Author of all things, did you really know my wish? Then why have you done this? You have let the years take her away from me. I would go to her. But I know that I cannot; not now, not yet. Is she waiting for me?

"I have been with Vatu," I say and it is not a lie, or not completely. They do not question me.

Chapter Twenty-Eight
Returning

When I arrive, I am nervous. I knock on the door and a maid opens it. She hesitates for a moment, just a moment. And then she bows and lets me enter. Unead comes to welcome me. She looks older and her hair is shot with grey. Greba must have told her I have returned because she is not surprised to see me, or at least she betrays no surprise. She always was good at hiding her feelings.

She bids me enter and invites me to sit in the courtyard while she fetches Irid. I sit under the spreading night jasmine and inhale the sweet smell. Irid enters. She is small and delicate and unchanged; still beautiful. I had thought that on my return she would seem older as if she had grown past me, but it seems she has not. She is slim and childlike. She also betrays no emotion. Instead she seats herself before me and bows. She does not raise herself up but waits for me to speak. Unead retires to her pavilion and leaves us alone.

I think about why I am here, why I have returned. What has she done in my absence? Greba would know that I would return, all the twelve would know. But still it is many years; ten I would guess. Has she taken a lover? It is a question that I dare not ask myself. But then neither Unead nor Greba would allow that. They know that if she did I would kill her, and them. Greba would be reborn, but there would be no rebirth for Irid or Unead. For them, death would be final. They would go to the darkness and not return. She has not been unfaithful. Unfaithful to what; to a forced marriage used to control her father? Unfaithful to what; a husband absent for ten summers? Unfaithful to what: not to love?

She still has not moved nor spoken. It is I who must speak and it is I who must find words. I must find them.

"You are well?" Is that all I have to say? When she entered the courtyard, I feared so much. But she is well.

"Yes, husband, I am well." She speaks but does not lift her face. I would look on her perfect face. She is mine to command.

"Rise." And wordlessly she stands. Now in the lamp light her pale skin seems to glow. Her eyes are still down cast and she avoids my gaze. She is made up perfectly, as if she were awaiting someone. She is dressed in finery and her hair is combed and set to perfection.

My sight lingers over her dress; it is of fine white silk and embroidered in brown and green thread. The pattern is of blossoms falling. It is cut and tailored to perfection. The sleeves cover her delicate wrists; her head is bowed and her hair coils over the nape of her neck. She does not look at me.

"Are you glad to see me?" I say the words and she looks up briefly. She is startled.

"Yes, husband," she says, but I cannot tell from her eyes if her words are true. It seems it is possible to lie to the dark after all. How I wish they were true. How I wish she loved me. How I wish I could believe that she loved me. I have made her a toy and slave. She has been a pawn in the game I play with her father. Why should I hope for love from a slave? Why should I hope for love at all?

It is what we all hope for. You whisper again in my ear.

Can you not leave me in peace? Are you here to mock me? I have said that love cannot touch me. But now it seems I wish that it could. What is love? Can you tell me that, author of all things? Do you know what it is? Is it what you desire also?

It is what we all desire and what we cannot know; to be loved. We must believe we are loved, we wish for evidence. We find evidence where we can, in a glance or in a touch or in kindness. It is by giving love that we find this most. A kind act is its own reward. An act of kindness is evidence that we can love and if we can love then why cannot others around us love also?

I have never been kind; it is not my nature. It is not the nature that Vatu has written upon me. Do I have a true nature? Is there some part of me not shaped by him or by the reborn soul that resides in me? And if there is, then where does it come from? The need for love; where does that come from? Have you written this upon me, author of all things? Have you made this weakness within me?

It is our weakness that will make us strong.

"Do you love me?" the words escape my lips and as I speak I know that they are the wrong words. They are the words of need and anger and doubt.

"I love you." When I say the words I am free. It matters no longer if she loves me. She does not answer or look up. She is shaking slightly. Why is she afraid? It is because I have made her afraid. Is there no way to go back and change things?

No, the author of all things shakes his head.

It is not possible to go back. He will not allow it. But it is possible to go forward and change things. I can change things. If she does not love me then I can be kind. If she fears me then I can be soft. I have given her many fine things, but till now I have never thought to give her love.

"I have missed you." Whose words are these?

Does it matter?

There are sobs in the darkness, soft ones that are barely more than intaken breath. But in the silent, endless night they are like thunder. Algria is weeping. Her tears drop soundless to the cavern floor. How long has she lived in the darkness? What have I done to her? I have been both torturer and saviour. I buried her in darkness and now I will raise her up from this tomb. I walk towards her and reach out to where I hear her breathing. She does not draw back when I put my arms around her. I am shocked to feel how thin and bony she is. She is dying. If I leave her here, she will die. She will starve to death and wither to nothing more than bones. It will be her skull that is used as a cup and her bones and flesh that feed lichen and moss.

She says nothing but does not push away. If she is to live I must take her from here. I take her hand and lead her. She follows after me.

"Where are we going?" The words are barely a whisper, it is all the strength she has left. We move onward until we reach a point we can go no further. My fingers brush against stone, darkness solidified.

"Where are you going?" It is him, it is Vatu.

"I wish to leave. I know that you can kill us if you want. I know that I am powerless before you. You know everything. You have not been deceived."

"Who are you?" the darkness asks, and I find that I cannot answer, because I do not know the answer. But another voice answers for me.

"I am Algria, you have held me here. But I will escape." Her voice is as soft as snowfall. It settles into the silence and melts away.

"How will you do this?" Vatu asks. He is playing with us.

"He will lead me out of here, or I will die." There is a stirring in the dark. Only I know that it is laughter.

"Who is he?" Vatu mocks.

"Just a man," Algria answers.

Is that all I am? In the end, is that all I am? I was once something more, it seemed. Now I am just a man in the dark. How can just a man stand against Vatu? How could even the High Priest stand against him? All my power and all my greatness came from him; have I really given all that away? It seems I did once in another lifetime. Now that I am just a man, will that be enough? I am still holding Algria. She is no longer shaking and I seem to find strength coming from her and a power. I cannot explain it.

"Will you let me leave?" I ask.

"I will let you do anything, beloved," Vatu replies.

I turn again to the wall and this time my fingers touch cold bronze. It is the door. The latches open and the door swings open. We bow low enough to walk through. Algria does not have to do more than nod her head forward. I had not noticed how small she is before, but then in the dark, why should I?

A gasp of breath, straighten up, turn and close the door. It is still dark but there are lanterns nearby and I lean down to light one. In the past they would simply light at my command, but I am him no more. The past is done. The light hurts Algria's eyes. I shield the lantern with my hand. There is enough to see by, more than enough. She is weak but is able to walk. She is smiling. We have not escaped, and I do not know where to take her. Vatu may have let us leave but will the twelve and will I, will the High Priest let us go? I cannot walk out of the tower. I must find another way out. Is there another way out? I have exchanged one prison for another.

Still, Algria seems better. Her breathing is more regular.

"We have not escaped," I tell her. But she does not stop smiling. I do not know if she was smiling before. In the dark, I could not see her face. I look at it for a moment. It has been so long since I have seen it. It is not how I remember it or rather, the sight of it corrects my memory; yes, it is like this. It is as if I have been trying to remember a poem that I had forgotten. Only a few lines came to mind; now I see it all. How could I have forgotten? Now that I know all the words, it is more like a song than a poem.

Algria is not able to walk far. She is very weak but she seems stronger and happier as we follow the tunnel away from the cavern. She is humming softly to herself. It is a tune I do not know, or if I know, then I have forgotten it. It seems familiar, but I cannot place it. There is really no choice as to which way we go. The tunnel will not fork for some miles. I must hope that I do not meet any of the twelve. They would love to meet me here, weak and unable to defend myself, stripped of my priesthood. They would slay me instantly. My only comfort is that none of them know about Algria. Only Kong knew about her, but he is dead and reborn.

I must go and go quickly, but Algria cannot move any faster. With our lantern on, any of the twelve will know that someone is here. I am loath to extinguish it after the trouble it took for me to light it. Algria keeps looking at the light and each time she does, it seems she gets stronger.

When we reach the first crossroads, I must decide where to go and hide. I say decide, but I can think of only one place that the twelve seldom go. They never go. It is my grave, my many graves. Only once have I been there. But I remember that the graves were not visited, other than when the twelve took my ashes in the urn and placed them there and when Arraio stole my bones to carve. They do not mourn me, and besides, I am reborn and they must teach me. I am not found in ashes or urns. It is Vatu's conceit to have them place my ashes there. It is only Vatu who mourns my passing and welcomes my return. It will be safe, at least for a while.

Now that I am heading towards my tomb, I feel safer. It is unlikely that I will meet any of the twelve or any others. I had thought once that Vatu had built these tunnels only when I needed them and that he parted rock and darkness before me and closed it behind me. It was a childish thought, but I think it again now, and wonder if he will close the tunnel while we walk and bring an end to it all. In the tomb we will be able to rest.

It is a long journey but other than occasional stumbles, it is uneventful. I ask Algria what tune she is humming.

"Do you not know?" she asks, and I tell her I do not.

"It is a common tune from my village. I sang it there as a child. It is a children's rhyme."

"I know no children's rhymes."

"No," she replies. "How could you?"

There is much more to be said and I must find the words to say it. It is hard and confusing to think on these things from the past. Memories shift and collapse; pieces do not fit together. I am a liar and will not tell the truth. It must be said. I must say it or write it. I must make it real. Once I thought this whole world was nothing more than my plaything and that all things in it were at my command. I stood on the top of the tower and watched the people of the city go about their business. It was my business. I directed them. They did my will. I thought that was enough. I thought that was what I wanted. But it is not. What do I want? I want them to live free. I want to live free. I want to be free of this world at least for a time.

This world is not my plaything. Algria is right when she says this world is hell. But this world is all I have and if there are other worlds, then how can I escape to them? Are they not hell also? Would I escape only to a worse torture and torment?

And memories? How do you escape them? Give them up. But if I lose them, then what do I become? It is memory that makes me what I am. If I lose my memories, then it is not me who escapes, but someone else. If I lose my memories, I die and am reborn a new person. Forgetting, is that a kind of death? And if so, then does not a part of me die every second? I do not know. I cannot recall that which I have forgotten. It may be that once I was completely different from what I am now.

These thoughts I keep to myself and do not share them. Who would I share them with? Who would understand what I try to say? Who would care? I do not share them with Algria, although perhaps I should. She is wiser than she seems. I had thought her just a foolish girl that two men fought over and condemned her to death. But she is more than that. She is a heretic; true, but then, so am I. I am a believer in her faith. She was a believer before me. What does she know of this world and how to escape from it? For all her talk, she is still here. It is I who have helped her escape.

"Where are we going?" she asks.

"There is a place we can be safe," I tell her. "At least for a time we will be safe. No one goes there. We can rest there."

In the lamplight, I can see her smiling.

"It would be good to rest."

But what have we been doing if not resting? We have rested for years in Vatu's dungeon.

"Tell me about this place."

"There is not much to tell," I say. "We will be there soon. Save your strength for now."

She is leaning into me. She is struggling to walk. I should carry her, but when I reach down to lift her she pushes me away.

"I must grow stronger," she says. Or else I will die, she does not say.

Eventually, we turn a corner and the cavern of tombs opens before us and the light of my lantern stretches out. It is vast. The domed ceiling reaches over us and the terraced floor falls down to the centre of the cave.

"It is like a theatre," Algria says.

No, it is no theatre; there are no performances here. She steadies herself and walks away from me. She follows the winding path that circles around and around the cave. She is looking at the wall and the niches in it. She does not reach out or touch any of the urns.

"What is this place?" she asks again. Her voice fades in the vast empty space. The air is thick with unspoken answers.

She starts to walk back to me.

"What is this place?" In her eyes there is a look of panic. Why? She has no need to fear.

"It is safe here," I tell her. "No one will come here."

"I can believe that," she says, "but, why? Whose ashes are in these jars?"

"Mine," I say. "This is all of me. This is where all my ashes rest. In every urn is me, and I am in every urn. This is where I will finish, like every other one of me."

She is looking around and says nothing for a while, taking in the vastness of the space.

"How many?" she asks.

But I cannot tell. It is impossible to count the graves.

"This might not be all of them," I say. "I have no way to tell if there are more elsewhere."

She nods and keeps looking around.

"The others, the twelve, do not get buried here. There is another chamber where their ashes are... scattered."

"Do you remember any of it?" Algria asks.

I shake my head. "Sometimes, I think I do. Sometimes it seems that I have, or that somehow they visit me. But how can I tell? How can I know what is real? I might remember some things or maybe I am just remembering what someone has told me. I am like a tablet that Vatu writes the same thing on, over and over."

"But each time on a different tablet," Algria tells me.

"Perhaps." I shrug. "It is difficult to know. The things I trusted are lies."

It is as if the earth I stand on has crumbled away. It is as if I stand not on the ground but on water and that I am sinking into it deeper and deeper. When I return to myself, Algria is holding my hand. When I look at her, she has a sad look. Is she sad for me? She is seeking to comfort me. She is seeking to do me a kindness, a small kindness in the dark. It is by such small kindnesses that we make the world better. I am grateful that she is kind to me. I hold her hand and try to smile at her.

"This will not be your final resting place."

When the words are spoken, I know them to be true. I will not end up here. I have escaped. Somehow I have escaped. I will not return to this. It has taken me a million lifetimes to escape. I will not go back. How long have we stayed in darkness when we needed not, years and years we stayed. How many years have passed?

Chapter Twenty-Nine
Rape

The time to think on these things is past. It is time to be practical. The tombs are colder than the tower. We will need to either make heat or build shelter. We will need food and water. And we must think how we will escape.

The great thick tree roots hang down and at the edges of the chamber reach the floor. We will not want for firewood at least. I lead Algria to the side of the chamber, to a place where the tree roots are thick and form a sort of cage of roots. It is like a room with walls of roots. It is a good place to rest. It feels safer. I draw a knife and start to cut into the roots. The bark is thick and tough. I had thought to cut them down but it is hard work. Inside, the roots are moist and fleshy. I cut some of the thick, fibrous root and suck. The moisture is sweet tasting and refreshing. I pass some to Algria and motion to her. It seems in the place of my death, there is life and sweetness. It is strange to think on it.

I go around the tombs and collect cloth that had been draped over the urns. Much of it is perished and moth eaten, but there is enough so that in the little cage of roots we can rig up the cloth to form a sort of tent. In our tent we are warm and comfortable. It feels safe. Although I know that we are not. It is only the fear that the twelve have for this place that keeps us safe. I wonder why they fear it, why they keep away. I have only been here once before, and only with Hilketa. I had not realized at the time that he was afraid. What did he fear; was it only death? Surely we who have faced death a thousand times should no longer fear it. Death should be the least of our fears.

I turn back to Algria and when I do I see that she is sleeping. In the lamplight, she looks very peaceful. Her breath comes easily and evenly, and her sleep is still and calm. What is this that I feel now?

I walk along the rows and rows of tombs. They have scarcely been disturbed from the day that I was interred in each and every one. The footsteps of the twelve lead to the grave and then away. At each grave there is a cluster of footsteps where they waited while my ashes were placed against the wall. They did not linger; why should they?

I have seldom come here and now I must stay here for... how long? I cannot say. But I am here. I am not trapped and I can leave just as soon as I no longer wish to stay with Algria. I can leave as soon as I wish, I need only to desert her and leave her alone to die in the dark. Is that a trap? If it is, then who has made it? It is a trap I have made for myself. Was I right after all; is love a weakness? I cannot afford to be weak. Or what, what if I am weak? The twelve will kill me and I am reborn. But I will die and be reborn no matter what. It makes no difference; weak or strong, it is all the same. Perhaps true strength is recognizing your weakness. Now I sound like a heretic. I am a heretic. I should sound like a heretic; it is what I am. It is what I have become.

Now I am released, now we are released and the other. What now? The darkness is lifted from us and we are free, but what of him? Will he betray us?

I have wandered. I have let my thoughts cloud my eyes. I have moved farther into the maze of tombs and urns. I turn and see footsteps, single footsteps. They are not mine. They are not mine from another life. I follow them to see where they lead. I must see who has been here and what have they done. I know that Arraio comes and collects my bones from the ashes. Perhaps it is him who has left the footprints. I should follow and see, I should see what he has done. I should find a clue to who he is. If I will stay here hiding, then I must know who I am hiding from. Why is he here? The footsteps are not so old. They are spaced regularly and far apart. Whoever it is, they are moving quickly and assuredly. They know where they are going. That is not Arraio; he moves furtively and cautiously. It could be Hilketa or Greba; they are both strong and certain in their walk. But why would they come here? It is true they both hate me and they may come here just to glory in my many deaths. But it does not fit; it will not do. This is not the answer. Neither of them ever act for any reason as petty as gloating.

The footprints lead a long way and the path is now broken and worn. It has not been kept up. None of the paths have been repaired. It is strange to think that once someone laid those paving stones. How many centuries ago was that? A million? But the footprints are not old. They are fresh. They were not here when I came with Hilketa; of that I am sure. I would have noticed. I would have seen them. I am sure. The footprints have become closer and then they turn and run parallel to each other. They are deeper. The person has stopped and is standing still. He has turned and is looking at something. There are imprints ahead where he has knelt down and there is some disturbed ground. I turn and look. He has written something in the dirt. I read it.

I know you are here.

That is all that is written, and beside it is a symbol. It does not say anything, it is just a single letter. It is the letter K. It must be Kong who has written this. It must be him. He must know that I am here. When I see the letter I feel something different. Is this fear? Am I afraid? The thought is ridiculous, that I should fear Kong. I fear nothing. And yet, I am hiding in a graveyard.

How can he know this? The Kong that I knew is surely dead. I killed him and he has been reborn as a child. A child can do nothing. Why should I fear a child? He can do nothing. He can know nothing. But, Kong is clever. He is not wise, but he is clever. He could leave clues for himself the same as I have left clues for myself. I have found them, some of them, so why should not he? His clues will be simpler and easier. Perhaps he has given clues to others of the twelve. He is also a blank tablet that Vatu writes upon. What has Vatu written there: hate, madness and fear? Why does he write these things? Could he not find something better to write? Could he not make Kong more than he is? Vatu is a mystery to me. I thought once that I knew his mind but now I see that it is impenetrable. It is a dark tower, a fortress. It cannot be breached.

Perhaps he has tried to write things differently. Who knows what he has tried to write upon us. Is that why we die and are reborn, so that he can try and write again what we have marred and spoiled? But if so, then he has failed a thousand million times to correct us and to make things right. He is a failure.

After a hundred million lifetimes, I have done something new. I have escaped and I have changed. Have I defied Vatu or have I simply done what he was waiting a hundred million lifetimes for me to do?

I must return to Algria. I cannot leave her alone. It is not just me who is in danger and who I fear for. She is not safe. If Kong comes looking for me and finds her, then she will be in danger. I should not have left her. Running, I can see the light of our lantern shining through the fabric of our makeshift shelter. She is safe, she must be safe. If she were not, then I would know. Kong could not have taken her without her calling out. She is safe.

I wake and find that Irid is gone. I think that she has gone to wash after our closeness. I think she has gone to tend to her duties in the house. The curtain is open, and the moon is rising. The rays of light rest on the glass case of the purple moth that hangs from outside the window. I am happy, but I wish that she was here to share my joy. She is everything to me and if I am not the same to her, then what of it? It is enough to love, to be loved is something we cannot command or control. To love is its own reward.

I lie still and pull the coverlet over me. It is cool here compared to the heat of the tower. We are farther from the Sun, but it is still warm and my coverlet is light. I close my eyes and think that I will sleep. But sleep does not come.

I can hear stirring in the house. Maybe Irid is seeing to her duties, but I would rather she would be with me. I think to rise and find her, but that would not be seemly. I compose myself. She will return soon enough, for duty's sake if nothing else. She is always dutiful. I cannot stop a smile crossing my lips when I think of her. She is calm and modest. She will not fail to do her duty even though she need not. She is the daughter of one of the twelve and the wife of the High Priest. There is nothing she needs to do or that should be denied her. But she too is a prisoner. She is hidden here and we pretend she is simply the daughter of a courtesan and a merchant. We pretend that she is married to a scholar. No, we pretend that I am now no longer a scholar but an apprentice to Greba. We pretend and hide and we have made a prison for her as before Greba made a prison for Unead. It is not right that we should do this. We should set them free. It is like the moths in the glass cage. Irid is right, we should set them free to flutter where they will. I look up to the case. In the moonlight, I can see almost nothing from where I lie, so I stand and walk to the window. I still cannot see any moth flying, and when I get to the case I see the moth is dead. It is lying on the bottom of the case. It is broken and crushed. It has not just died but has been taken and squashed against the bottom of the case. Who would do such a thing? I cannot imagine Irid doing such a thing and none of her maids would dare to do such a thing. Has Greba come and crushed this moth in the night? It seems such a trivial thing. It would not be like him. I doubt he has ever come to our pavilion. I do not doubt that seeing me with his daughter causes him pain, but he would not come. He would not do this and neither would Unead.

My mind is racing. A thousand possibilities, but only one is truly possible. There is an intruder in the house. Someone is here who does not belong. Who would do this? There is only one answer. Why has he come here? There is only one answer. I am afraid. I feel fear. I rise and dress silently and quickly. I will find him and I will kill him. He will not do this. I will not allow it. I climb up and enter the house from our pavilion. I will find him. I will find them. In silence I walk through the halls into the courtyard. I will find her. He will not take her from me. The servants should be rising, but there is no noise. It is possible they are dead. He could kill them. I walk into the moonlit garden and I can see footprints. I know who they belong to. They lead past the jasmine and twining woodbine. The early moonrise scents rise up, but there is another scent. It is the scent of iron and salt; it is the scent of blood. It comes to me faint and fading on the breeze. It is almost covered by the scent of blossom. But I smell it and again fear rises within me.

This is not how it should be. I have turned my back on hate and darkness and turned to love and now you have done this to me. This is not what I was promised. If I still walked in darkness then there would be none of this fear.

I begin to hear the servants stirring in the house. My fears are unfounded. The house is safe.

I hear a sound and turn. It is Irid. I can see her by the well collecting water. She should have a servant do it. My heart leaps when I see her, but then the scent of blood comes again and I see the footprints on the stone flags. Irid turns to me and looks. She is safe and yet she is not. Kong has been here. It is his footprints and his blood. Then I see she is washing herself where Kong has been. He has forced himself upon her. It would have been better if he had killed me, and that is why he has not.

I take a lantern and inspect the house. The servants are all alive, but they have been drugged. Kong has blown powder into the house. Traces of it have gathered in the corners as a white dust. This is how he was able to get so close to me. This is why I did not waken. How could he know about Irid? Who has told him? Who has betrayed us?

And why only come and reveal his hand now? Why did he not slay me while he could, or slay Irid? It is incomprehensible. What is his design?

Unead has risen. No words pass between us. But then words are not required. She is dressed, as ever, in fine clothes, and she moves with that same grace and ease, but there is a wariness about her steps, and her hand keeps moving towards where she has concealed her knife. She is afraid, if not for herself then for her daughter. Greba is not here, but I think that Unead will try to send him a message. She cannot send a servant directly to the tower. That would reveal us, but she must let him know. Greba will have planned for this for many years, there will be a way to let him know.

Unead and Irid are busy, I approach them and I see they are instructing the servants to pack up their belongings into a wagon. No servant is sent to Greba or to any intermediator. Their absence will be message enough. They have planned for this day and are ready. Irid looks up at me and smiles. She is glad, for her it is an escape.

"Where will you go?" I ask.

Irid bows to indicate that she does not know, but Unead looks at me directly. She will not tell me.

"Will you stop us from leaving?" she asks. "Will you keep us here now that we are discovered?"

She knows I will not. She knows that I will not let them die, not by Kong's hand, not here, not now. I will let them leave and perhaps I will never see Irid again.

"Greba will know where to find you," I say.

Unead looks at me again and I can see that he does not.

"Bid him farewell," she says. "He was always good to me and to

Irid."

I want to protest and to say that we can set up elsewhere, but I will not speak such foolishness. It must be this way. If they have been discovered once, they will be discovered again. It would bring danger upon them. Greba has been prepared for this for many years. He has had time to think things through. It is safer this way.

It seems that I must lose Irid on the very day I truly found her; all those years of waste.

"Come with us," says Irid. The words are both a plea and a challenge. I could give up everything. I could escape. I could be free.

It is moments like these when everything turns. It is like a hinge that can twist two ways.

Chapter Thirty
Love

When I return to the shelter, Algria is sitting up. She is eating bread.

"Look," she says and points to some loaves, a flask of wine and some dates.

I want to dash the bread from her hand. Has she not thought that Kong may have poisoned it? But I know he has not. If he wanted her dead then she would be dead already. He would have had no need for tricks.

"Where has it come from?" I ask, although I know the answer.

"A man came while you were away. I say man, but he is little more than a boy. He is barely as old as you. He left these things and said he would bring more. He said to tell you that he is your friend."

So, we are discovered and he will make use of us.

"You must stay here," I tell Algria, "at least for now."

"Where will you go?" she asks me.

"I will go to face them."

I put my hand to my throat and I find a snare. Around my neck is the amulet. He has given me it. I am High Priest.

There is no other choice. I must go. It is what I most desire. It is freedom. It is what I have hoped for. I have realized it; this is what

I have hoped for. It is my chance. I call him to me, and he is here.

"I set you free," I say. But really, I am placing him in my cage. I am putting him where I have been. He will take my place. He will be caught.

"I am free," he says. But that is a lie too. He is caught in the darkness. He is trapped in Vatu's chamber deep below the earth. He thinks that is freedom? It is not freedom. Perhaps there is no such thing as freedom. Perhaps I am going just from this captivity to another. Are all cages just the same? It seems that I desire this one. I will go to this new captivity, if that is what it is, and I will go willingly. Is that what freedom is, to be willingly captive?

"I leave all of this to you," I tell him.

He does not reply, but just looks at me. I think back to when we first met. I remember the shock of seeing myself for the first time. Now there is only weariness. In his eyes there is only weariness. And what is in mine? Hope?

He turns and looks around the courtyard. He sees the quiet bustle of the servants packing.

"So, you have been discovered."

"I will go with them," I tell him. Is he surprised when I say this? He turns and looks at me.

"He will follow you."

"Not if you are here. He will not know that I am with them."

He shrugs, he does not look convinced, but it is my best hope; they will not be searching for me, only for them.

"Where will you go?" he asks.

Now it is my turn to shrug. If I knew I would not tell him, but that is foolish. He can always find me. We can never be free of each other.

It is time to go. The wagon is packed and Irid and Unead are waiting. None of the servants will accompany us. If one of them has betrayed us then they will not get the chance to betray us again. We will not slay them. Instead we pretend that we are taking a trip and will return to our household when the trip is over. There is no greater sign of panic and flight than a house of murdered servants.

"I must go now." Why, where is he going?

Greba is waiting in the upper chamber when I ascend the tower. I greet him. Should I tell him about the discovery? I think that Unead would have sent for him, but she has not and he will not accompany them. It seems this was his plan, or her plan. They have gone and he will not see either of them again. I look at him and he stares back but says nothing. There is nothing to say. I wonder where they have gone. Greba is writing directives and will send them out. We are working, but no words are spoken between us.

I send for Kong and Hilketa. If they are old enough to cause trouble, then it is time that they had work to do. It is time to keep them busy. When they arrive, Greba hands them a pile of reports.

"This is your duty now; I have done your work for you for long enough."

Hilketa sits and starts to read the tablets that are given to him. He places them in separate piles. He will answer them. He motions to Kong and hands him a report. I look and I see that I am no longer needed here. Nor is Greba. I leave them to their work.

I should go to Vatu and speak with him, but I will not. Where will I go; back to the darkness? It seems that I must be the High Priest. I have been left here. He has left me here. He has made me what I was; I am the High Priest again. I am a fraud.

I return to my chambers; I have not been there for so long. It is strange to sit in there and to touch the things that once were mine. It is no different than when I left. There are a few things laid out on a table. There is a flute, my flute. And there is a tablet. The tablet is blank; it has been wiped clean and there are no words on it. What did he write there and why did he clear the words? I put my fingers to the clay. How often has the tablet been smoothed over; how often have words been written and then erased?

If I knew the words, if I knew what I had written, I think I would know everything; I think I would know the history of the whole world. I think I would know the truth. I have lived a lie over and over again. This world is a lie, it is a trap. Somewhere there is a way to escape. I will find it. If I could know what is written, then I could find a way out of this world.

Will you tell me the way? Will you show it to me? Can you not let me go? You have kept me in this trap. I am nothing more than a plaything to you. Why will you not let me go free?

Unead takes the wagon and drives off. I thought we would go with her but we will not. We will go our separate ways. It is right; there is a better chance to escape if we go alone. Irid would have a better chance without me, but she wants me to come with her. I should have said no; it would have been safer, but I cannot leave her. I hope that she will not leave me. It is a different type of trap, but it is still a trap. Maybe all of life is a trap. All we get to do is choose which trap we are caught in. I have chosen this one and I hope that I do not regret my choice. Will Irid regret her choice? She is in a trap too.

She hands me a bag and puts it over my back. I do not ask what is in it. She has one of her own she is carrying. She is no longer dressed as a courtesan because that would attract too much attention. Now she is dressed as a maidservant, like a maid sent out to market by her mistress. I think she is clearly too pretty to pass for a maid and say so.

She turns and looks at me. She does not bow demurely or avert her eyes. She smiles slightly and says that I am wrong and that there are plenty of maids prettier than the courtesans of the tower, but that most men do not look at them. If they are dressed shabbily or show low status, men do not look. What is beauty anyway, she asks? I am not sure. It is a question I have thought about before. What was it that Hilketa said all those years ago? I can no longer recall his words. Instead, I admit that I do not know what beauty is. I ask Irid what she thinks beauty is.

"Servants don't have time to think about these things," she replies.

We walk through the streets of the inner city. No one stops us. We manage to leave the inner city behind, and now we are walking through the outer city. I ask Irid where we are going, but she just tells me to hush. Servants don't talk amongst themselves while going about their business. We make our way between the clay brick walls and down alleyways. It is farther than I have gone from the tower for many years.

We do not follow the main thoroughfares. There is no need; we are on foot and Irid leads me by shortcuts between the houses. It is a long way to walk, and we reach the city gate just before the moon slips down below the horizon. We will not be allowed to leave the city before morning. I ask if we will find lodgings for the night but Irid shakes her head.

"Our mistress will not waste money on paying lodgings for

servants."

It seems we will sleep outside propped against a wall in one of the alleyways. I wonder how it is that Irid knows so much about the ways of servants. She takes some bread out of her pack and tears it into two parts. She hands me the larger of the two pieces and starts to eat the other. I hold the bread and look at it. I will be hungry tonight; this is meagre fare. But I have been hungry before. I have been so hungry that I have eaten mosses and dug for roots in black soil. It will be hard for us at least for a while, but we are together and that is what is important.

There are other servants sleeping in our alley. I sleep propped against the wall with my sack for a pillow. I lean against it as much to prevent it from being stolen as to make myself comfortable. I am tempted to look inside the sack, but a servant would not. It is none of his business what he has been asked to carry. The sack is not sealed shut. Some masters would seal the sack and if the seal is broken, the servant would be beaten and perhaps killed. It is to stop the servant from stealing the goods being moved. The fact there is no seal implies that I am to be trusted. It also suggests that the goods I carry are of little value and thus I am less likely to be robbed.

Irid is asleep. Even though her whole world is changed, she is asleep. I cannot sleep; there are too many thoughts going through my mind. My life has changed as much as hers; I am high priest no longer, and now what am I? It is something I must think on. I must find a new purpose. What is my new life?

I had forced myself on Irid. It is by virtue of my power as High Priest of Vatu that she is mine. Now that I hold no power, how then is she still mine? I gave away my power at her request. Come with me, she said. And in the moment I agreed, I became powerless.

When I turn and look at her, I wonder if she is still mine. Her eyes are closed in sleep, but the light from street lamps bathes her face and turns it into perfect smoothness. I long to touch her and to stroke her skin and hair. Her features are so perfectly composed it is hard to believe she is asleep. Perhaps she is awake, but I have seen her lie in perfect repose so many times, I am sure she is not awake.

If she were alone, would she be safe here? Would she have perhaps stayed in lodgings? If I had not come with her, would she have stayed with Unead? Her life is so much more complicated because of me, and because of Greba. She should hate us. All women should hate men. We give them reason enough. I have certainly given her reason to hate me.

In the morning, we buy fruit from a stall and eat it. It is a meagre breakfast, as befits a house servant. This is what my life will be now.

After we have eaten, we line up to leave the gate. It is slow waiting for the guards to inspect the papers of those leaving. They are making sure that no runaways escape from the city. Each person leaving, high or low, must have the required paperwork. All except for one, me, the High Priest. He does not need to show paperwork. He is above that, as I once was.

But now I must wait like all the others. That is not to say that all wait equally. We are not quite the lowest, but we are close to the lowest and so we will wait the longest, or close to the longest. It is midmorning before the guards finally call us forward. Irid presents our papers. They have been prepared just the day before and Unead's signature is on them. It is a risk, but it is less risky than using a fake signature. The guard barely looks at them. We are so unimportant that he does not care. What does he care if a few runaways escape? There is only starvation and death for them. Or they will be caught and killed. He has caught thousands of runaways. It is a small thing. I look at him and I can see all of him in a single moment. He does not care for the brutality that some of the guards like to show the runaway: torture, rape, beatings. It is distasteful to him, but he does not care. To him the runaways are nothing and if the other guards wish to act out their base natures, then what of it. His nature is not such, his only vice is indifference. He thinks of us as less than real; he thinks of us as characters in a book or in a play, less than that. We are not of sufficient interest to merit inclusion in a book or play. We are peasants and servants. We are slaves; it is a word we do not use, but it is what we are. Avoiding the word does not change the fact. We are all slaves to one thing or another. I have chosen to be a slave to the author of all things. I have changed my master. I am no longer slave to the dark. I hope my master is kind to me, and to Irid. Be merciful, author of all things, if mercy is within you.

I find myself saying a prayer, a heretic prayer that the guards will let us pass. He holds our papers in our hands and in a way he holds more than that. In a way, he holds our lives. Should he identify that we are not house servants but runaways, then surely our lives will be over, or at least the lives we hoped for.

It seems like an age but must surely only be an instant until he waves us through, handing the papers back to us. He is handing back our life, the life we imagine. But then I realize that nothing is ever as we imagine, never. It is not my life he hands back to me, but only my hope. Still, it is enough.

We walk away from the gate with the crowd of people travelling out to the dark lands. I want to say so much. I want to ask Irid about so many things. But there are people within earshot and these things cannot be discussed now. I must trust her. It is my wish that she shares the same dreams that I do. Somehow we will make them real, if not in the way we imagine, then in some other way.

We are heading along the river. If we had money we could pay for a place on a barge and let the water take us to a new life. But we have no money, or rather a house servant would have no money and so we must appear to have none. I am certain there is money in either my sack or Irid's, most likely both. Anyway, where would the river take us to? We do not know where we are going or at least I don't. Each step is simply a step into the unknown.

We walk in silence, as is befitting. Servants do not speak to each other, it is discouraged. It is through talk that plots and schemes are hatched. It is through talk that rebellion is organized. Servants do not talk to each other, at least not in public. But they must, for plots are hatched and rebellion is organized. I have read the reports, but they are hatched and organized in private. In secret trysts, lovers plan escapes, or the murder of a master who has forced himself upon a servant, or mistress that is cruel.

In private, plans are made to steal goods and sell them or to hide weapons. It is in secret that the doctrine of the heretics is shared.

We will have our secret moments.

Irid walks in front and I walk a few paces back and to the side. It is fitting, a female servant is usually prized more than a manservant. There are few manservants that serve in the house. It is mostly for heavy work or for guarding gates and doorways. A female servant is more highly prized; they will attend to household duties, they will cook and clean. They will attend to the mistress and, if they are pretty, perhaps to the needs of the master as well. They are not courtesans, but some use them as such. It is not unheard of and many house maids will die after a mistress discovers her husband's infidelity. It is a small thing to kill a servant. Such a thing will not be questioned.

When the moon is at its highest, we stop and rest. We sit on a mossy bank at the side of the road. We have some fruit from this morning and more of the hard dark bread that we ate last night.

Now the road is quieter and we can speak when it is clear of travellers. I should ask Irid all the questions I have stored up and perhaps she has questions for me. But I cannot find the words. I search for them but they escape me. How do I ask if she hopes for the same thing as I do, when I do not know what I hope for? How do I say that I am sorry for all the cares I have given her, when if I had not done as I had done, I would not be with her and I would not be free? I am glad we were discovered. I am glad I have left the darkness behind. How can I say these things?

And what words can she not find; what would she say but cannot? The silence is a gulf between us that cannot be crossed by words. And then after she has eaten, she reaches and takes my hand in hers. No words were needed after all. There are some things better than words, many things.

There is no intimacy here. How could there be? We are at the side of a road where many people are passing. We are runaways. We are fugitives that dare not speak to each other. And yet it is in this moment that I feel closer to Irid than ever. I have never felt so close to her before. I hope that I can keep this moment and make it mine, like a jewel for me to keep and from time to time hold in my hand and admire over and over again. This jewelled moment, the moment that finally I knew for certain that all my hopes in her were true, the moment that I first knew that she loved me.

Chapter Thirty-One
Together

As we travel away from the Tower of the Sun, I realize that we have no destination. We will not meet up with Unead. All we are doing is running. Is this Greba's great plan, to run like rats until we are hunted down?

Now the roads are quieter and we walk slower. Perhaps there are no hunters. It is possible that Kong has lost interest in us. What does he have to gain now anyway? Does he even know that I am gone? I have sent my other self to rule in my place.

Irid is no longer dressed as a house slave, she is dressed as a peasant and so am I. Her clothes no longer fit her as she has begun to swell around her stomach. At first, it was a shock, but why should it be? It is only what all couples do. We will have to stop and settle. She cannot go on walking day after day, and she is getting weaker. We could stop at a town, but what would we do there? We still have money, lots of it. But we do not wish to attract attention.

Almost anyone travelling is watched. Only merchants travel and they must have papers. Everywhere they go, they are searched for contraband. They are not trusted, and we do not have merchant's papers. I think that Unead must have had permissions to travel and sell, but we are not with her, and we do not know where she is.

"We must stop," I say to Irid. "You cannot go on and besides, running further will not help."

She looks at me doubtfully. But I can see that her strength is nearly spent. Perhaps we could buy a horse to carry her. But when I suggest it, we both know that would not be possible. No one cares about peasants; the poor can travel as they like, no one cares, but the poor do not ride horses unless they are stolen.

We stop in the mid moon and lie back to watch the clouds pass over the white, half-round face. I have some bread and offer her some. She eats it, and her face looks painfully thin. She has been ill most mornings and has difficulty keeping food down.

"Where will we stop?" she asks. "Where should we hide?"

There is no point in hiding, there is no point in running. I reach out and place a hand on hers. It is still fine and soft. It is not a peasant's hand. We cannot hide that way. I look at her face, still so delicate. It is a wonder that no one has sought to take her from me, other than Kong.

"It is your child, not his," she says. How can she know? It is only what I wish to hear. She is telling me what I wish to know. No man can ever know these things for certain.

"But it could be his?" I say.

There is bitterness and reproach in my voice even though I try to keep them from it. Does she hear it? Does she think I blame her? I have no wish to, but I do, even though I am to blame. It is I who brought him to her. If I had left her, then he would have had no interest in her. She will not deny it. She will not lie to me and for that I am grateful. The painful truth is better than any delusion.

"I should have killed him." But I did kill him; over and over, so many times. It made no difference. He always returns, no matter how often he is destroyed.

We are stuck. We cannot go on. We must face up to the truth.

We are in a dark forest. There is a path but it leads nowhere. Here is as much a trap as anywhere else. We must make a new path; one only we have walked.

After she has eaten and rested, I help her stand. She follows me through the trees. I stop and look back. I can no longer see the road. A bit further on I stop again. Here the trees have thinned out. The ground is wet at the edges of the glade where a spring issues out. I could dig a well here. There is stone to line a basin. I gather wood and start a small fire. Irid begins to cook some rice. It is very peaceful.

Other than birds and wind and water, it is silent. Other than the crackle of fire and the bubble of cooking and the breath of us, it is silent. Other than the rubbing of cloth as we move or the crushing of grass as we walk, it is silent. No words are spoken, none, but both of us know this place is as good as any other.

In silence, we eat rice and some dried fish. I am thinking about where to build our house, and how. I am thinking about the well I must build, and how I will collect food from the forest. I will have to hunt for meat. I will need to rig up a shelter first. Over by the trees would be a good place. But the house should be on the gentle rise where the ground is drier. I will build a foundation of stone and then use timber for the walls and floor. The roof can be made of rushes cut from the wet ground by the well.

After I have eaten, in silence, I rise and go to work.

Now we are alone or not alone; we have each other. The work is harder than I thought and there are some days that I return to our shelter too exhausted to sleep. There are plenty of rocks lying about to make the foundation of the house, but the wet ground makes them difficult to move. I need to lever them up out of the soil and as they lift, I can hear the sound of the mud sucking against me. It is a week before I have made a low walled enclosure. On top of this, I set lengths of round wood, then build up, fixing them into place. I cut more wood and this time I split the logs lengthwise. I am grateful that our sack contained an axe and a whetstone. Even so, it is hard work. I fix the logs crosswise to form a floor.

When it is finished, Irid comes and walks on it. She is laughing in the moonlight. She is not strong enough to cut logs or to help with the floor, but she helped levering some of the bigger stones, and she fashioned the fixings for the floor. The floor is strong and flexible. I think perhaps I should have waited until there were walls and roof to protect my floor from the weather. Irid says that if that is how I feel, then perhaps I should pull the floor up again. She is mocking me and we laugh together.

I am a poor builder, how could I be anything else? My hands have never known harder work than to lift a pen or play a flute or to strangle someone to death. Honest labour is a new experience. When the moon is down and we are lying together, Irid will take my hand and trace her still delicate fingers over the calluses. I am not ashamed of them. I thought I would never do this, but part of me has lived the life of a peasant before. Not a peasant I remind myself, a prosperous merchant's son. I try not to think of that, of how I slew them all in my jealousy. I wonder briefly if the other me will come here seeking revenge. It would be just, but it would be monstrous. Is murder ever really just? I do not think so.

It is a good time for us. We have water and we have food. Some days, I go hunting. It is something else new to me. I am not a quick learner. Mostly, it is rabbits I catch in my snares or small birds like thrushes and finches. I think a bow would be better, but in the dark, even by moonlight, it would be difficult to shoot anything so small, and I would need to be very close to catch deer.

It is good to go hunting. I had thought that it would be a cruel thing and often I feel guilty about killing rabbits and birds. But it is what I am, a carnivore and a hunter. It is how we live, by the blood of animals.

We have plenty of firewood, and we still have plenty of money in the sacks we brought from the City of the Sun. When it is close to summer, I go into town and purchase some seed. I buy peas and corn. It will not be a big crop, but it will help. I would like to have grown rice, but I would have to clear a field down by the well. I'm not sure how good a crop it would give. There is so much for me to do.

When I come back to the farm, it is a farm now, at least in my mind. Irid makes bread with the flour I have brought. She makes it into a ball of dough by mixing it with water and oil and then places it on a large rock at the edge of the fire. It is rough and charred when she takes it out. She is no better a baker than I am a farmer. It seems we must learn together.

When I tell her this, she laughs. This life is far from the one we lived before.

"Do you miss it?" I ask her. And I think of her fine clothes, her servants and her fine pavilion.

"It was like a cage," she replies, shaking her head. "There is much more to life than just comfort. Do you miss your life?"

"No," I answer, "it seems that Kong has set us both free."

"I'm still afraid," she tells me. "But, not of the same things as before. I'm not sure what I'm afraid of. I'm certain no one will come looking for us here. I don't need to fear you either."

"Were you afraid of me?" I ask.

"Yes," she replies, "to you I was just a hostage to be used against my father."

"And now?" I can barely stand to hear her reply.

"Now it is just us."

Raising the walls and roof is harder work. It is not physically more difficult, but it requires more thought. How will I raise a timber? How will I make it fast? First I build a frame flat on the ground and then I pull it upright with ropes. Again, Irid helps, but even so, it is difficult. I draw plans in the dust while I rest and when the moon is down and it is too dark to work. I make small models with twigs and string. Our house will not be large. It will be little more than two rooms. There will be two small windows facing the moonrise and a low door between them. It is something I have never done before and it is challenging, but we are making progress. The walls rise slowly and then quickly. Once I have two walls raised it is easier. I have finished building the frame and I am now thatching the roof.

When that is done, we move in. The house is small, and we sleep on a pile of dry moss wrapped in blankets. There is a hearth where we keep a small fire going, and we bring water from the spring every day. It is basic; it is a home such as any runaway slave or peasant would build. It is warm and dry. It is so different from the fine house that Irid dwelt in before and so different from the tower. But it is not so different from the house I lived in with Tanden and Huneko, or the village that I sent the Black Death to consume. They are hard thoughts that come to my mind when I think of them.

We talk little, Irid and I. What would we say? It is a joke the author of all things has played on us. It is a good joke, but still. I am freer here than when I ruled the whole of the shaded land.

Irid is kind to me. When I look in her eyes I see no reproach for what has been done to her. Nor does she complain about carrying the child. I should think more on that, and so should she. I have been trained in the ways of the body, but even so, I think it would be better if there were some other women here to help. It is usually women who deal with these things. It would be better if I took her to the village to deliver her child. When I say this, she shakes her head.

"We cannot do that. People would want to know more about us."

But I do not think she is correct. No one cares about the poor unless it is to take from them. If we have enough money to pay for a midwife, no one will care. There is a village not too far away, but she is insistent that she will not go. There may be someone hunting for us. I wonder if she is right. It is possible that things have changed since we left the tower.

I am afraid, but now it is a different type of fear. I am afraid for Irid and for the child. And there is another fear that I will not say, and neither will she. But I think back to that morning when I wakened from sleep and found her washing herself after he had been there. How I wish I had killed him. I will kill him someday. I will make him pay for all that he has done, in his current life and in the ones past. I will make him pay for it all.

And yet there is something. We are happy. When I look in Irid's eyes, I no longer see fear or distrust. There is something else there now. And at night, when we lie together, she reaches out for me in her sleep and her hand nestles in mine. It is still small and delicate, but her skin is no longer the soft skin of a courtesan, or a rich man's wife and plaything. If she longs for fine silks and servants and the refinement of the City of the Sun, then she does not let that longing show.

The time of the child coming is near. Irid is unable to move freely. There is still much work to do. There is furniture to build, and I want to patch some cracks to make the house more wind tight. I want to make a paved area outside the house and to make a small kitchen garden so we can grow food when the Sun is out. I would like to get a proper stove and a bathing tub. I would like to make a bed and cot for the child. There is always more to be done. When I talk to Irid about what needs to be done, she tells me that the house is fine.

I can no longer go hunting; I will not leave her. The child could come any moon round. How I wish her mother was here. There is a fear within me. Unspoken fears rise up; she might die. This is something that I have done to her. Had we stayed in the City of the Sun, she could have made sure this would not happen, or that there were those who could help her.

She is not afraid, and there is no blame or anger in her voice or eyes. But of course, she is trained to keep all emotion from her appearance. I trained her to do that. I can never know for certain what she feels. But then can you ever know what anyone feels or thinks? Sometimes we do not even know what we feel and think, not really. These things are hidden from us. Even when we think we know, we are deceiving ourselves. All life is a mystery. I think of all the things that I have learned in my life, and I think on those who have taught me. I have trusted them. I have had faith in them, but I do not know if they were lying or were mistaken. If these truths are false, what then replaces them? It seems that all things are taken on faith.

But my thoughts are disrupted by a low moan. I turn and see Irid. There is excitement in her face and she is looking to me.

"It is starting," she says.

There is little that I can do to help. I hold her hand and try to comfort her. I laugh silently as I realize that I know now exactly what she is thinking. It seems that somehow it is possible to know another's thoughts. I am wrong.

Each minute, each second, takes forever. Irid's skin is pale and covered with a thin coating of perspiration. Endurance is what is needed, and it is what she does. The birth is bloody and long. But it is not me who endures. It is different for me. I can do little. I give her tea made from the bark of willow and wash her body with water.

It seems to go on forever, and then it comes. It comes quickly; a new life. I leave them together. She holds the child and feeds it. She is tired and must sleep. The child will live. Why do I even doubt that it will? I go out to the well to fetch water and to think.

But he is there, the author of all things. His words come. *I know what is wrong with you. You think this is not your child. You think that Kong has cheated you of this. A child, it is the thing that all men value most and all men doubt. No matter how they must trust in the fidelity of a woman.*

I doubt so many things. I doubt her and myself. I doubt the child. I hear the voice of the author of all things. Can you take my doubt away, I ask him, but he shakes his head. It is a thing he will not do.

You must realize, he tells me, *that no child is yours and that no life is yours. If you are the child's father or if Kong is the child's father, she is not yours, nor his. She is her own, and she is mine.*

When I return, I do not trust myself to look at the child and not hate her. The author of all things says no. He says that to hate is always wrong and to love is always right. He says I am wrong to hate Kong, although he does not say that I should trust him. I wish I could be as the author of all things wishes. I wish that I could unravel things back to before the child was born, but even that would not be enough. I wish I could erase things back to before Kong raped her, back to before I took Irid from Greba. But even that is not enough, I would have to go back to before I was born, before I was conceived. Further back. There is no end to the unravelling.

Would you erase everything? the author of all things asks. *Is there nothing of worth? Can you not see what I have given you?*

I shake my head. Anger rises within me. This is what he has given me. It would be better if the child died. I could take it and dash its head against the stones around the well, or smother it with a blanket. I could take it and leave it in the forest for the beasts. It is a frail thing that I could snuff out so easily. I have killed so many times before. It would be so easy. This child could be the child of Kong. How can I let it live?

We could have another, the next child would be mine. It would be as if we were the first parents of the whole world. There would be only us.

Chapter Thirty-Two
Farming

But I find that I will not slay the child. I ask the author of all things to take this thing from me. Let it die in its sleep or choke or die of any of a thousand other ways. But the author of all things whispers that he will not.

The child is given to you. It is a gift. I will not take it back. You will not slay the child because to do so would make you once again a monster; what would it make me if I killed the child?

But the author of all things has killed many children too. Each child that dies of famine or of neglect; why has he not saved them if he is all-powerful?

I have saved them, he tells me, but I do not believe him.

You could ease my mind with just one word. Tell me the child is mine.

But if it was not yours, would you have me lie to you?

I would know one way or another.

Will you believe my words? You have said already that you do not believe me. If I tell you this, it's just another thing for you to doubt. Then what? You have heard my words; I have told you to love the child. No matter what, Kong is not the father of this child. Even if he has forced his seed upon Irid, he is not a father to this child. He will never know her, nor will he love her. That is something only you can do. It is something that Kong can never be. It is my gift to you. It is what will make you better than you are, become a father, her father.

When I re-enter the cottage, Irid and the child are both

sleeping. I add wood to the fire and settle in a blanket. I leave the child with her mother. The two of them sleep. Too many thoughts still go around in my head. How foolish I have been. I have allowed Irid to become precious to me and for her I have given up my priesthood, even if that priesthood is a sham.

I am both joyous and full of regret. My mind switches back and forth. It is as if I am two men.

It is many days before Irid regains her strength. During this time she feeds the child and lies in bed. I bring her water and help her to wash. I cook rice and bring it to her. Sometimes she offers the child to me, holding it out to me.

"Here, take her," she says.

When I hold the child, I understand the words of the author of all things. The child is not mine; I am hers. I find a smile playing on my lips. I find a softness within me. I, who have never been gentle, am gentle now.

Irid feeds the child, but the child is still hungry. I boil rice, and strain the water into a skin bag. Irid dribbles the rice water onto the child's lips and she licks it. Eventually the child learns to suck from the skin bag. Sometimes the child is hungry and Irid is asleep, then I take the child and feed her from the skin bag.

The child grows. She is healthy and will not die, although she cries a great deal and seems always to be hungry. I am glad the child will not die.

I say to Irid that we should name the child, but she says that we cannot, that all children can be named only on the dawn. I have no knowledge of women's ways, but it seems strange to wait to name a child. What will happen if the child dies before Sun-up? Does the child go into the darkness known only to the author of all things? I must ask him, but when I do, he does not answer.

Sunday will come within a moon turn. If we will plant crops and harvest, then I must go and buy seed. Irid is strong enough now to care for the child without me. I have cut a great pile of timber and will drag some on a sledge into the town and sell it. We have gold, lots of it, but it is better that people can see that our money has come from somewhere. I will need the sledge to bring back the seed. A cart would be better, but I am not skilled enough to make wheels, and a sledge is better over the rough ground.

I set out dragging the sledge behind me. I wish I had a horse or a mule to pull it for me. But runaway peasants that settle in the forest do not have horses or mules. I consider buying a horse. I will decide when I get there. I have enough gold, but it would mean having to build a stable and feed it. I am not sure we will grow enough to feed the three of us, never mind feeding a horse.

When I reach the road, the going is easier. It is almost a day's walk to the village and it takes longer dragging a load of timber. I will get there late and will have to stay over. I have left early, but I shouldn't have bothered. I should have stayed over on the way. I could have taken blankets and slept by the road.

There are a few people heading to the town. I am not the only one that needs to buy seed before Sunday. A man carrying a sack falls in with me.

"If you let me put my sack on your sledge," he says, "I will help you pull it. That way you'll make better progress and it will be better for my back."

There is sense in what he says. I stop and ask to feel the weight in his sack. It is heavy but not too heavy.

"What is in it?" I ask him.

"Oak galls," he tells me. "They are used to make dyes fast or to make ink or tan leather."

I agree to let him put the sack on the sledge and hand him one of the ropes to tie around his waist. Together we drag the sledge. It is easier with two of us.

The man tells me his name is Baso. He says he lives by himself. Mostly he lives by what he collects from the forest, and what he can hunt. But he likes to grow vegetables on Sundays.

"There is nothing sweeter than a fresh grown cabbage," he says. He tells me that when he has harvested them, he salts them and pickles them.

"It helps keep scurvy away," he tells me. "You should get some cabbage. Rice and corn are all very well, but there is no variety; a little pickled cabbage will make a plate of rice taste sweeter."

I agree with him and decide to get some cabbage seed as well as rice.

"And radish," he suggests.

Baso is taller than me and broader. But he is quick and nimble. He is pulling more than his share on the sledge and for that I am grateful, and also relieved. A man who will work hard is usually an honest man.

I ask him where he will spend the night when we get to the town.

"I have a sister there," he says. "She is never very pleased to see me, but she will feed me and let me sleep in her shed. To be fair, it is her husband that does not like me around. He fancies himself to be something and does not like to be reminded that his brother-in-law is nothing. Besides, I'm not comfortable in their house."

I ask Baso if there is a cheap inn where I could stay. He says that he will ask his sister. For the rest of the journey we make small talk, and not much of that. It is hard enough work dragging the sledge. When we arrive at the town, I ask Baso what the name of the town is.

"It is called Basseriko," he tells me. It is a small village really, much smaller than the town where Tanden and Huneko lived. The village has no walls, and the market is set up just on the outskirts. There is no village square, just two rows of sturdy houses facing each other. At one end of the village there is a well. It is the only settlement for many miles. So, although it is small, many people have come to trade. It is unlikely that I will find an inn to stay in, but Baso says that it might be possible to stay with him in his sister's shed. He points it out to me and tells me to come with him. He knocks on the door and his sister comes out carrying a lantern. The moon is almost down.

She looks at her brother, then at me.

"Who's your friend?" she asks.

"Just someone from the road," replies Baso. "Can he stay in the shed tonight?"

His sister looks uncertain.

"I don't mean to trouble you," I said.

"It's not that," replies his sister, brushing her greying hair back. "Come on, then." And with that she pulls out a small key from her coat and leads us behind the house. She unlocks the door of the shed and lets us in, then hands Baso the key.

"I'm holding you responsible for him," says his sister.

"I'm sure he'll be fine," Baso replies.

His sister still looks uncertain, but she says nothing and leaves. Later she comes with two bowls of rice. I eat mine and then lie down. I am very tired and go to sleep almost straight away.

When the moon rises, Baso shakes me by the shoulder until I'm awake.

"The market will be open now," he says.

It is not much of a market. Traders have come to the village and put their goods on display. Some of them have erected tents, but most of the goods are shown on top of low wagons. I sell my timber to one of the traders, and then go looking for seed. I buy rice and cabbage seed. I buy a small bag of salt and some vinegar. There is a trader selling dried fish, and I think it would be good for Irid's health to have some. I have finished buying my goods by high moon. I have packed my sledge and think about setting out. The sledge is much lighter than it was when it was loaded with timber, but still I am reluctant to start pulling just yet.

Some of the traders have horses that they use to pull their carts, but most have only hand carts. I look to see if any of them will sell a cart. I think of Huneko and his cart and I wonder what became of it. It will be burned. I'm sure all that village will have been burned. Yes, I burned it. I made sure that all of it was destroyed. I made sure that all that remember it were destroyed. Only I remember it now. It is a pile of black ash.

Eventually, I head out for our cottage. The sledge is light and I make better progress than I made coming, even with Baso's help. It is possible that I will be home before the next moon rises. The thought fills me with pleasure. I am not sure why.

Irid will be tired. She will make me rice and then I will sleep by the fire while she and the child rest. I am tired enough that I could sleep for a moon turn, maybe more. I should have brought her something pretty from the market, but there was nothing in the market pretty enough for her. Once, she had only the finest. It seems foolish to think of bringing her a ribbon or trinket.

I trudge on and as I do, my mind wanders to her again and again. It is better to think of my pretty wife than to think of the long walk ahead of me. The road is quiet, and I do not pass anyone either coming or going. I am glad that I set out early from the fair. I have no wish to have to stop and let others pass me on the road. It is better to keep the sledge moving. When I leave the road, it is more difficult. Roots and stones snag and catch the sledge. Still I must push on; to stop now when I am so close to home would be foolish. I am so tired and each step forward is laboured and slow. But it is not far now. I will keep going. Eventually, I will arrive and Irid will be waiting for me, with the child.

Although there is no path, I can see the tracks where I have passed before. I need simply follow them. I had thought it would be easier to travel this way than when I left, but for some reason, it is harder. I cannot stop. There are people waiting for me.

When I reach the clearing, the moon is still up and by the sliver of light it gives, I can see our cottage. It is dark, and there is no smoke coming from the hearth. I drag the sledge to the side of the cottage and cover the seed with sacking that I weigh down with rocks to keep it from birds and beasts.

I push the door open, and Irid whispers, "Who is there?"

"Only me," I reply. "Who else did you think it would be?"

"Of course," she says, "it could only be you."

She gets up and lights a candle. The moon has now slipped below the trees. By candlelight, she raises the fire from the embers on the hearth and swings our iron pot over the fire.

"It will be ready soon," she tells me and hands me some bread. "Here, eat this just now while you wait."

"I am more tired than hungry," I tell her, but I still eat the bread. It is a few days old and dry. Irid has gone to fetch me water. While she is gone, she leaves the child with me. I hold it, and while I do, the child looks at me with unblinking eyes.

When she returns, she takes the child. It does not take long for the broth to cook. It is made with hulled barley, and is thick and salty. There is a little meat in it, from some game that I caught before I left. Irid sits watching while I eat.

"How was the journey?" she asks.

"Good. It took longer than I thought. That is why I am so late."

"I am happy that you are back so soon, husband," she says.

"It is good to be back," I tell her. And it is. I am pleased to see her and to see the child.

"I meant to bring you something," I continue, "but there was nothing much to bring. I could have brought ribbons or something. Next time you can come with me and decide what you want for yourself."

"Thank you, husband," Irid says.

Things have become so formal once again. The closeness we shared when we travelled is starting to fade. There is now distance between us. Perhaps there is always distance and closeness is an illusion. Perhaps I imagine the whole thing and there is nothing changed at all.

There is not much to say about the time before Sunrise. I prepared the wet ground beside the well for the rice seed. I levelled it and made low walls of earth to hold the water in a shallow pool. I carried the seed down to the pool and left it there. I have prepared a short bed and planted it so that the seed will spring up when the Sun rises rather than having to plant it during Sunrise. When the seedlings are tall enough, I will have to transplant them and then weed the beds. If we are lucky, there will be fish spawned in our rice bed. The fish help to control the weed growth, and they can be left in runoff pools to catch during the year.

I have made a small cradle for the child. After I have harvested the rice, Irid will name the child. I have asked what she will call the child, but she says it is bad luck to tell the name beforehand.

We sleep outside on blankets and we lie facing the Sun. It is cold, but we have lit a small fire. The child is lying in the cradle. When the first light of dawn slips over the forest, we rise. Irid is holding the child, and she reaches out to the Sunlight as if she could catch it in her hand. I close my eyes for a few moments and feel the warmth of Sunlight on my skin. Even this far from the Tower of the Sun, it feels good. I head off to check the rice seedlings and to plant the cabbage and onion seed that I have bought, leaving Irid and the child to play in the Sun.

It is hard work farming. Even when I lived with Huneko, I did not have to farm. It is the bending that is difficult. I have to plant and hoe and weed. The rice seedlings have shot well, and I lift them to plant into the paddy. I wade into the water and push the seedlings into the soft wet mud. I am pleased to see that there are small carp swimming between the planted rice.

This far from the Sun, I will only get one harvest. But I must still watch that the vegetables do not bolt. I need to water them frequently and harvest them just as they are fully swollen, but before they begin to shrivel. The cabbages are ready first. It is possible that I might have had two harvests of cabbage, but I would have had to have bought more seed, and it would have taken more of my time. The onions do not need to be lifted. I simply wait until the flowering spike begins to show, then break it off.

The rice paddy needs constant weeding. Even with the fish eating the weed, I need to lift and pull to prevent the pond from becoming clogged up.

Chapter Thirty-Three
Hope

Irid brings me some water and rye bread to eat.

"It is a good harvest," she says.

"Yes," I agree. "There will be plenty for us. It will be more than enough to keep us through the year."

While I work, she comes and helps clear the paddy field. The child is held in a drape of cloth over her back.

"Who would have thought to see a fine lady work in a field," I say, and she laughs. It seems that the closeness is back.

"I am no fine lady," she tells me. "Not now."

I am leaning over cutting leaves from cabbages and putting them in a sack. Later I will chop them and pickle them in brine, vinegar and salt fish.

"Do you miss it?" I ask.

"I miss my mother," she tells me, "and my father. But other than that, no. It seemed every day I lived in fear."

"Fear of what?" I ask.

"Of you mostly," she replied.

"You should still fear me," I say. I have said it in jest, but when I say the words I know it is true.

Irid stops and looks at me.

"All women fear their husbands," she says, "but I will not fear you. I know you meant it lightheartedly, and now you are thinking that I should not trust you, and that you do not trust yourself. All of my fears did not stop Kong, and all of my fears will not stop you. I will not live in fear anymore. If you betray me, then there is nothing I can do. I do not think that you will. I choose to believe in you. I choose not to fear."

They are not the words a fine lady says to her lord. They are not the words of poets. But they are the sweetest words I have ever heard.

As the Sun goes down, I drain the paddy. Irid chases the fish into the runoff pool and one of them is left floundering in the retreating water. She lifts it and carries it in a pot to the pool. Soon the pool is thick with fish and herons are circling around waiting to rob us of our catch. I wish I had bought a net to put over the pond. Irid is busy weaving a cover out of fern fronds. They will wither and die, but they will protect the fish for a while. I will make a netting with heather roots tomorrow. If I had my bow, I could shoot a few herons and we could have game.

We are less busy now, and Irid is walking through the wet meadow collecting flowers. In her hand are bugloss and rue, birds-foot and vetch; they are small and mean flowers that no one ever thinks of and yet in her hand they are like the finest blossoms.

She comes and lays the flowers by the child's crib. I watch her as I gather the rice from the field. She gasps when she reaches the cradle.

"What is it?" I ask more sharply than I meant to.

"I don't know," she replies.

"Is the child all right?" I ask, and I am surprised at how anxious I am. It is possible that something may have injured the child while we worked. Sundays are dangerous; there are beasts and insects that can harm a child.

"I think so," Irid says. "I am not sure."

"Not sure? What do you mean not sure?" and I leave the basket of rice in the field and run towards the child.

When I arrive, the child is looking up at me. She seems well except for one thing. Her skin is glowing golden. Her hair and eyes are glowing. There is a golden light shining through her blanket. It is her that is shining.

"What is it?" asks Irid. "What can it mean?"

I am speechless. Words will not come. There are no words. What is the good of them? They can explain nothing. The child is glowing. As the Sun sets and darkness starts to return to the clearing, she glows brighter and brighter.

There is no answer to any of the questions we ask. Why? How?

There is no answer to any of that. She glows with the light of the Sun. It is and there is no reason or cause other than it is.

"She is like a candle in the dark," says Irid.

Indeed, she is a light that will attract things in the darkness. Already moths have gathered around the crib, flitting in the fading Sunlight and in the soft glow from the child's face.

We stand together for a while and then, before the Sun sets, Irid lifts the child, then runs to the well. I follow after her, and there I watch as she holds the child under the water for a few seconds. I think for a moment that she will drown the child, but then I realize that it's some woman's ritual for naming her child. When she lifts the child from the well, drops of water scatter, lit by the glow of her skin. They are like diamonds. But when they land, they run away to nothing.

Irid says one word: "Alaba." It is my daughter's name. It is who she is.

Now Irid has wrapped her again in cloth and leaves me to finish the harvest in the dying embers of the Sunlight. She goes into the cottage, taking both the child and the cradle with her. I continue to harvest our rice. I gather it up in baskets. Later, perhaps tomorrow, I will thresh the grain, but not tonight. I have lit a fire and sit. Irid comes and joins me later. She has the child with her, Alaba with her. She is still glowing, but the light from her is fading.

Irid has brought bread and dried fish. She has brewed tea from the flowers that she gathered. It is fresh and green and I am glad of it. It is better than wine or beer. She has a cup of water from our well and she hands it to me. I look and see that the water is shining.

"What can it mean?" she asks.

"I do not know, but I am a heretic," I tell her, although she does not look surprised. "I no longer follow the darkness. I have looked in the dark and I have found no answers."

"Have you found answers in heresy?" she asks.

"Some, but not all," I admit.

"And does your heresy have an answer for this?"

"Perhaps, but the child is well and lives. Is that not answer enough for now?"

"For now, yes," says Irid, "but what will become of her?"

"The light is fading from her even now," I tell Irid. "Maybe that is the end of it, and it is done and over."

"And what of this?" She holds the cup of water up. It is still glowing as bright as ever. I take it from her, but I am afraid to let the water touch me. Who knows how the water might change me.

And yet nothing changes. We still live alone, just us two. Irid is healthy now and helps with all that we do. We build a porch to store food and gear. Every day we have the same routine; it is the same routine as small farmers everywhere. We rise with the moon, we hunt, we gather food, we cook food, we eat, we sleep.

Only Alaba changes. She is growing fast. There is still a faint glow from her skin and hair, but now it is weak and it will not shine through her clothes. She learns to sit up and feed on rice gruel. She learns to follow things with her eyes and make noises. She learns to crawl.

Mostly Irid cares for her, but it is a pleasure when she hands the child to me for a few moments. It is of course a thing that men should not do, to care for a child, but it is not so unusual amongst the poor that men care for their own. There is a need for it and so they must, but also, they have less honour to lose than warriors and priests. I have no honour. I am the lowest of men in the whole of the dark lands.

I have turned my back on honour. What value has it? It will not feed the hungry or heal the sick. Honour will not aid the weary or strengthen the weak. It is simply a burden we place on the shoulders of men and I am well rid of it. If I am to be despised because I have no honour, then I will despise honour and those that seek it.

Honour is just another word for vanity. I do not imagine that I am too great a person to care for a child. Nor I am too great a person to eat the flesh of hunted beasts. I am not too great a person to rest when I am weary. Let the vain guard their honour and let them starve and sicken and weary. I am well rid of it.

But there is one that I wish will think well of me. I wish that Irid thinks well of me. I wish that she thinks of me as deserving of her affection. I wish that she has affection for me, and that she thinks well of me. All I do now is for her and for our child, for Alaba. It is the sweetness, not of riches, but of living together. I find myself content with cold rice eaten around the fireplace watching Alaba in the arms of her mother. It is a finer thing than any, finer than watching swordsmen duel or dancers. It is finer than feasting. Finer than ruling or judging. It is enough and better than any other thing.

I worry that it is not enough for Irid. I worry that she will tire of this life of toil. My mind drifts to ways to make her happy. There are only small things we can do. We are still hunted, I am sure. If we did not have the child, we would be running still. What is the best way to escape the hunt? Is running really any safer than staying? But do we have a choice? We cannot take the child and run. We must wait here like mice in a hole.

"They will find us."

Irid says nothing. At first I think she has not heard. I think that I have not said the words out loud. But then I see that she is holding the child tightly and shaking ever so slightly. I move beside her.

"We can hide. We can pretend this is real. In the end they will come."

"It is real," she says. "It is just not forever, nothing is. We cannot save ourselves, but we must save her."

When I was High Priest, what would I have done to a glowing child brought before me? I know the answer; the child would not be allowed to live. Vatu would not allow it to live.

"This must do for now. I have said that I will not live in fear. There is nothing else we can do."

It is almost as if I am back in the cage of darkness that Vatu built for me. And yet it is different and if he takes me back there, I will be free. As long as I have no fear, I am free.

"What can we do for Alaba?" I ask.

The brightness of her skin continues to fade. Each day it gets paler but it does not disappear. She will never be able to live freely like we do. When he finds her, he will kill her, and us. Our lives will be over. Irid will go into the darkness where the author of all things will take her and lead her into a new and better life. Alaba too must be taken by the author of all things. I will be reborn into this hell as I have been reborn countless times before. The mountains, the rivers and the seas will be unmarked by my passing.

All things must die, whispers the author of all things. *You must die, she must die, the child must die.* It is a whisper not of despair but of hope. If death will come regardless, then we do not need to fear it or to run from it. We can live instead.

Chapter Thirty-Four
Lies

The tower is no place to keep Algria. She cannot be hidden here, not in her condition. The twelve are aware of her and seek to destroy her, and through her destroy me. It is what they do, destroy things. It is what I do.

She is swelling up and the child within her grows, but as it does, fear grows within me. I cannot treat her well. I can treat her as no more than a courtesan, which is what she is, or what she was. I no longer have her in my quarters, but in rooms near the base of the tower. I should move her into the City of the Sun, but if I do, I am not sure that I can keep her safe.

Kong will kill her if he can, and perhaps some of the others. They are wary of me, as well they should be. Perhaps I should slay them all. Perhaps I should wipe them all out. It would save Algria from them. But Vatu will not allow it. He will not have all his disciples slain, not to save a woman.

I wonder if in all the lifetimes past, there has been a time where all of us have been reborn at once. Has a plague come and taken us all at once? Who brings the reborn to the tower then and who will train them in the ways of darkness? And as I think on it, it is clear that this happened a hundred thousand times. In the immensity of time, all things have happened. And when it happened, Vatu has brought us back to him and trained us in his ways. There is nothing new in life or in darkness. Not even this, that I should defy him, is new.

I do not visit Algria often. I am busy with the running of the state of darkness. There is always much to do. I am reminded that I should kill Greba. Now that Irid and Unead are lost, I have no hold over him. But something stays my hand. I cannot think why I let him live, but I do.

I tell myself that it is because I can use him against Kong and Hilketa, but it is not that, or at least not only that. It is true that Greba seeks to slay Kong. He will have revenge. If I wished Kong dead, then it would be as easy to do it myself.

Greba follows Kong when he goes to the outer court to indulge his perversions. Kong sets traps for Greba. Assassins lie in wait. But there are no assassins that can match Greba.

It amuses me to watch Kong struggle to slay Greba. It is possible that he will succeed. His fear makes him more and more desperate. He can see Greba following him and knows that if Greba finds him alone, then that will be the end of this life for him.

You would think we stopped fearing death. We who have died countless times before. We should fear it no more, but we have not conquered our fear, we fear it still. We fear it more than ever. We are like drowning men with our heads above water, we struggle to keep above each wave, even though we know we are only delaying the inevitable.

We know so little about death. We know less than those who have truly died. Each time we drop below the waves, Vatu pulls us up again to struggle all over again. When I think on it, I realize how cruel it is.

I am standing at the door to her cell. I hesitate to enter. She is well cared for. I have instructed the servants that she is to be well treated. It is not so unusual to have high placed prisoners in the tower, so my instructions are not so strange. The rooms are about three stories up and have a small window looking out onto the inner court. They are well lit with lanterns and a soft breeze cools the room. But they are still cells. The door is locked.

I should not hesitate; whatever we have to say to each other, we must say it. The door unlocks with a gesture of my hand and opens. I enter.

Algria is sitting on a divan. She must have known I was here because she is looking straight at me.

"Are you comfortable?" I ask.

"Yes, High Priest," she informs me.

"Is there anything you require for your comfort?" I continue.

Algria shakes her head. "No, great one, I believe I have everything that you can provide."

She is angry and is right to be.

"This is for your safety," I tell her.

"As you say, great one."

"How is the child?" I ask.

"Waiting to arrive," she says.

"And when is the child expected?"

"Soon."

"I have come to see that you are well."

"I am well, or at least as well as can be expected. The child will come soon; within a moon turn, I am told. May I ask, great one, what will become of me and the child?"

It is the question that I need to answer. None of the twelve knows who Algria is or what she might tell them. None of them knows why I have held her prisoner. How long has she been held prisoner? Long enough for Kong to grow to be a man.

In the lamplight I can see that she is no longer young or no longer in her youth. She is still beautiful, but the time in the dark has taken a toll on her. I should have silks and cosmetics brought so that she can dress like a courtesan. It is what she was, even if it is no longer what she is.

I must say something. I cannot let silence defeat me. She is no longer looking at me. Words struggle to leave my throat and it is Algria who breaks the silence.

"What will happen when the child comes?" she asks.

"The child will be cared for, as will you," I tell her. It is not what she means. I motion and servants bring food on trays. They set the trays before us. There is rice with vegetables. It is not a fine meal, but better than most prisoners can expect. There is even wine to drink. It is good wine too, from the valley and made from Sun-ripened grapes. I pour a glass and offer it to her. She holds it in her hand and turns the glass, letting the light from the lantern pass through both wine and glass.

"Are you not concerned that I might use this to cut my wrists?" she asks.

Normally prisoners would not be given glass or knives.

"The thought had not crossed my mind," I replied. "I know I need to keep you safe, but I did not realize that I have to keep you safe from yourself."

"You think that this is such a wonderful life you have provided for me, that I would want to prolong it?"

"Circumstances," I say, "they make prisoners of us all."

"Even of you?"

Especially of me, I want to tell her. None of this is by my wish. If I could, I would let her go, but if I did then they would surely kill her, or worse. They would take her and torture her until she told them everything. I am a prisoner of the dark as much as she is. There is at least the escape of death ahead for her. For me there is only rebirth and a return to darkness.

"I am not a prisoner," I say, but I am not sure who I am speaking to. Who is listening? If I am not a prisoner, then what am I? If I am truly free, then why can I not do whatever I wish?

"This is not why I have come," I say.

"Then why have you come?" she asks.

I have come because I am concerned for her, and for the child. I have come because I miss her and the closeness that we once had. I have come because something of her draws me near.

"I have come to speak with you," I say.

"About what?" she asks.

"Heresy," I reply. "I wish to understand heresy."

"So that you can destroy it."

"Yes." There are ears that might hear my words.

"I have told you all that I know, and I wish that I had not told you that. Why do you not just kill me? This has become a game. It is long and dull."

"You misunderstand. I know you cannot tell me who the heretics are or how they are organized. But you can tell me what they believe and why they choose to keep that faith in spite of all evidence of Vatu's greatness."

Algria starts to eat rice, that way she has an excuse not to answer me. She puts her hand over her mouth as she eats like a courtesan.

"I have only your best interests at heart," I continue as she eats. It is a lie that I would tell any prisoner. Anyone listening would think it a lie. It is not such a strange thing for a captor to tell his prisoner. When I say the words, I thought that I would wrap the truth in a lie. I thought that I did indeed have her best interests at heart. But if I do, then why is she a prisoner? I have wrapped a lie in the truth.

"What would you have me do?" I ask, and manage to keep the desperation from my voice.

"If you do not know what to do," she says, still covering her mouth with her hand, "then you must ask your master."

Does she mean Vatu, or does she mean you, author of all things? Vatu is no longer my master; he is my captor. Are you my master, author of all things?

Only if you wish me to be.

I am my own master. I have no wish to have a new one.

"What do you think Vatu would have me do?"

"He would have you let me go and provide me with riches to support myself and my child," she says. She was always quick to jest.

"I will ask him," I say. "It may be that you are right." As soon as the words are spoken, I regret them. I know only too well what Vatu will wish for Algria, or for any prisoner. He will wish them death. The darkness is just and it finds all guilty. That is justice; there are none that are innocent. All are deserving of death in his eyes.

"Yes," she says, "it may be that he is more merciful than you are."

Surely she knows that he is not. Surely she knows that he will kill her. Does she seek death? Is this life not better than death, no matter how miserable?

"The dark one is merciful in his own way," I say. I am well versed in the words of the High Priest. I have learned them from the twelve and from Vatu himself. Lies come so easily to me now. It is nothing.

"Will you not drink the wine?" I ask. She has put the glass back down on the tray without taking even a sip.

"I don't think I should," she says. "It is not good for the child."

The child will come soon. It is my child, or Kong's, or perhaps Hilketa's or perhaps some other's. I have no right to ask, but the unspoken question lies between us like a river of dark water that cannot be crossed. Why do I wish to cross it? What do I think lies at the far bank? What we had for such a short time is now gone. She does not trust me, and in my way, I do not trust her. If I was wise I would kill her, but that is the wisdom of the dark. The author of all things urges me to free her. *It will be for the best,* he says. But he is not my master. I will have no master. I will not risk my own life for hers.

But the author of all things whispers in my ear: *Your life is not endangered by her. The twelve seek to take your life now, the knowledge she has will not change that, nor will it give them power over you.*

But I think of how I had power over Greba. How I used love against him as a weakness. I think of how I held a knife to the throats of Irid and Unead and how, because of that, I held a knife to his.

The author of all things is not all knowing and all wise. In this he is wrong. I cannot set Algria free. Where would she go?

I could set her up as a courtesan in the inner court. But if I did that, then the twelve would descend upon her. They would destroy her, they would devour her. How is that merciful? How does throwing her to the wolves save her? This is the best I can do for her, at least for now. Here she is safe even if she is not free. When the child comes then perhaps I will have to think again. Until then I will hold her here, close to me and safe.

Yes, that is it, wait. The child will come soon, even though the moons have seemed to slow and each moon turn to stretch a thousand lifetimes. Wait. Endure. These are the gifts that have come to me from a thousand lifetimes in darkness.

I reach out to touch her. It is a moment of weakness, and instantly I draw back. Does she notice, and what does she think? Does she know that she is still dear to me?

I rise and take my leave. There is little point staying longer. I am wasting my time. My words are of no value. They leave no mark. I think she will ask me to stay, but she does not. It is like I thought, I am nothing to her. There is no point in this. I motion to the servants to gather the trays.

"Leaving so soon," she says. She is mocking me, and I should have her put to death for that alone.

Still so proud, says the author of all things. *Can you not see that she is afraid? Have you learned so little?*

It is not the place to answer him, not here. But I have learned only what he has taught and if I have learned so little, then what does that say about his teaching? If I do not understand, then why will he not explain it to me?

Chapter Thirty-Five
Enduring

There is much for me to do. There is always much for me to do. It is many moon rounds before I return to Algria. A note is brought to me informing me that the child has come. Doctors have been called from the inner court, and women. The child is well. I am still angry and wish to stay away. What is this to me anyway? The twelve and I have no children. We have nothing. The child is nothing.

But I do not stay away; I cannot. When I enter the cell, Algria is sleeping with the child beside her, a boy. I do not wake Algria. Instead, I look at her for a while and then leave. I will return another time. The child made no noise when I entered, nor did it turn to look at me. It is I who gave the child life and yet I am nothing to it. It thinks only of sleep and feeding and the warmth of his mother. There is nothing I can do for the child. I cannot feed it nor care for it.

I am in the throne room; that is what we call it. Where I sit next to the seat of darkness and dispense justice. Most of my work is not done there. Most of my work is done in a back office where I pore over tablets and dictate to scribes. Even the justice I dispense is decided elsewhere. I do not sit on the throne of darkness. That is the seat of Vatu. I have no power but that which he gives me. I have no power at all. Vatu does not sit on the throne either, not often. The dark spirit resides in all places, most especially in men's hearts. Once he dwelt especially in mine. Does he know that I have deserted him? Does he know that I am a fraud and that I was never his? How can he not know, but if he does know, then why does he let me live and rule in his name? So many questions, so few answers.

I sit beside the throne and cannot feel him near me. Here, beside him, I can feel nothing. I wonder if it is all a lie. But then I think on all that I have seen. He is real. I have seen him not with my eyes. You cannot behold darkness, but I have felt him within me and around me. I have heard his voice. But now there is only silence when I think on him. I should run. I should escape. But to where?

The author of all things will not guide me. Why will he not take me by the hand and lead me from this? Can he not save me? Can he not save Algria and my son?

It will be time soon for Vatu to open the Sun. It will be time for me to call him from his darkness to open the black box and let the Sun shine across all the lands. What then; will he heed my voice? Will he know me for what I am and destroy me? If I run, what then, surely he will hunt me down. You cannot escape from the dark. There are no secrets from darkness. He will destroy me and set another in my place. Perhaps he has done this many times before. There is no way to know the beginning of things. Only Vatu can comprehend the dark, only him and the author of all things.

When I retire to my dusty office, I gather my stylus and a tablet. I inscribe my wishes, my commands into the wax. Each gentle press into the wax forms the words that I am too cowardly to say, and the act I am too cowardly to do. I tell myself that I am wrong, that this is the best way. But I still feel like a coward. Besides, just because I have written it does not mean that it will happen. I would have to give it to one of the servants to follow out my command. Right now it is little more than an exercise. I can erase the words at any time. I can smooth the wax back to nothing. I can stop it any time I wish.

But I do not stop. I know it is the right thing to do. I must end the torture both for her and for myself. It is right.

I have finished scribing. I sit and look down. I run my fingers across the words and read them in the dark. I know what they say. It is what I should say and what I should do. Why do I even hesitate? I am resolved to do it and call a servant to me. But when I hand the tablet to him, he looks confused. The tablet is blank.

Perhaps I should do this myself anyway. Why am I afraid to see her? I imagine her lying sleeping in her cell with the boy. The child's eyes are closed, and he is making soft noises in his sleep.

I reach out to my other self and look with his eyes upon Irid and the other child. She looks thin and worn. The child is healthy but there is something else. It glows like moonlight.

Anger rises up within me. I was trapped here by him. He has everything that I wish and cannot have. Anger, envy and hate; they are gifts of darkness. I take them to my bosom and nurse them like a mother nursing a child. Why should he have what I cannot? What has he done to deserve freedom when I am a slave?

But Irid and the child are hidden from me and I will never find them. The child is mine; they should be with me. What a great trick I have played upon myself. What a great trick the author of all things has played; to deny me all the things that are mine.

He has come to mock me, the author of all things. He tells me that there is no trick and that I should leave darkness.

Let the gifts of darkness go, he says, *they will bring only destruction.*

Why should I care what they bring when I have nothing? Let the whole world burn if it will. Let poison pour into all the world. Why should I care? Death and destruction are the only things that I have.

I take my stylus and scribe my command and hand it to the servant again.

"See that it is done," I say, and he bows and heads off.

It is better that it is done now. It is merciful. I do not go to see that my commands are obeyed. I do not wish to see her. It would seem there is nothing for us to say. It is what she wished anyway.

I sit and imagine her face when the guards come to move her from her cell. She will ask what is happening, but they will tell her nothing. She will wonder why I do not come myself. Perhaps she will think me a coward. Maybe she will try to resist. That would be foolish. The guards will not harm her but they will not be gentle. When they take the boy, she will surely protest. But it is the right thing. The boy at least is innocent and deserves to live. This is all that I can do. I am not a monster. I will send the boy far away. I will give it to someone to take far away from here. Another discarded child. There are thousands of discarded boys.

I will never know my son. That is the order of things here. We do not kill our offspring. There is no need to. I sit and look around at the servants waiting on me. How many of them, I wonder, are children of the twelve or even of my former self. Maybe less than I imagine, not all of the twelve have tastes that incline to women. And courtesans do not bear children. You cannot work and earn when your stomach is extended or when you are nursing a child. Not unless a man's tastes run a particular way.

Why am I thinking of these things? I am not condemning the child to such a life. In fact, I am saving him from such a one. Once the boy is given to fosterlings, he will be forgotten by the rest of the twelve. When they see that I have discarded him and have no interest in him, they will lose interest too. It is such a strange thought that the High Priest would care for a child that perhaps only Greba or Hilketa will have thought of it. Kong will have thought it too, he is the greatest danger to the child. But I will have a distraction for him. Algria will still be here. That will keep him occupied.

There are so many things I still have to do. I have a thousand things to do and so little time. Time is pressing together; the end getting closer and all things to do crash into each other like colliding continents. They compress and buckle and swell up. Even small things are now mountains. To talk, to speak, to walk, to eat; these things are now like great weights pressing down on me. I strain against the pressure and push on. Each step I take, it is as if I am dragging the earth and the moon behind me. I am trying not to bring time forward, but to make it stop. Soon it will be time for me to return to the dark and face Vatu. I cannot refuse. If I do not go, then the Sun will not be opened. It is my task to bring the darkness, so that the Sun may come.

I am braced against time, but no matter how I resist, eventually my grip will give way and I will slip forward. Even these last few moments have come and gone and the inevitable is nearer.

But I cannot bring the end closer either. I cannot bring the darkness forward. I can only wait. I can only endure. I am almost done. I will finish this.

Each moon round is like the last. I do not go to Algria, but I see her angry, tear filled eyes. When I close my eyes to sleep she is there, glaring at me.

"Why have you betrayed me?" she asks. "Why have you stolen my child from me?"

I do not ask for understanding, or for forgiveness. These things are not for me. The dark asks for neither understanding or for forgiveness. But I am not the dark, I am not Vatu. I have done what I have done to cheat the darkness, not bring us to him. I do not ask for understanding but what I have done is right. Perhaps she does understand, and forgives me. It is right what I have done, she will forgive me when she understands.

Continue, endure, that is all I can do. And yet I wish to see her face again. It is a face that for so long I have touched but not seen and now I can do neither. Is she beautiful, I ask. I try to picture her but find I cannot. All I can see is her eyes. They accuse me of betrayal. But if she thinks I have betrayed her, she is wrong. There is nothing I can do to save her or to save us. We will be destroyed. And then I will destroy everything. I want to smash the whole world into nothing if I cannot have what I want.

The author of all things taunts me; *what do you want?*

Must I say it? Are you not all wise and all knowing? Can you not tell what I would have? Can you not give me what I would have? Can you not make me whole and free? Must I beg you like a slave for what I want? If so, then I despise you as a tyrant no better than the darkness.

He does not need to defend himself. Everything I say is true and not true. He is a tyrant, but is not. He has forced no one to do anything. It is me who has trapped myself. If he forced his will upon me then he would be a tyrant indeed. He seeks only to persuade me to do other than I will.

I wish him to leave so that I may do the things he wishes to persuade me not to do. Can he not see that what he wishes is impossible?

He withdraws from me.

Soon it will be time, and then it will be too late. My will is subject not to the author of all things but to darkness; that is my true master. I was a fool to think that I could escape. The twelve have gathered and they seek me to lead them. There is no choice, there was never a choice. It is all just a dream and nothing.

No words are spoken, but it is time. I walk the tunnels of darkness to the bronze door. All light is extinguished and at my touch the door swings open. I bow and enter, but the twelve wait outside. They are afraid. They should be. Soon I will be consumed by the dark.

He is waiting for me. There was never any hope. He comes and surrounds me and I breathe him into my body. In the dark there is only the sound of my breath and heart and somewhere the dripping of water. There is no incantation or magic, there is just him inside me, possessing me. My eyes are open but do not see, they are no longer my eyes, and it is no longer my feet that walk back to the twelve. Vatu bows and walks through into the dark tunnel. He sees without light the twelve trembling before him, before me.

Chapter Thirty-Six
Fire

My lips move, but it is not my voice that speaks.
"What do you wish?"

Then the pleading comes; open the box, master.

It is a plea that I have heard a hundred thousand times and I walk as they bid me to the top of the tower. They trail behind me, both fearful and beseeching. Nothing stands against the dark. Light and life are trapped and captive to my will.

I stand at the top of the tower, and my box is before me.

"What do you offer me?"

Twelve maidens dressed only in gold are brought before me. I see Algria. She is looking at me. Surely she knows. The twelve begin to play their musical instruments and the maidens smile as they dance before me. Their eyes are wanton, and their flesh is as dazzling as the gleam of gold from their rings and wristbands and necklaces. They still think that this is just a dance and that if they please me they will be rewarded with something other than death and burning.

She is looking at me. She alone of all the slave girls is not dancing. In her eyes I can see cold anger. What did she expect? I could never have saved her. The music rises and the other girls dance provocatively. They are fools. Soon the Sun will open and burn them to ash, they will not be missed.

It is the oldest lie that men tell; that a woman can exchange love for power. We do not share our power so easily and Vatu does not share it at all. They will dance and when the dawn comes, they will fade like dreams. They are not real; they are phantoms.

No words can be exchanged, not now. If she had anything to say then she cannot say it now, not here. I stride forward and look at Kong. It is he who has brought Algria here, but I cannot gainsay him. Even if these lips were mine to speak with, I could not.

Vatu is in my mind. He is telling me that he can save Algria if I will. He is telling me that the darkness can be merciful. He is telling me he knows everything, that he always knew everything. I am a fool, he tells me.

But he is not angry, he says. It is him, not Kong who instructed Algria to be sacrificed. The twelve obey him even when I do not. Now I have no choice but to obey. He holds my body in a dark grip and billows out behind me like a shadow.

I have a choice, he tells me. I can submit to the darkness.

He is mocking me. He could slay me now at a whim and bring me back to start this game all over again. He could do that. Or he could let me slip from his grasp and let me fade into the abyss.

What is the point of that? That would just let you escape.

I am ungrateful, he says. He has made a whole world for me to live in. This is my world, he made it for me. I do not understand and I have never understood. Why am I so blessed? Why am I so cursed?

I do not need to understand, I need only to obey. He is merciful. He will take Algria and put her in rooms, fine rooms like my own and only I will be able to find them. She will be mine.

Is that not what you want? he asks. He will possess her. She will be loving and sweet. Her tongue will be soft and her words honeyed. She will have eyes for no other. *I can do this,* he says. *The darkness keeps its word. Obey and everything you wish for will be yours.*

I am staring at Algria with eyes that are no longer mine. No words can pass between us. For a moment I am tempted. If I could, I would save her.

This is not salvation, this is damnation. That is what Vatu offers me. It is bitter to taste, this freedom that the author of all things promises, but it is not freedom. It is something completely different.

Before I can choose, Algria begins to dance. She is graceful, but it is not a dance of seduction. She is dancing a dance of death and of freedom. She is looking at me and her eyes are telling me farewell. If the author of all things is kind, she understands.

As the slave girls dance, Vatu takes my body; I lean forward and open the box. It is dawn. A finger of daylight slips between the black edges of the box. Their faces shine in the light, but slowly the crack of dawn, the sliver of Sunlight, widens and strengthens.

Now it is hot and soon the Sun raises blisters. They burn deeper into the skin. They are wounds now, weeping pus and blood. The blisters spread. It is like paper in a fire. The blisters grow. The dancers cry out in pain but keep turning. Now they are turning this way and that. The air is full of the smell of charred flesh. The gold draped around them begins to melt. It runs in burning rivers over their blistered flesh. Algria is looking at me and her mouth is open in a wordless scream.

You could save her still, Vatu tells me.

I wish I could turn or close my eyes but Vatu holds my eyes and head still and makes me watch. Algria's beautiful hair catches fire and her fingernails melt. She tries to shield herself from the Sun with her hands and arms but the flesh of her hands fall from her bones like the tenderest of meat.

Her eyes look towards me and I watch as they dry and shrivel and burn. She is still making gestures as if she would speak, but I can hear nothing except the roaring of the Sun. Now the flesh is being consumed from both her face and body. She is like a skeleton standing. And then that too is consumed. Her bones blacken and crumble to ash. Then even her ashes are burned to nothing. Nothing can stand against this; nothing except the darkness. The light is more terrible still than the dark. The other dancers too have been consumed.

Vatu is laughing.

"Why must it be so?" I ask.

Because I wish it, he tells me, *because it is my will. You cannot defy me. I can take everything from you. I will take everything from you. I will hunt them down and I will destroy them. This is the price of your defiance.*

But I know even if I submitted to Vatu completely, the dance of fire would still go on. I could only save Algria by condemning Irid.

She will not escape, he tells me. *I have seen your mind. I know that he lives and that you hold her dear. I have seen the child,* he tells me. *I will find her and she will be consumed. I have consumed the whole world. I have consumed the Sun.*

If my eyes were mine, I would weep. Algria is gone and I realize now that she was precious to me.

Love is the word you seek, says Vatu mockingly. *I have*

consumed love. I will draw it from you and leave you with nothing.

Inside I know that I will always love Algria, that she will always be precious. I could never have saved her, but I could have loved her better.

More dancers are brought and the twelve continue to play the music of death. I do not know how many slave girls the Sun consumes. In my mind I see the twisted delight that Vatu takes from their death. He is a monster, it is only now that I see it.

How many times before have I stood here accepting his will and watching as the dancers burned? It is only now that he has taken Algria that I realize how monstrous he is; how monstrous I am. But I am powerless. He has taken that which I loved and destroyed it. He will take everything I love and destroy it.

"Why?" I ask him. He does not answer, but I know why.

It is because I do not love him. I have never loved him, will never love him. He will destroy everything I love.

"I will fight you," I say without words, but he can hear me.

He hears my deepest thoughts. He is laughing. It will make it all the sweeter for him. How can I hope to stand against him? In the brilliant day, I am filled with darkest despair.

It is now midday. Vatu has opened the box to its widest. The heat is intolerable. The twelve retire to the rooms below. They will remove their protective gowns and cool themselves in baths of water before they are asked to come again. It is just we two that still stand in the Sunlight.

Although I do not burn, it is painful. It is the lot of the High Priest to do this. He is the vessel of darkness. I am the vessel of darkness. But darkness is my vessel too. I am surrounded by darkness, I am inside the darkness as much as the darkness is inside me. Years innumerable I have stood in darkness and held the Sun box open.

I can no longer think. I simply endure. Nothing lasts forever, not even torment.

I last forever, says Vatu.

His silent voice rings through my head. I cannot argue with him. He is all-powerful and all-knowing. He endures forever. It would be a small thing to give everything to him. But I know that I will not live forever, I will not. The torment will fade like it faded every other year. The Sun will return to its box. The night will close in again. We will find peace.

Only if I wish it, says Vatu. *I could hold this box open forever.*

I do not know if that is true. It might be. I know that I could not; that the heat and exhaustion would eventually take a toll on me and that I would perish.

I do not need you to hold the box open, Vatu says.

And that is true. When I was a child, those years that I was a child, he opened the Sun without me. A child could not endure this. So then why does he need me? Why does he call me back, life after life? It is true what the heretics say; this is hell, my hell. Vatu endures only so that he might torture me. I am punished for my crimes.

The darkness is just, says Vatu.

And it is now that my eyes open and I see things for what they really are. I see myself for what I really am. I pray to all the gods to forgive me. But Vatu is laughing because it is a million lifetimes too late for that.

When the trumpets of the twelve blow and they return, more dancers still are brought before me. I watch as they are turned to ash. How many times have I seen this play acted out over and over? I am the author of this play. It is only right that I should be forced to watch. I sicken inside to think that this once gave me pleasure, and I sicken further to think it gives pleasure still to the twelve and to Vatu. Monster is not a big enough word for me or for them.

Inch by inch, the lid of the box is lowered and the burning light diminishes. If I cared, I could look and see all life in the dark lands quickened on this day, quickened by the Sun and consumed by it. Inch by inch the Sun closes, like a blossom drawing petals of glowing flame in upon itself. The twelve sing songs of praise to the dark one but my ears do not hear them, even though it is I who wrote these poems eons ago.

Inch by inch, shadows lengthen and return. The cool returns, a light rain falls and drops of water hiss and bubble on the ebony box.

Then suddenly it is gone. The day is over and night time has returned.

Vatu gives a great triumphant shout that all can hear. He has done his part. He has brought light to the world for one day. It is up to the people to make sure that is enough.

I lead the twelve back to the abode of Vatu. They follow me and eventually, I enter through the brass door and close it behind me. Now Vatu should slough from me like a snake sheds its skin. That is the way it is always done, but not this time. He holds me loosely like a glove, but does not let me slip from his grasp.

"Why have you not let me go?" I ask him now that my lips are able to move by my will.

"Because we have work to do together, you and I."

"What do you wish me to do?" I ask. "I am your servant."

We both know that I am lying. If he lets me go I will run from here and from him. I will never do his bidding again. There are no secrets from the dark. I have said it many times, but only now do I know that it is true.

Vatu does not bother to tell me that I lie. I am closed out of his mind, and I cannot hear his thoughts.

"Can you not guess the work I wish to be done?"

I know what he will compel me to do. I will have no choice but to obey. I cannot resist his power. It has always been thus. I close my eyes and think of Algria, but when I do, I see her beautiful dark skin turning to ash. I see her eyes turning towards me in horror.

"I will not do it," I say, "not willingly. I have already let one love die to please you. Why should I help you kill another? Is it not enough that I am here with you?"

"Even you cannot comprehend the dark," Vatu says, but he does not enlighten me.

"Come," he says, and like a child led by the hand, or like a dog on a leash, he takes me out into the open night. Strings of darkness bind me still, but I find I am in the market square. I have a purse full of gold and I purchase a wagon.

Before I know it, I am driving the horse and leading the wagon out through the night. Most of the city is asleep after their efforts of the day. But a guardsman opens the gate and I travel on in darkness. The moon has not risen and the stars are gentle and faint, but it is as bright as full noon to me. I can see everything. Vatu is within me now. He is leading the horse in the darkness and holding me upright in my exhaustion.

"Where are we going?" I ask.

Vatu does not answer.

I offer a prayer. Great author of all things, is this your plan for me? I realize this torture is just and more than just. But will this hell endure? Will you not take the others out of this hell? Why must you torture them too?

The author of all things does not answer. Perhaps he is too busy weeping, as am I.

Chapter Thirty-Seven
Reunion

I have travelled far. I have travelled alone, except for him. It has taken long for us to find them, almost a year. Neither he nor I know where they are so it was not possible for Vatu to rip that knowledge from us. Instead we have had to search and follow the faintest of memories that come to me, and the urge to find him. It is that same urge that drove us together that very first time. It is like magnetism, but it is weak when we are far apart as we are now. It is only the faintest drift in direction. I would have fought against it, but my body betrayed me. And also there is Irid.

We do not talk, Vatu and I. There is nothing for us to say to each other. He is tired of taunting me. When I do not rise to his bait then it must be dull sport. I do not resist him. I do not seek for him to explain. I have no wish to comprehend the dark.

We are in a village and it is little different than a thousand others. It is mean and poor. I cannot believe that Irid is here, and when we search we find that she is not. Vatu tries to make me look through the other one's eyes, but he cannot make me do it. I am not sure why. But I am glad. Perhaps I will escape; the other me, that is. It is a foolish hope. I should not let hope rise but I have no energy left to fight; I can fight neither hope nor darkness, both can do with me as they will.

"He is near. They are near." Vatu's words are spoken with my lips. He is right, I can feel that closeness. My feet start to stumble in his direction. Can he feel my closeness too? If he does, why will he not run? I wish that he would run. But also I wish that this was

over. I go to walk away from the village, but Vatu stops me.

"We will wait here."

There is no inn, but he takes my body and leads me to a house. The homeowner comes as he knocks at the door.

With my voice he asks for lodgings. The houseman is not certain. He looks at me with contempt.

"We don't put up beggars and strangers."

I feel Vatu's urge to unleash himself, but Vatu restrains his urge.

"I have money." As if money is the answer to all questions.

"How much?" Perhaps it is.

I hand the houseman two coins. It is much more than the lodgings are worth. He looks suspiciously at them and then leads us to a mean outhouse. There is a rough bed stuffed with straw. It is dirty and the straw needs changed, but Vatu does not care.

"And food," he says with my voice.

The houseman goes grumbling away. He returns with a flask of water and some old bread and cheese. He hands it to me and leaves.

"Eat," I command myself and when I refuse, I force the bread and cheese into my mouth. We have played this game many times. Vatu will not let me starve. I cannot escape from him that way.

When the moon rises, we set out looking for Irid. We leave the wagon and walk out along the road by moonlight. We have asked in the village and the houseman tells me there is a forester who comes occasionally with a load of timber for sale. Why Vatu is convinced that this is me, I do not know, but he is. We walk and as we do, we look for a path leading off the road. We follow a few dead leads; the tracks of deer and other animals that fade out to nothing. It seems we are mistaken; Irid and the child are not here. I am glad, or would be if it did not mean that once again we must move on.

Vatu will not stop. He is certain that they are here.

We follow another trail. In places we can see the tracks of a sledge in the ground. I can feel him close. Now we need no trail. I am like a hound straining at the leash to find myself. Now Vatu does not drive me on, but simply follows me. I cannot resist it. I hope that he can feel it too, and that he runs.

I can feel it, he is here and he has brought the darkness with him. I am drawn to him as much as he is drawn to me. I cannot resist. I leave the house and head into the woods. I head straight towards him. There is no time to think. Irid looks up startled as I jump to my feet and rush out. I can hear the child crying as I step into the forest and leave the clearing behind. I am running towards him. I think that I can stop the darkness. I think that I can save them. It is the only thing I can do. Let the darkness kill me if it will. Only I pray, let them live.

I almost run past them. He is running too and the forest has become a maze that we move around in. But we are led to each other by that instinct that is in both of us. We stop only a few steps from each other. We look into each other's eyes. His eyes are filled with darkness. They are not his eyes, they are Vatu's. He has been devoured. Now Vatu will devour me. He will devour the whole world if he can.

Why does he not run? Why does he not run as fast as he can and keep running? You should run and not stop. But he cannot hear me because I cannot speak. Vatu will not let me speak. Vatu will not let me run.

There is a moment of perfect stillness. It is a pause in time. We are still for a moment and in that moment everything is in balance. It is a perfect stillness. It seems to last forever. And then the moment is over. What was possible is possible no more. There can only be this. Things are written and cannot be unwritten.

In the perfect stillness there is a sound like thunder. It is the sound of air parted by black lightning. A leap of black electricity jumps between us. In an instant everything is changed. I am discarded. Dark strings are cut and I slump. My lungs, now emptied of darkness, suck in night air, cool and moist. I lie face up on the mossy ground, and above me, the trees reach up shadowed fingers to the moon. I am like a newborn child, weaker than a newborn child. Vatu has abandoned me. I am deserted. I breathe and cannot speak or move. There is nothing I can do now. I close my eyes and reach out. If there is anything there, then help me. Help Irid and the child.

It is like a wave coming over me. Darkness returns, but this time it is not the darkness of deep places and dark hearts, it is the darkness that brings life to all things, it is the darkness that lies between stars and at the centre of all things. It is bigger and deeper and older than Vatu. It fills me and gives me the strength to move. I have given myself to darkness, but it is a different darkness, a better and a stronger one.

The darkness lifts me up and I stand and look towards the other. I stumble after him. Now Vatu is in him. There is nothing that he can do to stop himself. He is dragged to the clearing in the wood.

Why are they not running? Why do they not run and keep running? I shout and this time my lips move and the words are spoken, screamed. Do they not hear; do they not listen? I see her standing holding the child. She is looking into his eyes. Can she not see that they are no longer his eyes? Can she not see the darkness that lives behind them?

"Run," I shout, but they do not run. They stand looking into his eyes. They are waiting for death. They are waiting for their world to end. She is looking at him; what is it that she sees that stops her from screaming?

When Vatu enters my body, all my will is taken from me. I turn away from myself and walk back to the cottage. Irid is standing at the door holding Alaba. I want to cry out to her but I can do nothing. All I can do is watch with eyes that no longer belong to me. It is as if I see through smoked glass. It is as if there is a wall of glass between myself and the world. I want to fight him, but I cannot. I am possessed completely.

I have no will of my own. Darkness runs through my veins and wraps around my bones. Dark fingers caress my brain and dark thoughts become my thoughts. I look at Irid. What does she see? I can see no fear in her face. There is something else there that I cannot tell.

Now that I have found her, what happens now? Will Vatu rip her apart? Will he let darkness crush her into a pulp? What is it he wishes to do? He could slay us all. He could slay me and bring me back as a child to be schooled once more in his ways. I wonder if I have rebelled before, and when I think on it, I realize that I have always rebelled, and that I have always failed, because I am here. If I had succeeded then I would not be. I feel the dark lust for blood and destruction rise up within me. I reach with my own hands and wrap them around her throat. It would be a small thing to twist that graceful neck in a way that will leave her dead, to set her free.

But Vatu will not let her die so easily. He wishes to torture her and to torture me. He has been playing with us all along. It is still a game to him, although it is deadly earnest to us, or if it is a game, then it is a game of life and death.

There comes a shout from a stumbling ruin of a man who is walking towards us. He is telling Irid to run. But it is too late for that. She is caught like a bird in a snare. There is no longer any chance to run. She has two choices: fight or die. She has no choices; she is as good as dead already. It is just a question of how she dies. She can die slowly and painfully or quickly. And even that choice is no longer hers. Some things are written and cannot be unwritten.

Irid looks at the shambling man and then at me, at the man she has shared her life with and who has given her a child. Mesmerized, she looks at him and then at me and then at him again. She can see no difference.

"Who are you?" she asks.

I answer, "We are both one, we are both the High Priest. He is me resurrected before I have died, or I am him after he has died. We no longer know which is which. And neither does he."

"What will you do to me?" she asks. Her voice is steady and calm and she stands tall and unbowed. "What will you do to him?"

Vatu answers, *"Torture, and death."*

It is what awaits all of us. It is what the darkness brings to us all.

"Why?" she asks, but this time Vatu does not answer. I withdraw my hand from her neck. The shambling man is coming closer. I turn and Vatu strikes him, sending him again to the ground.

"Run," he says, repeating it over and over. But he is not dead. Why is he not dead? Vatu reaches for him and lets dark bands wrap around him, crushing him. Then he turns. I turn back to Irid and for the first time Vatu sees the glowing child; for the first time, he sees Alaba.

He laughs and his laugh is not gentle. He spreads out, engulfing all of us. He is a dark whirlpool that leads to deeper darkness. We are powerless to resist even though I am released. We are carried on dark tides and washed onto a dark shore. He has taken us back. It is as if all our efforts are to no avail. It is as if the little play Irid and I acted out in the clearing of the forest was no more than a folly performed in the darkness of the tower for Vatu's amusement, and now he has dropped the curtain and ended it all.

Chapter Thirty-Eight
Tower

"**W**hy am I here?" Irid asks.

"To die." The words uttered with finality.

We are in the chamber of the Sun, and Vatu has released me. Before us, Vatu coils and uncoils like malignant smoke.

She looks around the chamber. The box of the Sun sits in the centre of the room. It is an obsidian block that even the Sun cannot melt. She holds Alaba close, as if she can protect her. But nothing can protect her, or Alaba. This chamber will be their last place in this life.

I am not there; I am lying barely alive in the clearing.

"Save them," I whisper and miles away I hear my own voice.

"If I can," I tell him. It is enough, and I see him smile and lie back on the earth. But it is not enough for me. I cannot save them. I am powerless before the darkness.

I can feel him reaching out to me, sending me the last of his strength. He should keep it, he will need it. I can see he is wounded and may die. But I, who am not wounded, will almost certainly die also. We will perish and Vatu will start the game anew. It is hopeless.

I lie bleeding on the ground. This is my end and I am glad. I will die here in the open and beasts will consume my flesh, and my bones will dissolve into the earth. Let the gods be merciful to me, and let them not return me to this hell. I have done what I could. If it is not enough, then let the author of all things be graceful. I close my eyes and he is near me.

"Will you take me to the next darkness?" I ask him. But it is not darkness, it is light he leads me to. It is the same light that came for Huneko, and that I hope came for Tanden and Nino. It is an escape from this place. I ask the author to lead me there.

If you wish, he says.

Do I wish it? What peace there must be in death. It is sweeter than wine. I reach out towards the light and to those that I loved and loved me. Algria is there and I hear her voice. I long to be with her and tell her I should have fought harder for her. She is telling me that she forgives me, that there is nothing to forgive. She is saying that this world, this hell, is too much for any one man to stand against, that all that anyone can ask, is that we desire to do well. I wish that I could have done more. I wish that I had taken her far away. But no matter how far I run, death would have found us, as it has found me now.

"I am ready," I say.

But I am not. I cannot go and leave things as they are. This hell is my hell, it is of my making, and it is I who must right things, if not for me, then for those still here. I think of Algria's child, the boy hidden far from my reach. I think of Irid and Alaba. I cannot desert them.

Then what will you do? the author of all things asks me.

I do not know what to answer.

"What I can," I say.

I feel life returning to me. I look up and see the sky above me. I feel the warmth of moonlight on my broken skin. My blood stops seeping into the earth, and instead, strength seeps from the earth into my body. I drag myself to the well that other hands dug. There is a vessel of shining water.

Drink and be made whole.

I do as I am commanded and the living waters enter my body.

In the well, I wash away the dirt and blood from my skin. Tears fall from my face, but they are not tears of despair or pain, they are tears of gratitude.

I am grateful, author of all things, that you have given this chance to me, that I may make things right.

As the moon sets and the great white face leaves the sky, I realize that I am not alone, that I have never been alone, that the gods are with me, that they are always with me.

"Give me the strength," I pray, "that I may be able to do what I must."

The gods lift me to my feet and lead me through the forest back to the road. Our wagon is there and I lift myself onto the driver's seat. I have loosened the reins and I let the horse pull me, step by step, forward. I am going back to the City of the Sun. I am going back to rescue my child, the child that I abandoned. I will not let her perish.

The chamber is lit with many lamps so that it is not dark. Even so, I wish it were. Then the shadows might conceal the deeds that will be done here. The strength that he gave me, his dying strength, sent as he lay in the forest, is enough for me to stand. I walk between Vatu and Irid and my child. If he will slay them, then let him slay me first. Then at least I will not need to see them die. I will not see them tortured or burned by the great fire of the Sun. I can hear a distant echo of its fiery voice call out to me.

"Step away from them," Vatu commands. But I refuse.

"Why are you doing this?" I ask him, but I know why.

He is doing it because he is afraid. In the darkness he has only me; I am both his victim and his desire. Without me, he is nothing. Without me, he is just a shadow. He fears losing me. That is why he has brought me back time after time, countless times. Without me, there is nothing.

"I will destroy you," Vatu says.

"I do not fear destruction," I reply. "I know what you want, and you will not get it."

When I speak, I realize that he is weak and afraid. That it is his own destruction and ending that Vatu fears. If he loses me, then he is lost. But he does not lose me. He coils towards me, seeking once more to enter me and engulf me. He will devour me once more, and I will be helpless.

I turn once more to Irid. I wish to see her one last time with my own eyes.

"I loved you," I tell her, and speak the words that I have not spoken for a millennium. They are words I failed to speak to Algria; the words that hung between us in the darkness and kept us apart.

"I loved you," I have the strength to say it one last time before Vatu devours me again, and just in time to hear Irid's voice. It is soft and yet it echoes through the chamber, the words dancing over and over.

"I know."

Is it only now that the truth is spoken; I have loved her, and she has loved me. Only at the end can we see things for what they really are. Only now that it is too late, can we find the words we dared not say.

"I loved you too."

Vatu is not gentle when he takes me. It is like a violation. He forces himself upon me. I am powerless to resist. The strength that came to me in the forest clearing far away is brushed aside as if it is nothing. I am encased in black ice that freezes my soul. It is glacial, both slow and irresistible. Nothing can stand against Vatu's will, not even the very mountains. They will bend or be ground to sand. I will be ground to sand.

I move back behind the box of the Sun. Vatu drags my body there. I am nothing more than a black chess piece moved by his hand. It is all I have ever been, but I have been moved by other hands than his.

Behind the box, I lift the lid just the barest part. A knife edge of daylight inches towards Irid and the child. The child is still glowing softly, in Irid's arms. Through all of this she has slept blissfully. I am grateful for that. It is one less thing for me to worry about. Let the child die silent and asleep. I wish only that I could give the same to Irid.

When the light reaches Irid, she will scream in agony. She will drop the child and hold her arms out, but it will make no difference. The child will scream and burn. The remembrance of this will be with me always.

The focus of the light moves along the floor. Irid backs away from it until she has nowhere left to go. Behind her are the basaltic walls of the tower. She presses herself hard against them as if she could push her way between the cyclopean blocks. But the massive walls do not yield to her urging. They do not part and let her escape. It is not her bidding they obey. There is no escape.

Irid looks at me with resignation. She accepts her fate. There is nothing I can do for her or for Alaba. They are doomed. I reach out to find strength to fight Vatu, but there is none. I curse him. I curse the darkness.

The blade of Sunlight has now reached Irid. It is not strong enough to burn through her clothing. It traces a line and rises up and rests around her midriff. There is so much I want to say to her, but I am mute.

Can you see how I am fighting for us even in the dark grip of Vatu? And for our child; I am fighting for our child. Can you not see how I am struggling to halt Vatu?

I will my arms to push the box closed but I can do nothing. I will my eyes to turn away but they are no longer my eyes, they are no longer my arms. I am his completely.

The thin line brushes Alaba's skin, and it is as if a flare has been set off in the chamber. She glows with even greater brightness, a brightness not so much less than the Sun's. And then a flash lights the whole room. The child turns and stretches in her sleep, unaware of what is happening to her.

Vatu shouts with rage. A torrent of angry, hateful words comes from my throat. His anger causes me to shake, and black tendrils like creeping vines snake out towards Alaba. He will take her and destroy her. But he is thwarted in his desire. The brilliant light burns away the darkness. Vatu evaporates into a haze. Vatu pours forward like a stream of darkness, but is dashed apart by the burning light. He cannot touch her. He cannot reach her, nor can he reach Irid. It is in balance, darkness and light. Neither can gain the upper hand. Vatu is powerless while Alaba shines, but Alaba cannot destroy the darkness, she can only drive it away. As long as the Sun feeds light and power to the child, there is balance.

But what if Vatu closes the lid on the box of the Sun? The thought comes to me unbidden, and I try to banish it from my mind. I can feel the cool, dark obsidian beneath my fingers and I try to jerk it open more. If there is more Sunlight, then perhaps Alaba can burn the monster to oblivion. It is possible that she can destroy him completely. Is it possible that we can be free?

The balance continues and then a struggle begins within me. One half strives to open the Sun to its fullest. Let it be a touchstone for the child and let her destroy Vatu and all of us. The other strives to close the box.

Vatu draws back from the child and gathers around me, while the light shines brighter still. He seeks to hold me and I seek to resist. I try to open the box and yet a black impulse urges me to close it. Once more there is balance, but it is a temporary one.

Inch by inch, glacially slow, the lid moves downward. My aching limbs weaken, and my will is taken by his. I am powerless, and as the Sun lowers, the shadows return, both to the room and to my mind. He has taken me again. The Sun is closed. Vatu has won. The child still shines bright enough that he dare not touch her, but he has not perished.

Vatu hisses angrily. He ebbs and flows in dark currents around the child, but he dares not approach her. A thousand dark snakeheads dart towards her and then withdraw. He is still weakened. Irid is looking at me with astonishment. Her hands are burned where she holds the child. But she does not let her go. Instead, she draws the child to her as if she could protect her from the shadow.

Chapter Thirty-Nine
Escape

B ut she cannot protect the child; it is the child that will protect us. She can save us. The child will save us all.

"No," Vatu cries. *"I will destroy her."*

He summons the twelve to him, and the doors of the chamber burst open as the twelve enter. Greba recognizes Irid and stands motionless while the others push past him, eager to do their master's work. They look around without comprehension. Vatu departs from me. He towers over the chamber, like a pillar of cloud. His voice rings out.

"Take her."

The twelve—no, eleven, Greba is still too stunned to move— rush forward, thinking that Irid is the subject of his wrath. Beldura grabs Irid, and Kong lifts Alaba in his foul, dirty hands. I am free again and step forward, striking him down and taking the child from him.

"The child," Vatu screams at his priests, *"take the child from him."*

Again they are confused, but then they step forward. Not even the twelve together could defeat me if I was strong, but I am weak, so weak from Vatu's torture. It is the work of a moment for them to overpower me and take the child from me. Even without Greba, they are able to do this. I resist and Irid struggles against Beldura, who holds her, but Irid has no power to defeat one of the twelve. She struggles, but to no avail. He slaps her hard, and she bites his hand, but then he pins her arms and she is powerless.

Kong has taken Alaba again. I see her shining face and his ugly demeanour. To think I ever thought the child might have been his.

Hondatu and Gorroto are holding me. Hilketa is standing before me, looking into my eyes. He is seeking answers. That was always his weakness. He seeks to know rather than to act. What a fool, can he not see that wisdom has no power? What does he seek to know? Does he think that I would tell him? As if he could understand what has happened.

Kong is holding the child, and on his face is gloating victory. He does not understand anything except that I have been destroyed. He will lead the twelve for now, until I am reborn, or perhaps forever. He thinks it is a victory. He stands before me smiling as if this were all his plan, and that he has done this to me. I am content; let him be the plaything of Vatu from now on.

I wait for the killing blow, but none comes. Instead, Vatu motions for the child to be removed and Kong hands Alaba to Irruzura. He bows and leaves the room. I hear Irid calling for her child.

"Bring her to me," she shouts, and then Beldura strikes her again and she is silent.

Greba has still not moved. I try to catch his eye, but he will not look at me. Why should he? He has reason enough to hate me and now he has more. I have brought his daughter to this. I have brought Irid to destruction. How I wish that I had let her die of poison when Greba sought to withhold her from me.

I think that Vatu will have us killed now. If it is to be done, then better that it be done quickly. I struggle against the hands that hold me and they drop and release me. I am still the High Priest, even if Vatu has ordered them to restrain me; old habits die hard. They are used to obeying me. It is something they will have to unlearn, I think. I step towards Beldura and he backs away. I take Irid and hold her. She is calm; much calmer than I am.

"Why did you bring me here?" she asks.

"I did not," I tell her. She understands.

Vatu has coalesced into hard dark stone. He is like a statue of black marble.

Hilketa looks towards Vatu and asks, "What is your wish, great one?"

There is a rumble of dark thought. The tower seems to shake

as Vatu's dark mind thinks.

What is he waiting for? It is death he wishes for us, and now there can be no games; no cat and mouse. He must kill us. It is better done quickly. We have seen his weakness. He has been exposed. Those things we have seen must die with us. The child, my child can destroy him. It is the child who must live, not us. Kong has her now. But Vatu will have him take her and kill her.

Just for a moment, I think perhaps she is Kong's child, and that perhaps that thought will come to Kong also. But even if it does and even if it were true, it would not stay his hand, not for even one moment. He has no mercy, he is not like Greba. Such ties do not bind him; that is not Kong's weakness. It is my weakness and my strength.

It is as if an age passes. Vatu stands before us and in his eyes I see doubt. Ten of the twelve stand before him; Zauria has gone with Kong and Alaba. I stand next to Irid. It is surely the end for me and for Irid.

Vatu is still hesitating. I think he will kill us both and when I step forward and push Hilketa aside, he does not resist. Vatu is here and needs no help from the twelve to decide my fate. I guide Irid towards the door. Spikes of darkness shoot out and impale me, stopping me. The black spears pierce my thighs and side. Blood pours from my wounds. I am impaled on darkness. Irid cries out and then tries to break the spears and release me. It is surely the end for me now. I turn to Irid. She is as yet unharmed. Maybe her father can save her. Clearly now I cannot. I am weak with loss of blood and shock. I remember those lessons with Hilketa from years ago. I know well that I will die soon. Hilketa has come to stand beside me. He is staunching my blood loss. He is holding a vial of poppy juice that he wants me to drink and take away the pain. Why? What is the point, the pain will end soon enough. It is like I said, it is better that it be done quickly. My head starts to droop and Irid helps Hilketa tilt it back while he pours the liquid down my throat. As he does, sleep comes to me. It is surely eternal sleep.

My rest is not eternal. Vatu will not permit me to die, or at least not so easily. The darkness heals me. It is a rough healing. He takes my flesh and pulls it together and new blood spurts through my veins. My body is scarred and twisted, but I am made whole. Damaged organs grow back and replace themselves. I am truly the creation of the darkness. My broken mind is pieced together. Why? So that he can fracture it again? So that he can slay me again? Is that why Vatu has brought me back so many times; to kill me over and over again? Should I die a death for each death I have meted out? But with each life, I have slain more and more. I can never balance what I have done. There is not enough blood in the whole world to pay for my crimes.

The dark spears are replaced by a leash of black. I am now a dog on a leash. I am Vatu's dog. I am a disobedient cur that he has whipped to the point of death. I look around and Irid is still there. She is still alive. Others of the twelve are there also, but not Kong and not Greba. He will have no wish to see Irid's death. Although he will have wanted to see mine. Perhaps he is with the child, his grandchild. He will make sure that Kong does nothing to her unless commanded by Vatu. Or will he? Am I just letting foolish hope rise within me even now?

The roof of the chamber twists open and the walls peel away at Vatu's command. Now we are standing on the topmost point of the tower. I have been here before many times. I look up, thinking of the times I sat here with Hilketa, but there is no moon. Instead, I look towards the place of justice. How many have been cast from this very point in the name of Vatu's justice? It is fitting that he cast me from it too. It would be merciful.

None of the twelve will meet my eye, not even Hilketa. I look around and see how weak they are. If I am to perish here, then so be it. I am not afraid. I step boldly to the parapet and prepare to jump. The fall is over two hundred feet. I can see the inner court lit by lamplight and the courtiers going about their business. Once I stood here and considered them as ants, now I see they are less than that, and more.

Vatu tugs at my leash and sends me sprawling to the floor.

"No," he says. He will not permit it.

Irid is in his dark grasp too.

"She is pretty," Vatu says, *"not as pretty as the other one, but more refined."*

She does not speak and neither do I.

"This one?" he asks. *"Will you save this one?"*

It is the same choice, and this time I consider it. But the answer is the same. If I did, then it would be the end for Irid anyway.

He has my answer and so Vatu takes Irid to the place of justice and drops her from the tower. She does not scream. But I can hear the sound of breaking bones. It is a soft sound. But it rends me inside.

"*Now,*" says Vatu, "*bring the child.*"

A door opens like a dark, toothless mouth, and from its gaping maw come both Kong and Greba. Greba is holding the child and there is blood on Kong's lip. Greba has not been gentle with him, but then why should he be? It is strangely comforting to see that Greba has Alaba. But it will do no good. Greba will not defy Vatu and if he did, then his fate would be the same as mine.

Greba looks around for Irid. I shake my head. He makes no sign that he has seen my gesture. Irid is dead. I know how much a blow that is to him.

The child is still sleeping, miraculously sleeping. Here in the Crowtower, where her mother has been murdered and surrounded by the foulest of monsters, she sleeps. It is enough to make me laugh, almost.

Greba is cradling the child gently, and I realize that he must have cradled Irid too when she was a child. It is strange to think of him so, but then, is it stranger to think of me as a father and as a husband? The author of all things has taught me that love is not a weakness, but strength. How strange to think Greba has found that strength. Did you teach him, author of all things? Did you whisper to him and teach him the secrets you taught me? And when we are at our last desperate moments, why is it that the strength you taught us has failed? Is the darkness stronger than love after all? Is Vatu the master of this world despite all the whisperer's promises?

Alaba's glow is clear but faint. It shines on Greba and by the silvered light, I can see on his face something that I cannot quite comprehend. It is something I cannot read. He is holding his grandchild just moments before her certain death and murder. He should not be content, nor should he be at peace. What have you promised him, whisperer, that you have not promised me? What is the secret that even now after all I have done and suffered in your name, you deny me?

I try to close my eyes. But as I do, Vatu tears my eyelids from my face. Blood flows and obscures my vision until Hilketa stops the bloody tears with greasy ointment, probably pig's fat. However this plays out, I will see it all. I must watch every minute of it. Vatu will not be robbed of his triumph.

"I will not," I say and my voice is the cry of the raven.

I will defy him to my last breath.

"It does not matter," says Vatu. *"You could not save her anyway."*

It is true, there was never any other way it could end but this. I want to hold her one last time, to kiss her and tell her it will be well. But I cannot. When I walk towards Greba, Vatu's leash restrains me. All I can do is watch.

Kong takes the child. Greba does not resist, nor does the unreadable look on his face change. Alaba stirs momentarily as she is passed. She passes from each member of the twelve to the next. All of them have held the child for the briefest of moments. All of them are guilty of this murder.

"What crime has she committed?" I ask. "This is not just."

There is no place for justice now. Hilketa is holding her. Although he will not pass her to me, he is angling the child so that I can look into her shining face.

There are no more words, just silent commands.

The child is carried to the edge of the tower and cast over. I leap forward to catch her and tumble over the edge. Vatu's black leash jerks me to a stop and I hang over the edge. Bones are broken, and the wind is taken from me. I swing back against the wall of the tower, hanging only by the black noose around my neck. I cannot breathe. My hands reach for the falling child but to no avail. She is like a flaming torch dropped from a great height. Her brilliance tumbles through the air like a falling star. But when she reaches the ground and is united with her mother once more, the light goes out. There is only darkness now, and even without eyelids, I cease to see. And I cease to breathe and to feel and to think and to be.

Chapter Forty
Endings, Beginnings

My ashes are brought to the place where all my ashes lie. I am crammed into an urn of clay. The twelve bring me here and then leave. There is no singing and no memorial. My shade rises and cries out. All the shades of a million lifetimes hear and do nothing. But I will not stop. I call them to me. And each comes in turn. The nothingness that is me is added time after time. Each of us added together time after time. A million nothings should be nothing, but it is not quite so. A million, million shades come and join together.

"We do not have to stay here, brothers," I tell them. Are they listening? They are still coming million after million, each giving what little they have left to me.

"I will not stay here," I tell them.

It is not hate that drives me on. It is not hate that makes me rise from the dead. It is not hate that makes me into something more than a ghost. It is love. A teardrop falls onto my ashes. It is my teardrop. I am whole. I am not whole. I am partially whole. I am not alive. I am partially alive.

Heavy feet of dust and clay drag as I leave the tombs and wind through the darkness.

"I will escape," I say. The wind carries my words like the hiss of dust blown across a floor. No one meets me in the darkness and it is well. It is well for them. I am a shadow and a cloud.

I enter the library and as I walk, my feet leave no trail in the dust. Deeper and deeper I travel until there are only the footsteps that I placed there a million lifetimes ago. When they stop, I lift the tablet and run my fingers over it one more time. In the darkness I read only by touch. Every word I have written and now I take these words and place them on the shelf. There a thousand thousand tablets there. It is all written, but they are not in the right order.

Deeper I go. There are no longer books on the shelves. There are papers, documents almost perished by age and by fire. There is a red ball suspended in midair. There is a set of broken spectacles. There is a child's toy with wheels abandoned by a grieving parent. There are children's clothes. There is a shadow burned into stone. There are paper cranes; nine hundred and ninety-nine paper cranes. Some are as tiny as flies. There are piles of twisted metal and rubble. I lift a blackened steel cross and set it across my back like a sword. There is a timepiece that has stopped and a bell that is ringing.

There are other things too; there are fingernails black and long and dreadful, lengths of skin that slough from bodies, eyes that melt to nothing and secret hidden illness, vomiting and death. As I walk, I feel my body burning with black light as intense as the Sun. Blood flows from every part of me. There is a hat of straw lying on the shelf. I put it on and it burns and stabs at me like a crown of thorns.

I weep a river of tears and on the river I float away. When I stop crying, I am in a new place entirely.

I am lying across the wagon, too weak to move. The horses make way without my urging, but they are travelling slowly. I look up and watch the stars as they twist around the sky, weaving in and out. There is no cover to the wagon and a light rain runs down my face. I open my mouth and drink. The water enters my mouth and then runs down my face. I close my eyes. I am not sure how long I lie in the rain. I am soaked to the skin.

The rain is chill, but the water brings healing and renewal. I can feel the stiffness lifting from my limbs. I can feel my wounds heal slowly. I have slept and I am still weary, but I am stronger and best of all, I will live.

Why has Vatu spared me? Perhaps he thought I was dead or would die when he left me. He has taken Irid and Alaba to the tower. I have failed. There is nothing I can do for them now. There is a lightness to my body. I reach out to myself and find that I cannot reach him. Perhaps he is dead, or maybe Vatu now possesses him completely.

For the first time I feel free of all purpose. I have failed and now there is nothing for me except to live, and to let the wagon carry me where it will. But then the whisperer returns. Why will he not leave me be? As the wagon sways to the gentle march of the horses, it is like a mother rocking a child and yet I cannot sleep.

What now, whisperer? The author of all things speaks. He tells me that there is more that I must do. Is this why I still live? Has the author of all things robbed me of death? A purpose; that is what he gives me now. It is a hard blessing. There are others I must save, even if I can do nothing for Irid and her child, or for Algria. There are others that need to be saved. I realize now that this was always the author of all things' plan.

"You have always known," I say and the words echo back to me. I have always known.

Onwards the horses travel. I no longer care how far or where. Let them lead me to oblivion. Let the sky fall upon me and crush me. All that I have loved is taken from me. But the whisperer will not let me go. He leads the horses where he wishes. He heals me, at least my body he heals. I am well. I sit now when the horses move.

How long do I travel? What now is my purpose? Be merciful, I cry to the gods, but they must be deaf or dead or so stony hearted that they do not care.

The horses have stopped and I am sitting in the wagon outside a small town. The guards do not stop me when I lead the horses into the town and to the stables. There is a small inn and I find that in the wagon there is money enough and more for my lodgings. As I walk to the inn I notice that all the townsfolk are watching me warily. I must look a dreadful sight. My priest's robes are now so torn and dirty that no one would think me other than a runaway. I stop and look around. There is a young girl playing games with string. She is making patterns and loops. She holds her hands high above her head and I see the pattern. It is a circle made of ellipses. It is the sign of heresy. I am in a town of heretics. If they knew who I was, then they should surely kill me.

I walk to the door and call. There is a man and a woman waiting and they usher me in. The woman brings water and some bread for me to eat.

"We have been waiting for you," the man says. "You are Utas."

The woman returns and in her arms is the child. It is covered head to foot by heavy cloth. Although no part of the child is exposed, I can see that it is broken and twisted.

"I do not understand," I say.

"Nor do we," the woman says. "A man brought her here. She was almost dead. But her bones have healed and she lives. She is very weak and may still die. He told us you would come for her. He said that you would save her."

"Who is she?" I ask. I hold the child and weep. They do not answer me.

Glossary

Agana: a guard of the inner court murdered by Amantae.

Algria: girl fought over by Agana and Amantae, a heretic.

Amantae: a guard of the inner court, accomplice of Kong.

Arraio: one of the priests of Vatu.

Baso: a forester met on the road.

Basseriko: a town near the High Priest and Irid's home.

Beldura: one of the priests of Vatu.

City of the Sun: city nearest the dark tower, contains the inner and outer court.

Estira: one of the priests of Vatu.

Hondatu: one of the priests of Vatu.

Gezuri: one of the priests of Vatu.

Gorroto: one of the priests of Vatu.

Greba: one of the priests of Vatu.

Hilketa: one of the priests of Vatu.

Hoga: a scholar, tutor of Irid, murdered by the High Priest.

Huneko: foster father to the High Priest.

Irid: daughter of Greba and Unead.

Irruzura: one of the priests of Vatu.

Izain: govenor of Urrunak, executed for confiscating property and killing leading citizens of Taiga.

Karo: the false name given to Unead by the High Priest while pretending to be a scholar.

Katilu: peasant woman, mother of the reborn Kong.

Kong: chief of the priests of Vatu.

Lappura: one of the priests of Vatu.

Nino: foster sister to the High Priest.

Saco: a small village by the river, birthplace of Amantae.

Taiga: a prosperous weaving town.

Takur: a prisoner at the dark tower, formerly a guard in the outer court.

Tanden: foster mother to the High Priest.

Tuathan: a farmer, suitor of the widowed Tanden.

Unead: wife of Greba.

Urrunak: a province of the dark lands.

Vatu: the dark spirit who keeps the Sun in a box and opens it once a year.

Zauria: one of the priests of Vatu.

Zigoro: one of the priests of Vatu.

About the Author

David Rae lives in Scotland and grew up in a world where hordes of workers spill out of factories, a world where fog and smoke shroud all kinds of creatures, a world where ruined castles, factories and houses are haunted by ghosts, gangs and memories. He lives in a world where witches have been burned at the cross and martyrs have been hung on the Gallowgreen.

Since a child, he has tried to capture that world in words, poems, and stories. He has read every trashy novel, every children's book and every comic that came his way. Thank God for public libraries.

He studied Botany, Architecture, Mathematics, Computers, Geography, and Ecology. He worked in a candy factory (not as an Oompa-Loompa), as a scaffolder and ditch digger. He has worked as a draftsman and as an ecologist, as a statistician and as a policy maker. He is married and has four lovely children and now lovely grandchildren. And he continues to read and to write and marvel at the world he lives in.

Lightning Source UK Ltd.
Milton Keynes UK
UKHW010708080721
386832UK00003B/644